DIANA & DESTINY

DIANA & DESTINY

CHARLES GARVICE

WILDSIDE PRESS

Published by Wildside Press
wildsidepress.com

CHAPTER I

DIANA

DIANA stood erect on the small platform on which her desk was placed and, looking down upon the eager faces upturned to her, raised her clear, sweet voice in the first notes of the evening hymn; and the children took it up with swift and glad promptitude, and, wonderful to say, sang it in tune; for Diana had taught them to sing as conscientiously as she had taught them to read and write; and they had been apt scholars, as is always the case when the teacher's labour is a labour of love.

When the last notes had died away, Diana said—

"We will now sing the first verse of 'God Save the King,' children," and the girls attacked the national anthem as if they had expected the command; for this was the break-up for the Easter holidays, when, for a week, the little schoolroom would be silent and deserted, and Diana would be left in solitude.

"Thank you, dears," she said. "And now you are going to have a week's holiday, I hope you will all be good girls; indeed, I am sure you will. Good-bye—and don't forget me!" she added, under her breath.

"Good-bye, teacher!" came the chorus, and the children began to tramp out; but some of the elder ones came up to the tall, slim schoolmistress, who looked very little older than themselves, shyly offering their hands.

Diana shook hands with them, saying a kindly word or two—which would be proudly carried home by the recipients—and, bending down, caught up a tiny dot of a child who had become entangled in the group, raised her in her arms, and kissed her.

"Take Susie home carefully, Annie," she said to one of the girls. "Good-bye!"

When the last of the children had passed through the door into the sunlight, Diana leant against the desk with loosely folded hands and looked round wistfully; and, as she stood thinking of her children whom she loved, all unconscious of her beauty and grace, she made a picture which would have stirred an artist to the depths.

She was tall and slim, as has been said, with the lithe grace and ease that belong, or should belong, to youth; her face was almost a perfect oval, the dark hair, ruffled on her forehead by the hand that had swept it aside in the ardour of teaching, was soft and silky; the eyes were grey, the illusive grey which at times becomes violet and well-nigh black under the shadow of the long lashes; and the mouth small, and yet as expressive as the eyes. It was a charming face, and possessed some quality beyond that of mere beauty, which instantly impressed all who looked upon it. Perhaps it was the slight droop or curve of the mobile lips which hinted at a strain of melancholy in the girl's nature; or it might have been a touch of wistfulness, a reserve in the eyes when she was silent or lost in thought. At other times both eyes and lips could smile, as the children who eagerly watched for that smile well knew. However the effect was caused, it was there, and it lifted Diana from the ranks of the ordinary and commonplace women of the village in which she lived and taught.

Presently she awoke from her reverie, and, after tidying the schoolroom, picking up a book here and a slate there, which the children, in their haste to be gone, had not put away, she closed the outer door behind her and passed into the small garden which divided the schoolhouse from the teacher's cottage, and surrounded the latter.

Here she lingered, looking dreamily at the flowers; for Easter was early this year; the too often procrastinating Spring had come along briskly, and the beds were glowing modestly with forget-me-nots and narcissi, wallflowers and tulips; all of which had been planted and tended by Diana herself.

After a time a middle-aged woman came to the door of the cottage, and, shading her eyes with her hands, looked for a moment or two in silence at the graceful figure of the girl as she bent over the flowers; then she said in a low, subdued voice—

"Tea is ready, Diana;" and Diana followed Aunt Burton into the sitting-room, where she had laid the tea. The room was tiny, of course, and it was plainly furnished; but the taste which displayed itself in Diana's plain dress and white collar and cuffs, made itself obvious in her surroundings; it was the room of a lady.

"The flowers are early this year, Aunt Mary," said Diana, as she arranged some narcissi and tulips in the vases. "I don't think they have been so fine since we came here. Let me see, how many years is it?"

"Three next June," replied Mrs. Burton, in a toneless voice.

"Is it so long! Ah, yes. I got my certificate in May, didn't I? What a day that was!" She smiled and looked thoughtfully at the fire. "We thought that I should be too young, do you remember? But I wasn't. I suppose I passed because I was so eager, so anxious. It meant so much to me, didn't it?"

The elder woman nodded and glanced at the beautiful face with a curious wistfulness and a hint of pity.

"Yes, Diana. It's a hard life; hard work, I mean."

Diana shrugged her shoulders slightly. "I suppose it is. Oh yes, I am often very tired; but it is no worse than other women's work; it is better than that of most. I am my own mistress, to a great extent; and there are the long holidays; and—and the children!"

Her pale, weary-looking face lit up, and she smiled to herself.

"So one may say that you are quite content, Diana?" asked her aunt.

"Oh, quite—or nearly," replied Diana. "Of course, there are many things I want; oh, ever so many. For instance, I should like a larger playground, a separate room for the tiny children; a girl's gymnasium, a laboratory—"

"Oh, the school!" broke in Mrs. Burton, with a listless impatience. "I was speaking of yourself. It's lonely here;" she looked round for an instant, but her eyes, with their intent look, came back to the girl's face. "You never see anyone but the Rector or the school inspector; never go anywhere but to Lowminster—"

"And very seldom there," said Diana. "Oh yes, it's quiet enough; and sometimes I feel just a little dull; but it might be so much worse. Do you remember"—her voice grew low and a little tremulous—"do you remember the time in that attic in London, Aunt Mary, when we had only two shillings and tenpence left?"

Mrs. Burton's face paled and her lips twitched.

"And we should have had no money for the rent if you had not received some by post? Do you know, Aunt Mary, I often wonder where that money came from so opportunely," she broke off.

Mrs. Burton rose quickly and turned away to place the kettle on the fire.

"It was money owing to me," she said in a dry voice. "I suppose you want the table. I'd better clear it off."

"I'll help you," said Diana promptly.

"No, no, you sit still," said the elder woman. "You sit still; you're tired."

"I hope not; for I've a great deal to do between now and by-by. I've all the children's exercises to correct."

When the table was cleared she got the books out and began work. The light faded and the rays of the early moon poured a silvery glow on her bent head and pale cheek. She rose to light the lamp, but paused at the open door and gazed out on the fairy-like scene. It was too tempting to be resisted, and Diana, flinging one of Aunt Mary's precious antimacassars over her head, went out. A belated bird, which had been deceived by the unusually warm Spring day, was singing in one of the elms, and, listening to it half-unconsciously, Diana sauntered through the garden and down the road.

It was a night for dreams; and Diana was dreaming of the past which Mrs. Burton's words had recalled. As far back as she could remember, she and Aunt Mary had lived alone together. Of her parents Diana knew next to nothing. They had died, so Aunt Mary had said, when Diana was quite a child, and had left her to Mrs. Burton's care. The aunt and niece had lived the hard and grinding life of the self-respecting poor; but, though it had left its mark upon the elder woman, it had spared the child, though she had fought her way through the squalid surroundings of a dreary London back street to the schoolhouse in the little village of Wedbury.

Diana, as she walked slowly down the road, scented with the blackthorn and the primrose, and thrilling with the notes of the birds, shuddered as she recalled that attic in London; and asked herself why she was not even more happy and grateful for the change that had come into her life.

"But this isn't finishing the exercises," she murmured. "I must go back. To-morrow there will be no work to do. A whole week's holiday! I wonder whether the children will be as tired of it as I shall be!"

She stopped at the bend of the road and looked down at the reddish haze rising from the town of Lowminster that lay in a hollow five miles away. It was a garrison town, and, consequently, a gay one; with plenty of shops, a theatre, and a music-hall; but Wedbury lay outside the line of railway, and the quiet village was rarely troubled by its bigger and noisier sister. Diana's visits to it were few and far between, for she remembered London too distinctly to be fascinated by a provincial town, and loved the lanes and the woods, the brooks and the rivers of Wedbury too well to care to leave them.

As she turned away, to return to the cottage, the moon disappeared behind a cloud, and at the same moment she heard the sound of wheels behind her. The lane was narrow and dark, so she drew back against the hedge to let the approaching vehicle pass.

It was a dog-cart with two gentlemen in it, and immediately after passing it pulled up, and she heard one of the men say—

"*I* can't find the matches. Sure you gave 'em to me, Grayson?"

"Dashed if I can remember," replied the other. "My head feels like a hot potato. Here, hold the reins, Mortimer, and I'll feel for the box. There you are! Confound it! You've dropped it! Do you think you can get out?"

"I can get *out* right enough," retorted Mortimer. "The question is, can I get *in* again? I'll tell you what it is, we've both had too much, old man!"

He alighted, laughing, and began to hunt for the match-box; and Diana saw, by the light of the lamp, that he was a certain Captain Mortimer, one of the "gentry" of the locality. He was in evening dress, with a light overcoat; his face was flushed and his movements unsteady and uncertain.

He found his box at last, lit his cigar, and handed a match up to his companion; but he seemed to be really doubtful as to his ability to return to his seat, and leant against the body of the cart with indolent indifference.

"Yes; it was a warm evening," he said, with a laugh; "but if we're a bit bad, what about Dalesford? He has drunk twice as much as we have."

"Oh, Dalesford!" exclaimed Grayson, with a short laugh. "He can *take* twice as much. But he went the pace to-night, right enough."

"He must have lost pretty heavily," remarked Mortimer.

"That wouldn't matter. He never cares whether he wins or loses."

"That's as well, seeing that he usually loses," commented Mortimer drily. "He's had a long and a bad bout this time. By George! it would have knocked most of us under; but Dalesford's got the stamina of a—a horse, and is as hard as nails."

"Come on up," said Grayson, with good-natured impatience, "or we shall have him running into us."

"Is he driving?" asked Mortimer, as he climbed with tipsy carefulness into the cart.

"No, riding!"

"Phew!" was the significant comment. "I wouldn't insure him!"

"Your money would be safe enough," said Grayson. "Hold on tight, Mortimer!—Get up, old lady!"

Diana waited until they had driven off, then she went slowly toward the cottage.

The man of whom they had been speaking was Lord Dalesford, the only son of the Earl of Wrayborough, one of whose family-seats stood embowered amid the trees on a knoll a couple of miles from the village. The earl and his son were very seldom there, and Diana had not seen either of them; but she had heard some of the stories of the father's eccentricity and the son's wildness, which had now and again trickled through the various social strata to the simple folk of Wedbury, who regarded the Wrayborough folk and all pertaining to them with a mixture of awe and reprobation, which had a spice of pleasurable excitement in it; indeed, the district generally was proud of the questionable distinction of possessing the maddest and wildest and most charming of noblemen as their landlord and chief, and "heir-lord."

Diana forgot the incident before she had got through the remainder of her work; and gathering up the books and extinguishing her lamp, was going up to bed, whither her aunt had gone long since—when she remembered that she had left the garden gate open. Treading on tiptoe that she might not wake Mrs. Burton, she went out and closed the gate. The night was so beautiful that she lingered, resting her arms on the top rail and looking up at the clouds as they sailed across the moon. Suddenly she heard the sound of an approaching horse, and turned quickly to beat a retreat, when the rhythmical beat of the hoofs ceased abruptly, so abruptly that she stopped short and listened. For a moment all was silent, then she heard a sound as if the horse were plunging, and a man's voice crying out with surprise and anger.

Convinced that something unusual had happened, Diana, obeying the impulse of the moment, tore open the gate and ran down the road. The moon emerged from behind a cloud, and, as she reached the bend of the road, she saw a strange, an appalling sight.

CHAPTER II

LORD DALESFORD

A HORSE was rearing and plunging, its bridle held by a man who was striking with a heavy stick at the rider. The blows fell fast and thick, but the man on the horse sat tight, though he swayed to and fro in the saddle, and with his hunting-crop, endeavoured to ward off the blows and return them. Neither man spoke, and only the sound of the sticks, as they met in the furious onslaught and defence, and the pawing of the plunging horse, broke the silence.

Diana's heart leaped in her bosom and the blood rushed fiercely through every vein. She was only a girl, but the spirit of a woman thrilled through her and nerved her; and with a cry she ran towards the combatants and fairly flung herself upon the assailant.

Startled and amazed, for he had not heard her approach, the man uttered an oath and swung round upon her. She saw his face, for a moment, a moment only; saw the bludgeon, for it was more of a bludgeon than a stick, raised to strike her; then she felt, rather than saw, the horse between her and the impending blow. The stick fell with a heavy crash—but not upon her; there was a momentary struggle; then, all bewildered and confused, she saw the assailant dart across the road, leap the rough fence, and disappear; then she felt a strong arm round her waist, a man's hot breath on her cheek.

"Are you hurt? Don't faint—if you can help it! Are you hurt? Did he hit you? —Still, Jess, still!" This was to the horse, who, quieted by her master's voice, ceased to tug at her bridle and stood still, but trembling.

"N—o, I am not hurt," said Diana. "I am—only frightened."

"Frightened!" he said, with a smile of pleasant irony. "That seems scarcely possible, after your plucky conduct. If you had not come to the rescue—and it was indeed a rescue!—I don't know what would have happened. You must be a very brave woman—girl!" he added, as he looked in the light of the moon at the slight figure.

"What was it, who was it?" asked Diana, as she drew away from his arms, and, womanlike, put her hand to her hair, which had been disordered by the struggle.

The young man shrugged his shoulders.

"A tramp turned into highwayman by tempting circumstances," he said carelessly. "It's of no consequence, as far as I am concerned; he got nothing. But you! You must be very much frightened, upset, even if you are not hurt."

"I am not hurt," said Diana. "But you—he was striking at you—"

She broke off with an exclamation of dismay; for she had raised her eyes and saw a thin streak of blood running down his face.

He met her horrified gaze with a reassuring smile, and drew his hand across his face.

"Oh, that's nothing," he said. "But for you I should have fared much worse. It was a heavy stick—" He stopped, and his face grew dark with suppressed anger; but the next moment it was overspread by the pallor of pain and weakness, and he staggered slightly and stretched out his hand to the rail of the fence beside them, as if for support.

"You *are* hurt," said Diana, very quietly. "Is it your head—"

He drew himself upright and smiled down at her grimly, but she saw that he did not see her; that he was by sheer force of will keeping himself from fainting.

"What shall I do?" she asked of herself more than him. "If I had some water, brandy! Will you come—do you think you can walk as far as the cottage—"

He forced a laugh. "I could walk a dozen miles," he said huskily. "I assure you that there is nothing the matter—"

The blood was streaming down his face now, and Diana, interrupting his obviously untruthful assertions, put her hand on his arm pleadingly.

"Please come with me; it is not far."

He shrugged his broad shoulders and walked beside her. When they got to the door she took his hand, in her anxiety, and led him into the dark room.

"One moment. I will light the lamp."

She did so. He had removed his hat and was standing, vainly trying to stanch the blood from the wound; but he was still smiling the pleasant, half-cynical smile.

"I'm giving you a great deal of trouble," he said, as he took a glass of the brandy which Aunt Mary always kept "for medicinal purposes only." "I'm awfully ashamed of myself. If I had been quite sober—I mean quite wide-awake—I should have seen the fellow come out at me; but he was upon me before I had pulled myself together. Oh, I don't think I can let you bother any more!" he broke off, as Diana brought a bowl of water and a sponge.

"You cannot go home like that," she said, glancing with a shudder at the blood. "I will call my aunt—"

He caught her arm with an expression of undisguised dismay.

"O lord, please don't disturb her!" he said. "The whole thing isn't worth making a fuss about. I've had as bad a knock as this at football, and infinitely worse out on the frontier—India. I'm all right, I assure you. I'll just sponge—Thank you!"

He bent over the bowl, but did the sponging so clumsily, sending the water down his neck and over his shirt-front—not that the latter mattered, for its once immaculate breadth was already irretrievably ruined—that half impatiently Diana took the sponge from him and continued the operation deftly.

In doing so she parted the thick chestnut hair and disclosed an ugly wound, the result of a blow which would have knocked most men out of time.

"It's an awful wound!" she muttered, between her teeth. "I wonder it did not kill you—or stun you, at any rate."

"Got a thick head," he said. "It runs in the family. We're the biggest stupids and dunces in the county: always were. It would take a poleaxe, at the very least, to down me. How pleasant the cold water feels."

"I will get some fresh," said Diana, in the low voice in which they had all along spoken, lest they should wake "Aunt Mary."

While she was gone he sat up and looked round him. He was in great pain still, and still saw through a kind of mist—he had not yet seen Diana distinctly—but his narrowed eyes took in the tone of the room, its neatness and obvious refinement.

"You are still very pale," said Diana. "Drink some more brandy while I try to bind this round your head. I have been thinking, trying to remember exactly what happened."

"Yes?" he said politely, but with no great display of interest. "What did happen? The only thing I remember was seeing the fellow at my mare's head—"

"The horse—I'd forgotten it!" exclaimed Diana.

He smiled. "Oh, Jess? She's all right; she'll stay outside nibbling the grass until I go to her. I've trained her well, and she is rather fond of me. I was half or quite asleep, I fancy. But he woke me up pretty quickly," he added, with a grim smile.

"You saw him, saw his face?" asked Diana. "You would recognise him?"

He shrugged his shoulders. "Oh no, I saw him for a moment or two—the whole thing was crowded into just a moment or two—but I don't think I should recognise him."

"Nor I, I fear," said Diana. "One thing struck me: he did not look quite like a tramp.—Pshaw! how awkward I am! This stupid bandage *will* slip off as soon as I tie it."

"That's all right," he said, with polite indifference. "Not like a tramp? How so?"

"Well," hesitated Diana, for nothing is more difficult than an accurate description of a person seen momentarily and under such circumstances, "he was better dressed than a tramp. I think, I am not sure, that he wore a blue serge suit, with a dark, thin overcoat. It came open in the struggle. The coat collar was turned up, and I did not see his face until he turned on me—"

"Ah, yes!" he said quickly, and with a frown. "I think I caught sight of him at that moment. I got upon him just in time."

Diana looked at him with her brows drawn.

"Y-es. If you had not—" She left the sentence unfinished. "It is a pity that you did not ride after him."

"Well, no," he said quietly. "I could not have left you."

"But when you saw I was not hurt— But you felt faint—"

He nodded and shrugged his shoulders. "And if I hadn't, if I had been all right, I should not have gone after him. Why should I? It was, so to speak, a fair game. And he won. And I've an idea that he did not get off scotfree. My hunting-crop is a heavy one, and I felt it hit something once or twice."

"But the man ought to be caught and punished," urged Diana, to whom this easy-go-lucky philosophy did not commend itself. Your true woman can forgive a thief—"Poor man, he must have been starving!"—but finds it difficult to extend the same mercy to a man guilty of a murderous assault such as that which Diana had interrupted. "He was a dark man with a moustache—"

"There are one or two dark men with moustaches in the world," he said easily. "Pray don't trouble yourself any more about him. A man who plays that kind of game always comes to grief in the end. Some night he'll be laid by the heels and meet with his deserts. Besides—well, frankly, I should hate the fuss of a prosecution and all the rest of it. If I had caught him I should have thrashed him and let him go. It's the easiest way of settling such matters. And now"—he rose and took up his hat and hunting-crop—"I have only to try and thank you—" He stopped with a significant gesture. "No, I'd better not make so utterly futile an attempt. But I can express my regret that you should have suffered so much anxiety, should have run such a risk, and been put to so much trouble, on my account. And I do that with all my heart."

He peered at her in the semi-darkness of the cheap paraffin lamp—the lamp so rich in scent, so poor in light—and Diana, blushing a little, shook her head in depreciation of her part in the affair.

"The pluckiest thing—! But I will not try to tell you what I think of you," he broke off. "Good-night—and thank you!"

He held out his hand, and it closed over her small white one with a grasp that made his assertion that his assailant had not got off quite scotfree easily credible.

Diana drew her hand away and stepped back into the shadow. At the door he paused and looked over his shoulder at her with a smile grave and grateful, then went out very quietly, with an upward glance at the window above the porch.

Diana stood until the sound of the horse had died away, then she sank into a chair and looked round the room, as if she were asking herself if the whole affair had really occurred or were only a dream.

As she sat there mentally re-enacting the dramatic incident, it occurred to her that it would be wise not to tell Mrs. Burton anything of it. She knew how terrified her aunt would be, and how for the future she would dread to let Diana out of her sight; for she was a nervous woman, full of apprehension and quick to take alarm; it would be an actual kindness to keep her in ignorance of the episode.

Diana got up and removed all traces of her very amateurish surgery, set the room straight, and at last—it seemed ages since she had finished the exercises—went to bed. It is easy enough to do this, but it is not so easy to sleep; Diana lay awake for some time, and when she fell asleep, her slumber, usually as placid and untroubled as that of a young child, was haunted by the vision of the rearing and plunging horse, the sound of blows and an angry voice, the sight of blood which stained her hands beyond cleansing.

And in her dreams, strange to say, she saw the face of the assailant quite plainly; saw that at the corner of the thin-lipped mouth there was a scar, as of a cut, about a couple of inches long. It was only in her dreams that she discerned the face thus plainly; when she awoke in the morning, the remembrance of the man's countenance was as dim and vague as it had been on the preceding evening.

"You look pale and tired this morning, Diana," Mrs. Burton said, as Diana stood at the breakfast-table cutting bread-and-butter. "Did you have a bad night? I thought I heard you come down again and move about in the kitchen."

Diana bent over the loaf and coloured uneasily; and she would have liked to make a clean breast of it; but she glanced at Mrs. Burton's careworn face, with its chronic expression of anxious apprehension, and replied—

"Yes; I was moving about, aunt. But I am all right this morning. I am going for a long walk; to the top of Oak Hill, if I can; and you will find that I shall return with a tremendous colour and a perfectly appalling appetite."

She set off soon after breakfast and tried to forget the incident of last night; but, of course, she failed to do so. Highway robbery—or attempted murder, which was it?—are not daily occurrences in the lives of village schoolmistresses; and once or twice she caught herself thinking of Lord Dalesford; for she knew that it must have been he. The opinion, founded on hearsay, that she had formed of that nobleman had not, of course, been favourable; and it was not much more so now. He seemed to her to be a reckless, dissipated man, whose only object in life was the pursuit of pleasure of an ignoble sort, in which drinking and gambling figured conspicuously. Brave—oh yes; he had shown plenty of courage! And good-natured: but, perhaps, it was sheer indolence and the desire to avoid trouble which had held him back from any attempt to find the footpad. And yet, easy as it was to censure and condemn Lord Dalesford, something within her pleaded for him. Not his good looks alone, though they were striking enough, but a certain easy good-temper apparent in voice and manner, and that indescribable something which proclaims the Man.

She thought of him so much that her quick, maiden sensitiveness became annoyed.

"Bother Lord Dalesford!" she said, with a certain irritation. "For Heaven's sake, let me forget him!"

But though she succeeded in driving him from her thoughts, she was reminded of him again as she went down the hill into the road; for the Wrayborough carriage passed her. The earl was seated in it—a tall, aristocratic man, who looked little more than middle-aged, though his hair was white and his face lined with fine wrinkles. He leant back in the stately barouche, with its powdered and richly liveried servants, one gloved hand, as small as a woman's, resting on one side of the carriage, the other toying with his eye-glasses. His lordship was strikingly handsome, and Diana saw where Lord Dalesford had got his good looks. As she happened to step into the road almost abreast of the carriage, his lordship quickly raised his pince-nez and scanned her. The sight of a pretty girl had always brought a smile to his face, and Diana's beauty brought one there now. It flashed in his dark eyes, which were as bright as a young man's, and curved the delicately-cut lips. With a swift elevation of the eyebrows he raised his hat, as if

14

with an instinctive recognition of, and tribute to, her youth and beauty. But Diana, who was not prepared for the salute, let it go unacknowledged, and the carriage rolled past her, leaving a trail of dust behind it.

There was more dust the next day, for a number of carriages drove through the village and up the road to the great house.

"There is a big dinner-party at the Hall, a bachelor party," Mrs. Burton remarked. "It was to have been yesterday, but Lord Dalesford met with an accident the night before; fell from his horse coming from Lowminster. He was intoxicated, they say."

Diana coloured at the partly unjust inference.

"He—he may not have been—I—I mean, so bad," she said, rather stammeringly.

She lay awake that night and listened to the carriages as they drove away from the Hall. From some of them came bursts of laughter and snatches of song; and the horses of one vehicle, a mail phaeton probably, went by at a gallop.

Unacquainted with the great world though she was, Diana could imagine the sort of dinner-party it had been; and, half-unconsciously, she sighed as she turned on her pillow and strove to shut out the discordant sounds. Why were men so foolish and so wicked?

By the fourth day, if she had not forgotten her adventure in the lane, she had ceased to dwell upon it. She had spent a very happy day. Finding it impossible to get on any longer without the children, she had gone to some of the cottages and carried off half a dozen of the smaller ones for a picnic in the woods. They had a delightful time, and Diana, having restored the healthily tired and supremely happy children to their complacent mothers, went slowly homeward.

Mrs. Burton met her at the door.

"How late you are, Diana," she said. She looked more anxious and nervous than usual, and Diana made haste with a soothing response.

"They were so happy! And they begged to stay 'a little longer, and a little longer, teacher!' " she said, smiling. "I'm sorry if I've kept you, Aunt Mary. Why are you so anxious, so fearful of something happening, dear?"

Mrs. Burton made a nervous gesture with her hands.

"I'm not always so," she said wearily. "But to-night— What is that?" she broke off.

Diana, who was in the act of filling the teapot from the kettle, paused and listened.

"It is someone coming up the path," she said easily. "Don't be frightened, Aunt Mary; it is only the postman."

She took the letter from the man, who lingered for a moment or two to exchange a few words, country fashion, with the pretty school-lady, whom he, in common with all the other young men in Wedbury, "worshipped from afar."

Few letters came either to Mrs. Burton or Diana, and she looked at this one curiously; for it was addressed to her in a handwriting painfully distinct and formal—a business letter evidently.

As Diana opened it, Mrs. Burton watched her from the doorway, and she started as Diana uttered a half-suppressed exclamation, and, looking up with surprise, said—

"How strange! I wonder what it means? 'Fielding'! I never heard the name before. Listen, aunt!"

"DEAR MADAM,—I have a communication of such importance to make to you that I think it would be better if I could do so personally—I mean, by word of mouth. It would give me great pleasure to come down to you, but stress of business renders it quite impossible; and I am compelled to ask you to be good enough to come up to me as early as possible; in fact, to-morrow, if you can do so. I am presuming that your aunt, Mrs. Burton, will accompany you.

"I ought to say that there is nothing in the nature of my communication to alarm you; indeed, quite the contrary. I am, yours very truly,

"JOHN R. FIELDING."

"Fielding!"

Mrs. Burton echoed the name, her hand pressed to her heart, her face deathly pale. "Don't go! You must not go, Diana!"

Diana rose and went to her.

"But why not, Aunt Mary? Do you know him? He is a lawyer, I suppose; his address is Lincoln's Inn. Why are you trembling so? What is the matter?"

Mrs. Burton struggled to regain her composure.

"Nothing—nothing," she said, drawing a long breath. "Yes; he is a lawyer, and we must go."

CHAPTER III

DIANA'S INHERITANCE

To soothe her aunt, Diana made light of the letter, and treated it as quite an ordinary one; but she lay awake a greater part of the night wondering who Mr. Fielding was and what his communication could be.

They caught the early train from Lowminster, fortunately a quick one, and, reaching London, took a cab to 106 Lincoln's Inn. During the journey Mrs. Burton had scarcely spoken, and for a greater part of the time had sat with closed eyes; and as they approached the office her pale, wan face assumed an expression of dogged resolution, as if she were preparing herself for some ordeal.

A clerk in the outer office received them with solemn dignity, and went to announce their arrival to Mr. Fielding. The office was a very old-fashioned one, handsome but grimy. There were cobwebs in the beautifully moulded cornice; dust lay on the furniture and the rows of books; the clerk had moved noiselessly; an air of silence, a hint of mystery, as if the place were haunted by the shades of dead-and-gone secrets, brooded over the building. Diana began to grow nervous, for the first time. The inner door—there were two, one being covered with thick baize—opened, and the clerk, with a gesture and a bow, as if speech were golden and not to be wasted, ushered them in.

Mr. Fielding rose from his chair at the table, and looked from one to the other with a piercing gaze, which was masked behind a smile of welcome. There was a faint surprise as well as keenness in his sharp eyes, as if he had not expected to see so beautiful, so ladylike a girl. He was a middle-aged man with a clean-shaven face and thin, set lips, and his expression, when the smile had faded, was that of alertness, of watchfulness, as if he were on guard and standing ready to parry a thrust or deliver one. The hand he extended to the two ladies was soft but firm, and it closed over Diana's as if he were taking her into custody.

"I am delighted to see you, Miss Bourne," he said, in a low but soft voice. "And you, Mrs. Burton. You are looking extremely well," he added to the latter, "and not in the least changed since I had the pleasure of seeing you last." He uttered the conventional falsehood without a flicker of the eyelid, and waved them courteously to the chairs that had been placed for them by the clerk, so placed that the light fell directly on their faces, enabling Mr. Fielding to watch them easily. "I hope my letter did not alarm you. A lawyer's letter, whatever its nature, is, I know, never very welcome to a lady. You are still at Wedbury; still at the school? You see, I know your whereabouts, your movements." He smiled and nodded at them both impartially.

"Oh yes," replied Diana, "I am still schoolmistress there; and hope to remain so."

"Ah, yes," he assented, looking above her head and beyond her, his lids half lowered. "Let me see, they give you—your salary is—"

"Eighty pounds a year," said Diana, with modest pride. "And an extra sum for light and firing."

"An extra sum for light and firing," he repeated, quite gravely. "Just so; an extra sum for light and firing. And I take it that you are quite happy and contented?"

"Oh, quite, quite!" Diana assured him, her eyes glowing, her lips parted in a smile. "It is the dearest little school and the cosiest little cottage. And the children—ah, well, I don't think that there are such dear, good children in any other part of England. I wish you could come down, and see them. Perhaps you will some day? Wedbury is a very pretty place, and the scenery is famous."

"I am afraid it is very improbable that I should ever visit Wedbury; for if I went it would be to see you, Miss Bourne; and I do not think you will remain there much longer.—I beg of you not to be alarmed," he added quickly, as Diana changed colour.

"I—I was afraid the inspector had been making some complaints," she said apprehensively.

"Not at all," he said. "I happen to know that everybody concerned appreciates your work. What I meant was that it is probable you will be leaving Wedbury at once and of your own accord."

He paused for a moment, then he looked at Mrs. Burton. "Miss Bourne does not remember her father, I suppose?" he said softly. "Ah, no, it isn't possible."

"My father died when I was quite a baby," said Diana, in a low voice.

"Just so," he assented. "At least, so, for the best reasons, you were given to understand; but it was not quite accurate. As a matter of fact, your father died only a few months ago."

As he spoke, he filled a glass with water and unobtrusively placed it on the table within reach of Mrs. Burton; but she disregarded it, and sat, with white face, staring at the wall before her. Diana uttered an exclamation half of grief, half of surprise. She scarcely realised the significance of the communication, but was conscious of a sense both of injury and bereavement. Why had she been kept in ignorance of her father's existence; why had he never come to her, sent for her? As if he read the unspoken question in her face, Mr. Fielding said, in the same low, deliberate voice—

"Your father, Miss Bourne, was a somewhat singular man; he was eccentric and erratic; a man who was so fond of—travelling that he could not remain for any length of time in one place."

While he was speaking, he was watching the elder woman, and, though his face was not turned to her, he managed to convey a warning, to put her on her guard. It was skilfully done, and Mrs. Burton was conscious of his intention, and sat rigid and stonelike.

"When your father left England some years ago—he never returned—he was a poor man. He went to America, where he met with the trials and the opportunities which poor men find so abundant there. For some time, he endured the usual hardships of the man who is struggling to exist, and years elapsed before I heard from him. I was his lawyer."

He paused, and glanced openly at Mrs. Burton, and now with a distinct warning.

"He was then at a place in South America called Chaquetta—rather a pretty name, evidently Mexican. At that period, it was quite a small place, and your father was, in the parlance of business, quite a small man; but Chaquetta grew, and so did your father. There are mines of various kinds in Chaquetta, and your father became connected with some of them. He engaged in other enterprises, and made money. From time to time, he forwarded me certain sums, to hand to Mrs. Burton, who had charge of you—"

"I have kept an account," said Mrs. Burton hoarsely. "I have still some left; all that was spent was spent on Diana—"

"Aunt Mary!" exclaimed Diana remonstratingly, the tears starting to her eyes.

"My dear lady," said Mr. Fielding quickly, "I am quite aware of that. I think I ought to tell you that I have kept myself acquainted with all the details of your and Miss Bourne's life since her father dis—left England. I am quite sure you have been an efficient and affectionate guardian."

"Oh yes—yes!" Diana broke in. "Aunt Mary has been all the world to me—mother, father, brother, sister—all the world."

"Quite so—quite so," said Mr. Fielding reassuringly and soothingly. "Let me see; where was I? Eighty pounds a year, I think you said, and light and firing? A nice little income—very nice. But, as I said, I think you will have to surrender it. As I told you, your father died three months ago." He tapped some papers on the table. "I have all the dates and particulars here, and will give them to you before you go, so that you may look them over quietly, and by yourself. He died—suddenly, but he had, fortunately, made his will. It was a very short one, on a sheet of weather-stained paper; but I am glad to say that it is quite valid. Glad to say, because— Let me read it to you."

He took up one of the papers, and with a glance at Mrs. Burton, read aloud and impressively—

"I, Benjamin Bourne, leave everything of which I am possessed to my daughter, Diana Bourne, who lives in England, under the care of my sister, Mary Burton.
(Signed)   **"BENJAMIN BOURNE."**

Diana's eyes were full of tears. "My father! Oh, why did I not know him? Why did he keep away from me? He must have remembered me, must have been fond of me, to have left me this money!"

Mrs. Burton did not speak; Mr. Fielding looked from one to the other silently, as if to give Diana time to recover from her very natural emotion. Then he said—

"As Mrs. Burton is aware, your father's remittances ceased some time ago, and I feared that he had fallen into bad luck."

"I do not care—about the money," said Diana. "It is his thinking of me—"

"But there was some money," said Mr. Fielding. "You do not ask how much. I think you will be surprised when I tell you that it was a very large sum. In fact — Eighty pounds a year, with light and firing, I think you said, Miss Bourne?" he broke off, with a curious smile;—"in fact, when your father died, he was interested in all, or nearly all, the flourishing concerns in this place with the queer name—mines, factories, land, house property. He died worth, as far as I can ascertain, considerably over a million of money."

Mrs. Burton drew a long breath, and clutched the arms of her chair, and Mr. Fielding, as unobtrusively as before, pushed the glass of water a little nearer to her. As for Diana, her still tear-dimmed eyes opened widely, and her lips parted, as if she were amazed; indeed, she scarcely realised the significance of the lawyer's statement.

"A million of money?" she said at last. "Do you mean that he left this money, all of it, to *me*?"

"That is exactly what I have been trying to break to you," responded Mr. Fielding, "and I trust I have succeeded in breaking it gently. Good news is often a greater shock than bad. And now you understand why it is not very probable that you will remain at Wedbury, teaching school at eighty pounds a year, and light and firing." He leant back, and smiled, and rubbed his hands together, with an air of satisfaction and enjoyment.

Diana put her hand to her brow, and shut her eyes. She was trying to realise this thing that had happened to her; but, for the moment, all that she could think of was that she was going to leave Wedbury, say good-bye to the children she loved.

"Let me think," she said. "A million of money. It belongs to me. Then we are rich?" She stretched out her hand, and clasped her aunt's, and smiled at her through a mist of tears. "Rich! Oh, Aunt Mary, the things I will buy for you!"

Mr. Fielding nodded approvingly.

"There are a few things better even than money," he said, with a smile. "And one of them is a loving and a tender heart. I congratulate you, Miss Bourne, and you, Mrs. Burton—on its possession. Oh yes, you can buy all sorts of things; in fact, there are not many that you cannot buy. And you want to begin at once. Of course, of course! Now, here I can help you." He took some bank-notes from a drawer, as if he had put them there in readiness, as he had, and held them out to Diana. "There is a little money to go on with. Of course, I will open a bank-account for you. Presently, you will be spending a great deal of money. You will want to buy a big house, a large estate in the country, a house in London. I know of one in Park Lane that would just suit you."

Diana had pressed the notes into her aunt's hand, and she turned to Mr. Fielding, with a rather frightened air.

"A big house, an estate—a house in London?" she breathed.

He regarded her with a smile; then he glanced at Mrs. Burton. It was a questioning glance, and she answered it by a flicker of her eyelids and a twitch of her thin, pale lips.

"Ah, well; no, not at once," he said. "All that may come a little later. Just at first, you will like to become accustomed to this vast fortune of yours. Now, I wonder if I might venture to advise you?"

"Yes—oh yes," responded Diana quickly. "We shall be very grateful, shall we not, Aunt Mary? You have been so kind, so considerate. Yes, pray help me; pray tell me what I ought to do."

"Well," he said, leaning forward, and looking at her with a curious expression, as if he were on his guard, "if you are so good as to allow me to advise you, I should say: Don't launch out just at first. In fact, if I were you, Miss Bourne, I think I would say nothing about this sudden—good fortune of yours down at Wedbury. There is no need to make this vast legacy public. The newspapers are so eager to get hold of anything sensational; they would jump at the chance of making a story of this sudden acquisition of wealth; would—rake up—er—I mean, allude to your father's long absence." He did not look at Mrs. Burton, but he saw her hand grip the chair tightly, and her lips writhe. "In fact, you would become public property, and as famous—I was going to say as notorious—as the latest fashionable beauty, or a popular actress. And, I am sure, you would not like that kind of fame; would not care to see your portrait in the society journals, with some such line as this under it: 'Miss Bourne, who inherited over a million of money from her father, whom she had not seen since childhood.'"

Diana winced, and shrank back. "Oh no, no!" she said, in a low voice. "I would rather—"

"Not possess the money," he said, with a nod of approval. "Quite so. Now, I would suggest that you—and Mrs. Burton"—he nodded to the elder woman reassuringly and encouragingly, as if he should say: "There is no need for alarm; all is well"—"take a trip abroad for a time. You can go round the world, if you like. You have almost enough money to construct a railway to the moon. Go where you like, stay as long as you like, enjoy yourself. While you are away, I will look out for a nice little house to which you can come when you are tired of globetrotting. Then presently you yourself shall choose a larger place, an estate suitable to so wealthy a young lady, a house in town, and the rest of it. Oh, but forgive me"—he broke off, with an air of apology—"I am taking it for granted that you will wish me to remain in the position of your solicitor and adviser."

"Yes, yes," said Diana eagerly. "Of course I do. I shall be only too grateful if you will be my friend, as you were once that of my father, and will take care of this money, and will look after Aunt Mary and me."

Mr. Fielding smiled. "The latter will be the pleasantest part of my duty, believe me, Miss Bourne," he said, with a smile. "I have your late father's affairs in hand, and I will go into them, and watch over your interests. You will stay in town for a time, of course; I should recommend—." He mentioned one of the grandest and most expensive of the London hotels.

Diana's face fell, and she looked at her aunt wistfully.

"Oh, must we?" she said hesitatingly, and with evident reluctance. "I—I should like to go back to Wedbury at once. I may have so short a time to stay there; and I want to see as much of my children—before I leave them forever."

Mr. Fielding laughed, and for quite a minute his keen eyes softened, as they dwelt upon the girlish face of the great heiress, whose eyes were dim at the thought of leaving a parcel of school-children.

"Very well, then," he said. "Go back, by all means. But you must write to me; come and see me whenever you want to do so. Please do not forget that you may have as much money as you want. Ah, yes; we will open that account. I'll go down with you to the bank at once."

He rose, and rang for his hat, which the clerk brought and offered to him with an air of one performing a religious ceremony. Mr. Fielding drew on his gloves, looking under his eyelids smilingly at the two timid women.

"Come, then," he said. "The bank is not far; we will walk, shall we?"

He opened the door for them to precede him, and Diana passed out. Mrs. Burton was following her, but paused, and, going back to the room, picked up a glove which she had let fall from her nervous hands. Mr. Fielding waited for her, and she drew near to him, and beckoned him to approach. Her lips moved for a second, but silently, as if the words she wanted to speak would not come; then she said, in a whisper that was almost audible—

"You will not tell her?"

He raised his eyebrows, and regarded her with faint surprise, as if he pretended that he did not understand her.

"Tell her? My dear lady, what is there to tell Miss Bourne?"

Her lips quivered, and she plucked at them, with a shaking hand, her eyes fixed imploringly on his.

He shook his head at her rebukingly.

"My dear Mrs. Burton, let the dead past bury its dead. Why should you and I disinter it? Not only shall I not tell this charming and beautiful girl that which you and I know, but I shall *forget* it. I have done so already. Let me advise you to do the same. We shall only be following the example of the world. Everything is forgotten. Tell her! It would be worse than cruel—it would be foolish. We lawyers are obliged to be cruel, but, believe me, we are never fools—if we can help it.—You have found your glove, Mrs. Burton? Right! Then come along. Sorry to keep you waiting, my dear Miss Bourne. Your aunt dropped her glove. What lovely weather! The sun is shining on you, my dear young lady! May it long continue to shine!"

22

CHAPTER IV

FAMILY COUNCILS

DALESFORD rode home quite quietly—for him; and much to the surprise of Jess, who was accustomed to going hard when her master was on her back, especially at night.

A groom came across the stable-yard to take the horse, and Dalesford signed to him to lead the mare under the lamp, and passed his hands over her carefully. There was a bruise on her shoulder, and Dalesford pointed to it and bade the groom bathe it.

"A fall, my lord?" asked the man, looking up at his lordship's stained fore-head—the bandage had long ago been transferred to Dalesford's pocket—where a spot or two of blood was showing.

Gurdon, his man, was waiting for him, and, as he took his master's hat, at once saw the wound. But he was too well trained to make any remark, or to ask any questions; and, having valeted Dalesford, respectfully bade his lordship "Good-night." Dalesford responded courteously, but absently, and, as the man reached the door, called him back.

"I met with an accident this evening, Gurdon," he said. "Call me a little later, will you? And, Gurdon, there is no need to mention it, please."

"Certainly, my lord," responded Gurdon, with a slight air of surprise, as if the injunction was quite unnecessary.

After he had gone, Dalesford lit a cigar, sank into an easy-chair, and smoked and thought hard.

"I suppose that fellow would have settled me if she had not come up," he said to himself. "A plucky girl. He very nearly struck her, the hound!—and beautiful, too, I think—I wish I could have seen her face distinctly—a musical voice—a lady, evidently. What's she doing in that cottage? Ah, yes, the school cottage. That is it, of course. She is the schoolmistress. I should like to see her again. I wonder what her name is."

He took the handkerchief from his pocket, and examined it. There was the faint trace of some initials, which had been partly erased by the demon washer-woman.

"I'll ask—I must call—"

His pale face coloured, and he frowned; for it had suddenly occurred to him that to meditate a flirtation with this girl, who had, in all probability, saved his life, was a mean way of requiting her heroism. The kindest thing he could do would be to refrain from intruding upon her: the world does not approve of friendship between the heirs to earldoms and young and beautiful schoolmistresses.

It was an unusually virtuous resolution for Dalesford, and he registered it with a certain amount of reluctance, for Diana's face and voice haunted him pleasantly and invitingly. He went to bed at last and slept the sleep which comes so readily to him of the sound constitution; but, when he was awakened in the morning by Gurdon, he was annoyed to find that his face was disfigured by a bruise across the temple, and that the edges of the wound had swollen.

Gurdon respectfully suggested the doctor; but Dalesford laughed.

"Nonsense! You used to be rather good at black eyes and cuts, Gurdon; surely you can cope with this."

"Yes, my lord; but that was—your lordship wasn't—was younger then," he said, as he did his best with warm water and court-plaster. "The earl's compliments, my lord, and will your lordship breakfast with him?"

Dalesford nodded. "All right. Half an hour."

In half an hour he sauntered down the corridor, and was admitted by a footman to the earl's own rooms, a luxurious suite, which overlooked the terrace, lawns, and park. The earl was leaning back in a chair at the breakfast-table, his thin, upright figure wrapped in a dressing-gown of rose-du-barri satin, his white hand turning over his letters.

He raised his brilliant eyes—they shone like onyx—as his son entered; and, as they rested on the bruised forehead, the delicate, dark brows went up slightly, but he said, with his ordinary expression of bland serenity, and with a cheerful nod—

"Good-morning, Vane! Good of you to take compassion on my solitude. Fine morning, isn't it? Have you seen the paper? Red Pepper is scratched. Did you back her? Ah, yes; so did I.—Fish, Benson. Thanks! Don't wait."

When Benson and the footman had gone, the earl, without raising his eyes, said, in a smooth voice—

"Late last night, Vane?"

"Yes, rather, sir," replied Vane. "Had a—fall." He knew that he would have to volunteer an explanation, that his father was far too courtly to ask for one.

"Not a bad one, I trust?" said the earl sympathetically, feeling free now to raise his eyes, and look, but not too keenly or curiously, at the bruised forehead.

"Oh no; mere nothing," said Dalesford casually.

"No? I am glad. All the same, I think we will postpone the dinner-party until to-morrow. May I look at my letters? You have yours, I see."

Vane nodded, and took up one or two; they were mostly bills and reminders, more or less gentle, that they were overdue.

"Same as mine, I suppose?" said the earl, with a smile and shrug of his shoulders. "They should pass a short act making it a criminal offence to send in an account more than twice in twelve months. But Parliament never does anything that is really useful. By the way, talking of bills—most unpleasant and incongruous subject for so charming a morning!—Starkey wants to see you—very badly, I think, judging by his manner."

Mr. Starkey was the earl's steward and business man, the unfortunate gentleman who spent his days in an attempt to manage the family affairs.

"Does he?" responded Dalesford, with languid surprise. "Why on earth should he?"

The earl laughed softly. "I imagine that it is because he has long since discovered that it is of no earthly use his seeing me. Frankly, Starkey—bores me. I feel for him, I sympathise with him. I would not be in his place for—for double the salary he—doesn't get, as I told him the other day. The fact is, Starkey has the unpleasant knack of making me feel uncomfortable. He reminds me of Edgar Poe's raven that was always croaking 'Nevermore.' You remember? Charming poem. You don't read poetry, I think, Vane?"

Dalesford shook his head.

"Not very often, sir. But what is the matter with Starkey?" he asked, as he went to the sideboard, and surveyed the breakfast dainties with an indifferent air.

The earl shrugged his shoulders slightly. "The same old story. I told him yesterday that I always know so well what he is going to say that I could say it for him. And, by George! I think he could as easily voice my responses. Might I trouble you to bring me the caviare? Thanks! So it was not a bad fall last night? Vane, I should take it as a favour if you would get rid of that mare, or ride another one."

"It wasn't the mare's fault, sir," said Dalesford. "I—wasn't keeping a sharp lookout; the night was dark—"

"Quite so," stepped in the earl blandly, but with a certain gravity behind his smiling eyes and serene tones. "But, some darker night, she will throw you, and you may not come off so easily. Pardon! I know how excellent a seat you have. I mean, you may come to utter grief. I dislike playing the part of Cassandra—that is reserved for poor Starkey!—but I should like to remind you that you are the only son I possess, and that I am looking forward to your following me, though a worse one to follow you could not find! Candidly, my dear Vane, I should not like to think that I was going to be succeeded by that unmitigated blackleg, your cousin, Desmond March. And, if anything should happen to you—which Heaven forefend!—he must so succeed."

Dalesford nodded reassuringly. "Nothing is going to happen to me, sir," he said. "I'm as hard as nails."

"I'm delighted to hear you say so. But permit me to remind you that the hardest nails are sometimes broken."

"When did you hear from Desmond March last?" asked Dalesford.

"I—really forget. He wrote to Starkey—again poor Starkey!—some little time ago, saying that he had—'got on to a good thing' was, I think, his phrase, and that he only wanted a thousand pounds to make his fortune. Starkey, I believe, wrote and told him that we, the family generally, also needed a thousand pounds, and wanted them very badly. I don't know whether that settled the matter, or whether it did not. Did not, I should imagine, from my past experiences of Desmond March's pertinacity."

"He's a bad lot, I'm afraid," remarked Dalesford absently.

"He is a very bad lot, indeed," assented the earl, with cheerful confidence. "Now, if *h* would take to riding a mare of uncertain temper—"

Benson came to the door. "Mr. Starkey, my lord."

"My good Benson, did you not tell him that I had not yet come down?" the earl asked, with gentle reproach.

"Yes, my lord; but one of the men had told him—"

The earl groaned. "Ah, well! Shall we have him up, Vane? Come to think of it, it is a capital opportunity—"

"Just as you like, sir; oh yes, certainly."

The earl nodded to the faithful Benson, and Mr. Starkey was admitted. He was a middle-aged man, whose hair had been prematurely whitened and his face lined by the cares of state, the unintermittent struggle to make both ends of the Wrayborough finances meet, and who had never yet been able to witness that meeting.

"Mr. Starkey!" said the earl, in accents of pleasant surprise. "How good of you to come round. Pray join us! Benson, a chair for Mr. Starkey! I'm afraid the coffee is cold; you shall have some freshly made."

"Thank you, my lord," said the steward, in a grave, almost sombre, voice. "I have already breakfasted—hours ago."

"Really! How—how commendable! My dear Mr. Starkey, I have not the least doubt in the world that you owe your excellent health to your admirable habit of early rising. Now, I—and, I fear, Dalesford, here—have acquired a rooted objection to facing the day until it has been properly—aired.—Yes, yes, pray smoke, my dear Vane!" he added, as Dalesford drew out his cigarette-case, and glanced at his father for permission. Mr. Starkey declined the proffered cigarette.

"I never smoke until the evening," he said solemnly. "I find that I keep my brain clearer."

"Ah, yes!" assented the earl. "But where you have no brains—Vane, I assure you, I was speaking of myself only! And now, you want to talk, Mr. Starkey, I know! I'll leave you two—"

He rose with the alacrity of a young man, and prepared to make his escape; but Vane gently caught the rose-du-barri dressing-gown.

"No, you don't, sir!" he said laughingly. "I wouldn't be left alone with Starkey for—for any money."

The earl shook his head reproachfully, and sank back into his chair; and the unfortunate steward, leaning forward in his, looked from one to the other, with an expression of despair, and an impatient resignation produced by a long and painful experience.

"I did want to have some talk with you, my lord; and I am very glad that Lord Dalesford is present. It is difficult to find you together—"

The earl nodded. "Dalesford is too clever for you," he said, with self-depreciation. "You can always run me to earth, but it's not so easy to catch him. Well, you've got us both this morning, and I hope you won't spare him. Just talk to him as you talk to me; I should enjoy it above all things!—That's a Turkish you are smoking, Vane? Thank you!"

He leant back, with half-closed eyes, and a smile of anticipatory amusement on his handsome face, which goaded Mr. Starkey into abruptness.

"I think Lord Dalesford ought to know our position—exactly how we stand, my lord."

The earl nodded complete approval.

"Certainly! Ah, yes; let him have the figures, Mr. Starkey," as the steward took some papers from his pocket. "Perhaps he will understand them; I never do! Do they teach arithmetic at Eton now, Vane? I am sure they didn't in my time.— But I beg your pardon, Mr. Starkey!"

"Things are very serious, Lord Dalesford," said Mr. Starkey, addressing the son, with intense gravity and earnestness. "The affairs of the estate were in a bad way when I came into the office. My father did his best—"

"A most admirable man!" murmured the earl.

"—Did his best; but the tide had begun to set, and he could not stem it, though he tried to do so. I have been trying as hard all my life, and I have failed, as he did, and with a stronger excuse, my lord, for the debts have been accumulating. Such encumbrances as ours are like a huge snowball that grows bigger and bigger the longer it rolls."

"Clever simile!" murmured the earl. "So apt and true!"

"At one time, we were able, with more or less difficulty, to raise money to pay the various interests, as they fell due; but, lately, the difficulty has been much greater, and I find it almost impossible to provide the large sum necessary to meet the accruing charges on the mortgages."

"Then why not sell some of the property?" asked the earl, as if he were making a suggestion as novel as it was brilliant. Mr. Starkey glanced at him with mild despair.

"Which, my lord?" he asked laconically. "Wrayborough has its mortgage; Glenaskel and all the Scotch property is held in lien by the Insurance company; the Lancashire mines are dipped as deep as I dare. The London property is covered by the Aaron loan—"

"The château at Avranches?" suggested the earl.

"Sold four years ago. Surely your lordship remembers! It was to pay the stud accounts."

"Yes, yes! Pardon! Of course! Stupid of me! But my memory is one of my weakest points, as you know."

"Then the revenue—I mean the revenue from the land, the estate generally— has been decreasing rapidly for years past. It has always been difficult to get the rent, for the tenants"—he groaned—"have been, and still are, under the impression that they need not pay until they choose, and cannot understand any pressure —"

"No, no; there must be no pressure, Mr. Starkey!" said the earl. "Bless my soul, they wouldn't understand it! It would be cruel—cruel to us, as well as to them. Why, my dear fellow, I should never be able to face them, never be able to ride over the place. Tut! tut! The mere idea of pressure calls up the distressing picture of the Ejected Tenant; smoking roof, family and furniture out in the road;

women and children crying, and the men wringing their hands, and cursing the landlord. No; no!"

"Exactly!" exclaimed Mr. Starkey, with mild exasperation. "My hands are tied—"

"My dear fellow, all our hands are tied!" retorted the earl cheerfully. "We live in democratic times— Surely you're not going, Vane?"

"I was, sir," said Dalesford, with a smile. "I don't understand politics, and I want to see how the mare is. Look here, Mr. Starkey; I quite understand that we're in a bad way, and I'm sorry, as much for your sake as ours.—But we've always been in a bad way, haven't we, sir?"

"Certainly, always," said the earl, with prompt acquiescence.

"And Mr. Starkey has always pulled us through, and always will, I'm sure. You see, you understand the whole thing, know the ropes so well. Take my advice, sir, and leave it all to Mr. Starkey."

"Very good advice. I will!" responded the earl.

With a nod to Mr. Starkey, Lord Dalesford left the room. The earl looked after him, and sighed and smiled; he was fond, very fond, and proud, very proud, of his handsome, stalwart son.

Mr. Starkey rose, and put the papers back in his pocket; and he also sighed; for he, too, was attached to the heir of Wrayborough, and would have liked to save him from the impending ruin. He stood lost in gloomy thought, and the earl, sympathising with him, said, at last, "Things *are* bad, I suppose, Mr. Starkey. Is there anything you can suggest?"

The steward raised his heavy eyes, then dropped them again, under the gaze of the earl's brilliant ones.

"You have, I see! Pray speak out!"

"There is one way out of our difficulties, my lord," said Mr. Starkey in a low voice. "I—I feel a certain delicacy; I hesitate—"

"But why, my dear sir? I am quite sure you would suggest nothing that would be painful or derogatory to our position; I mean yours, as well as ours, of course."

"It rests with Lord Dalesford," said Mr. Starkey, still hesitatingly.

"Yes? I am much relieved to find that it doesn't rest with *me*. What is it? What is it you want him to do?"

"To marry, my lord," said Mr. Starkey desperately.

The earl raised his brows, and laughed.

"My dear sir, I wish to Heaven he would!"

"And—and marry money," said Mr. Starkey.

The earl made a grimace.

"You—you put it somewhat bluntly," he said ruefully. "But"—after a pause —"you are right. Yes; you are right. It is an unpleasant way out of the difficulty; but, if there is no alternative, why—poor Vane must do it. But who is to tell him so?"

Mr. Starkey frowned. "If I may suggest, your lordship would be the proper person—"

The earl smiled grimly. "I may be the proper person—but I'm hanged if I do it! Now, you, my dear sir, you who know how extremely necessary the step is—"

Mr. Starkey gripped his thin, long hands behind him, and set his teeth.

"Something must be done!" he said almost defiantly. "And I see no other way of saving the estate from ruin. It is—forgive me if I speak plainly, my lord—"

"My dear fellow, you always speak plainly," murmured the earl, with a stifled sigh.

"It is time Lord Dalesford married. I cannot forget that, if anything happened to him—"

"My dear Mr. Starkey, don't, for Heaven's sake—*don't* make matters worse by croaking!" implored the earl.

"—That the title and estate—what there is left of it!—would pass to Mr. Desmond March," went on Mr. Starkey. "The mere thought of such a—a calamity—"

"Then, for Heaven's sake, don't let us think of it!" broke in the earl.

"And, speaking of Mr. March, my lord, reminds me that he has written to me again. It is a—well, threatening letter this time. He threatens that, if we do not send him the money he asks for, he will—well, come to the Hall for it, and demand it in person."

The earl shuddered visibly. "My dear Mr. Starkey, such a visitation must be warded off, at any cost. Send him five hundred pounds, and—and tell him to go to the devil!"

"He has gone there long since, my lord," remarked Mr. Starkey grimly. "Five hundred pounds! I'm sure I don't know where I'm to find—"

"Try him with two hundred and fifty," said the earl persuasively.

"And—and Lord Dalesford, the plan I suggested?"

The earl rose, and sighed.

" 'Pon my word, my dear sir, I couldn't tell him he must marry for money. You must. Not that it matters which of us undertakes the task. He wouldn't do it. He would laugh at either and both of us."

Mr. Starkey went to the door, but was arrested by a cough and a murmur from the earl.

"Oh, Mr. Starkey, I shall want a few hundreds by the end of the week."

The unfortunate steward opened his lips, shut them again; then, with something between a sigh and a groan, said—

"Very well, my lord."

As he passed out, a footman came up, with a letter on a salver.

"For you, sir."

Mr. Starkey opened the letter, read it absently for a minute, then he stifled an exclamation, and nervously wiped the beads of perspiration which had started to his brow. Of course it was a demand for money. He turned, as if with the intention of re-entering the earl's room, but hesitated, and, at last, with a gesture of despair, walked slowly and heavily down the great staircase, with Black Care close behind him.

CHAPTER V

TUBBY, CHAPERON

"MR. FIELDING, I wonder whether you would mind very much if I called you my Fairy Godmother?" said Diana.

Mr. Fielding leant back in his cane rocking-chair, and smiled. He had had an excellent dinner, prepared by a cook of his own choosing, and was enjoying a mild—a very mild—cigar, through the smoke of which he was regarding, with intent appreciation, the girl reclining in the chair beside him.

They were seated on the terrace, under a broad verandah, which ran the length of what the house agent had called "the most recherché residence in Berkshire." Before them lay a lawn like green plush, broken here and there by beds of flowers, which rivalled the hues of the peacock that strutted about in the red glow of the sunlight. Beyond the lawn ran that most wonderful of all rivers, the placid, silver Thames, its deep blue broken by white spots—the swans that floated near the landing-stage. A pine wood rose behind the house, and filled the air with the delicious and health-giving odour of terebene. Noisy London might have been a hundred miles away, for the only sounds that broke the stillness were the cry of the peacock, the rustle of the swans' wings, and the notes of the nightingale, who was just tuning up for his nightly concert.

"You shall call me what you like, Miss Diana," responded Mr. Fielding, with the affability he always displayed in Diana's presence.

"Thanks, very much!" said Diana laughingly. "And, really, the old lady in the red cloak and high poke hat, who appeared to poor Cinderella, and did the conjuring tricks with the melon and the mice, did not better deserve the title than you. Why, yes; I was just Cinderella. And you came and waved your wand, and —and here I am! 'With my pockets full of money,' with everything the heart of man—I mean woman—could wish for! It is marvellous, and you are the most effective Fairy Godmother that ever lived."

"You enjoyed yourself abroad?" he asked.

"Oh yes, yes! I had, sometimes, dreamed of seeing all these wonderful things, but I never thought my dream would be realised. 'Enjoyed myself'? Yes, indeed! The days passed like a vision. I used to start awake at night, and ask myself if it could be true that I, Diana Bourne, was travelling on the Continent like a princess incognito. It was so hard to realise that I could go where I liked, stay there as long as I liked, or move when I liked. That I was rich enough to put up at the palatial hotels, travel first-class—do you know, Fairy Godmother, that that little matter of first-class, instead of third, helped me more than anything else to realise the—the change that your wand had wrought for your Cinderella? Only the rich ride first-class, you know—and, then, to feel that I could buy anything I wanted— Ah, you can't understand the delicious thrill that used to run through me as I gazed into a shop-window, and coveted some of the things in it, and then suddenly remembered that I could walk in and buy them without counting the cost!"

"And you bought a great many things?" he said, with a man-of-the-world's enjoyment of the naïve confession made by the beautiful lips, half-parted with the smile of happiness.

"Oh, dear, yes! All the things I didn't want. That's it, you know. To be able to buy the things you don't want! Whenever I saw anything that I thought Aunt Mary would like, oh, the joy of stalking in, and saying, 'I'll have that, please!' Poor aunt was frightened at first, and rebuked me for extravagance; and I don't think she is quite resigned even yet."

"You travelled a great deal?"

"Oh yes! However beautiful the place was, there always seemed to be a still more beautiful one a little farther on. Yes, we covered no end of ground. France, Germany, Switzerland, Italy—it would fill a geography! And everywhere we were made much of, and treated as if we were, indeed, princesses. It was the money, of course—"

"Not altogether the money," he murmured smilingly, as he looked at the beautiful face, the graceful figure clad in its costly dress of black lace, upon which sparkled the few diamonds Aunt Mary had persuaded Diana to buy.

"And, at first, it seemed as if I could go on, and on, and on until I had gone right round the world; but, presently"—she paused, and her eyes grew dark and dreamy—"but, presently, I—well, I was homesick; I wanted to see 'the white cliffs of old England,' to hear the dear old Cockney twang, the broad, country drawl; to see the green fields—there are no green fields like those of England!— to hear the railway porters shrieking the stations by names quite unlike their proper ones; to breathe the London smoke, and hear the cows lowing as they turned home at milking-time. You see, I mixed it all up together—town and country. I wanted them both. I wanted Great Britain—England, Scotland, and Ireland! All of it!"

She drew a long breath, and looked wistfully, lovingly, at the scene before her.

"I wanted—home! And then, when I felt as if I should die if I didn't get there, you—you Fairy Godmother—found me this beautiful house—why, it's a veritable fairy one! I could have cried aloud when you brought me here, and showed me this pretty place, with its gables, and its broad eaves, its dainty rooms, and its lovely gardens!"

Mr. Fielding smiled, with self-satisfaction. "I had an idea that it was just the place you'd like, Miss Diana."

"It's a dream!" said Diana rapturously. "To-morrow, I'm going to spend the whole day going over it; I haven't seen half of it yet! Janet, my maid—that's another thing I'm not quite used to yet; a maid, who insists upon helping me dress, and won't let me do my own hair, or mend a thing!—Janet tells me that there are cows—actually cows! And a dairy! Do you think I shall be allowed to make the butter, Fairy Godmother?"

"I'm afraid not!" he replied laughingly.

Diana pretended to pout. "That's just the one drawback of being disgustingly rich. I find you can't quite do as you like. And the horses! There are the big carriage horses; and there's the dearest mite of a pony; I felt inclined to pick it up and kiss it! And I'm going to learn to ride. Yes! Years ago"—her voice grew softer, more dreamy—"I remember watching the ladies riding in the Park. I was a tiny child, rather shabby—oh, very shabby, and—and sometimes rather, oh, very hungry. And I used to watch them—not enviously, for that would have been absurd, but as if they were denizens of another world, as if they had come out of heaven just—just for a ride, and were going back there. And now I am one of them!"

She was silent a moment.

"If—if I should ride in the Park, and saw a shabby little girl looking at me, I should think of that other one, myself, years ago; and I—well, I should want to lift her on to the saddle beside me."

Mr. Fielding nodded, and looked at her thoughtfully. He was not easily moved to sentiment, but very often he was quite touched by some such speech of Diana's.

"It's the quaintest, the prettiest village here," she went on. "The children were coming out of school as we drove through. And the people looked so nice, and prosperous—and touched their hats, and curtsied. Do you think—I wonder whether they would let me visit the school, and go and see some of the people? Do you think they'd mind?"

Mr. Fielding laughed. "My dear young lady, they'd be delighted, I'm sure. But"—with sudden caution—"you must be careful! They're certain to be always having measles, or whooping-cough, or something; they always do in healthy villages."

Diana laughed. "Oh, I'm not afraid of I. D.'s," she said.

"I. D.'s?"

"Inspectors' abbreviation for Infectious Diseases," explained Diana glibly. "They're dreadful things: they close the school." She was silent for a moment or two, her thoughts wandering back to her own school, her own children there at Wedbury, and she recalled the pain of parting with them.

"Oh, I must, I *must* go and see the school! I'll have the children up here, on the lawn. And give them buns and milk. Nothing in the world is half so good as a bun, a real, indigestible bun, you know."

Mr. Fielding smiled again. "Oh yes; I can see that you will slip into the part of Lady Bountiful, and that this pretty place will be soon overrun by noisy children—and snuffy old women."

Diana nodded defiantly, and laughed softly. At this moment, one of the French windows behind them opened, and Mrs. Burton came out, in her quiet way.

"Are you sitting here without a shawl, Diana? You will catch cold," she said, in her low, nervous voice.

"Shawl me no shawls, Aunt Mary!" exclaimed Diana gaily. "It's quite warm —it's Italy in England! Come and sit down, and talk with Fairy Godmother!"

She put her white hand—there was now the glitter of diamonds, instead of inkstains, on the beautiful fingers—to draw her aunt down; but Mrs. Burton shook her head.

"No; I have a great deal to do," she said, and, after a nervous glance at the lawyer, she re-entered the house.

"And Mrs. Burton? She enjoyed her long trip?" he asked.

"I—I hope so. No; I'm afraid she didn't. Poor Aunt Mary! I think she was homesick the day we left England! The months must have seemed very long to her. I was selfish to stay—but she would not hear of coming back till I, too, longed for home. Poor Aunt Mary!" Her brows came together thoughtfully, wistfully. "I wonder why she is so—so nervous, so full of nameless fears and forebodings? I had hoped that the change—I mean, all this tremendous sum of money, and the change of scene—would have dispelled her nervousness; but it has not. Do you know what is the cause of it, Mr. Fielding?"

Mr. Fielding coughed, and looked straight before him.

"Your aunt is too old to be affected by the change," he said. "I mean, that her early life, the struggles and privations— My dear young lady, you can look back at the little girl who watched the horses in the Park, and smile. Fortune came to you before it was too late—strange to say! You can forget—well, no, not forget, but look back without bitterness; you are young. But your aunt—"

Diana looked at him wistfully, as if she were not quite satisfied with his explanation.

"Aunt Mary is not bitter," she said. "No; it is not that. It is as if—it is so hard to describe—as if she were always dreading lest something should happen; as if she were waiting for some trouble—"

"Hush!" he whispered warningly, as Mrs. Burton came out again, and put a shawl over Diana's shoulders.

"Your dress is thin," she said, "and the evening is growing chilly."

She was gone again, almost before Diana could thank her.

Mr. Fielding looked after the elder woman, with a frown.

"Mrs. Burton will be—better, now that she is back in England," he said.

"How late the light holds!" remarked Diana presently. "Look, they are only just beginning to light up in that house on the other side of the river. How big it looks, though one can only see a bit of it above the trees. Who lives there, do you know?"

Mr. Fielding shook his head.

"I haven't the least idea. But you will soon know, for the people will be calling on you before long."

Diana laughed. "Do you think so? I hope the natives will be friendly. But, perhaps"—rather hopefully—"they won't call."

"They may or they may not," he said. "Of course, if they knew that you were —well, a millionairess—"

Diana made a little deprecatory gesture.

"Don't! I've taken a dislike to the word. I don't want to be sought after for— my money."

"I know, my dear young lady, I know," he said soothingly. "That's why I bought this small place—though it's a pretty expensive one for its size—instead of buying an estate with a mansion suitable for a person of your wealth. I might have purchased one of the historic houses—"

"I'm glad you did not," Diana cut in. "I'm not ashamed of my riches, but— but I don't want to flaunt them. During our travels, I met some people who were all diamonds and gold-dust—you know what I mean?—and I don't want to seem like them. No; this beautiful, this fairy house, with its quaint gables, and unexpected turnings—do you know, I lost my way in one of the passages—corridors, I suppose I ought to call them?—is more than sufficient for me."

Mr. Fielding regarded her contemplatively.

"You are a strange girl," he said. "Most young women would have been only too delighted to reign in a big place, to make aristocratic friends, and—and seize upon the advantages which such wealth as yours gives."

"Yes; but consider!" said Diana, leaning forward in her chair, and regarding him gravely. "Only a few months ago, I was—well, just a schoolmistress at Wedbury, with eighty pounds a year, *and* lights and firing." She mimicked his voice, and he laughed. "Then you came with the wonderful story of this inherited wealth, and I blossomed into a—hateful word!—millionairess. At first, it seemed as if I had inherited the whole wide world. Then, presently, I realised that money cannot buy everything; that, though nearly everyone bows down to it, it is, after all, powerless to wave the magic wand which lifts us to happiness; and— Ah, well, I'm glad you didn't buy a historic mansion, and compel me to play the great lady. Here, at Rivermead, I can be 'a simple, single lady, living at her ease.' You are sure you have not told anyone that I am—I am disgustingly rich?"

"Quite sure," replied Mr. Fielding, with a smile. "You can—well, conceal your golden hoof as long as you please." He stifled a yawn. "There is something in this air that makes me sleepy. And I have some letters to write before I turn in to-night. I think I'll go to the study."

Diana laughed. "Is that what you call the dear little room on the left of the hall, the room with the book-shelves? All right. I'll tell them to send you in some —is it whisky-and-soda?"

"Whisky-and-soda it is, Miss Diana," he responded. "The drink that gives an edge to giddy youth and a support to venerable old age."

When he had gone, Diana leant back in her exquisitely comfortable deck-chair, and looked before her with half-closed eyes. Not yet had she realised the change that had come into her life, and often, in her sleep, she awoke fully convinced that she was still the schoolmistress of Wedbury, and oppressed by the fear that she had over-slept herself, and was late.

She lay in a reverie for some time; then, aroused by the striking of the church clock—she meant presently to "do" that ancient church thoroughly—she drew her shawl round her, and, liberating herself from the embraces of the too comfortable chair, strolled slowly to the landing-stage.

The moon was nearly at its full, and the river—well, even a minor poet could not have done justice to it to-night. The water shone with the keenness of a Damascus blade. The shadow of every withy stood out like the tree itself, the murmur of the weir sang a mystic and soul-soothing song.

Diana stood on the landing-stage, looking out over the river, her spirit in perfect harmony with the scene; and it came like a shock to be suddenly awakened to the prosaic by hearing a girl's voice chanting—

> **"If I love you, and you love me,**
> **And we love each other, then—**
> **How happy we shall be. For I love you**
> **And you love me—"**

She looked in the direction of the musical voice, and saw a punt coming down-stream. A man was punting; a young girl—Diana could see her long brown hair streaming down her back—was half sitting, half lying, in the stern. She was dressed in white, with a shawl drawn across her girlish bosom, and on her lap was a fat pug.

The man was tall, and partly in evening dress; that is to say, he had taken off his coat and waistcoat, and had tied a handkerchief round his waist, so that he might punt with ease.

It was a pretty picture, and Diana regarded it admiringly and wistfully, because the young girl seemed so happy. And, for all her wealth, Diana had not, as yet, tasted perfect happiness; she knew that there was still something lacking in her life.

Loath to break their solitude—there was no sound other than that of the girl's voice—she drew back into the shadows; and, with a strange sense of loneliness, watched them.

The punt came swiftly down the stream, so swiftly that the nose of it nearly touched the landing-place, and the pug leaped to the end of the punt, sprang ashore, and ran, sniffing and panting, toward Diana.

"Oh, Vane!" cried the girl in the punt. "Tubby has gone ashore! You must go after her! Aunt Selina would never forgive me if I lost her."

The man shrugged his shoulders, and sent the punt to the landing-stage. Then he dropped the pole, and stepped out.

By this time Diana had conquered her nervousness, and, with the pug jumping up and yapping at her, confronted the man.

"I beg your pardon—the dog," he said apologetically. "Ah, here she is. I am very sorry—"

He stopped short, and looked fixedly at Diana. It was not only the beauty of the face upon which the moon was shining, but the vague sense of having seen it before, that arrested his words. If he had not quite forgotten the young schoolmistress, who had rendered him such signal service on a certain night, his memory of her was dim and uncertain.

But Diana had recognised him, and waited—wondering. He frowned for a moment, in a puzzled fashion, then took up the burden of his apology.

"The little beast jumped off the punt—I drove it too near your landing-stage. Pray forgive it—and me—for trespassing."

He packed the dog under his arm, raised his straw hat, and strode back to the punt. Diana had not spoken. For some reason, which she could not have explained, she was glad that he had not recognised her. She had no wish to renew her acquaintance with "the wild Lord Dalesford."

"Have you got it?" the young girl in the punt called out. "Oh, Vane, how tiresome! Give her to me!"

She held out her arms, forgetting that, in doing so, she was releasing the punt which she had been holding to the landing-place; and, of course, it swung downstream. She staggered slightly, nearly lost her balance, and quite dropped the pug into the water.

"Vane!" she cried, with a girlish shriek. "I've let it fall overboard!"

"So I hear!" said Dalesford coolly; he knelt down, and snatched the dog from the water, holding it up, dripping, and gasping indignantly.

"Oh, look at it! It's wet through! Whatever shall I do? Aunt Selina will have a fit if I take it home like this—a series of fits. Look at its eyes! They're bulging dreadfully!"

"It's all right," said Dalesford. "The little beast will be dry by the time we get home. Don't worry, Mab."

"Oh no, it won't!" she responded tragically. "It takes ever so long to dry, and Aunt Selina will be fearfully angry. She won't let me come out with you again, Vane!"

There was a touch of pathos in the girl's voice, which made Dalesford lay the pole down, and take the pug from her.

"I'll dry him on my coat," he said. "No, I can't; I left it on the bank. Confound Tubby!"

Diana had been watching the comedy from a coign of vantage in the shadow.

"Perhaps you can dry it with this," she said, offering her shawl.

The girl in the punt sprang ashore, exclaiming gratefully—

"Oh, how kind of you! But, really, we ought not to— Must I?" as Diana gently pressed the shawl into her hand. "Vane, give her to me! Oh, you troublesome little wretch! There, there!"

The shivering pug stared at her resentfully, and squirmed under the process as the girl rubbed it dry.

"So very, very kind of you! It's my aunt's dog, and she makes no end of a fuss over it. My Aunt Selina, you know— But, perhaps you don't know? Lady Selina Dashwood. She—we—she and I— Vane, what are you grinning at?"

"You seem to be getting a little mixed, Mab; that's all," he said.

"No, I'm not—not a bit," retorted the girl indignantly. "She and I live up at the house there. And Vane, my cousin—I mean, Lord Dalesford—is staying with us."

Dalesford raised his hat. "Please let me continue the introduction," he said, with a smile. "This young lady who dipped Tubby is my cousin, Lady Mabel Dashwood. She would bring the obnoxious little brute—"

"No, I didn't!" retorted Lady Mabel. "You know very well that you said, 'Let her come,' Vane!—The introduction isn't complete yet. This is my cousin, Vane —Lord Dalesford."

Dalesford raised his hat, and seemed to wait; and Diana said, with a smile—

"My name is Bourne—Diana Bourne."

As Dalesford had not sought to learn the name of the Wedbury schoolmistress, it brought no reminiscence to him. But Lady Mabel exclaimed, with renewed interest—

"Oh, I know! I heard that you had taken Rivermead; that you were coming to live here. What a beautiful little place it is! I am so glad to see you. We have heard so much about you."

"So much about me?" echoed Diana.

"Yes; people, especially country people, will talk, you know. Some of them said that you are a famous opera singer—"

"My dear Mabel!" chided Dalesford, in a low voice.

But Diana only laughed.

"I'm sorry to disappoint you," she said. "I am not famous for anything. I am simply—myself."

Lady Mabel drew nearer to her, and looked up at her with a smile.

"How—how prettily you said that! Merely yourself! And that's enough, isn't it? And, in your case, quite enough! Oh, I wish I knew you! I mean, I should like to know you. I'll ask Aunt Selina to call, may I? You won't mind—Tubby is nearly dry now. But I've wetted your shawl; it's soaking! We'll bring it back to you. May we? No; that won't do, for then Aunt Selina will know that Tubby got wet. But you'll let us call?"

"I shall be very pleased," said Diana.

"Come, Mabel!" Dalesford called from the punt.

Lady Mabel held out her hand to Diana.

"I hope you'll let us be friends!" she said, her large eyes expanding girlishly. "I have no friends, excepting Vane, and he"—eyeing him accusingly—"is only a man—and a cousin!"

She held Diana's hand until Dalesford called again to her; then she sprang into the punt, and Dalesford, raising his hat, sent the boat up-stream.

"Oh, Vane, what a beautiful—what a perfectly lovely girl!" cried Mabel. "—Sit still, you tiresome brute; you're dry now!—Did you ever see such beautiful eyes! And such a mouth! I—and I'm only a girl!—wanted to kiss it! What you must have felt! But you are one of those men who never enthuse. I'll get Aunt

Selina to call on her. I want to know her, to see more of her. Now, *that* is my ideal of perfect womanhood!"

"Is that so?" asked Dalesford; but, though his voice was indifferent, he was mentally disturbed. For the face, the voice, had impressed him, and recalled vague memories.

And Diana? His presence, the artless words of Lady Mabel, had recalled the night she had helped him, dressed his wound. She returned to the house, half amused, half wistful.

CHAPTER VI

MR. MARCH'S ACCOMPLISHMENTS

In dealing with Mr. Desmond March, one has to resort to superlatives. For instance, he was one of the handsomest men in London—and there are several good-looking men in that little city—one of the best-dressed, the most beautifully mannered, the cleverest in the art of living by one's wits, and the most unscrupulous of all the professors of that grimly fascinating art.

He was the heir presumptive to the Wrayborough earldom and estates —"what there was left of them," as poor Mr. Starkey would have said—and had gone through the usual curriculum of young men of good birth and position. Eton and Oxford had done their best—or worst—for him, and he had made a faint, a very faint, pretence of reading for the Bar, at which he would undoubtedly have shone; but there was a bad strain in Desmond March, and it spread, and spread until it permeated the whole of him, and made him—what he was: a spendthrift, a wastrel, and a cumberer of the ground, a man without principle and without an object in life, save that of living for the hour only and for the pleasures thereof.

As the heir presumptive to an historic title, he had the *entrée* to the best society in England—that society which circles round the throne itself, and keeps our aristocracy sweet in the nostrils of the people; but Desmond March had long since dropped from the Olympian heights, and descended to the smart set, and the openly vicious one which hangs to its fringe.

There is a certain set of men—and women—in London of whom it may be said that no one knows how they live; and Desmond March belonged to it. He had an allowance from his uncle, Lord Wrayborough, but it was always mortgaged by bills and I.O.U.'s before pay-day. Even the sums which he was able to extort, by threats of inflicting his presence on the earl, were swallowed up, spent, dissipated almost before they were received. He was in debt to every tradesman he employed; and yet they kept up the supply of beautiful clothes, of choice wines, and cigars of the best brands, of costly orchids for his buttonhole and table, and of all the little luxuries which were more vital to Mr. Desmond March than absolute necessaries, for they knew that there were only two lives between their aristocratic and good-for-nothing customer and the peerage; that something "might happen" to his cousin, Lord Dalesford, any day, and then—ah, well, they would be paid some part, at least, of their accounts.

And, indeed, they—and other people, who ranked above tradespeople— found it difficult to refuse anything to the well-bred scamp with the pleasant voice and smile, the ingratiatory, fascinating manner.

There was scarcely anything reprehensible that Mr. Desmond March did not do, and do with so charming an air of irresponsibility, that vice almost assumed the aspect of virtue. He drank heavily, but—like most of the family, alas!—he could carry with ease, and a clear head, an amount of champagne that would have driven an ordinary man under the table, or into the police-court. He gambled—there was no keener hand at écarté, baccarat, bridge, even among his own sharp set—and he was a terror to the mothers of young lads just starting on the perilous voyage of life, lads who were as fascinated by the charm of his manner as a bird is by the glitter of the serpent's eye.

Now and again society rang, shrieked, with indignation at the ruin of some promising young nobleman, or rich man's son, by the handsome-faced, soft-voiced Mr. Desmond March. But nothing happened, and that gentlemanly rook sailed on, with unbroken wing and unruffled plumage.

Actions at law, even criminal prosecutions, were sometimes threatened, but the keenest and most astute were unable to substantiate a charge of unfair play; and the scandal was hushed up, and forgotten—very often for the sake, and in the interests of, the lad who had been plucked.

And the women, alas! the women of the smart set especially, were on Desmond March's side; the man was so irresistibly frank and sweet-mannered that it was difficult, well-nigh impossible, to believe that he could be guilty of the merciless cruelty of which rumour accused him. "Oh, no doubt there was some mistake; he could not be so bad as he was painted." He was skilful, as well as lucky, at cards; and, "of course, he won, and the losers didn't like it." "Well, they weren't obliged to play, were they?"

On the evening Diana had lent her shawl to dry Lady Selina's pug, Mr. Desmond March sallied from his flat in Hans Crescent—the luxurious suite of rooms which had proved a veritable hawk's nest to many a wealthy young man who had entered it with pride, for Desmond March was exclusive and sparing of his invitations, to leave it plucked and shorn of nearly all his feathers—and, with a choice Havana cigar between his lips, sauntered down Pall Mall.

He had risen at midday, had breakfasted and lunched wisely and well, had read his letters, turned over the pages of a French novel, and, at length, the day well advanced, had been turned out by his valet a model of well-groomed, well-dressed, and debonair manhood.

The devil, we are told, goeth up and down like a roaring lion, seeking whom he may devour; but there was no roaring here; there was more of the graceful panther about Desmond March, the sleek-footed, beautifully marked leopard, than the fierce and openly voracious king of beasts; and women, as they drove past in their carriages, turned and bowed eagerly, as he lifted his irreproachable hat, and greeted them with his winning smile.

He was going to dine at his club, one of the most expensive and exclusive of the fast ones, the Apollo; but, as he reached the handsome building, he paused, glanced at his watch, and, turning aside, went down the steps by the Duke of York's Column, and through the Mall and the Horse Guards' gate, past the House of Commons to a street off the river.

It was a small and shabby street, and Desmond March stopped at one of the smallest and shabbiest of the houses and rang a shrill bell.

The door was opened by a maid-of-all-work, with a corrugated brow, and shrewd lips half opened with a Cockney impertinence; but the lips closed at the sight of the handsome face and the brilliant, smiling eyes, and she drew back, and jerked her shoulder toward the stairs.

"Yes, Miss Edgworth is in, sir," she said, though he had not made any inquiry.

"Thank you, Emma," he said. He paused a moment as she shut the door, and he touched a soiled and commonplace bit of ribbon on her bosom with the tip of his perfectly gloved finger.

"Not quite right, I think, Emma. Get yourself a piece of blue—light blue; that's your colour."

The grimy hand closed over the shilling, and she stood at the top of the kitchen stairs, and looked after him admiringly, murmuring—

"Ain't 'e 'andsome! And 'ow 'e knows! Yes, blue's my colour right enough! Ah, 'e's a purfeck gen'leman, 'e is!"

The perfect gentleman went slowly up the stairs, and knocked at a door on the first floor, and a soft and gentle voice bade him "Come in."

As he opened the door and entered, a young girl looked up from a table placed near the window, a table strewn with drawings and drawing materials, over which she had been bending. She was a pretty girl, small and slight, a girl with a pale face and sad blue eyes. Looking at her, one would have been reminded of a forget-me-not, a forget-me-not whose colour and fragrance were not quite washed out by the rain and the scorching sun.

The pale face flushed as she saw who her visitor was, and she rose, and went to him, not with outstretched hand, but with a feverish, wistful welcome in her eyes and in her suddenly tremulous lips.

"Desmond! You have come—then? I—I scarcely expected—and yet I hoped —"

"Yes; I got your letter, Lucy, and here I am, you see. What! Did you think I should have the bad manners to ignore a lady's invitation?"

She looked at him with a touch of reproach in her eyes, as if she resented his tone; then she sighed, and sank into the chair again.

"Yes, I hoped— And yet, perhaps, it would have been better for me, for both of us, if you had not come. It would have been hard to bear, but—"

He let his hand fall lightly on her shoulder, and took up the drawing on which she was at work.

"Pretty, undeniably pretty," he said, holding it up, and surveying it with critical admiration. "You do that sort of thing very well, Lucy—deuced well. But I am afraid there is not much oof in it, eh?"

She took the drawing from his hand, and shook her head.

"No. It is badly paid. They have cut down the prices again—it is a bad time for this sort of work; this kind of magazine is not selling well. And there are so many eager for employment. I am very lucky to get this to do—it is a series, see!

41

But I don't want to talk of my work, Desmond, but of myself, and—and you," she broke off, the colour flushing her pretty face, her eyes uplifted to him appealingly.

"You couldn't choose a pleasanter topic, my dear Lucy," he said lightly, and he bent to kiss her; but she drew back, and put up her thin hand, with its long, flexible fingers, to keep his lips from her.

"No—no! Wait; listen—oh, listen, Desmond!"

"My dear child, what am I doing but listening? And, by George, I'd rather listen to you than Melba herself!"

As he spoke, he stroked the soft, golden hair at her temple, and this time she did not draw back; for she loved the man, and his touch was joy to her.

"What is it, birdie?" he asked, after a pause, during which she had been trying to escape from the spell of his caress.

"I—I want you to remember your promise," she said, in a low, fluttering voice. "Ah, Desmond, you have not forgotten it, forgotten how many times you have made it!"

"Faith, no!" he responded, with a pleasant laugh. "And I'm going to keep it —"

Her face lit up, and she turned to him, with her blue eyes glowing.

"—Some day," he added smoothly. Then, as her face fell, he went on, in a soft, seductive voice, "And I'm hoping that day may soon come. See here, dearest; you know how I stand—up to my neck in debt, relying entirely on the generosity of that old uncle of mine—confound him! As it is, I don't stand too high in his good graces; a marriage—well, such a marriage—Tut, tut; don't force me to be brutal! But, my child, you know what the world, his world, would call it. 'Imprudent' would be the least word for it. You're the sweetest, the dearest girl in all the world, but, unfortunately, you weren't born in the purple, and, worse still, you're not an heiress. Now, Lucy, you're too sweet, you're too fond of me, to want to ruin me, to ruin us both?"

She leant her head on her hand, to hide the tears that rose to her eyes.

"That's putting the thing with cruel candour, birdie," he said; "but, you know, it's the truth. Wait, dearest, wait until the old man goes off the hook, till that precious cousin of mine breaks his neck—"

His face darkened, the eyes flashed with an ugly light, and the girl shuddered.

"Don't, Desmond!" she said. "I—I don't like to hear you speak of them so!"

"No?" he said cynically. "And yet they stand between you and me, my child. Well, well; we'll let them alone, But you see how I stand, and you won't refuse to be reasonable. Patience, a little more patience! Meanwhile, why shouldn't we be happy, Lucy! We'll dine at Prince's to-morrow, and go to the theatre—"

"No—no!" she broke in earnestly, rising as she spoke, and moving away from him. "I'd rather not. I'd—I'd rather not go with you. We should be seen. Besides, I'd made up my mind to—to—not to see you again—"

He looked at her, with a faint smile, then shrugged his shoulders, and took up his hat.

"Well, you know best," he said, with an air of resignation. "You discard me, eh, Lucy? Is that what it means? The only woman in the world I care for! Well, I'm not surprised. I'm not worthy of your love, your trust—I'll go. The only girl —the dearest, sweetest—"

He was a superb actor; and yet it was not all acting. There was only one person in the world Desmond March loved, and D. M. were his initials; but it cost him something like a pang to lose this pretty young creature who loved him.

"Good-bye," he said, in a low voice; and, with a sigh, he moved toward the door.

But before he could reach it, she had flown to his side, and her head was on his breast.

"No—no! Don't leave me, Desmond! Oh, I—I can't bear it! Don't leave me! I'll—I'll go with you to-morrow! Oh, I'm weak—weak! But I can't help it! I can't lose you!"

With a smile of satisfaction, he pressed her to him, and kissed her, murmuring the words for which women give their souls; and she clung, sobbing, to him.

When he had gone—and, having got his way, he did not stay long, for Desmond March did not like a woman in tears—she went back to the table, and stretched out her arms, and let her head fall on them.

"Oh, God help me!" she moaned. "I love him! I love him! I cannot let him go!"

CHAPTER VII

DINNER AT SHORTLEDGE

To DIANA the sudden reappearance of Lord Dalesford seemed to glide into the fairy-tale of her altered life with the happy consistency of the unreal. But she was not so foolish as to make a hero of romance of him; indeed, she tried, as she had done some months before, not to think of him. And found the same difficulty.

She told Mr. Fielding, as he sat at an early breakfast, so that he might catch the morning train, of her meeting with the heir to Wrayborough and his pretty girl-cousin, and Mr. Fielding laughed, with cynical appreciation.

"I know something of the Wrayboroughs," he remarked. Who was there in the fashionable world that Mr. Fielding did not "know something of"? "Lord Dalesford is a fine fellow; and yet—" He was silent a moment; then he went on, "I think that idea of yours, I mean of saying nothing for the present of your wealth, is rather a good one. Lady Selina? Ah, yes. One of the Dashwood family. I remember her. Quite a *grande dame*. The kind of lady who would have gone to the guillotine with a smile of scorn on her face for the people, the common people, thronging and howling round the tumbril. So you've made the acquaintance of Lord Dalesford? Hem!"

Diana blushed. Should she tell her Fairy Godmother that she had made Lord Dalesford's acquaintance a long while ago? She did not. When she had driven Mr. Fielding to the station in the light, but comfortable, dog-cart, she returned, and went over the house, and found it as delightful in all its details as the general view she had already obtained of it. It would be happiness to live in such a place, to wander about the pretty gardens, to drift on the silver river, to saunter in the pine woods; and, if "they" would only let her, to make the acquaintance of the children and the "snuffy" old women in the village!

The latter desire was nearer fulfilment than she guessed, for that afternoon, as she was hesitating between a walk, a row, or a drive, the servant announced, "Mr. Selby."

Mr. Selby was the Rector; he was a bland, comfortable-looking cleric, a widower, with one boy, who was at the rectory cramming for Oxford, and he had accompanied his father, with an air of resignation; "calling" being one of those ceremonies which Bertie Selby, like most lads of his age, considered more honoured in the breach than the observance.

But, as he entered the cool and exquisitely tasteful drawing-room, and Diana rose to greet them, his air of social martyrdom fled, his handsome, boyish face flushed with a lad's swift and generous admiration, and he could scarcely take his eyes off Diana's face. It was as instantaneous a conquest as that of Lady Mabel.

Mr. Selby himself was almost as quickly prepossessed, and long before they had finished tea, both father and son were convinced that Miss Bourne would be an acquisition to the parish.

To Diana's modest and faltering request that she might be permitted to see the schools and the children Mr. Selby hastened to give a hearty assent.

"My dear young lady," he said fervently, "we shall be—er—delighted to see you at any time, and most grateful for your kind assistance. I will send you the current number of our parish magazine. You would perhaps like to join the Dorcas Society, and the—"

"Yes, I should like to join them all!" said Diana eagerly. "Please let me!"

Bertie had scarcely been able to put in a word edge-wise up to now; but as his father turned to address Mrs. Burton, who had sat in nervous silence, the lad, looking wistfully through the open window and still more wistfully at Diana, said—

"I say; mightn't we go into the garden? The guvnor," in a lower voice, "will talk shop till it's time to go, or you have us turned out."

With a laugh and a girlish nod, Diana went out with him.

"Oh, I'm jolly glad I came!" he said, with the fearless candour of his age. "And I wanted to shirk it. 'Calling,' you know!" he made a grimace. "You've no idea of what it's like here; but you precious soon will. I pity you! You'll be swooped down upon by all the old tabby cats in the place, and made to go to all their tea-fights, and listen to their talk. And it's maddening; all scandal and backbiting; and all about nothing; because, don't you see, everybody's so beastly respectable that they never do anything worth talking about. I say, what a jolly place this is! I've never been here before. Good tennis lawn, too. Do you play? But of course you do!"

"A little," said Diana.

"Won't you have the court marked out?" he inquired eagerly.

"Oh yes," replied Diana. "I've only just come here—"

"And may I mark it?" he broke in. "I mean that the gardeners never do it quite right, don't you know—always want someone to overlook 'em. I'll come to-morrow morning, if I may."

"That will be very kind of you," said Diana, smiling at him with a gratitude which made his eager eyes radiant.

"That's all right, then," he remarked, with a sigh of satisfaction. "You've got a skiff and a canoe, I see. I'm awfully fond of rowing. Perhaps you'd let me scull you about sometimes? The river's jolly about here. And we might have some picnics. Fond of picnics? Right, ho! Oh, I say, I think we shall get on first-rate—I beg your pardon!" he broke off, abashed by his temerity; but Diana's frank laugh put him at his ease again.

"I'm going up to Oxford, you know. But not till October, thank goodness!" he added. "I hope you'll let me come over very often; you just tell me when I'm a nuisance; I'm an awfully good hand at effacing myself. I shouldn't like to be a bother to you. Here's the guvnor! I thought he was fixed for another half-hour.— Coming, sir!—I say, you'll be at home to-morrow morning, won't you? I shall want someone to hold the tape—we won't have the gardeners, they're always so stupid. You will? Good!—Yes, sir!—oh, bother! And—and we were getting on so well, weren't we? I mean— Oh, I say, I'm so glad I came this afternoon. To-morrow! You won't go and forget, will you?"

The Rector went his way, to trot round the parish with his favourable report of the new resident; and Bertie turned up soon after breakfast the next morning, and he and Diana were soon engaged in spoiling their clothes with a pail of whitening, and the marking-machine which, so it appeared, required two pairs of hands for its management.

He stayed to lunch and to tea, and would have remained to dinner if he had not remembered that he had done no work that day. But he was back again the next morning, and, having coaxed Diana into the skiff, had the unspeakable felic-ity of rowing her up the river. Every now and then he rested on his oars and gazed at her, as she leant back in the stern seat, with an admiration so boyish in its outspoken candour that Diana was forced to respond to it with a smile that sent him back to his sculls, glowing with satisfaction.

In the afternoon he accompanied her on her visit to the school, and stood be-side her with an air of proprietorship that amused the staid schoolmistress and made the pupil teachers giggle. Diana's heart beat with delight at the pleasure of getting among children again; and she went from class to class, eagerly asking questions and looking at the lesson books.

"Oh, that was good!" she breathed, as they came out. "Do you think they'd mind if I looked in once or twice a week, Bertie?" He had implored her not to call him Herbert, much less "Mr." Herbert.

"If I ran the show I should be only too jolly glad if you looked in once a day —and stopped there!" he returned. "Hello, here is the Dashwood carriage," he broke off as an old-fashioned but extremely stately barouche, drawn by a pair of fat and sluggish horses, rolled past them. A tall and very thin lady, of aristocratic mien, leant back among the cushions and surveyed the landscape patronisingly through a gold lorgnette. "That's Lady Selina! Awful swell, Lady Selina; so are all the Dashwoods; but she's the most awful of the lot. Not that I know very much about them; for, of course, they're a cut above us. I see 'em occasionally. My guvnor goes there to dinner once or twice a year, and they do him very well; but I always notice that he's particularly glad to shuffle out of his dress-coat. Funny thing, a parson's dress-coat! Ever seen one? Oh, you will presently—and to get on to his old brier pipe. Lord Dalesford's staying here just now. Splendid chap! He was at my school, you know."

"Where they were all splendid?" put in Diana teasingly.

"Oh, come, you know, if you're going to chaff a fellow!" he said laughingly. "Seriously, he is splendid. Good all-round man. Played cricket for his county; was in the Eton team that beat Aston Villa; won the Coronet sweepstakes; pulled stroke in the Oxford boat in his year—"

"An Admirable Crichton, in fact," commented Diana laughing.

"Never heard of him. What was he? Anyhow, he couldn't beat Dalesford. Pity he's such a wild chap. Mad as a hatter, you know."

"But I don't know," said Diana; adding quickly, "But I'll take your word for it, Bertie. Must you go? I'm sorry! But you'll come over to-morrow and help me to arrange the tea for the school-children."

"Oh yes," he assented. "Not that I'm much good at a muffin scramble; but I'd do anything for you, Miss Bourne."

The next afternoon, as Diana and Bertie were playing tennis, or rather, as they were squabbling across the net over the disputed score, the pair of fat slugs reluctantly dragged the Dashwood carriage to the entrance to Rivermead, and a servant scurried across the lawn to announce that Lady Selina and Lady Mabel were in the drawing-room.

"There!" laughed Diana, vainly trying to smooth the hair which had become ruffled in the romp which they had flatteringly called tennis. "There are these 'awful swells' of yours. Now you will come in and help to entertain them."

"Not I!" he retorted emphatically. "I'll stay here and smoke a cigarette until they've gone. I've met Lady Selina before—'Oh, and so you are the Rector's son?'—but never again with you, Robin! I don't mind facing fire and water for you, Miss Bourne; in fact, I should enjoy doing so; but not Lady Selina, thank you!"

So Diana went alone; very much alone, for Aunt Mary had gone on an expedition to Reading, shopping. Diana found Lady Selina seated on the edge of one of the Chippendale chairs, seated bolt upright as if she had swallowed a poker and was not quite sure of being able to digest it. Just behind her was Lady Mabel, who looked up eagerly and winningly as Diana entered. Of course, Lady Selina was the first to speak.

Dropping the gold-handled pince-nez, she said, in her stateliest fashion—

"How do you do, Miss Bourne?"

She said it rather jerkily; for, though she had been somewhat prepared by the Rector—the carriage had been coming from the rectory when Diana saw it yesterday—Diana's beauty and grace took her by surprise. "My niece told me of your courageous rescue of my little dog"—here Lady Mabel was guilty of an unmistakable wink at Diana—"and I am glad of an opportunity of thanking you. It is an extremely valuable dog, and so intelligent that, I regret to say, it compares favourably with most of the human beings whom it is my misfortune to know. Are you fond of dogs?" she asked abruptly.

"Oh, very," said Diana promptly. She was not at all overcome by Lady Selina's stateliness; perhaps Lady Mabel's wink had somewhat stultified it. "There's a collie here—he belongs to the farm—who, much to Aunt Mary's annoyance, will come into the house. And I love a fox-terrier—"

"Collies are treacherous, and fox-terriers are mischievous," broke in Lady Selina, solemnly and with the air of an authority. "If you were fortunate enough to secure a pug like my Tubby, now— I hope you like your house and the locality. The Rector told me that you have settled here for some time, and that you take an interest in the parish. Quite right and proper. So do I. But I have so many claims upon my attention— Mabel, why do you stare out of the window?"

Mabel, who had been gazing at the vision of a young man in flannels, with a cigarette between his lips, drew herself up primly and looked as if butter would not melt in her mouth.

"I am here, at Shortledge, for only a few months in the year— My dear Mabel, are you listening to what I am saying?"

"Yes, Aunt Selina," responded Lady Mabel meekly. "I was looking at—at the flowers. How beautiful they are, Miss Bourne!"

With ready sympathy and comprehension, Diana took up a pair of scissors with which she had been doing fancy-work.

"Would you like to pick some for me? I want some for the dinner-table to-night. Please do!"

With a grateful glance—again it was almost a wink—Lady Mabel, the tomboy of the family, escaped by the French window.

Bertie heard her and looked up gloomily; but his expression changed as his eyes took her in. She stood before him uncertainly for a moment; then, with a toss of her long hair, she said—

"You are the Rector's son, aren't you?"

Bertie raised his cap and flung his cigarette away—a notable sacrifice of the goddess Nicotine.

"Yes. And you're—"

"Lady Mabel Dashwood," said Mabel. "I say, what a jolly place, isn't it? And isn't Miss Bourne splendid?"

"Splendacious!" he returned. "So—so—jolly, too!"

"So beautiful," corrected Mabel severely. "I've never seen anyone so lovely; so—so—"

"Say jolly; that's what you mean," he advised. "And so you're Lady Mabel Dashwood! Well, I'm not afraid!"

"Afraid? Why should you be?"

"I said I wasn't afraid!" he retorted. "Care to play tennis? I was playing with Miss Bourne before you came. And I daresay she wishes that she was playing now."

"I think you're very rude!" said Lady Mabel, flushing hotly. "No; I don't want to play."

"All right," he said serenely. "Let's sit down and talk. Wonder whether they'll send us out some tea—oh, here it comes. You pour it out. Ladies always pour out, you know. I say—"

"Well?" demanded Lady Mabel, intent upon the teapot which, like most teapots, seemed inclined to pour its contents into everything except the cups.

"Isn't she stunning?"

"Who?"

"Who? Why, Miss Bourne, of course! I say, this tea seems very strong. Can't I have some more milk?"

"I've given you more than half already. Yes, isn't she? So beautiful and so—so—I want a word."

"Try charming," he suggested.

"No; that won't do. So—so—I've got it!—so lovable!"

"Yes; that's the word," he assented, with an emphatic nod. "She seems to take a fellow's breath away, doesn't she? Gives him something to think of when he wakes at night—"

Lady Mabel returned his nod. "I think she's fascinating. She's so—so simple and yet so *comme il faut*—"

"Eh? What?" he questioned. "Oh, do let's have a game of tennis. No shoes? Let me see!" Mabel held up the small foot, clad in the regulation shoes with high heels. "Well, of all the— How on earth do you walk in them?"

"Very well, indeed, thank you!" she retorted. "I could walk you three times round the lawn—"

"Done with you!" he responded with alacrity.

So it happened that Lady Selina, coming in search of her niece, found that young lady sprinting round the lawn in apparent pursuit of a young man who was leading, and jeering, twenty yards ahead.

"Mabel!" she exclaimed, in stern accents.

"Yes, Aunt Selina!" responded Lady Mabel meekly; but as she broke off the contest and walked to her aunt, she murmured to Bertie, "You haven't won! It's a drawn game!" And I regret to state that she added "Yah!"

When Bertie went into the house—he was a well-bred boy and "saw" the Dashwood ladies into the Dashwood carriage—he was duly lectured upon his misconduct, and informed that his lecturer, Miss Diana Bourne, to wit, had been formally invited to dine at Shortledge.

"Well, I pity you," he said compassionately. "My guvnor took me to one of their dinners, and I shall never forget it. It was too awful for words. 'Eaven 'elp you; I can't!"

Notwithstanding Bertie's warning, Diana was not afraid of the dinner at Shortledge. You see, she stood on the impregnable rock of her own modesty. She was just the mistress of Rivermead, no more. Not the owner of a million; for that was to be concealed, according to the compact made between her and her Fairy Godmother.

Bertie came round the next morning, waltzing across the lawn, to the great annoyance of Bob, the collie, who had been seated in meditation at Diana's feet.

"Oh, I say!" he exclaimed jubilantly. "I've been asked to dinner at Shortledge!"

"I thought you didn't like dinner parties, and that you commiserated me for having to go," remarked Diana. "Don't tease Bob; I'm sure he'll bite you!"

"Oh no, he won't. Only one dog has ever bitten me—and he died. Yes, so I do; but this is a very different affair—you're going, you know!"

"And Lady Mabel will be there," added Diana, with a twinkle in her eyes.

"Oh, if you're going to chaff me— But she is rather jolly, isn't she? I'd no idea any of the swells could be so decent."

"You'll be able to finish your walk—round the dinner-table," suggested Diana.

The young scamp grinned.

"Yes. I say, if Lady Selina hadn't already told the guvnor to bring me, I shouldn't have got an invitation after she'd caught us sprinting yesterday afternoon. I reckon Lady Mabel got a wigging on the way home."

"I think Lady Mabel can take care of herself," said Diana.

"That's so," he assented emphatically. "Rather pretty hair, don't you think?" he remarked.

Diana suppressed her laughter as she said, "She's a very pretty girl, and she will be a beautiful woman."

"Yes; I think she will. She'll marry some belted earl or bloated aristocrat of some kind or other, I suppose."

"No doubt," assented Diana drily. "Nice to be a belted earl, Bertie."

"Oh, I don't know," he said; but he sighed.

On the night they were to dine at Shortledge, Aunt Mary was in a tremor of nervousness.

"I thought we had come home to be quiet, Diana," she said. "If you could only go alone! The idea of having to meet all those grand people makes me—unhappy."

Diana laughed, to reassure her.

"But we found the grand people we met abroad the simplest and most easy to get on with, dear," she reminded her. "Lady Selina is rather stiff; but I think it is more a matter of manner than mind. And you look so nice, Aunt Mary! I'm ever so proud of you. And everybody who meets you likes you."

"I'm not of any consequence," said Mrs. Burton humbly. "It is you—"

"Well, I look nice, do I not?" Diana laughed; and she pivoted round that her aunt might see the handsome black lace dress which Diana had bought in Paris.

She wore no jewellery that night; not even her modest diamonds; but the white rose in her bosom was more effective than any gems could be, and, if candour may be indulged, a more suitable ornament for a girl of her age than the costliest gems.

Mrs. Burton looked at her with an admiration that was subdued by an air of sadness, almost one of apprehension; but she said nothing, and they were soon on their way. The road to the big house on the hill wound through the pine woods, with an occasional glade giving a glimpse of the usual scenery round a nobleman's country-seat; and Lady Selina lived in a style suitable to her rank; the great hall, with its stained oriel window, its family portraits, and its air of historic antiquity, impressed Diana not a little; the number of servants, in their rich liveries, not at all; for had she not stayed at some of the palatial Continental hotels where the state is absolutely ducal?

When they were shown into the drawing-room, a magnificent apartment, decorated by Inigo Jones, Lady Selina rose from her arm-chair to meet them, and, as she scanned Diana's dress, without appearing to do so, her greeting was extremely gracious. The Rector and Bertie, and a wife and daughter of a neighbouring squire, were already there, trying to look cheerful during the trying ten minutes before dinner; and Lady Mabel came forward demurely, but with a mischievous twinkle in the corner of her downcast eyes, as if to assure Diana that she was only on her best behaviour because Lady Selina's watchful eyes were upon her.

The tall clock in the hall chimed eight, and Lady Selina looked towards the doorway, through which the butler came to her.

"Why are we waiting?" she asked in a severe tone.

"His lordship, my lady!" he said.

"Lord Dalesford is not returning from London to-night," said Lady Selina. "We will go in, Thompson."

Mabel slipped up to Diana.

"Yes, he is!" she whispered. "I wired to him that you were coming. Hush! here he is! I can hear his step."

Dalesford entered as she spoke.

"Found I could get back, Aunt Selina. Sorry to keep you waiting," he said, as he went round, and shook hands, without a glance at his fellow-conspirator. "Hallo, Bertie! Glad you're here! Going up to Oxford? Lucky dog! Wish I were!"

He offered his arm to Mrs. Burton, and the Rector took in Diana; but Diana was, of course, placed on Dalesford's left. He saw, at once, that the elder lady was nervous, and did not want to talk, and, after a commonplace remark or two to her, he turned to Diana, with an eagerness which was not wholly suppressed.

"I've been hearing a great deal about you from Mabel," he said. "In fact, she has now only one topic of conversation—Miss Bourne. If you had a brother, I should have reason to fear a rival. As it is, you have quite cut me out of my place —until now the first one—in Mabel's affection. I hope you are settling down in your new house, and that you like the neighbourhood?"

Diana made the suitable responses to these courteous commonplaces, and, Lady Selina leading the Rector into parish affairs, the conversation became general. Presently Diana joined in, and Dalesford leant back, and listened, looking at her, as he was now free to do, with intent attention. Once more he was troubled by a vague consciousness of having met her before; but he could not fix the memory, and he gave himself up to noting her wonderful beauty and grace. The simplicity of her dress, costly though he knew it to be, struck him; but it was the simplicity of her manner—it occurred to him that it was the most perfect "form"—and the girlish enthusiasm, indicated by the subdued eagerness of her voice, the faint flush on her cheek, as she talked of the school-children, and the poor of the parish, and of the things that might be done for them, which impressed him most. She was quite a new experience in womanhood for him, for most of the girls of her age whom he knew might now and again play at "slumming," while it was in the fashion, but were not so intensely and actually interested in the poor, "and that kind of thing," as this girl.

"She's good," he said to himself, with a momentary distaste and misgiving; but it was only momentary, and disappeared, as, in response to some sally of

Bertie's, she laughed, not loudly, but with a frank, girlish laughter that convinced him that she was not a prude.

As the dinner went on, Lady Selina's stiffness relaxed—the three young people were just three too many for her, and presently Dalesford found himself in their ranks, and laughing as freely as they.

But there was no smile on Mrs. Burton's face. She was not exactly a skeleton at the feast, but she sat almost silent, and with downcast eyes, which were raised now and again to Diana with a curious expression of pride alloyed by doubt and anxiety, almost hidden under her lowered lids.

The gentlemen did not sit long over the admirable Dashwood claret, and soon followed the ladies into the drawing-room; the wife and daughter of the neighbouring squire were at the piano, the daughter singing; and Dalesford, after standing for a moment or two in front of the fern-filled fireplace, went out through the open French window to the terrace, and stood looking at the starlit night, and the slowly rising moon, but thinking of Miss Bourne. Beautiful and "good." It seemed to him, the man of the world, a quaint combination.

Presently Mabel slipped out, and, linking her arm in his, pressed it.

"So glad you came home, Vane! Isn't she lovely in war-paint and feathers? And isn't it jolly to hear her talk? Aren't you glad you left the London rabble, and came home like a good boy? Oh, who's that singing? It can't be that young Selby? Fancy a boy singing! It's so like a girl. I'm glad I haven't got a voice. But he sings well, doesn't he? Don't tell him so, though, Vane; he's quite conceited enough already. Ah, here he is!" she broke off warningly, as Bertie came out, his honours thick upon him. "What was that you were singing?" she asked. "Something about 'Love me a little, love me well'? What do you know about such things, I should like to know?"

"Not much," he retorted, "but I'm quite willing to learn. Perhaps you'd give me a lesson, Lady Mabel?"

"Thanks; I've got something better to do than teach schoolboys," she retorted scornfully.

"Schoolboy! Why, you are only just out of the nursery yourself!" remarked Bertie.

"Here, you two, if you want to quarrel, go down on the walk; I want to smoke a cigarette in peace and quietude," said Dalesford, and, taking Mabel by the shoulders, he pushed her laughingly down the steps, and trundled Bertie after her; and their fresh young voices ascended to him, as he leaned against the balustrade and smoked thoughtfully. Suddenly he straightened himself, and turned. Diana, who had been playing an accompaniment for the squire's daughter, was moving past the window.

"Won't you come into the fresh air, Miss Bourne?" he asked her.

Diana glanced round. The ladies were gathered about the Rector, discussing a threatened bazaar, and Diana wanted to listen and join in; but, after a moment's hesitation, she went out.

"Moon's late to-night," he said. "I'm afraid they're boring you, aren't they?" He jerked his head toward the chattering group.

"Oh no," she replied. "They are talking about the most interesting things. But," with a smile, "I don't suppose you consider them so."

She glanced up at him, as she spoke, and noticed the hint of world-weariness in his handsome face, that touch of sadness which indicates satiety and the fact that Vanity Fair, for all its seeming joyousness, is but a tiresome business, a feast of Dead-Sea fruit.

"I daresay," he assented reflectingly. "I'm afraid I'm rather difficult to interest. Don't think me a sentimental bounder, please. But, you see, a man of my age has run through most of his interests."

"A man of your age," said Diana, glancing up at him with a quiet smile. "Are you so old? Not much older than I, surely?"

He laughed down at her rather grimly.

"Old in experience and—" "Sin" he was going to say; but checked himself. She looked so girlish, so pure, in the starlight that fought with the more garish light streaming through the window, that he shrank from the word, from the vein of thought that it might lead to. For the first time in his life, he wished that—that he had led a different kind of life, that he could meet this virginal purity of hers on equal ground. Bertie's voice, as he squabbled amicably with Mabel, just below them, struck on him accusingly. He was once as free from vice and guile as the boy there!

"What a lovely view!" said Diana presently.

He woke, with something like a start, from his reflections. "You can see it better from the end of the terrace," he said. "Shall we go and look at it?"

They walked there, side by side, and he pointed out the spire of the church, the chimnies of Rivermead.

"This is my father's favourite view," he said. "He is coming here next week. I should like you to know him. He is"—he hesitated a moment—"one of the last of the old brigade. He would like to know you; and I think you'd get on together; though, Heaven knows, you haven't much in common— What have you dropped?" he broke off, as Diana bent down, as if searching for something.

"My rose," she said. "Bertie Selby gave it to me—they have beautiful roses at the rectory—and I mustn't lose it."

He paced back on the terrace, and found it.

"Here it is," he said. "Let me try and fasten it more securely."

"Thanks. I can do it," she returned; and she essayed to pin it into the bosom of her dress; but the pin missed it, and the bud dropped to the ground. She tried again, with like ill-success.

"Tut! tut!" she clicked, between her teeth. "It *will* slip!"

Dalesford started, and caught her arm.

"By Heaven!" he exclaimed, between his teeth. "You are the girl—it has come upon me like a flash! You are the girl that saved me that night at Wedbury!"

Diana looked up at him with a smile of amusement, which faded as she saw the sudden earnestness of his face.

"I was waiting to see how long it would be before you knew me, Lord Dalesford," she said.

His hand fell from her arm, but his dark eyes were still fixed on her, with a startled, an intense, gaze, as if he were recalling the past; as if, at that moment, a link were being forged between that past and the present.

"I am—a fool!" he said at last, and with a strange, deep note in his voice. "I ought to have remembered you the other night. And I have never forgotten you. No, never! How could I? But—but"—he looked at her with a puzzled frown —"how does it happen that you are here, at Rivermead? You were the schoolmistress at Wedbury! Yes? What does it mean?"

Diana's heart beat fast. If she had obeyed the impulse of the moment, she would have told him the whole truth. But she shrank from it.

"My—my father died, and left me some money," she said falteringly.

He drew a long breath, and nodded.

"I see! You are the same girl. I saw you only indistinctly. I was—I had been drinking. I—I beg your pardon. But that explains why I did not recognise you. And I have thought of you so often."

"Yes?" said Diana wonderingly.

"Yes! There is scarcely a day or a night that I haven't thought of you," he said almost grimly. "How brave you were! Fancy a girl, a mere girl, cutting in between two men, and risking a blow, a deadly blow! And you washed my wound—I've got the scar still—and—oh, the whole affair is stamped on my memory! I've never forgotten it, thought of it often! And here you are—an acquaintance, a friend; may I say a friend?"

Diana looked up at him, with a smile.

"Yes; if you wish, Lord Dalesford."

"A friend!" he repeated, with a subtle note of satisfaction. "And you live at Rivermead, close here; and you're dining here to-night! By George, I can scarcely realise it!"

He drew nearer to her, and looked down at her with a kind of subdued eagerness, of pleasure, of delighted surprise.

"And we are friends. We can meet, you and I! Miss Bourne, I've laughed at the long arm of coincidence as a convenient invention of the novelists; but here we are, aren't we? You and I!"

"Yes," said Diana, smiling, though her heart was beating fast, for his tone of delight and satisfaction affected her strangely.

"And we are going to be real friends? I am staying here. Aunt Selina keeps a room for me—bless her! And I shall see you now and again, every day. What? Don't say 'No!'—the girl who rescued me in that plucky way that night! Good lord, I can scarcely realise it! Let me look at you!—I beg your pardon! But it seems so unreal, so impossible!"

He asked her, by a gesture, to turn to the light flowing from the window, and smiling—and blushing a little—she did so.

"Yes! It's the same! I thought I should never see you again. I meant to do so, but"—he paused a moment—"but you are a schoolmistress no longer. I'm glad you have taken Rivermead, that your father left you some money. I hope he left you a great deal."

"Enough to live upon," said Diana, with downcast eyes.

"Yes? I'm glad! And to think you are the girl I have dreamed of, that I have longed to thank as you ought to have been thanked—"

He caught her hand, and raised it towards his lips; but Diana drew it back.

"You never discovered who it was that attacked you that night?" she asked, with a novel shyness, for he was regarding her intently, as if he were more engaged with her than her question.

"No," he said absently. "Some footpad."

Diana shook her head. "Highway robbery is out of date. It belongs to the medieval novel. Is there anyone who would be benefited by your death, Lord Dalesford?"

"No; there's no one—excepting my cousin, Desmond March," he added mechanically.

"Desmond March," said Diana. "What kind of man is he?"

Dalesford laughed. "The kind of man of whom you can have no conception, you pure, sweet woman-angel—I beg your pardon, Miss Bourne. He's a—a—raff of the most pronounced type. Oh, don't misapprehend me! He's the pink of perfection, the glass of fashion, and the mould of form—have I got that right? I'm bad at quotations. Oh no; my esteemed cousin, Desmond March, is above highway robbery and assassination.—What a noise those young people are making; they will have Aunt Selina upon them presently!—And you are the girl who dressed my wound that night!—Yes, Aunt Selina, here I am! Mabel? Oh, she is talking astronomy with young Selby.—We must go in, I suppose," he said, in a low voice, to Diana. "You and I have a—shall we call it a secret?—between us."

CHAPTER VIII

AN ENGLISH SUMMER

DIANA leant back in the carriage, as she and Aunt Mary drove home from Short-ledge, and looked at the moon dreamily, and with a shadowy smile on her parted lips, for she was feeling strangely happy.

Everyone, from Lady Selina downward, had been kind to her, and this, her first formal introduction to society, had been an extremely pleasant one. As usual, these people of high birth had proved simple-mannered and kindly natured. But it was not Lady Selina's graciousness, nor Lady Mabel's outspoken admiration and girlish affection which suffused Diana's spirit with the warm glow of happiness.

It was the few minutes on the terrace with Lord Dalesford, his joy at his recognition of her, his delight at their meeting, at the idea of friendship between her and him. Why, she asked herself, should he be so glad to meet her again, to find that she was the girl who had come to his rescue that night, which, in the altered present, seemed so far off, so vague, so unreal?

A vain girl would have found the reason without any difficulty, but Diana was singularly free from vanity, and she let the question go unanswered, while she asked herself another: Did she like Lord Dalesford to be pleased at meeting her again? Did she want the friendship he had almost claimed?

She told herself that she ought to be indifferent to his pleasure, that she ought not to accept, or yield, the friendship he offered and asked; that between Lord Dalesford and herself there was a big social gulf; and that, if there were not, he was not the kind of man whom a young girl should take for a friend. But, though the voice of wisdom and prudence strove to make itself heard, something whispered that, notwithstanding his reputation, and the faults with which rumour liberally endowed him, she could not help feeling pleased with his pleasure, and—yes, gratified by his reminder that there was a secret between them.

She could not help thinking of him. He was so unlike other young men she had met. That air of his, of serene conviction that the world had been made for him; the perfectly self-possessed manner in which he took it for granted that everyone was in the best of humour with him; that life was a case of "roses, roses all the way," impressed her. It had been more than pleasant to listen to his deep, musical voice, to look at his handsome face, to note the unconscious ease and grace which marked his every movement. Even the admission of his faults, the candour which took it for granted that everyone knew he was good for nothing, told in his favour; for Diana, young and inexperienced as she was, knew that most men are given to putting their best goods in the front window. But Lord Dalesford seemed to say: "Here I am—no good. But, all the same, you've got to like me, you know."

And how much and generally he was liked! It was evident that Lady Mabel adored him; that Bertie regarded him as the model of manliness; that even Lady Selina was fond and proud of him. What a pity it was, thought Diana, that he should waste his days in the dissipation to which smaller men were given!

As for Dalesford's reflections, they shall not be set down. Indeed, he himself would have found it difficult to do so; but he paced up and down the terrace long after the others had gone to their rooms, and, smoking hard, recalled the beautiful face, the violet eyes that had met his so modestly; the voice that recalled the night he had first heard it; and, when, at last, he turned into the house, he murmured, "There is no one like her, no one!"

"I'm going to row down to Rivermead," he said to Mabel, the following afternoon. "You can come, if you like."

"Mabel had far better employ her time hemming these handkerchiefs," Lady Selina remarked severely. But Mabel knew that this was not to be taken as a command, and she was down at the boat quite as soon as Dalesford.

He pulled down-stream almost silently, only half-listening to Mabel's chatter.

"Oh, they're playing tennis!" she said, as they came in sight of Rivermead lawn. "And, of course, that Selby boy is there," she added, with the tolerant contempt with which a girl regards the seniority of a lad who is only a year or two older than herself. "Tennis! I'm glad I told them to put our shoes in.—Here we are, Miss Bourne! We can make a foursome, can't we?"

"Might one suggest that it would be as well to wait until you are asked?" said Dalesford, as he fastened the boat, and took Diana's hand.

She had come towards them with a smile, and without, she fervently hoped, a blush; but the blush was there, and it heightened her loveliness in Dalesford's eyes. He had thought she must surely have looked her best last night, in her "war-paint and feathers," as Mabel had put it; but he questioned whether she did not look still more beautiful in her plain white dress and simple hat, which accentuated her slight figure and sweet, girlish loveliness. And there was a hint of shyness in her greeting which was too subtly delicious for description, like the fragrance of the flowers amidst which she moved.

"None the worse for last night's dissipation, I trust?" he said, holding her hand a moment or two longer than was necessary. "Sides!" to Bertie. "Oh, I'll play with Miss Bourne, if she'll accept me for a partner."

"What nonsense!" Mabel began to remonstrate, but, catching Dalesford's eye, she added hastily, "All right! But you'll have to play your best, Mr. Selby— if you've got a best. From what I saw of your play as we came down the river—"

"Now, you two!" Dalesford broke in laughingly. "If you are going to squabble, we shall beat you easily."

Dalesford was, of course, a good player; as Bertie had said, he was good at most games; but he played very badly that afternoon, for his heart was all a-quiver with the proximity of the slight figure that moved so swiftly, so easily, with the sound of the laughing voice that contended over the score. Diana was absorbed in the game, and yet she was conscious of a novel sense of enjoyment; surely, the sun shone more brightly, the birds sang more blithely, the perfume of the flowers was sweeter than it had been half an hour ago!

They played until Aunt Mary came out, followed by a couple of maids with the tea; then the girls sank, breathless, into rustic chairs, and Dalesford dropped on to the grass at their feet, leaving Bertie to hand the cups and bread-and-butter. Strangely enough, no one of them proposed to renew the game; and, presently, Bertie and Mabel wandered across to the fruit garden, Aunt Mary went back to the house, and Diana and Dalesford were left alone.

"It's just the right time for the river," he said. "Shall we go?"

Diana looked round for the other two. "I'll call them," she said. But, before she could do so, he remarked—

"Oh, let them alone. They'll be much happier with the peaches!" And, after a moment's hesitation, Diana rose, and they went down to the boat.

She leant back in the soft-cushioned seat, and Dalesford let the boat slowly drift with the stream, now and again taking a pull at the sculls, sitting half sideways, but only half, so that he could see the face opposite him. The mystic beauty of the water and sky wooed them to silence, and for some minutes they drifted without speaking; but presently, with the skill of the man of the world, he led her into talking, and got her to tell him of her travels, of the famous places she had seen, the people she had met. Every now and then, he made a comment, or asked a question which drew her on; and, as he listened, he felt as if she were all unconsciously revealing her sweet, unstained nature, as if he were looking at a vision of the "pure womanhood" of whose existence he had been hitherto sceptical. With the admiration that stirred his senses was a reverence which thrilled him with an aching of the heart for his own unworthiness. With an almost audible sigh, he turned the boat round.

"I feel as if I had been with you on your travels," he said. "Strange, I've been all over the same ground, but I didn't see so much in it. And now you are going to settle down? I'm glad. Must I begin to pull?" he asked regretfully, as Diana looked at her watch. "The time has passed very quickly. I wonder whether you would join us in a picnic to-morrow?"

"Not to-morrow," she said, a trifle wistfully. "I am going to read to Mrs. Baker's little girl; she has been ill, and declares that a fairy-story, a real fairy-story, does her more good than beef-tea and jellies."

"Oh," he said casually. "And who may Mrs. Baker be?"

"She lives in the cottage with the green shutters, at the end of South Lane," replied Diana unsuspectingly.

And she was still unsuspicious that they had met by anything more than chance when she saw him sauntering up the lane next afternoon.

"Let me carry your basket," he said, after they had exchanged greetings.

"But you were going the other way," she reminded him.

"Was I?" he said. "All ways are the same to me. That's the great advantage of being a lazy man, with no object in life. Now's the time to read me a lesson on the wickedness of sheer indolence."

Diana laughed.

"Why should I?" she said frankly.

He looked rather discomfited for a moment, then he retorted—

"I was under the impression that it was the duty of the 'good person' like yourself to speak the word in season."

Diana looked at him gravely.

"I wonder why nearly everybody scoffs at goodness," she said very gently.

"Sour grapes," he responded. "Some of us couldn't be good, if we tried. But I wasn't scoffing, by the way. No! Is this Mrs. Butcher's—Baker's? What's her name? I suppose I may be allowed to wait for you?"

Diana looked her surprise. "Why, I shall be twenty minutes, or half an hour!" she informed him.

"Well, I can endure my own company for as long as that," he said. "I'll sit on the bank there, and smoke or go to sleep, while you read to that lucky young person inside. What's she done that she should have a beauti—an amiable young lady to read fairy-tales to her?"

"She has been ill," said Diana.

"Oh! And, up to the present moment, I have been under the foolish impression that health was a blessing," he remarked, addressing the sky.

Diana went into the cottage, and up to the sick-room, where the convalescent child greeted her with affectionate eagerness.

"Why, Mary, what beautiful grapes!" Diana exclaimed, casting an eye on a basketful on the table.

Mary flushed, and pursed her lips with an air of great secrecy.

"Yes, miss, aren't they lovely? But I mustn't tell you who gave them to me. I promised!"

"Promises are sacred, Mary; and I won't even try and guess. But, really, I'm almost ashamed to put my poor peaches beside them. Never mind! Here they are!"

She took out the contents of her basket, and read her fairy-story; and, having tucked up the child cosily, went downstairs, where the mother was waiting to express her gratitude.

"And it do seem, miss, as if your goodness to Mary was catching; for another of the gentry has been to see her, and he brought her the loveliest bunch of grapes— There, now! Tut! tut!" she broke off penitently. "And I promised not to tell! I can't think how it slipped out, miss—that I can't."

"I don't suppose it is of much consequence, Mrs. Baker," said Diana, with a tone of shy pleasure in her voice; and she was still smiling as she left the cottage; but the smile was driven off as she came to the figure lying on the bank.

He sprang up to meet her, and flung the cigarette away.

"You said twenty minutes," he remarked, with an air of long-suffering patience. "You have been gone two hours and a quarter."

"Exactly five-and-twenty minutes," corrected Diana, looking at her watch. "Did you cut the grapes yourself, Lord Dalesford?"

He glanced at her shamefacedly, then laughed.

"So Mrs. Butcher—Baker betrayed me?" he said. "Well, it's the first good action I've been guilty of, and I'll try and not do it again—if you'll let me off with the option of a fine."

"Yes, I will," she said, her eyes beaming on him. "There is an old man, an old woodman, in the next cottage but one. His great and crying need is tobacco—"

Dalesford groaned. "Oh, I say! Well, I'll send him some cigars."

"No," said Diana, in a matter-of-fact way; "cigars are no good. I tried him with some, and he said that he couldn't taste them. It must be tobacco—that very black stuff, like old rope. And you mustn't send it; you must take it, because he likes to hear someone talk."

"Talk!" he echoed, with dismay. "Why, what on earth could I have to say to him!"

"Tell him about—about the shooting. Oh, anything that will interest him."

"I will," he said grimly. "I'll tell him about a certain *dame sans merci*, who sets her devoted adherents impossible tasks.—What's the man's name?"

In time, most of the sick children and old women in the village got accustomed to seeing his lordship and Miss Bourne walking down the village, his lordship carrying a basket or a book, and listening intently to the young lady at his side; and, presently, the children began to share their allegiance to the beautiful young lady from Rivermead with his lordship from Shortledge; for, when Diana was out of the way, Dalesford, at first shyly and awkwardly, always produced a packet of sweets and other delectables from the yawning pockets of his loose shooting-jacket, and never failed to present them to the surrounding brats without awful threats of corporal punishment if they "told on him" to the lady who had gone upstairs.

It was not all visiting the sick and needy with these two. There were picnics, boating expeditions, tennis, tea and dinner parties, at which they were continually meeting; and each day Diana was growing accustomed to the society of this young nobleman, and insensibly forgetting his evil reputation. Indeed, a change was working in Dalesford—a remarkable change. Hitherto he had found it impossible to remain from London, and its questionable amusements, from the theatrical supper-parties, the baccarat-tables, the feverish excitement of the race-meetings, for longer than a few days; but the days slipped by on tiptoe, and still found him at Shortledge, and found him content to be there. And if he did run up to town, it was only for a few hours; for he was restless while he was there, and eager to get back to the simple delights at which he had once scoffed.

Of course, this sudden infatuation of his for country life, for tennis and boating, and the rest of it, was noticed by both gentle and simple of the place; but, though some of the latter nodded, and smiled, and whispered to each other when Diana and he passed, Lady Selina had no suspicion of the cause of his long visit.

As a matter of fact, she and all his kin had come to regard Dalesford as invulnerable; and it certainly would not have occurred to her as possible that he should fall in love—with matrimonial intent—with a person of so little consequence as Miss Bourne, charming though she might be.

But a sharper pair of eyes was coming on the scene!

CHAPTER IX

CHILDREN AT PLAY

THE afternoon of the school treat arrived, and not only Diana, but all her friends, including the servants at Rivermead, were in a state of wild excitement. If they had been going to a fête of royalties they could not have thrown themselves into the affair with greater enthusiasm. The piles of buns and cakes, the pots of jam, the scores of dolls for the girls, and the balls and tops—they were "in" just then —for the boys, were discussed, counted, arranged in the methodical order insisted upon by the mistress of the feast, Diana, who superintended everything, and worked her willing slaves unmercifully.

The excitement extended to Shortledge, and was caught by even Lady Selina, who for days beforehand had driven to and from the village, with Tubby on her lap, yapping at everything and everybody, and adding to the confusion.

"The place is quite stirred up since Diana came," said Mabel, to whom it was "Diana" now. "She has awakened Sleepy Hollow. I declare, we're all changed; we've all been made to move ourselves. And some of us are improved. Vane, for instance—"

"You leave your elders alone, my sweet child," remarked Vane, who was seated on the balustrade of the terrace, smoking a cigarette.

"Vane is not half so slack—and, oh, think, Aunt Selina, how beastly lazy he used to be—"

"Beastly is not a word that should be used by a lady, Mabel," rebuked Lady Selina.

"Sorry, aunt; I caught it of that Selby boy. But it's true. And he's ever so much more polite and attentive—"

"The Selby boy?" asked Vane innocently. "Yes; I've noticed his 'attentions.' "

"No; you. *Nothing* could make Bertie Selby polite. But I suppose you'll draw the line at tea-fights, Vane? You'll go up to town, and come back when all the work's done, and say how fagged you are. So like a man!"

But, marvellous to relate, just after the proceedings had commenced, when the tables were laid, and the forms set, and the children were all agog with excitement, laughing, jumping, jostling, as children will do in their delighted moments, and Diana was going from one table to another, with plates of buns and cake in her hand, she heard a deep, but nobly resigned, voice at her elbow say—

"Anything I can do, Miss Bourne?"

The colour rose to her face, and she hastened to excuse its presence by exclaiming, with simulated petulance—

"How you startled me! Good gracious, no! What did you imagine you could do? But it's very good of you to come and offer your services, all the same, Lord Dalesford!"

"Thank you," he responded. "Yes; I admit that I feel rather out of place at a school treat, and I can't think what induced me to come. Do you think it's softening of the brain?"

"It can't be that, Vane," interjected Mabel, who also bore her burden of plates. "You've got to have brains to soften, you know."

"Don't pay any attention to this young person's impertinence, Miss Bourne," he said; "but, now I'm here, take pity on me, and let me carry something."

"He'll drop it, if you do," Mabel asserted. "He always upsets the tea, if he attempts to carry a cup at home, and he'll be worse out here."

"Perhaps you'll be so kind as to see that the children get into their places without crowding, Lord Dalesford?" suggested Diana.

"Certainly," he said; but he stood with his hands thrust into his pockets, and his eyes fixed on Diana, as she moved swiftly, easily, to and fro; her presence accompanied, as it seemed to him, by a halo of sunshine; and it was not until the bell rang that he woke up, helped by a push from Mabel, and began to marshal the children to their places. His way of doing it was scarcely regular, though it proved effective enough.

"Now, youngsters, no crowding!" he said, with that air of comradeship which children are so quick and so delighted to recognise. "Girls, sit opposite the cake; boys, opposite the bread-and-butter—else the girls will have no cake. Been a boy myself, and I know. Here, young man, you want a hand. Up with you!" as he helped one of the smallest urchins into his place.

Mr. Selby said grace, the feast began, and the ladies and gentlemen who were ministering to the wants of the children—who ate as if they had not seen food for weeks—were kept hard at it. Now, it was noticeable that Mabel and Bertie worked in double harness, and that, wherever Diana happened to be—and she seemed to be in several places at once—Dalesford was sure to be close to her elbow. He was not of much use at this part of the proceedings, and once, in lifting a kettle, he nearly succeeded in scalding himself and several other persons; but he appeared to be perfectly happy, and, wherever he went, the children looked up at him with a smile; for that easy-go-lucky way of his won all their hearts, especially the girls'.

"You don't think any of them will—explode?" he asked Diana, with mock anxiety. "I've got my eye on one or two cases that threaten to be fatal. That boy there, for instance, has eaten enough for a carter, and has drunk eight cups of tea."

Diana laughed. How happy she was! Happier than she had ever been at any other school treat; but, then, she assured herself, no other had been quite so successful as this!

"Oh no; he's all right. Do, please, see that they have enough."

"Oh, all right," he responded. "But mind, you take all the risks! It's your show, remember.—Now, my little man, try another piece of cake. What, no? Oh yes, you can. You stand up, and see. What! as bad even as that?—And, now, what do you do with 'em?" he asked, going back to Diana's side. "Let 'em lie on the grass, and recover?"

"Oh dear, no!" she replied, her eyes all alight with joy, her lips parted with what Dalesford thought an angelic smile. "They are going to play now."

Dalesford groaned. "You wouldn't be so cruel!"

"Yes. They are going to have skipping-ropes—"

"It sounds like sudden death—"

"And rounders, and cricket. And—and—I'm afraid the tiny ones will want kiss-in-the-ring."

"Thank Heaven that no one even with the grossest flattery could call me a tiny one!" he said. "What shall I do?"

"You can hold a skipping-rope. No, no! I didn't mean it, Lord Dalesford; I didn't, indeed," she broke off swiftly, as he looked round for a rope.

"Oh, in for a penny, in for a pound," he said, with an air of resignation. "I ought to be thankful that I'm not expected to skip. What's that fool of a boy doing?"

That fool of a boy was Bertie, who was having his pocket-handkerchief tied over his eyes, that he might be the first victim in blind man's buff, and who was "swung off" by mischievous Mabel with a heartiness that sent him literally spinning.

"Let me see, what shall I do?" murmured Diana, looking round eagerly.

"You will hold the other end of this absurd rope," said Dalesford firmly.

"Oh, must I? Well!—Not all at once, dears!" for the children all wanted to skip over the rope held by dear Miss Diana and his lordship. "Two—well, three at a time.—Oh, swing it faster, please, Lord Dalesford; this isn't nearly fast enough, is it, children?"

It was at this moment that a carriage came along the road by the green. It was bringing Lord Wrayborough from the station, on his visit to Shortledge—a visit that had been postponed from day to day because it was always impossible to keep the earl to a date. Lady Selina had left word with the butler that if a telegram should arrive while she was out, it should be opened, and, if announcing his lordship's coming, the carriage sent for him.

Hence it was that, all unsuspecting, his lordship was being driven past the green swarming with children, shouting and yelling as if their lives depended on it.

The earl leaned forward in the carriage, and surveyed the scene through his eye-glasses with a smile of wonder and satisfaction—and thankfulness that he was not in their midst. But, suddenly, he descried Lady Selina, seated on a form, with Tubby—still yapping—on her lap, and his smile broadened to one of cynical amusement. Then, still more suddenly, the smile gave place to a stare of wonder and amazement.

Could that be Vane at the end of that skipping-rope? Impossible! Vane at a school treat! And yet—yes, it *was* Vane! The eye-glasses dropped from his nose, and he sank back, with something between a sigh and a groan.

"The boy's gone mad!" he said to himself.

Then he snatched up his glasses again, and scanned the figure at the other end of the rope; and, as he looked, the smile which had begun to reappear died out suddenly, and his eyes grew keen and his brows rose.

"Ah, yes, I see!" he muttered. "Yes; mad, indeed!"

"Shall I stop, my lord?" asked the footman. "Lady Selina is there."

"No, no!" replied the earl grimly. "I fear I should be in the way. Stay; stop for one moment, just by the post there. One moment only, please; then drive on."

At the spot he had indicated, he knew that he could see the face of the young lady distinctly. He did see it, and looked long and keenly at it; then, as he motioned them to drive on, he fell back, and murmured, with a chuckle—

"By Jove, he has a good excuse for his madness!"

"Good gracious, there's Edward!" exclaimed Lady Selina, who caught sight of him as the carriage drove off; and, with Tubby under her arm, she hurried up to Dalesford.

CHAPTER X

THE HEIR PRESUMPTIVE

"VANE, your father has arrived—there he is! You must come!"

"Sorry! Couldn't possibly," he returned regretfully. "Couldn't leave Miss Bourne. She'd be torn to pieces by these young savages—they've lured her on to 'touch.' You go, Aunt Selina, and tell him I'm engaged in preserving an amiable young lady with a monomania for spoiling children," he added coolly; and, without waiting for her remonstrances, he went after Diana, who, indeed, appeared to be in the kind of peril he had intimated.

"Excuse me," he said, after they had been martyred for some time, and she paused, breathless, but laughing and happy; "isn't there something about the labourers being worthy of their hire? Isn't there any tea left for the victims who have been butchered to make this Roman holiday?"

"Oh, I beg your pardon! I am so sorry!" she exclaimed remorsefully. "I forgot! I'll get you some!"

"You'll do nothing of the sort," he declared. "Strange and incredible as it may seem, I wasn't on this solitary occasion thinking of myself, but of you. I've been under your orders all the afternoon; now it's my turn. You'll sit under that tree, away from this ravaging horde, and I'll bring you some tea, and—things."

"Oh, must I?" she said wistfully.

"That's it," he retorted. "You must."

He brought some "tea and things," and found her vainly trying to smooth her ruffled hair, and set her hat straight; and her delicious unconsciousness of this new phase of her beauty made his heart leap so tempestuously that his hand shook as he deposited the tray at her feet.

"No, no; I'll pour it out," he said. "You shan't do a thing. Why, you must be tired to death. Hold hard a moment!" He got a cushion, and placed it against the tree. "Now, lean back. How's that, umpire?"

"It is delicious!" she said. "I'm not tired—"

"Oh no; why should you be?" he inquired, with savage irony.

"But it's nice to rest. How kind of you to think of me, Lord Dalesford! But, indeed, you have been more than kind all the afternoon. And—and it must be so strange to you. You can't like it—"

"I do not picture heaven as an eternity of school treats, no," he said, as he poured out the tea. "Sugar?"

"And it is all the more kind and unselfish of you. I can't think why you have done it," she added innocently, and more to herself than him. "How one misjudges people!"

"Meaning me? Thank you very much," he retorted blandly. "I myself suggested softening of the brain—but it's softening of the heart. Miss Bourne—Diana—don't you know, can't you guess, why—" For the first time in his life, his voice faltered, his slow, assured fluency, his composure, deserted him; for her eyes met his, with a sweet wonder that confused, bewildered, and awed him. "Oh, don't you know? Can't you see that I'd do anything, go anywhere, to be near you—that I'm not happy when I'm away from you; that I count the hours, the minutes, that keep me from you, because—I love you?"

She understood at last. Her face flamed for a moment, then turned pale, and her hand went to her bosom, as if her heart had threatened to stop. Over her eyes, still fixed on his, flashed the swift maiden-fear, the swift questions of the heart; then her eyes were veiled from his eager gaze, and the long lashes swept her cheek.

"Are you so surprised, startled?" he asked more gently, pleadingly. "Think! Is there scarcely a day that I haven't spent with you? Have not I—the whole of me —told you, without so many words, that I love you, and want you? Oh, I can't—can't speak as I'd like to do. I—I feel like a dumb dog. But—but there it is! I love you. Will you try and love me? Will you be my wife, Diana?"

Now she must speak. Silence had been a safe refuge until now; but now she must speak, must answer him. But how should she? Did she love him? And—and, oh, was he not the "wild Lord Dalesford"—worse, the "wicked Lord Dalesford," unworthy of any girl? Alas! for the prudence of virtue, she could not dwell on this objection. Did she love him? That was the question.

"Speak to me," he said at last, after an unendurable silence.

She raised her eyes.

"I—I can't!" she said, almost piteously. "I—am trying. But I can't! I—I don't know. No; I did not guess, did not suspect.—I—thought it was just because you were amused, that—oh, I did not think! And I cannot think now!"

He took her hand, but, rising, she drew it from his eager grasp.

"No. Do—do not touch me. I want to think, to be sure."

"If you're only not sure you don't care for me," he said, catching at the straw; but she shook her head.

"No. Don't say any more, Lord Dalesford. I—can't answer you. I don't know. I want to think, to be sure," she repeated, with a long sigh, as of one driven to bay, and seeking escape.

Dalesford was a gentleman, as well as a lover. He rose, and looked at her—he was pale, and his lips were set straightly.

"I don't want to badger you," he said rather grimly. "I'll wait. But not long. I couldn't!" desperately. "I'll give you until to-morrow morning. And—and, for God's sake, let it be 'Yes,' if you can, for I feel as if my life were at stake! And it is! We'll go back now. No; I won't badger you, Diana!"

"No," she said, with a movement of her head. "I—I will go alone."

"You shall," he said; and, with an inclination of his head, he stood aside to let her pass, and watched her, with all his heart in his eyes, as she moved away from him, leaving him with so keen a sense of loss that his heart sank in fear and apprehension.

He did not come in to dinner until the soup was on the table, and all of them —and, be sure, the earl was included!—noticed how grave and preoccupied he was; but the earl greeted him with cheerful light-heartedness.

"Vane, you are looking fit!" he said, as he extended a white, bejewelled hand to the son he loved, and for whose future he was, at that moment, trembling. "The sight of you is the best tonic I know.—Selina, I have to thank you, no doubt, for Vane's bucolic air of health and contentment. Early hours, and the soothing charm of your society, to say nothing of Mabel's." He bowed to that young lady, with his most delightful air of old-world courtesy and worship of her sex and years. "I really think I shall have to remain with you for a month, at least. I've always been convinced that the air of this place is the purest and most bracing—" And so on.

He talked—he and Mabel—all through dinner in so light-hearted, careless, and bantering a tone that no one, not even Vane, suspected that he was filled with dread.

"Yes, my dear Mabel, you shall row me on the river to-morrow; and we will go and see your new friend, Miss Bourne— My dear Selina, Mabel has talked of no one else since I arrived, I assure you!—and we will have a good time!"

Father and son were left alone at last, and the earl rose.

"Shall we have a cigarette on the terrace, Vane?" he suggested, and he put his arm in Vane's, as they moved across the room.

"A touch—just a touch—of gout, I think," he said, apologising for the caress, for caress it was, and was meant to be. "May I trouble you for a cigarette? I always like yours so much better than my own. So you have taken to tea-fights, eh, Vane?" he went on, as he sank into a chair, and looked up at his son's face. "Well, well! there is nothing like change. By the way, that was a very beautiful girl you were—er—skipping with this afternoon. I happened to see her as I drove past. That was *th* Miss Bourne Mabel was raving about, of course?"

"Yes, sir," he said. "We weren't exactly skipping—"

"No, no; my mistake," said the earl blandly. "Who is she, Vane, do you know?"

"She was the schoolmistress at Wedbury—"

"Gad, yes! I thought I remembered having seen her. But how does she come here, fascinating all our people?"

"Her father left her some money," Vane explained rather shortly.

"I see. Er—may I ask—much?"

"Enough to live on," said Vane.

The earl nodded. "Ah, yes. Quite so! Very interesting. And—forgive me, my dear boy, a father's interest must be my excuse for my seeming impertinence— but—how far has it gone, and—er—how far do you mean it to go? Of course, I saw you. I—to be explicit—I saw your eyes, as they rested on hers: and mine are quick."

"Yes; I know, sir," said Vane. "How far? It rests with her. I love her—of course you saw that."

"Of course! But—er—"

"It all rests with her," said Vane gravely. "I have asked her to be my wife."

The earl winced, and his under lip quivered, but he uttered no exclamation; on the contrary, he said blandly, suavely—

"Yes. And—may one ask—what did the young lady reply?"

"She's to give me my answer to-morrow," said Vane.

"Enough to live upon, I think you said," remarked the earl contemplatively. Vane nodded.

"You mean that—that there will be trouble, sir?"

The earl smiled; it was a mirthless—indeed, a ghastly—smile.

"No. I mean that it will be—ruin," he said, in a low voice. "No, no! Don't let's talk it over! I hate—so do you—talking things over. Besides, there's a chance for us yet."

"A chance?" echoed Vane.

"Yea," with almost religious fervour. "Not much, seeing that you are—who and what you are, and that she is the daughter of 'somebody' who has left her 'enough to live upon.' But she may refuse you.—Did you hear Melba when you were in town, Vane? Gad, I don't think she was ever in better voice!"

And he talked of London, and the last race-meeting, until they parted; and it was not until he was alone, and trying to sleep, that the old man muttered sadly —

"A poor chance! I wonder how soon Starkey can get here to-morrow!"

The moment he had arrived at Shortledge, he had wired for that long-suffering gentleman.

The legislature, with a wisdom that does not characterise all its enactments, closes all the licensed places of public refreshment at the half-hour after midnight in London. But this is far too early for some folk, and the police, recognising that fact, are, consequently, blind to the existence of sundry unlicensed places where a thirsty and hungry man—thirsty and hungry for "pleasure" which shall not be limited to 12.30 p.m.—may procure food and drink galore, and a certain amount of doubtful amusement.

Most of these places are to be found in the region of Leicester Square, the historic square which, forms the centre of the metropolitan gaiety.

Here the electric light sets the darkness at naught; here it is, indeed, that the great city never sleeps; it is here that the rattle of the cab, and the song of the roysterer, is heard from dewless eve to gaunt, unsmiling morn. It is here that vice shows its gay and seamy side, that the footpad and the unfortunate touch elbows with the foolish rich and prosperous.

And it was on this pavement, on the night of Vane's avowal of love for Diana, that Mr. Desmond March, in company with some companions of like mind and character, sauntered in search of illicit supper, champagne, and amusement.

It was past two, the clubs had closed, and Desmond March was showing "life"— save the mark!—to the son and heir of an historic peerage, a vacuous youth, who regarded his mentor and friend as the most charming and faithful of guides.

The lad was half intoxicated already, but Desmond March, though he wore his immaculate silk hat on one side, and walked with a rakish air, was quite and dangerously sober; and, linking his arm in the boy's, he led him to the night house at the back of one of the narrow lanes off Coventry Street.

"I shay, March, old chap, what the deuce are you stopping at—hic!—this blessed 'bacca shop for?" inquired the young viscount, as Desmond March pulled up at the door of a seedy, neglected-looking shop, and knocked three times at the closed door.

It was opened very quickly, an evil-looking face peered out at them, a sign of recognition passed between March and its owner, and, the door being opened just wide enough to permit them to pass, the two gentlemen entered.

The man who had admitted them had disappeared; but Desmond March lifted the lid of the counter, and, pushing open a door, papered like the wall, went down a narrow and stuffy passage into a long room half filled with men and women, most of the former of whom were in evening dress, the women being richly attired—a few in good taste, but the majority in clothes of the loudest, and most garish vulgarity.

There were several tables in the room, at which some of the company were eating badly cooked food, served in silver-plated dishes, and drinking champagne of an unknown but vile brand, both food and drink costing twice and three times the usual amount. At other tables card-playing was going on, games at which the pigeon may lose anything the men who are rooking him please, and lose quickly.

A buzz of subdued voices filled the room, thick with heavy fumes of cigars; subdued because the farce of a visit from the police—who never came—was maintained as part of the fun and enjoyment, and every now and then there was a burst of laughter from the groups at the supper-tables, or an angry exclamation and an oath from one of the players.

It was a noisome, disreputable place, and a forbidding one, notwithstanding the rich apparel of its company, and the costliness of its drink and viands, and the glitter of jewels—not all false, by the way. But the young viscount felt quite grateful to his friend, Desmond March, for bringing him there—for was he not seeing life?—and at once lurched up to one of the card-tables.

"Want to play?" said March genially. "All right; but let's have some supper first." The lad wasn't quite primed enough. "Give us something to eat—the best you've got, Moss," he said to the proprietor, who smiled, and bowed, and rubbed his hands; for Mr. Desmond March was one of his most valued patrons.

"Yesh, Mishter March! Shertainly, shir! And champagne?"

"Yes. And some brandy," said Desmond March, with a significant nod.

While the supper was being prepared, he linked his arm through the young viscount's, and took him round the room, nodding to one and another of the company, and exchanging a word with some. And these considered themselves favoured by the notice, for Mr. Desmond March was somewhat of a king among this half-foolish, half-ruffianly crew.

The supper was brought, the lad plied with the vile wine, and still viler spirits; and, when he was "gone" far enough, March, with affected reluctance, permitted himself to be led to a card-table set apart from the others.

No one interfered, though the boy was evidently drunk, his hair dishevelled, his eyes bloodshot, his lips—through which issued spasmodically the latest popular song—swollen. This tragedy of the pigeon and the rook was enacted too often in this room to call for comment, much less interference, and March and his victim proceeded to play.

"Jolly nice place, this, March!" hiccoughed the boy. "Much jollier than the—hic—club. And you can play as long as you like. No beastly—hic—closing time!"

"No, rather not!" assented March. "My deal, I think.—Let me see; I won that. Yes.—And that's mine, too. What luck you have, Wally! But it will change; it will change, you see."

"It'll change, all right enough," echoed the boy. Then, with tipsy gravity, he inquired, "I shay, how much do I owe you, March? A deuce of a lot, I know!"

"No, not much. Don't bother about the money—here, give me an I.O.U. Can you see?"

He rose, as he spoke, to turn one of the gas brackets on the table; and, as he did so, a new-comer entered the den.

Now, though he was playing, "engaged in business," as one may put it, Desmond March had an eye for everyone, and everything that was going on in the room, and as he scanned, with a covert keenness, the face of the man who had just entered, a quick change came over his own; a light flashed in his eyes for an instant, and his lips came together with a peculiar twitch.

This latest visitor was a middle-aged man, with a face that belonged to that of the labouring class. The mouth was coarsely cut, the brows heavy, the eyes evasive, half-cunning, half-timid. His thick-set figure was like his face, that of the lower middle class, and he was dressed in a respectable fashion enough, but quite unlike most of the fashionable men present. In short, the man might have been taken for a well-to-do tradesman from the provinces, or a pilot who had exchanged his rough overalls and pea-jacket for his best suit. A commonplace man enough, so commonplace that, though several looked up at his entrance, no one gave him a second glance—not even Desmond March, who studiously kept his eyes on his cards.

The man stood for a moment looking round, as if he were renewing his familiarity with the scene; then he went, with the heavy step of the man who has known physical toil, to the counter for a drink, and, after drinking it slowly, loitered, exchanging a banter, as heavy as his gait, with the woman at the bar; then seemed about to leave.

But he hesitated, and presently gravitated to the table where Desmond and the lad were playing.

As he did so, and his eyes fell on Desmond March, he started, his face paled, and he turned quickly, as if about to go.

But Desmond March, without taking his eyes off his cards, and without raising or changing the voice in which he had been speaking, said slowly—

"No; don't go. I know you. Wait till I've done here. I want to speak to you."

The man stood, biting his thick lips, and looking, with a frown, at the handsome face, with its eyes still fixed on the cards, and seemed to hesitate, to rebel; but once again the smooth voice said—

"I know you—knew you the moment you came in. Wait.—Your play, Wally!"

The man hesitated a moment, then he went slowly to a chair, dropped into it, and sat staring uneasily at the door, as if he would have escaped even then, if he could have summoned up sufficient courage.

CHAPTER XI

GARLING

DESMOND MARCH did not hurry his game, did not even glance at the thick-set, commonplace man, who leant back in the chair, and, with a poor attempt at ease and nonchalance, waited Mr. March's pleasure.

Desmond March and his pigeon played until the latter could no longer see the cards; in fact, collapsed and fell across the table; then March leisurely put the I.O.U.'s the lad had given him into a pocket-book, and, dragging Lord Wally to his feet, administered a big glass of soda-water, and led him from the room. As they passed the man in the chair, March, without looking at him, said cheerfully—

"Back directly."

Having put the lad into a cab, and told the driver the address—"Better take him for a little round first, cabby," he said presently. "Here's a sovereign for your fare. Look after him!"—March went back to the room, and beckoning to the man, signed to him to take the chair Wally had vacated.

"What will you drink?" he asked.

"I'm not drinking anything," replied the man sullenly. "I've stayed because you asked me to; but I don't know you, sir, and I don't know what business you can have with me."

Desmond March nodded to one of the waiters.

"Bring some whisky—out of Mr. Moss' own bottle, please!—and soda-water," he said; then he handed his cigar-case to the man opposite him, and carefully lit a cigar for himself. There was in the action so plain an indication of conscious power, of superiority, that the man, as if hypnotised, lit a cigar and took the drink the waiter placed before him.

"You don't know me?" said Desmond March, leaning forward, and eyeing his companion with a smile of sardonic enjoyment. "My name is March. Recall anything?"

The man shook his head.

"Oh, come!" remonstrated March, with a shake of his head. "You knew me the moment you came up to the table; and you were going to bolt if I hadn't stopped you. A bad memory is a great drawback; I've always felt that, and cultivated mine. For instance, I can go back twelve years—yes, it's twelve years ago—and recall a very pleasant visit I made to a friend who held an official position under Government; in fact, he was the governor of Portland convict prison—"

The man had his glass half-way to his lips, but he arrested the action, and put the glass down. His ruddy face paled, his thick brows lowered, and his lips drew together; but he said nothing, and kept his eyes fixed on the handsome, smiling face opposite him.

"A very interesting visit it was," Desmond March went on, in a ruminating fashion, as if he were pleasantly recalling the time. "Of course, I went over the prison, and saw a great deal of the convicts. There's always a peculiar, gruesome charm about prison life—to the spectator; just as there is about the Morgue and the scaffold. Ever seen a man hanged? I have—got in with a press ticket. It's interesting. That cigar doesn't draw, I'm afraid. Take another!"

The man ignored the offer, and Desmond March resumed—

"One night, the whole place was in a state of excitement; usual cause—a convict had escaped. All the warders—guards, do you call them?—were up in arms, the alarm bell was rung, and the hue-and-cry was out in hot pursuit. The man had stunned a warder, got into the yard, and skimmed up a pole—they were repairing a roof, or something—to the outer wall. His name was Garling, and he was one of the model prisoners, and had earned ever so many good-conduct marks; but he had been playing the saint with an object, and was the last man likely to be suspected of attempting to escape. It looked as if he would get clear off, for the pursuit was at a loss for a couple of days; but, on the third, if I remember rightly, they found him, half-starved, behind a hayrick. Another drink?"

He ordered it, but the man took no notice of it when it was brought, and still kept his eyes fixed on March's smiling ones.

"I was present when the fellow was brought in. Poor devil! He had had a rough time of it! He was covered with mud and blood—one of the guards had been obliged to club him over the head, for, weak as he was, he had put up a fight for it. His clothes were torn, the skin hanging to the palms of his hands in shreds, and he was half-dead with exhaustion and disappointment. I had a good look at him, of course, and I shouldn't be likely to forget him, even if my memory wasn't as good as it is. I can see him now. There he is beside you!" he added, with a sharp change of tone.

The man turned his head, and saw himself reflected in a dingy pier-glass.

Desmond March laughed.

"Besides, he had an identification mark—a scar on his left arm.—Excuse me, that match has set your sleeve alight! Permit me!"

With an electric swiftness he caught the man's arm, forced back the loose sleeve of both jacket and shirt, and revealed a long, vivid scar. The man sprang to his feet, his face white as death, his eyes glowering under his thick brows; but Desmond March leant back, and, with a smile, motioned him to be seated again; and the man, after a moment or two, sank back into the chair.

"Now we've cleared the way, let us be comfortable, Mr. Garling," Desmond March said pleasantly. "Take your drink, light up another cigar, and—enjoy yourself. What on earth did you come here for?"

With a shrug of his broad shoulders, and a jerk of his head, Garling drank some whisky, and lit a fresh cigar; then he leant his elbows on the table, and re-

74

garded his tormentor, as if he expected some more questions, and he was not disappointed.

"Twelve years ago," said Desmond March, as if he were calculating, "you had two years to serve when you made a bolt for it. I remember, because they were surprised at your not waiting, seeing that your time was so nearly out. Why didn't you?"

Garling cleared his throat, and smiled grimly.

"The last year, the last month, the last day's the worst to bear," he said.

"And you had an extra term, or did they let you off easy?"

"They let me off—easy," said Garling, with dry irony.

"Let me see, what were you in for? Ah, yes, a little affair of a bank, and a safe. Why, of course: I remember! They used to call you the Ironmonger, because you were so good at negotiating safes and strong rooms. That was one of the interesting bits of information my friend the governor gave me. The Ironmonger. And it wasn't your first conviction. So they gave you your ticket, and you—now, pardon my curiosity, what did you do? Get into trouble again? Have you just come 'out'?" He glanced at the man's thick, iron-grey hair, which was of the ordinary length. "Ah, no; I see that you have not been in the jug lately. What has been your game, eh, Garling?"

Garling's lids dropped. Then he raised them, with a curious smile.

"If I was to tell you the truth, you wouldn't believe me," he said, and the smile broadened for a moment, then passed, and left his face grim again; but there was a strange, half-mocking expression in his eyes.

"I daresay not," said Desmond March. "That's the worst of having a bad name; you lose your credit and may as well be hanged at once with the proverbial dog. Been abroad?"

"Yes; I have been abroad," said Garling musingly. Then, suddenly, he said—

"And now let me ask you a question or two, Mr. March. I drop in here, just like any other man might do, for a drink, the publics being shut, and I run against a person that remembers me, and spots me at once. That person is a gentleman, a regular swell—though he does pass the time rooking a boy—a mere boy. No offence, sir—"

"None at all!" responded Desmond March cheerfully. "My young friend wanted to play, and you can't disoblige a friend, you know."

Garling nodded indifferently. "It's no business of mine; but, what I'm asking myself, and what I want to ask you, is—what is your game? Why couldn't you have let me come and go without interfering with me? You're a gentleman, Mr. March, a swell, and far above a common man like me; why did you want to pounce on me, and throw up in my teeth that I was once a lag; in short, what is your game, sir?"

Desmond March stroked his moustache, and looked at the man through half-closed lids.

"You wouldn't believe me, if I said I had none, eh, Garling?"

"I certainly should not!" was the prompt assent.

"And yet it's the truth," said Desmond March, with a smile. "When I saw you coming in, and looking like a respectable tradesman, or an engineer in a good way of business, I wondered who you were, why you'd chosen to come to Moss's little den—the last place for a respectable tradesman, you know. Then, when I recognised my old friend, the convict who had so nearly escaped, I thought it might be rather amusing to have a chat with you. You see, I'm a student of human nature; and you must admit that you are a quaint bit of character."

"I see," said Garling, with tightening lips. "It was sheer wanton devilry, eh, sir?"

Desmond March shrugged his shoulders.

"Call it what you like, my friend. But—who knows?—I may want you some day."

"Want me?" The man echoed the words resentfully.

"Yes. I'm a gentleman, as you say; but I'm a gentleman who lives by his wits —as you have seen. Now, to one of my profession, a man of yours is sometimes useful. Oh, don't look so black, my dear fellow; I'm not at all likely to ask you to exercise your well-known skill on a bank, or any other safe; but there may be several other ways in which you can be of service, and it is pleasant to know that you can't refuse to serve me, if I require you to do so, and that the service will cost me nothing, or next to nothing."

Garling scowled at him watchfully.

"You're making a mistake," he said at last. "You've got no hold on me."

"No? Let us see. Now, my good Garling, you have only just returned to England from abroad. How do I know? By your hands and face, of course. We don't get that peculiar tan in London town, or in any other part of England. It was got under a southern sky, Garling; and it hasn't had time to wear off."

Garling gnawed at his lips.

"You've sharp eyes, Mr. March," he remarked.

"Didn't I tell you I lived by my wits?" retorted Desmond March. "Then, again, those clothes weren't made in England—they're foreign, or colonial. Right again? And now for one more guess. Shall I hazard the conjecture that you, though a 'ticket' man, haven't reported yourself to the police for a long, a very long, time?"

Garling's lips twitched, and he glanced round the room apprehensively.

"It's all right," Desmond March observed. "They can't hear us. And, if they could, they are, most of them, too drunk to understand," he added contemptuously. "Now, if I am right in my conjecture, and I see by that expressive face of yours, Garling, that I am, I ought to do my duty as a good citizen, call a policeman directly you get into the street, and give you into custody. But it's lucky for you that some of us seldom do our duty. No; I don't care a hang whether you report yourself at Scotland Yard or not. But you shall report yourself to me, instead."

With a nod and a smile, he drew out his dainty pocket-book, extracted a card, and flicked it across the table.

"There's my address. Just look in, let us say, every Monday—"

Garling took up the card, glanced at it, crushed it in his strong hand, and, leaning forward, made a gesture as if to demand Mr. Desmond March's particular attention.

"Look here," he said, his face white, his voice thick with emotion. "You asked me what I'd been doing. Suppose—I say suppose—I'd been abroad, trying to turn over a new leaf, trying to earn a decent, honest living, and suppose I'd succeeded. Do you think that, having given the police the slip, got rid of the past, I'm going to drop back into being the tool, the slave, of the first fine gentleman that happens to spot me?"

"That's exactly the supposition I'm acting on, Garling," responded Desmond March. "Why, man, don't you see if you hadn't been on the square for some time past, if you hadn't a character to lose, you'd have told me to go to the devil long before this? You'd have whined and promised anything, everything—and made a bolt for it the moment you left me."

The man's deeply lined face worked, and he regarded the smiling one of Desmond March as if he were fascinated.

"Tut, tut! Give me credit for some small amount of penetration," March went on. "It's just because you are on the square, my good fellow, that you will do as I order you. You've come back to England, to dear old London—what a charm there is in it for the exile, isn't there? The little village with its cheerful pubs, its cabs, and its crowds, its little places like this of Moss's, its lighted streets and its fogs and muds. How you chaps, who have to bolt from it, pine for it, long for it! Oh, I know!—And you want to stop here. You've had enough of foreign parts— they're all beastly, aren't they? Yes! Here you are back again with some money in your pocket—"

The man started slightly and seemed to rouse himself from a fit of preoccupation, in which he had been listening only absently to Mr. Desmond March's smooth, soft voice.

"I'm—I'm a poor man, sir," he said, with his eyes downcast.

Desmond March laughed. "Just enough for a spree, eh? Well, have your spree; but don't forget that if I want you I shall require to know where to put my hand on you. Call it a whim of mine, if you like; but I've a fancy for keeping you on the string—"

Garling's face darkened and his eyes glowered.

"I'm a bad 'un to hold!" he said threateningly.

Desmond March laughed up at him. "I like holding bad 'uns.—What, is it closing time, Moss?" to the Jew, who came to them, rubbing his hands and with a deprecatory smile. "All right. An old servant of mine, Moss." He indicated Garling by a nod. "Strange to meet him here, eh? Yes; we're going. Come along, Edward." He clapped Garling on the shoulder—and smiled covertly as Garling started as if the action recalled unpleasant experiences. "Moss likes to keep early hours!"

Garling walked with him into the street.

"Good-night," said Desmond March. "But, I'm forgetting—you haven't given me your address!"

"Twenty-nine Old Ham Street," said Garling sullenly.

"Old Ham Street? Ah, yes, off the Tottenham Court Road. A laundress of mine used to live there. Nice quiet street; just the place for a respectable man. Call me a cab, please."

Garling started as if he were unaccustomed to receiving a curt command, and looked angrily at Desmond March as he leisurely lit a cigar; but after a momentary hesitation he stepped to the curb and hailed a hansom, and Desmond March got in slowly. Then he nodded to the man he had been baiting.

"Good-night. Don't forget—Monday!"

Garling stood on the curb looking after the cab with the passion he had been suppressing distorting his every feature; his lips writhed, his strong hands gripped each other, his massive shoulders shook. With an effort he controlled himself and pulled out a watch—it was a valuable one—looked at it and made a mental calculation.

"I could catch the Continental express," he muttered. "I could get away from the hound—curse him! What's he want with me? He's a scoundrel, though he's a fine gentleman. A card-sharping swell. He'll drag me back—back—back! Me who—who—! Why, when I think of all I've done; all I've given up—it makes me mad. Why, I could laugh!"

Something like a laugh, a hideous travesty of one, did burst from his lips. He stood on the edge of the pavement hesitating for a moment, then with a heavy sigh, the sigh of a man who has been fortune's football for so long a time that he has learned resignation to every decree of fate, however hard, he muttered—

"No, I can't go—I want to see her; I must see her, if it's only for once. What made me come here to-night? It was the solitude, the living alone, as drove me out for some amusement, anything to help me forget, to pass the lagging time. No, I can't go, and I won't."

CHAPTER XII

WHEN A WOMAN LOVES

DIANA waited until the school feast had broken up; and to the very last some of the children clung round her; indeed, she carried one child, asleep, in her arms to its home, one of the cottages on the road to Rivermead; but she had moved, and spoken, like a person in dreamland.

Could it be true that Lord Dalesford loved her? It had come so suddenly, so unexpectedly, that the surprise, the shock of his declaration confused and bewildered her.

He loved her! In the midst of the din and clamour of the children's voices his words rang in her ears, and in her heart; and every now and then she stopped short in what she was doing and gazed before her, with a scarlet blush burning in her cheeks; so that the young harpies surrounding her stared at her and demanded to be told what was the matter.

How well he had spoken, how handsome he had looked, how considerate and gentle he had been with her, and how patient! He was coming to-morrow. To-morrow—why, that was only a few hours ahead! And she would have to give him her answer. What should she say to him?

The most important time of her life had come; the hour on which all the future hung. And her answer? Did she love him?

She did not dare ask herself the question until she had reached the solitude of her own room; where she sat with her hands clasped in her lap, her eyes fixed, not on vacancy, but the mental vision of his grave, earnest face. And she could see it so plainly.

Lord Dalesford's wife! Her face flamed and her heart beat tumultuously with a sense of joy and doubt, and something nearly akin to dread.

For Lord Dalesford was not the sort of man she would have chosen—if she had not seen him, if he had not been by her side every day, as he had been since she came to Rivermead. She would have warned any girl-friend against marrying the man whom the world regarded as one of those who live the life of indolent ease and selfish pleasure. And yet—and yet—why did the thought of being his cause her to thrill, send a warm current through every vein?

How long she sat pondering, a voice in her heart drowning that of prudence, of doubt, even of conscience, she did not know; but presently there was a knock at the door and Mrs. Burton said—

"The supper is laid. Are you coming down, Diana?"

Diana answered in the affirmative, and after bathing her face went down. Mrs. Burton had not been to the school treat. She had pleaded a headache; but it was only an excuse for avoiding the function, as she avoided, whenever possible, any appearance in public. The meal had been laid in the morning-room, and Diana, as she went to her place, paused and, bending down, kissed her aunt, who was already seated.

Mrs. Burton looked up at her quickly, and noted the rapt expression in Diana's eyes; but she said nothing until she had dismissed the maid; then she asked—

"Did it go off successfully, Diana?"

"Oh yes," Diana replied. "Very." She hesitated a moment, then she said in a low voice, "Aunt Mary, Lord Dalesford has asked me—to be his wife."

Mrs. Burton laid down her knife and fork and looked at the downcast face as if she were stupefied.

"Lord Dalesford—has proposed to you!" she gasped at last, her face white and drawn.

"Yes," said Diana in a low voice, her eyes still downcast. "He asked me this afternoon—"

Mrs. Burton leant back, gripping her hands under the table.

"And—and what did you say? You refused him, Diana?" She spoke with difficulty, her breath coming painfully.

"No; he is coming to-morrow for my answer."

"It must be 'No'!" said Mrs. Burton, almost sternly.

Diana raised her eyes with grave surprise, and regarded the white face with alarm.

"No? Why, Aunt Mary?"

"Why?" repeated Mrs. Burton hoarsely. She was silent for a moment, her under lip caught in her teeth, her hands gripping each other more tightly. "It—it isn't a suitable match for you," she said thickly. "He is a nobleman—the son of an earl—he will be Lord Wrayborough. And you—you—" She stopped and her lips twitched.

"Yes, I know," said Diana quietly. "There is the difference in rank, position —"

"That's not the only objection," Mrs. Burton broke in tremulously. "He is not a good man, he belongs to the class— Oh, Diana, you won't do it, you won't do it!" Her voice broke to a wail. "He's not worthy of you; he doesn't know what love means; your way of life isn't his; you wouldn't be happy with him. No woman can rely upon a man of that sort—"

It was an unwise and unfortunate argument. Diana's face, that had been pale a moment before, now grew crimson, and a light came into her eyes which her aunt had never before seen shining in them.

"You are unjust, Aunt Mary," she said in a low voice, but it rang with a note of indignation. "You don't know him—you judge him by hearsay. And—and—if it were true, it would make no difference, it would not influence me."

"No difference? Would not—"

"No!" rejoined Diana, her face pale again now, but the light burning more brightly in her eyes. "If—if I loved him, nothing anyone, or the world, could say against him would matter. It would not matter if—if he were really bad."

Mrs. Burton stared at her with painful intentness.

"Are you mad, Diana?" she whispered.

Diana was silent for a moment, as if she were thinking; then she looked up.

"No; it would not matter. Where her heart goes, there a woman must follow. She doesn't wait to ask herself whether the man is good, bad, or indifferent; she loves him, and that is enough." She panted a little, under the strain of the emotion that thrilled through her words. "For better or for worse—ah, yes, that is it!"

She rose as she spoke and went to the window and looked out at the stars which were shining through the dusky night; and she still saw Vane's face, heard his voice.

Mrs. Burton sat with lowered head and twitching lips; then, with a deep sigh of despairful resignation, she said—

"I can say no more, Diana. You will follow your own will, I know; but—but —I have warned you!"

Diana went to her and put her arm round her neck.

"Warned me! Oh, why do you speak so sternly; why do you look on the dark side of everything—everything? Oh, forgive me, Aunt Mary! I have made you unhappy—I did not mean to do so! I know you love me! I did not mean to distress you!"

"No; it's not you," said Mrs. Burton, almost inaudibly. "Not you, Diana. It is —not your fault. Whatever happens—" She rose and, putting Diana's arm from her, went out of the room.

Diana lay awake through the night, listening to the striking of the hours by the great clock in the turret at Shortledge, the house where Dalesford lay—thinking of her, she wondered?

Mrs. Burton did not come down to breakfast. Diana went up to her room; but the door was locked, and in answer to her tender inquiry, Mrs. Burton said that she had a headache and wished to be left alone.

With a sigh Diana went down and tried to eat some breakfast; but she could not; and her eyes strayed to the window and across the lawn to the river. How soon would he come? And her answer? Oh, her answer!

Presently she heard the dip of the sculls, the boat glided to the landing-place, and, pale and red by turns, she watched him come quickly across the lawn. Even in that moment her heart thrilled with pride. How tall and graceful, how handsome, he was. She had never seen anyone like him—and he loved her!

She went through the open window to meet him, and he met her eyes raised to his for an instant, with an intent, questioning gaze.

"I am here," he said in a low voice. "No; not the house—" as Diana turned. "Come into the garden."

He did not say "Will you come?" she noted. He spoke in the tone of the man on the brink of the most momentous hour in his life.

They walked side by side, but he leading the way, all the same, to a seat in the shrubbery overlooking the placid river, and with a gesture he motioned her to be seated.

"I have come for my answer, Diana," he said gravely, quietly, but his eyes sought hers with an earnestness and eagerness that belied his apparent calm. "I love you—but you know that. Will you give yourself to me?"

Diana's heart throbbed, but she tried to still it; to answer the question put so masterfully, and yet so gently; but her aunt's words haunted her.

"Lord Dalesford, have you thought—have you considered the difference between us, the difference in rank?"

He looked at her with faint surprise.

"What on earth has that to do with it?" he asked.

"Your people—" she said, in a low voice. "They will think of it, if you have not—"

"Let them think," he said calmly, even with a smile. "I'm not asking you to marry my people. And you do them an injustice. Do you think they won't be proud of you, Diana?"

"Proud of me!" she echoed; but her heart glowed at his words, at the tone in which they were spoken.

"Why, yes!" he said. "Is that your only objection? Good heavens!" he laughed rather sadly. "I could find ever so many much stronger ones. Here's one of them. I'm not worthy of you, no man is; but I the least of all. My life—" His face darkened and he bit his lip. "But let the past go. Since I met you and loved you, I've been a different man. It rests with you whether I go back to—to that fool's life again or not. You can make of me what you will. But you know that, too. Dearest,"—his voice broke and he caught her hand,—"don't hesitate! Have some pity on me. It's life or death for me—this answer of yours. Let it be 'yes,' Diana, let it be 'yes'! I'm a bad lot, I know; but—but—" His voice failed him completely, and he sprang to his feet and caught her up to him. "But I love you, and I want you! And I'll spend the rest of my life in making you happy. No, no, it must be 'yes'; I'll not take 'no.'"

She felt his arms tighten round her; felt his lips on hers in a passionate kiss; and as they touched hers some thing seemed to go out from her soul to his. A moment before she thought that she had not known her own heart; but at the touch of his lips she was conquered, if the indescribable joy of surrender can be called vanquishment.

With a low cry he pressed her more closely to him, and she hid her face on his breast.

"Now, dearest!" he said, with infinite love, with the tender wistfulness of a man's passion, "tell me now!"

"Yes!" she murmured, raising her face and looking at him through veiled eyes.

"Dearest!" he whispered, his voice hoarse and trembling. "I—I can scarcely believe it. It seems too good luck to be true. Diana, give me one kiss, of your own accord, so that I may really know!"

It was the first time in her life that her lips had ever been raised to meet any man's; and, panting a little, she hung her head, longing yet dreading to bestow this sign of her heart's conquest. Then she slowly put her arms round his neck, and, with her solemn, joy-lit eyes gazing into his, kissed him on the lips.

It is such moments as this that transform this transient world of ours into an earthly paradise and make life worth living. These two mortals sat side by side, hand in hand, rapt in a joy beyond the power of words to describe.

The man asked himself why Heaven had bestowed this angel upon him; the woman why this man, this king of men, had bent down to love her, to raise her to his heart, his chosen, his mate.

Time glided by unheeded; the music of the river, the singing of the birds, the very rustle of the leaves made a harmony which sang of love divine, immortal. All the world lay between their hands; as they glanced at each other there flowed from their eyes a stream of electric sympathy, of mutual understanding, as if each had known the other since very childhood, as if they had been mated by Divine decree from the beginning of time; twin souls flying wistfully through space to meet and join here in this garden beside the silver river, to flow, like it, until they were lost in the ocean of death.

"And you doubted, hesitated, kept me in doubt," he said at last.

Diana hung her head, then raised her eyes to his.

"No. I never doubted," she said innocently. "I only thought I did. It seemed so marvellous, so—so—impossible that you—*you* should love me."

He laughed, but not loudly.

"Do you never look in the glass?" he asked. "Don't you know that you are one of the most beautiful women—"

"In your eyes," she whispered. "Oh, I'm glad you think so—glad!"

"And so—so—good! Good as gold!" he said in a lower voice. "I think that's why I love you, Diana. Jolly name—Diana. And it fits you. You weren't easy to get, dearest! But nothing worth having is—my treasure!"

She grew grave in a moment.

"That makes me remember—your calling me that. Your father—"

He drew her to him and pressed her warm, soft cheek against his.

"See here, Diana. My father will be delighted. He has always wanted me to marry. Good lord! I should have done so years ago if he had had his way. And as for you and him, why"—he laughed—"he simply worships beauty, and will make no end of a fuss over you. There's only one thing—" He paused a moment, and looked down at her with a smile.

"Tell me," she said.

"Of course," he responded. "No secrets, no concealment between us. We start on that basis, eh, dearest?"

"Oh yes, yes!" assented Diana.

"Right. Well, look here; you haven't made much of a match of it. You might have married a duke—oh yes, you might. If you'd run a season in town—Jove, how glad I am you didn't!—there's no knowing how high you might have flown. But you're my bird now, the captive of my bow and spear. Where was I? Oh yes," he went on lightly. "You have done very badly in a worldly sense, Diana. For we're as poor as Job. Fact!" as she stared at him. "Poorer than Job, for I don't remember that he was in debt. We are,—up to our necks. You and I will have to economise. It will be love in a cottage, don't you know."

She looked up at him quickly, and her lips moved. She was going to tell him that she was that hateful thing, a millionairess. Hateful? No, blessed! For could she not pour her money at his feet? A golden sacrifice on the altar of love. But she kept back the words. It was so sweet to be loved for herself alone that she clung to the flattering fact, to the delicious picture of the love in a cottage which his imagination had drawn.

"But we shall get on all right," he said easily. "We always have. And if we don't, who cares? Not I!"

"Nor I!" she whispered, a little guiltily. She would tell him to-morrow.

They sat and talked—for even when their lips were silent their eyes were eloquent; and the subject never altered, though they rang an endless variation on it, until a shadow fell on the path before them, and they looked up and saw Mrs. Burton.

She looked white, ill, and anxious; and Dalesford sprang up with a dash of colour in his face, a proudful look in his eyes.

"Mrs. Burton, Diana has promised to be my wife," he said, his hand fastening in a possessive grasp on Diana's arm.

Mrs. Burton caught her shawl to her bosom and regarded them with a strange expression.

"I—I wish you every happiness," she said. "Are you—coming in to lunch?"

"Are we?" he asked of Diana, who stood looking at her aunt entreatingly. "Yes? All right!"

"Mr. Starkey, my lord," announced a footman.

The earl was seated in the easiest of easy-chairs on the terrace at Shortledge, the *Times*, just arrived, on his knee, one of Vane's cigarettes—his father would never buy them, so that he might have the pleasure of receiving them from Vane —between his clean-cut lips.

"Heaven be thanked! Ask him to come here, please."

Mr. Starkey, of the anxious countenance, came through the house to the terrace, and the earl held out his hand and smiled at him ruefully.

"I received your telegram in time to catch the early train, my lord," said Mr. Starkey.

"Thanks, thanks! Sorry to inconvenience you, my dear fellow! But—well, the fat's in the fire, and there's the devil to pay. Sit down. Have a cigarette? No, I forgot."

"What is wrong?" asked Mr. Starkey, in the tone of a man who is accustomed to things going wrong.

"Everything's going wrong," replied the earl, with a gesture of his white, ladylike hand. "Vane is in love—"

Mr. Starkey frowned. "Yes? Well, my lord, that's not an uncommon occurrence with the sons of men."

"Yes; but he's in love with a mere nobody. A beautiful young creature, I grant you. Oh, very beautiful! One of those girls who—who— But I think you were never in love, Starkey?"

"I've not had time, my lord," said Mr. Starkey grimly.

"Really? Sorry! I feel for you. Well, this young lady is as lovely as a—a peri. I'm not surprised at Vane's infatuation. I only caught a glimpse of her for a moment or two, and I must confess—"

Mr. Starkey lifted his silk hat and looked into it gloomily.

"Who is she, my lord?" he asked in a rather tired manner; for he had come a long journey.

"A young lady who has taken a house here, on the river-side. A—a—I don't want to be offensive—but a mere nobody; a young lady who, to quote Vane's own words, was left, by her father, also a mere nobody, just enough money to live upon. He has proposed to her, and has, I take it, gone for her answer this morning."

Mr. Starkey wiped his much-lined brow.

"We are ruined," he said at last.

"Dear, dear me!" murmured the earl sympathetically. "Can anything be done? I fear not. You know what Vane is!"

"What is her name?" asked Mr. Starkey, in the dull tones of despair.

"Her name is—is"—the earl pondered for a moment—"ah, yes; Diana Bourne. She was the schoolmistress at Wedbury—"

"What!" exclaimed Mr. Starkey, so sharply that the earl started.

"My dear Starkey! What on earth is the matter with you?" For poor Starkey was smiling, grinning from ear to ear.

"Miss Bourne—Miss Diana Bourne! My dear Lord Wrayborough! What luck! What—what extraordinary good fortune!"

The earl looked at him as if he feared the excellent Mr. Starkey had taken leave of his senses.

"Good fortune! A—mere nobody!"

"Nobody be hanged!" ejaculated Mr. Starkey. "I beg your pardon, my lord! But this Miss Bourne, Miss Diana Bourne, is a great heiress!"

It was the earl's turn to exclaim, but he only raised his dark brows.

"What? I beg your pardon?"

"She's a great heiress!" repeated Mr. Starkey. "Her father—he died a little while ago—abroad—left her nearly a million of money! I know her solicitor, Mr. Fielding."

The earl leant back and fanned himself with the *Times*.

"But—but Vane evidently doesn't know this!" he said at last.

Mr. Starkey, joy overspreading his countenance, expressed his surprise.

"No," said the earl thoughtfully. "And for Heaven's sake don't tell him! He's just the man to cut up rough over it. Vane's Quixotic, Starkey; that's the word! A million, did you say? Good lord! No, no; not a word to Vane! Hush! here he comes; with all the conquering hero thick upon him! A million! Oh, my seven senses! Not a word, Starkey! Take your cue from me! For Heaven's sake pull a long face, my dear fellow!"

Dalesford came down the terrace with quick though long steps—his legs were long.

"Father—Hallo, Starkey, how are you?—father, Diana, Miss Bourne, has accepted me. Wish me luck!"

The earl, pulling the long face he had enjoined on Mr. Starkey, held out his thin, white hand.

"Really? Well, well! We wish you luck, eh, Starkey?"

CHAPTER XIII

ON THE ROAD TO WEDBURY

GARLING, the man whom Desmond March had lassoed so ruthlessly, trudged through the rosy dawn, which made even London poetic, to his lodgings in Old Ham Street, off the Tottenham Court Road, and, opening the door with his latch-key, paused and looked round with a covert watchfulness, and mechanically, as if the trick were a confirmed habit; then he went softly up to his room, which was at the top of the house; and before he closed the door of the room he stood and listened again.

It was the ordinary lodging-house bedroom—plain but comfortable. Garling looked round, as he had looked round in the street and at the top of the stairs; then he locked the door and inserted a small wedge of wood in the crack at the bottom, so that it would be impossible to open the door from the outside unless it were broken in.

There was a large wooden, iron-bound trunk, much battered, at the foot of the bed; he unlocked this, and, taking out an old leather wallet, extracted a roll of bank-notes, and, wetting his thumb, turned them over and counted them; he put some of them in his pocket, and, locking the box, seated himself on the top of it, his chin resting in his thick hand, his eyes peering under his heavy brows into vacancy.

The chimes of a neighbouring clock roused him from his reverie, and with a sigh he took off his coat and lay down on the bed; and, notwithstanding his trying interview with Desmond March, he fell asleep at once, with the facility of a soldier or sailor, or a man who has been accustomed to take sleep just when he could snatch it.

It was ten o'clock before he awoke; then he sprang out of bed the moment his eyes were open, and stood in the centre of the floor, listening intently. A little later he left the house and made his way to a grimy little coffee-house round the corner, and ordered some breakfast.

He had taken his seat near the window, but behind a dingy red curtain, so that he could see the street without being seen; and while he ate his breakfast of indifferent ham, and eggs which, like the curate's, were only good in parts, he watched the street and the passers-by with that peculiar interest which is displayed by the man who has been absent from a large city for a long period.

Nothing escaped the keen eyes; and every now and then his thick lips twisted with a faint smile of enjoyment as something characteristic of a London street passed under his notice: two errand-boys, playfully sparring on the other side of the road—a dissipated cat slinking home with a furtive air of guilt—the police-man stopping on his beat to exchange a few words with the housemaid cleaning the steps. These incidents, commonplace enough to the ordinary Londoner, seemed to afford Garling much entertainment.

Presently, a young girl came along the street—a slight, graceful figure, a pale and pretty face. She had a portfolio under her arm, and walked quickly, with a certain shyness and timidity which attracted Garling as much as, or more than, her face and figure had done. She disappeared, Garling watching her until the last moment from behind his curtain; and the sight of her seemed to awaken some memory, to evoke some reflection, which softened his rugged face. Having finished his breakfast, he drew his hand, nature's *serviette*, across his lips, paid the modest charge, surprised and fluttered the diminutive waitress by giving her a shilling, then went out.

He paused outside to light a cigar, a very strong but a very good one, and while he was doing so the young girl he had noticed came round the corner. He saw that her face was still paler, that she looked anxious and disappointed, and that she held her head much lower than when he had first seen her.

While he was watching her with interest, a milk-cart came dashing round the corner in the charmingly careless manner peculiar to those vehicles; the girl was crossing the road at the moment, and the cart was almost upon her, when Gar-ling, shutting his teeth hard on his cigar, sprang forward, and, catching hold of her, swung her out of harm's way.

The girl uttered a frightened cry, looked up, and saw how she had been deftly rescued, and stood, white and trembling, with Garling's gorilla-like arm still round her. Garling, with an oath that scared the milk-boy on his devastating way, now led the girl across the road.

"Narrow squeak that, miss," he said, with a rough kind of gentleness. "You ought not to walk about the London streets without knowing where you're go-ing."

"I know," she said apologetically; "it was my fault. I was thinking of—of many things, and I didn't see the cart. I have to thank you for saving me from what might have been a serious accident, a very serious accident to me."

She smiled up at him bravely, but wearily; she was still very white, and her delicate lips were quivering; indeed, her whole slight figure was trembling.

"I'm very glad I happened to be on the spot," said Garling, "and in time to pick you up out of the way of that fool of a cart. That boy will murder someone before he's much older! But you're upset, miss. You don't feel as if you were go-ing to faint, do you?" he asked anxiously. "How would it be if you came into this little place, and got a drink of water, and rested a little?" he added.

She glanced up at him timidly, apprehensively; but something in his rugged face, the kindly light in his eyes, gave her confidence, and reassured her. She felt weak, and scarcely able to stand, and she said—

"Yes; I think I will go in and sit down for a minute or two; but don't let me trouble you any further. It's a coffee-house—"

"Oh, it's all right," he said; "but I don't like to let you go in alone. I should like to come in and see you through this." He glanced at his watch. "I've got a quarter of an hour. Here, put your hand on my arm. And don't you be afraid. I've"—he paused a moment, and a curious expression flashed across his face—"I've got a daughter of my own."

She put her hand on his arm, and they went in; he called for a glass of water, and sat opposite her while she drank some; and he watched her with even a greater interest than he had displayed in watching the panorama of the street.

"Better now?" he asked presently.

"Thank you, I am all right now," she replied, with a smile; it was a smile with a dark shadow of sadness behind it, the shadow that lurked in the slightly drooping lips, and clouded the brightness of her blue eyes. "Oh yes; I am quite recovered. I will go now. I haven't thanked you, really thanked you, for your kindness; and you have been very kind."

"Don't mention it," he said, nodding at her in a fatherly way. "Better wait another minute or two, till you've quite felt your feet. Hope that hasn't come to any harm?" he added, as she examined the portfolio, which had come untied. "Something valuable?"

The question was so devoid of offence that the girl replied at once—

"To me, yes; but"—with a sigh—"not of much value to others, I'm afraid. They are some drawings, which I was taking to sell; but I have not succeeded in disposing of them."

His keen eye ran over her plain and inexpensive dress, and he nodded sympathetically and comprehendingly.

"An artist, eh, miss?"

"Oh, I'm scarcely entitled to call myself an artist," she replied. "I make drawings for magazines, and fashion-plates—and these are fashion-plates."

"I'm sure they are very clever," he remarked, looking so wistfully at the portfolio that she could not fail to see his curiosity; and, after a moment of hesitation, she opened the case and showed him the drawings. He bent over them, and turned them over with the reverence of the uneducated, touching them gingerly with his thick, strong fingers.

"They're right-down beautiful," he said, with unfeigned admiration. "Beautiful, that's what I call them! And you mean to say they wouldn't buy 'em? They must be fools! Why, every one of them—these pictures, I mean, not them idiots as don't know a good thing when they see it—ought to be framed. And I should like to frame them. See here, miss, I should take it as a favour if you'd sell them to me."

She laughed, coloured, and shook her head sadly.

"You cannot want a set of fashion-plates," she said.

"That is just what I do want," he responded. "I've spent such a long time in places where there aren't any fashions that this kind of thing is a treat to me, and I'd rather have it than the regular sort of picture. Besides, I should like to have 'em as a kind of—what do you call it?—soovenere."

The girl shook her head again. "Do you think I don't understand?" she said very gently. "You saw that I was disappointed because I had not sold my drawings; and—and you want to add to the kindness you have shown me by helping me, by offering me—"

"Excuse me," he argued. "Business is business. I'll pay you just what you were going to sell them for; no more, because you're a lady, as I can see, and wouldn't take it; no less, because I'm not the man to take advantage of a low market; that is"—with a grim smile—"where a lady is concerned."

The girl laughed mirthlessly, and, selecting the plate she considered the best, she held it out to him.

"Well," she said resignedly, "there is one—if you really want it. You shall buy it, and give me what the publisher would have given me."

"Right you are," he said, taking a five-pound note from his pocket and laying it on the table. "That's about right, I suppose?"

She stared, and blushed; then laughed, with sad irony, and shook her head again rebukingly.

"It is quite right—barring four pounds ten shillings."

"Why, I am ashamed of myself," he said penitently, as he quickly placed another note beside the first.

The girl regarded him with astonishment, and a touch of offence.

"I mean that the price is ten shillings."

"What!" he exclaimed. "You do this beautiful thing, this lovely lady in the swell clothes, for ten shillings? And they call this a just world! Well, I can see you won't take any more," he said, and he pocketed the notes and held out half a sovereign.

"Thank you very much," she said, as he dropped the coin in her cheaply gloved hand. "Now, I will say good-bye."

"One moment," he said, peering at the corner of the drawing; "there's a name here—Lucy Edgworth. That's yours, I suppose?"

"Yes; that is my name," she said.

"Now, suppose," he said, trying to speak in a casual way, "suppose I was to want some more of these, to frame and hang up in my room, you know—where should I write for them?"

"I live at—" she began; then she stopped, and, biting her lip, shook her head. "You will not want any more of them," she said. "I—I would rather not give you my address. I am not ungrateful; but—but it is not necessary. Good-bye."

She hesitated for a moment; then, with a trustful glance from her childlike eyes to the man's rugged face, she held out her hand. His huge fist swallowed it up, and he patted it in a fatherly way.

"Well, good-bye, miss," he said. "I was hoping that I might see you again; but you're right— I am a stranger."

"A good Samaritan," she said wearily. "Good-bye."

He looked after her thoughtfully.

"I suppose *sh'd* be about her age," he murmured. "I wonder whether she's as pretty and taking? Ah, well, I shall know some day—soon, I hope."

He called a cab, and told the man to drive to Waterloo. There he took a third-class ticket for Lowminster, and, getting into a smoking-carriage, lit a cigar, and made himself comfortable behind a newspaper. Just as the train was starting, two young men got in, and Garling, from round the side of his paper, examined them, as he examined everyone and everything that came within his purview.

They looked like clerks, and they lit the everlasting cigarette, and talked and laughed with the beautiful irresponsibility of youth.

Garling listened to them for a time; but their conversation—it was mostly of a sporting character, with football predominating—did not interest him, and he closed his eyes and went to sleep. He awoke, after a time, and heard the two young men still talking; but their voices were now lowered, and they were leaning forward to each other, as if they were speaking of something of importance; and Garling instantly closed his eyes again, but opened his ears.

"You see," said one of the men, "it's a touch-and-go thing. We're as certain as certain can be that the line's coming right through the property. Look here; I'll show you." He drew a paper from his pocket, unfolded it, and the two heads bent over it. "See? Right through it. And just think what a difference it'll make. It will turn a kind of fishing-village into a swagger watering-place. Everything is in its favour—situation, climate, surroundings. It's one of the most beautiful places in Cornwall; and it only wants this railroad to transform it into—well, into a gold-mine, for that's just what it would be. Now, my firm have got scent of this—Oh, they're sharp!"

"They're sharp enough," assented the other, with a nod.

"You bet! And, naturally, they want to get hold of the property. Once they had got hold of it, they could easily raise the capital to work the thing. And, I tell you, it's a splendid chance," he went on eagerly. "A lovely bay; a good sea frontage; hills at the back, with pine-trees, and all that; no end of sites for a casino, hotels, swell houses, villas, shops—everything you want."

The other man nodded. "I know the whole bag of tricks. You get a swell doctor, one of those Harley Street chaps, to go down and see it, and send his patients there, and write a letter to the *Times*, saying it's the finest air in England."

"Exactly," assented his companion. "You start a kursaal"—he called it "curse-all"—"and a band, and a ballroom, a club, and a pier; make the place pleasant and entertaining, and in less than no time you've got a property worth—"

"Half a million," caught up his friend eagerly. "Yes; that's just what could be made of Sunninglea."

Garling's thick lips mutely formed the word—Sunninglea. His eyes were tightly closed; he emitted a faint snore.

"How that old chap sleeps, doesn't he?" remarked one of the men. "A good name, too, isn't it? By George! I believe you get more sun there than in any other part of the kingdom; sun all the year round. Oh, I tell you it's a big thing!"

"But who does it belong to?" asked his companion; the other, after a cautious glance at the figure in the corner replied, in a lower voice—

"To the Wrayborough family. That is to say, they are the owners; but Drake and Drake hold the mortgage; and they're anxious to sell, because they've lent more money than they think it's worth, and—here's where the joke comes in—the Wrayborough people have authorised them to sell. They're hard up, you know—the Wrayboroughs, I mean."

"Fine old sportsman, the earl," remarked the other knowingly. "So's his son, Lord Dalesford—splendid chap. 'Pon my word, it seems a pity that they should be so blind to what's going on."

"Oh, I don't know," remarked the other; "business is business, you know. My people will have their claws in this thing presently, and they'll make a mint of money. Hallo! Here's the junction. We change here. Tumble out, old man."

In leaving the carriage, one of them stumbled over Garling's extended legs, and begged his pardon. Garling stretched himself, appeared to awake with difficulty, yawned, and told him not to mention it. When the train was in motion again and had got well beyond the platform, he sat up, and, with an alert expression in his rugged face, took out a note-book, and wrote down the names of the places and persons he had heard; then he composed himself to sleep again, and slept soundly until he reached Lowminster.

Without making any inquiries, he found the quietest hotel in the town, engaged a room, and, having eaten the usual hotel meal of chops, potatoes, and cabbage, set out for a walk. Again, without any inquiries or guide, excepting the finger-posts, he made his way to Wedbury, and late in the afternoon stood beside the church, and looked gravely about him. He had all the air of a man who had happened on the quiet, out-of-the-way place by accident; and it was in a manner of easy and casual interest that he stopped an old labourer and got into conversation with him.

"Pretty place, this," he said.

"Yes; it's pretty enough," replied the old man.

"Not many houses or people here, though," remarked Garling.

"No, not so many," assented the old fellow; "most of us goes up to the big towns; it's only the gentry as stops on."

"Ah, yes," said Garling. "Have a cigar? Prefer 'bacca, eh?" as the old man eyed the cigar-case doubtfully. "Here you are, then; help yourself. You're one of the old inhabitants, I suppose—know all the people, eh? Do you happen to know a Mrs. Burton?"

The old man lit his pipe, and shook his head dully.

"No? A lady as lives with her niece, Miss Bourne—Miss Diana Bourne," said Garling, a trifle huskily.

"Oh, you mean Miss Diana, the school-teacher," said the old man. "Why, of course I do; everybody knows she. You're inquiring for 'er, mister?"

"Yes—for a friend of mine," replied Garling, still more huskily. "He asked me to look them up if I was down in these parts."

"Ah, well, then, you're too late," returned the old man. "They be gone."

Garling's face fell, and he suppressed a sigh of disappointment.

"Gone, have they?" he said, as indifferently as he could. "How long ago's that, and where have they gone?"

"Oh, it's a long while ago," replied the old man wearily, "and I don't know where they be gone. Nobody does. They went quite sudden-like. Disappeared, as you might say. They lived in that cottage there, by the school. Beautiful young lady she was, and kind. Us misses 'er a good deal. No; nobody knows where they be gone. Well, good-evening to you, mister, and thank you."

Garling wished him good-evening, then sauntered to the cottage, and stood looking at it sadly and wistfully, as if he were suffering a keen disappointment. After a time he pulled himself together, and, with a shake of his broad shoulders trudged back to Lowminster. When he reached the hotel, he found a Bradshaw, and ran his thick forefinger down the column of S's. There was no station called Sunninglea. He rang the bell, and asked the waiter if he had such a thing as an atlas, and the man brought him a dingy, much-thumbed one.

Garling found the little fishing-place with the romantic and taking name, and traced the nearest station. Then he called for a whisky-and-soda, and sat and smoked and drank, his thick brows bent in a thoughtful frown.

93

CHAPTER XIV

CONGRATULATIONS

"My dear Vane, I wish you luck and every happiness," said the earl, with a fine smile, and holding out his hand.

As he took it, Vane felt and looked somewhat surprised. He knew his father too well to dread a scene; knew that his father had too correct a sense of the right of men, especially of sons, to go their own way; but he certainly did not expect that the earl would take the announcement so cheerfully.

"And so you are going to turn Benedict, eh, Vane? Well, the Benedict in the play hadn't a better excuse. She is one of the most beautiful girls I have ever seen, and no doubt is as amiable as she is beautiful; but I shall avail myself, at the first opportunity, of assuring myself of that fact. Your aunt and I will do ourselves the honour and pleasure of paying our respects to the young lady this very afternoon."

"You are very kind, sir," said Dalesford, in a low voice, and with an affectionate glance at the handsome face, with its smiling eyes and delicately curved lips. "I did not expect you to take it so nicely. I am grateful. Starkey looked rather flabbergasted!" Starkey had discreetly withdrawn. "I suppose he thinks that I have made a mess of it?"

"My dear Vane, it doesn't matter ☐☐ what anyone thinks; the die is cast, the Rubicon has been passed, and the only thing that remains to be done is to exercise our philosophy, and make the best of it; indeed, I am prepared to make the very best of it. I have this consolation, and this cause for congratulation—that your charming cousin, Desmond, will have his nose put out of joint. But we will not think of such an unpleasant person on such an extremely pleasant occasion. You look particularly well and happy, my dear boy. Ah, love's young dream!"

"Of course I am very happy, sir," said Dalesford. "I have got a prize. Diana is — But you don't want me to sing her praises, though I shall be very disappointed and surprised if you do not join in my song when you know her."

"This afternoon, my dear Vane—this afternoon! I will go and put on my best clothes, and my best manner, and I will do my utmost to cut you out."

"Of course, sir," responded Vane, eyeing his father fondly and proudly.

When Dalesford had left him, the earl sat for a minute or two chuckling over the comedy. Then he went to break the news to Lady Selina, which he did in his characteristic manner. He found her and Mabel in the morning-room, and, surveying them both with a comic air of dismay and resignation, he said pleasantly, though abruptly—

"Selina, your congratulations, if you please. Our dear Vane is in love, and, what is more, is going to be married. You cannot speak? I am not surprised. Contain your delight within reasonable bounds when I tell you that it is that most charming young lady, Miss Bourne."

Lady Selina gasped like a fish, and echoed the name in a sepulchral tone; but Mabel sprang to her feet, clapped her hands, and danced the first steps of a □□□ □□'□□□.

"Mabel!" cried Lady Selina. "Mabel!"

But the earl broke in upon the rebuke.

"Do not check her, my dear Selina; the child is right. It is a proper occasion for exuberant hilarity. Mabel, you can kiss me if you like."

Mabel sprang to him, and threw her arms round his neck, exclaiming—

"Oh, dear Uncle Edward, I am so glad! It is delightful news! She is the dearest, sweetest, loveliest—"

"Oh, come, my dear child, Vane spared me; do you be as merciful!"

"But you surely do not intend to encourage this—this madness, Edward?" said Lady Selina, with stern amazement.

"That is exactly what I intend to do, my dear Selina," said the earl. "Vane's madness is his own private affair, and I should not dream of interfering with it. Besides, we are all so painfully sane nowadays, that insanity of this kind ought to be encouraged. And, really, when you come to think of it, you will admit that it would not matter a brass farthing to Vane whether we approved or disapproved. It wouldn't have mattered to me at his age, and I wouldn't give the aforesaid brass farthing for any young man to whom such disapproval would matter. No; my dear Selina, we will face the inevitable with all the grace we can command. We will call upon the future Lady Dalesford this afternoon. Shall we have the carriage at four o'clock?"

"But—" began Lady Selina, still gasping.

The earl held up his hand, and shook his head, smiling pleasantly, but with a look behind the smile which effectually stopped Lady Selina's threatened expostulation and remonstrance.

"My dear Selina," he said sweetly, "be thankful for the goods the gods send us, and grateful that things are no worse!"

The reader does not want to be told that Vane was at Rivermead long before four o'clock. He was as passionately in love as any boy in his teens could have been. The joy, the ecstatic happiness, that thrilled through every vein of him was so novel, so strange, that he felt as if he had just been born into a new world, a world in which it would be always sunshine, in which every hour would be instinct with the delight of living; as if he had found an angelic being to share his existence, his every thought, his every breath.

He did not tell himself all this in so many words, for Vane, thank Heaven, was quite incapable of self-analysis and introspection. He only told himself that he loved her, this beautiful young girl, who was as good as she was beautiful, innocent as a child, pure as a star, tender as a woman; and he was filled with amazement that she should condescend to love him, and asked himself, with wonder, and a humility strange in a Dalesford, what she had seen in him.

"Dearest," he said, as, hand in hand, like child lovers, they walked in the friendly screen of the shrubbery, "my father is coming here at four o'clock. He is coming to know you—and to love you. And I think you will like him, Diana. He told me that he should try to cut me out," he laughed. "The dear old boy! Yes; you will like him."

"I hope he will like me," said Diana, just a wee bit timidly. "I am a little nervous, Vane. Lady Selina— But I will try to be brave, and not feel like a prisoner at the bar, who ought to plead guilty to the heinous crime of winning the affection of the son of the great and all-powerful Earl of Wrayborough. Seriously, Vane, your father must be very sweet and good-natured to—to accept me; for, after all—"

"I think that will do, dearest," he said. "When you disparage yourself, it gets on my nerves, and I want to throw up my arms, and shriek out, 'Listen to this angel, who stoops to love a mere mortal!' I suppose I may take it that you do still love me; that it isn't a mistake, that you haven't changed your mind?"

Within his encircling arms, Diana gave him assurance of her love. And the sun shone brightly on them. Moments of happiness are fleet of wing, and Diana started when she heard the Shortledge carriage roll up to the entrance. She was rather pale as she and Dalesford went into the drawing-room to receive the party; and there was a touch of reserve in her reception of Lady Selina's rather cold greeting.

But Mabel made amends for her aunt's stiffness, and, encouraged by the presence of the earl, who consistently spoiled her, she put her arms around Diana and gave her a girlish hug. Then Diana turned to the earl; and now there was a faint look of appeal in the beautiful grey eyes—an appeal to which the earl responded immediately.

Taking both her hands, and bending over her—he was very tall—he smiled at her, and in the voice which had won, in the old days, not a few women's hearts, he said—

"My dear Miss Bourne—my dear child, I have come to thank you for making my son happy."

The words, the tone in which they were uttered, went straight to Diana's heart; her eyes grew moist, and the hand which he held trembled. He drew her nearer to him, and kissed her on the forehead.

"An old man's privilege, my dear; indeed, a father's, for I have gained a daughter; and"—there was pathos in his eyes and in his voice—"I had not one before."

Fortunately for Diana's strained nerves, at that moment Mrs. Burton entered. Diana murmured her aunt's name, and the earl turned, with swift courtesy, to the anxious-looking woman with the haggard, weary face and downcast eyes, bent over her hand, led her to a seat, and expressed to her his pleasure in the engagement of her niece to his son. Lady Selina seemed to be still too benumbed to grasp the situation; but there was nothing for her to do but to follow suit with as much amiability as she could command; and Diana, seated beside her ladyship, received her congratulations and good wishes.

The tension was still great; but, fortunately, Mabel was there to relieve it. As usual, she was pining for the garden; and when her aunt turned to Mrs. Burton, with the automatic movement of a wax figure, Mabel tugged at Diana's sleeve, and whispered—

"Oh, let us come outside, and leave the old people to fight it out."

Diana shook her head smilingly, but wistfully; but the earl, whom no movement of hers escaped,—he had been watching Diana without appearing to do so, —came to Mabel's aid.

"Better go, my dear," he said, "or that tiresome child will give you no rest;" and Diana, with a blush, allowed Mabel to draw her out. Of course, Dalesford followed; but Mabel turned upon him indignantly.

"Oh, Vane, you'll surely let me have her to myself for a minute or two?" she exclaimed. "That's where men are so selfish! He doesn't remember that he'll have you for the rest of his natural life!"

"I'll give you five minutes," said Dalesford grudgingly; "and that's four minutes more than I can really spare."

Mabel made a grimace at him, and, linking her arm in Diana's, led her to a seat, into which she plumped Diana with gentle force.

"Now, tell me all about it, Diana—I've really the right to call you Diana now, haven't I? But, of course, you won't tell me anything; I shall have to get it out of Vane. And he'll be worse than ever; he's so conceitedly happy. And no wonder! Shouldn't I be if I were a man! And you are really going to be my cousin! Diana, you'll let me come and stay with you when you are married?"

Diana laughed, and blushed. "That will be a very long time to look forward to, Mabel."

"Oh no, it won't. You won't catch Vane waiting very long. He's too bad for that. And, oh, Diana, promise me now, now this minute, that I shall be one of your bridesmaids!" she said eagerly. "I suppose you'll have ever so many; but, mind, mind, you must make room for me!"

The blush faded from Diana's face, and she looked rather grave.

"I think it is very likely that you will be the only one, dear. I haven't any relatives, or girl friends, like other girls."

"Haven't you?" said Mabel, with wide-open and sympathetic eyes. "How strange!"

"Yes; it is strange," said Diana. "But there is only Aunt Mary."

"Well, that makes me safe, anyhow," said Mabel, with a sigh of satisfaction. "And how beautiful you will look as a bride, Diana! I don't wonder at Vane being so proud of you. You didn't see him while he was looking at you and Uncle Edward. And isn't he a dear old man—didn't he behave splendidly? There are times when I think Uncle Edward must be the nicest man that was ever created. But there! I knew he would go down before you. He adores beauty, and you are irresistible!"

"You are an irresistible flatterer," Diana assured her. "Yes; Lord Wrayborough was very sweet to me, and I—I am very grateful to him. I did not expect—but I must not say any more on that point. I am very grateful to you all for being so kind to me."

Mabel's eyes opened wide. "Kind to you? You mean because we are all so glad you accepted Vane? Why, my dear Diana, it is the best thing that could have happened to him, and all of us. Why, you just ▢▢▢▢ him." She coloured, and looked down shyly. "I am only a girl, but, of course, I know how important it is that Vane should marry, should settle down. Of course, I know he has been wild, like—like all the Wrayboroughs. But he is quite changed now. And you have changed him, you dear, sweet girl. Love you! I should think we should! Oh, here is Vane! What a bother!—Vane, I am sure the five minutes aren't up."

"They are, my sweet child, and you are wanted in the drawing-room."

"Of course that's a fib, but I suppose I shall have to go," retorted Mabel; and, stooping, she kissed Diana, and ran in, pausing at the window to throw her another kiss.

Vane was all aglow with happiness.

"What did I tell you, dearest?" he said. "I wish you could have heard my father singing your praises to Mrs. Burton. I haven't seen the dear old man look so happy for years. He told Mrs. Burton that our marriage would add twenty years to his life."

Diana looked up at him, with joy in her eyes, but still with a shadow of surprise in them.

"It seems so strange," she said. "I can't be blind to the fact that your people ought not to regard our engagement as a good thing for you."

He laughed. "But what more can you want?" he asked. "What will convince you? Diana, you are the only beautiful woman I ever met who was really humble-minded and free from vanity. I have got a prize, indeed!"

As he spoke, lifting a hand to his lips, a carriage came down the road, and stopped at the front gate.

"Good heavens! Another visitor!" he said disgustedly. "Yes; I suppose we must go in," he deplored, as Diana rose.

They went toward the house, drawing apart to a conventional distance when they got within sight of the windows.

"Why, it's my Fairy Godmother!" Diana said, as she heard Mr. Fielding's voice.

"Your what?" Dalesford asked.

"My lawyer, Mr. Fielding," Diana explained. "I call him my Fairy Godmother, because he has been so good to me; because he found me—"

"Found you?" echoed Dalesford.

Before she could give him any more information, they had reached the window, and Mr. Fielding, catching sight of her, came forward to meet her.

"I have just come in time, my dear Miss Bourne, to hear some important and interesting news," he said, as they entered the room.

He stood and smiled at her, his thin lips drawn together, his eyebrows raised, his keen eyes looking from her blushing face to Dalesford's.

"I was going to write to you," said Diana, in a low voice.

"Of course, of course," he said, with a little bow. "This is Lord Dalesford? Lord Dalesford, you will permit me to offer you my heartiest congratulations. I have just expressed them to Lord Wrayborough." He inclined his head to the earl, and, at the same moment, cast a glance, as if casually, at Mrs. Burton, who was sitting with her head bent and her hands gripping each other. "Yes; my visit is a happy accident, and I am delighted to have arrived at such an auspicious moment. I have just been telling Lord Wrayborough, my dear Miss Bourne, that you have been good enough to grant me the inestimable privilege of calling myself your friend, as well as your legal adviser."

He had taken a chair, and leant forward, with the self-possessed and alert manner which Diana remembered he had shown on her first visit to him at Lincoln's Inn. With his birdlike eyes, he seemed to dominate the situation, to hold the others, as it were, in his grip. With his fine acuteness, his quick, intuitive insight, the earl saw that this suave, self-possessed man of the law had something to say, and was going to say it.

"Most happy coincidence, Mr. Fielding," he murmured with a smile. "Particularly happy for me. I am delighted to meet you. Of course, I know the famous Mr. Fielding by repute, but this is the first time I have had the pleasure of meeting him. Let me congratulate our dear child here on the advantage of possessing so valuable a friend and so efficient an adviser."

Fielding bowed. "Thank you, my lord. You are very kind. Yes, I need scarcely say that Miss Bourne's friendship, which I esteem beyond words, amply rewards me for any exertion I may have made in my efforts in watching over her vast interests."

He laid a slight emphasis on the word vast, and Lady Selina caught it, and looked up, with surprise and sudden interest. Vane also heard it, and vaguely wondered why the lawyer should use such an apparently inappropriate adjective in connection with Diana's small means—"enough to live upon." But the earl's smile did not flicker; and he leant back, gently swinging his gold pince-nez.

"How vast they are," continued Mr. Fielding, still addressing the earl, "you may not, perhaps, be aware, Lord Wrayborough."

The earl made a non-committal gesture, and Mr. Fielding went on—

"I myself have scarcely arrived at a proper estimate; but I suppose I should not be far wrong if I valued Miss Bourne's estate at very little below a million."

Vane was standing near Diana, and he turned to her, with an exclamation, a swift inquiry, an expression almost of reproach. Lady Selina gasped like a fish out of water; Mabel cried "Oh!" and stared at the pale-faced lawyer; and the earl dropped the pince-nez, and leant forward, with an admirably feigned surprise, which gradually slid into satisfaction.

"My dear Mr. Fielding, that is a very large sum! Our dear Diana's interests are vast, indeed—"

Dalesford came slightly forward. His face was pale, and he was frowning.

"I didn't know," he said. He turned to Diana. "Diana, why did you not tell me?"

Diana hung her head for a moment, then looked at him appealingly.

"Why didn't you tell me, dearest? Why did you keep me ignorant of the fact that you were so rich, that you had so much money?"

"My dear Vane," murmured the earl remonstratingly, "I quite understand! There has scarcely been time. If I may venture to say so, Diana's reticence was quite right."

"Quite right!" echoed Mr. Fielding. "Lord Dalesford would have received from me the information of Miss Bourne's enviable position. This is not the moment for business details; but, perhaps, I may be permitted to supplement my rather startling announcement with a few particulars. Miss Bourne's father, my—er—esteemed client, died abroad, leaving the whole of his fortune, his immense fortune, to his only daughter and child. Mr. Bourne's state of health rendered it impossible for him to reside in England; and for many years he had not seen his daughter, who was left to the efficient and affectionate guardianship of her aunt, Mrs. Burton—"

He stopped suddenly, and rose, not abruptly, but in quite a self-possessed manner, for, though he had not been looking at her directly, he had seen the grip of her hands relax, and her thin form sway to and fro. She, also, had risen, and, stretching out her hands, as if groping in darkness, uttered a cry, and fell back in the chair.

So quick were his movements, notwithstanding his deliberate manner, that Mr. Fielding had caught her before she could fall to the floor. With a cry, Diana was at her side.

"Aunt Mary!" she exclaimed. "You are ill!—Oh, what is it? What has happened? What have you said?"

They had all gathered round the fainting woman, in amazement and dismay; but Mr. Fielding, still self-possessed and still master of the situation, said calmly—

"If you will ring the bell, Lord Dalesford— Thank you!"

A maid-servant entered, and she and Diana almost carried Mrs. Burton from the room.

All eyes were turned to Mr. Fielding, but he was quite equal to the occasion.

"An extremely nervous and highly strung lady—Mrs. Burton," he said quietly. "It is my fault. I ought not to have referred to her brother's death in her presence. It was inexcusable. Her state of health—"

"We will go," said Lady Selina. "Edward, Mabel. You will remain, I suppose, Vane?" Vane nodded.

"You must come and see me, Mr. Fielding," said the earl, as he shook hands. "Vane, this is very distressing. Take care of that dear girl."

They got outside, and the carriage drove off. Lady Selina leant back, as if she herself were threatening to faint; then she jerked forward, and, in a Cassandra-like tone, said impressively—

"Edward, mark my words, there is a mystery here."

100

The earl carefully adjusted his eye-glasses, and smiled. "There may be, my dear Selina," he said. "But there is also a million. And, if there were not," he added, after a pause, "Vane should have my consent to marry her! She has only one fault." He paused. "She is too good for him—or any man!"

CHAPTER XV

DAYS OF BLISS

IT is given to few of us, alas! to taste the perfect happiness which fell to the lot of Diana. There were times in which she stopped short in the middle of a walk, or whatever else she was doing, to ask herself what she had done to deserve such bliss; why she, of all the women in the world, should have been chosen as a favourite of fortune.

Only a little while ago, she had been a country schoolmistress, passing rich on eighty pounds a year, "with light and firing"; she was now "a great lady," and, more than this, ah, more than this! the betrothed of a man whom she regarded as the noblest, the prince of men. Saving for her wealth, she was a mere nobody, an insignificant person, and yet she had been received by the great Wrayborough family not only favourably, but with something like enthusiasm.

The earl led the way. He had been greatly taken with her on the day of the betrothal, on the occasion when Mr. Fielding had announced her wealth; and the admiration and liking grew into love. The qualities which had won Vane's heart won his father's, and it seemed as if the earl could not see too much of her.

He stayed on at Shortledge, so that he might be near her; and every day he had her up there, or paid a visit to Rivermead. He would call for her to go for a drive with him in the stately barouche, or would sit on the lawn, watching her and Vane playing tennis against Bertie and Mabel; but what he liked best was to recline in the stern of Diana's favourite skiff, while she pulled slowly up the river, or drifted down it, her hands crossed on the sculls, as she bent forward to listen to him.

And he was never tired of talking to her; sometimes of himself and his youthful days, but more often of Vane; of how he had won this race, or the other, or gained the prize for the high jump, or stalked an almost impossible stag under almost impossible circumstances.

He was proud, too, of her, and found a peculiar delight in witnessing the effect her beauty and grace made upon the friends to whom he introduced her.

"The girl's unique," he said to Lady Selina. "She ought to be ▮▮▮▮▮▮▮▮—middle class, but, marvellous to say, she is nothing of the kind; on the contrary, she is aristocratic from the crown of her beautiful head to the soles of her dear little feet. Until I saw Diana, I did not believe in nature's gentlemen and gentlewomen; but I do now. She has converted me. The solution of the enigma lies in the fact that she is so exquisitely natural. She has never done anything, she has never entertained a thought of which she should be ashamed. Her modesty disarms criticism; her womanly dignity, her innocence and purity would carry her, unharmed and unstained, through the rabble of Comus. In short, I have not had the pleasure of meeting an angel, but, given a pair of wings on those beautiful white shoulders of hers, and Diana would fully come up to my idea of one. And, with all this, she is going to bring money into the family. I don't wonder that Vane sometimes looks as if he were confused and bewildered by his good fortune. He must very often ask himself whether it isn't all a dream."

Needless to say, Vane was delighted at his father's affection for Diana.

"Upon my word," he said to her, "I am half inclined to be jealous. If he had seen you before I did, you might have been the Countess of Wrayborough, and my step-mother. Sounds nice, doesn't it, dearest? It's delicious to hear him talking about you, to see the air with which he alludes to 'my future daughter-in-law.' He's as proud as if he'd invented you—and he takes all the credit of our engagement. I don't know whether he's spoken to you about our marriage, but this morning he asked me when it was to be, remarked that he was an old man—as if the governor could ever be old!—and that the only thing he wanted was a daughter. May I tell him, dearest, when I can give him one?"

Diana looked startled, and shook her head.

"Oh, not yet, Vane—not for a long time. We are so happy! I want this time to last; I don't want to change it."

"All right," he said. "You'd better tell him so. But, seriously, dearest, don't keep me waiting long. I'm happy, so happy that sometimes I find myself laughing at nothing at all; but, all the same, I want you to myself, and want you very badly."

There were other reasons, besides Diana's reluctance to break the spell of this betrothal period, why the marriage could not take place at once. A great heiress is not nearly so much the mistress of her actions as are ordinary and less fortunate girls; there were business arrangements to be made in connection with her vast wealth; settlements to be drawn up, legal questions to be considered and decided; and lawyers are, of all the sons of men, the most slow and procrastinating; and Mr. Fielding declared, in a tone of finality, that the wedding could not take place for some months.

Vane was indignant, the earl almost as much so; but they both knew that it was as useless to oppose Mr. Fielding's decision as to run their heads against a brick wall.

It was now the time of the year when Vane and his father usually went up to Glenaskel for the shooting and stalking; and it was the earl who proposed that Diana should accompany them.

"Your Aunt Selina must come up there, and run the place, and act as chaperon." Lady Selina, who generally went to Homburg for the season, stifled a groan; but Mabel, who was in the room, uttered an exclamation of delight.

"Oh, Uncle Edward, how jolly! I love Glenaskel! And I may shoot, mayn't I, Vane?"

"Oh, have you been invited?" asked the earl, with an innocent air of surprise, but there was a kindly twinkle in his eye; and Mabel knew that she was safe.

"Don't let's have a mob, sir," said Vane. "Three or four guns will be enough. What about young Selby? I think Diana would like to have him."

"Oh, then, certainly he must come," responded the earl, in a matter-of-course voice. "Let me see, Diana can have that south suite of rooms."

"Really, Edward, I think you might leave that to me," remarked Lady Selina.

"Quite so, quite so, my dear Selina!" he assented hastily and apologetically. "But I should like her to be quite comfortable, and they are the sunniest rooms, you know, with the best view; you can see the river and the forest. By the way, the rooms will want doing up and refurnishing. Will you see to that, or shall I, Vane?"

Vane laughed. "I'll see to that, sir," he said.

The earl nodded. "Have everything very nice; don't spare expense. Let me see, what would be the best colour for her? Something with roses in it. You might sound her—delicately, you know, Vane. No, no; I'll do it myself. I'm better at that kind of thing than you are. I shall like it to be a surprise to her."

He was always planning a surprise for her. One day, it would take the shape of a charming pony phaeton, with a couple of miniature Exmoors; the next, some costly piece of jewellery, which he had chosen with anxious care; on another, an exquisitely bound book, or a volume of music.

It was a liberal education in old-world courtesy to see him presenting her with the orchid from his buttonhole; or leaning over her, his face wreathed with smiles, as she examined and exclaimed over one of his presents. And with what loving pride Diana wore the costly gems or the simple flower when she went out to dinner, with Vane and the old man worshipping in her train, as if she were a princess, or something still rarer in womanhood!

Little wonder that she almost feared to break the spell. One thing only marred her perfect happiness—Mrs. Burton's health. Ever since she had fainted, on the afternoon of the earl's first visit, Mrs. Burton had been weak and ailing, and Diana had been anxious about her. The doctor who had been called in said that there was nothing serious the matter, that it was a nervous trouble, which rest and quiet would dispel; but, though Mrs. Burton kept almost entirely to her own room, she did not recover her strength.

Diana sat with her for hours, and tried to interest her in the life that was going on about her; but Mrs. Burton could not be roused from the state of apathy into which she had fallen; and, while Diana was talking or reading to her, she lay back in her chair, her hands tightly clasped, her eyes fixed vacantly on the window.

It had been arranged that her aunt should accompany Diana to Glenaskel; but she was, evidently, not well enough to go, and Diana proposed to give up the visit and remain with her; but Mrs. Burton was so agitated by the mere suggestion of such a sacrifice on Diana's part that Diana was compelled to yield, and to promise that she would go alone if her aunt were not well enough to go with her. She would not hear of Diana giving up the most unimportant invitation for her sake; and became so excited when Diana offered to do so that the doctor impressed upon her the necessity of letting the sick woman have her way.

One day the earl and Diana were seated on his favourite spot on the terrace at Shortledge, talking of Glenaskel, and of the happy time they were going to have there. On the preceding day he had artfully learned from her her favourite colour —it was his own, old rose—and Vane had gone up to London to see the decorators. He had been charged by the earl to spare no expense.

The phrase was very often on the old man's lips now; and it did not strike a chill to Mr. Starkey's heart as it had been wont to do. For the announcement of Lord Dalesford's engagement to a great heiress had smoothed the financial way for the Wrayboroughs; and Mr. Starkey's once gloomy countenance had grown lighter and his voice less lachrymose, for he found no difficulty now in raising a loan which could be met by some of the money which Diana was going to pour into the Wrayborough empty coffers. He paid several visits to Shortledge, where he attempted to talk business with the earl. Diana now saw him coming across the lawn.

"Here is Mr. Starkey," she said.

The earl stifled a groan; then he smiled. "He has got a new hat, and how cheerful the man looks! It's all your doing, my dear girl.—How do you do, Mr. Starkey? Sit down. Let me order you a cooling drink. What! Still sticking to that absurd habit of yours of never drinking between meals? Don't say you've come on business, on such a beautiful day as this, and when you can talk on ever so many pleasant matters with Miss Bourne here."

Mr. Starkey said that he had come on business, and Diana rose; but the earl pressed her down in her seat again.

"Don't go, Diana; it is as much your business as mine now, you know. Besides, three heads are better than one, especially when one of the three is so extremely pretty and clever—of course, I allude to Mr. Starkey's. What is it, Starkey? Let's get it over before tea-time."

"It's rather an extraordinary matter, my lord," said Mr. Starkey, pulling a paper from his pocket. "You remember that property at Sunninglea, in Cornwall, which fell into our hands some years ago? I say 'you remember,' because I myself had almost forgotten it. It is a stretch of land, with a bay—an extremely pretty place, but by no means a profitable one. There are one or two small farms, but the rent from the whole of the property does not pay the interest of the mortgage—of course, it is mortgaged."

"You see, he says 'of course,' my dear," remarked the earl to Diana. "There is scarcely anything that is not mortgaged. The merry game began in our family generations ago, and, of course, we have kept it up. Well, Mr. Starkey?"

"The mortgage is in the hands of Drake and Drake," Mr. Starkey went on, "and they served us with a notice of foreclosure some time ago; in fact, I thought they bought it in."

"Well, there's an end of the matter, isn't there?" said the earl.

"Well, no, strange to say. Three days ago, I had a most extraordinary letter from a solicitor. He is a Mr. Jeffrey, of whom I know nothing. Quite a small man. He writes and informs me that a client of his, of the name of Brown, has purchased the property, and that he is willing to sell it to us at a small profit."

"Of course, you told him that we didn't want to buy it?" said the earl.

"I should have done so; but Mr. Jeffrey's letter contained a most extraordinary statement. He said that the main line intended running a branch to Sunninglea, and that, therefore, the possibilities of the place were enormous. I myself saw that at once, and I went round to him, and asked him the very natural question, why his client did not keep the property, and reap his own harvest? Mr. Jeffrey, who seemed a very sharp man—"

"Scarcely a necessary piece of information. My dear Diana, you heard Mr. Starkey say that this gentleman was a lawyer?"

"In polite terms, he advised me to mind my own business, pointed out to me that the sum his client was asking amounted to only a fair profit on his purchase, and took it for granted that I should accept his really very advantageous offer. I have satisfied myself, by cautious inquiries, that the railway company do intend running a line to Sunninglea, and I think we ought to buy it."

The earl smiled. "Would you not like to buy also, say, Buckingham Palace, and an estate or two in Wales?" he said ironically. "My dear Starkey, where is the money to come from?"

Mr. Starkey shot a sideways and involuntary glance at Diana.

"Oh, there is no difficulty about the money, my lord," he said, in a tone of cheerful confidence, which contrasted markedly with the melancholy one which, until recently, had been habitual with him.

"Oh, very well," said the earl. "Shall we buy it, my dear? Don't blush, and look so startled, for I've more than a suspicion that it will be bought with your money; eh, Starkey?"

Mr. Starkey coughed assent.

Diana, blushing still, laughed, and nodded.

"Oh yes, buy it, by all means," she said. "You say it is very pretty, Mr. Starkey, and that it will bring in a great deal of money later on?"

"You see!" exclaimed the earl, gazing at her admiringly. "Didn't I tell you that Miss Bourne's head was a clever one?"

"You forget that I was once a schoolmistress," said Diana, "and that I know something of multiplication and division."

The earl looked at her proudly—he liked her reference to her former humble station.

"All right," he said. "You've got your instructions, Mr. Starkey. Buy it, by all means; and, when you've turned it into a fashionable watering-place, we'll come down and stay there; eh, Diana? There's the tea. Come along, Mr. Starkey. And, by the way, better not say anything of this business to Lady Selina. She's always thinking we are trembling on the brink of ruin, and she will conclude we have taken leave of our senses."

106

CHAPTER XVI

GLENASKEL

THE journey to Scotland was made with so much of state, and ceremony, and luxury, that Diana, who still retained her liking for simplicity, was filled with amazement. It seemed to her that the whole of the express train would be needed by the apparently innumerable servants, the carriages, the horses, and the piles of luggage belonging to the Wrayboroughs; for, when he went north, the earl travelled with semi-royal state. It seemed as if every official connected with the railway station, to say nothing of the porters, had considered it to be his duty to see that the earl and his party started under the most favourable auspices; but the earl himself, and Lady Selina, and the rest of the family—indeed, the whole household—took the attention as a matter of course; and only the presence and conduct of Mabel and Bertie saved Diana from the conviction that the great Wrayborough family were more than mortal, and of different flesh and blood from the crowd of servants, porters, and inspectors who attended them with obsequious offers of service.

Mabel and Bertie were enjoying themselves like a couple of children off for the holidays; and very nearly behaved themselves as such. Regardless of the fact that an elaborate luncheon would be served in the saloon-carriage, they dodged Lady Selina, and loaded their pockets with Banbury cakes and chocolate, purchased at the refreshment-room; they bought piles of magazines and comic papers at the bookstall, and trotted up and down the platform, at the peril of their own limbs and the sanity of the luggage porters. Both of them had brought guns and fishing-rods, and Mabel, affecting to be anxious about their safety, continually insisted on Bertie's hunting them up among the stacks and piles of other luggage.

At the last moment, they pretended that they could not find room in the saloon-carriage, and smuggled themselves into a compartment, the only other occupant of which was an old lady, who was absorbed in a King Charles spaniel, which had been yapping from the window at the pug in Lady Selina's arms.

Diana and Vane had watched the confusion from a coign of vantage behind the luggage, and they, also, eschewed the luxurious saloon, and found an empty carriage. To Diana, the journey was the most delightful she had ever taken; for was not the man she loved by her side, to watch over her comfort, to point out the notable objects on the way, to hold her hand, and to whisper those short, sweet sentences in which love expresses itself so eloquently? They had to go into the saloon for lunch, of course, but they stole away again to their own carriage at the next stoppage, and remained undisturbed till the train ran into the little Highland station near Glenaskel.

Here Diana found fresh cause for amazement; for the state and ceremony which had attended their departure were as nothing compared with that which awaited them on their arrival. In an "orderly confusion" of carriages and servants, footmen in the Wrayborough liveries, and Highlandmen in kilts of the Glenaskel clan, of which the earl was chief, luggage fourgons, and a huge 'bus for the servants who had come down by train, the party was received by a crowd which astonished and bewildered Diana.

"Are you very tired, dearest?" Vane asked, as their carriage started. "It is not a very long drive to the castle; I know you will be glad to be there."

"I am not in the least tired," she said, nestling up to him all the same. "It is the happiest journey I have ever taken in my life; and I am thrilling with excitement. It is all so strange to me. I feel as if I were a princess of the blood royal; indeed, I can't imagine any greater fuss being made over anyone."

Dalesford laughed rather apologetically. "Yes, they do make rather a fuss," he said; "but it's their way of showing that they are pleased to see us; and I'm afraid that you will be still more surprised when we reach home. But you will like these people, Diana. They are true and staunch as steel; and there isn't a man of them who wouldn't go to the end of the world for us. But you will understand it all before you have been at the castle many days—many hours, for that matter. Look, dearest; there is the first glimpse of it."

Diana looked out of the window, and saw, in the twilight, a vast castle, set half-way up a hill, and rising from amidst a dense mass of firs. The size and grandeur of the ancient pile were intensified in effect by the misty light, and she gazed upon it in speechless admiration and something akin to awe.

A few minutes afterwards, the carriage, winding its way up a magnificent avenue, drew up in the courtyard of the principal entrance, the outer space of which was lined by Highlandmen bearing torches, which threw ruddy gleams in rivalry with the electric light that streamed from the apparently innumerable windows of the building. The great entrance doors were opened wide, and Diana, as Vane helped her to alight from the carriage, saw the earl standing, silhouetted against the lighted hall, waiting to receive her, with a state which accorded and seemed necessary to, and even consistent with, the presence of the crowd of retainers who watched the great earl and the young girl who would be their future mistress.

As Vane led her up the broad stone steps, flanked by great couchant lions supporting crested shields, a deep-throated cheer arose, and awoke the echoes of the hoary walls and the surrounding pine forest.

The earl took her by both hands.

"Welcome to Glenaskel, my dear!" he said; and, as he led her in, another cheer went up, the men waved their torches and, closing up about the steps, watched her eagerly as she entered the hall.

She was startled, and the tears sprang to her eyes. With an instinctive movement, she turned to Vane, who stood by her side, eyeing her proudly and fondly.

"That's meant for you, dearest," he said. "It's their welcome. Have they frightened you?"

"No, no," she said quickly. "Ah, they don't think so, do they?" As she spoke, she looked wistfully toward the door; and Vane, who read every thought of hers, took her by the hand, and led her back to the entrance.

"You want to speak to them, Diana?" he said.

She made a gesture of assent; her lips parted and trembled, as she looked down upon the stalwart men massed at the bottom of the steps, every eye upturned to her with an eager expectancy. For a moment or two, no word would come; then, in a low voice, but so distinctly that the words reached the farthest fringe of the crowd, and went to the heart of every one of the faithful fellows, she said just two words that mean so much when they are spoken from the heart—

"Thank you!"

It was all that was necessary; it was done so spontaneously, with such heartfelt gratitude, that Vane glowed with appreciation, and the earl murmured "God bless her!" As if to mark his sense of the fact that their welcome was intended for her, he kept in the background, and said no word.

The hall, its vast proportions and antique furniture and ornaments glowing redly in the light of the huge fire of logs in the open stone fireplace, seemed full of servants, male and female; but presently they dispersed, tea was brought in and served on the big oak table, and Diana was free to look round her.

She seemed to have entered an entirely new world, to have passed from the present to the past; for there was scarcely anything that was new and modern in the objects that met her eyes. The very staircase was of stone; the armour, the shields hanging on the walls, the trophies of arms and weapons of the chase, all spoke eloquently of the historic past.

And there were still wonders to come; for, when she and Vane were left alone, and there was silence, save for the laughing voices of Bertie and Mabel, as they went along the corridor, Vane took her into the great banqueting-hall, with its tapestried walls, its rudely carved fireplace, its decorations of antlers, coats of mail, broadswords and helmets; and from there to the drawing-room, which, though modernised in accordance with the luxury-loving present, was still eloquent of a bygone age, for here there was no electric light, and the soft gleam which fell on priceless furniture, old brocade, illuminated carving, and pictures of incalculable value, came from wax-candles in sconces wrought from the copper which had been found in a part of the vast estate. All was subdued in colour and design; but so impressive, so grand in its severity and dignity, that Diana held her breath, as, with Vane's arm round her, she looked about her.

Of course, he was not so much impressed. To him it was a familiar sight. He had played about the rooms in this vast castle as a child; and its grandeur, its feudal stateliness, were to him almost commonplace; but he tried to project himself into Diana's mind, and her appreciation and admiration gave him pleasure.

"Will you see any more of it, dearest, or shall we wait until to-morrow?" he asked. "I am so afraid you will be overtired."

"No, no!" she said eagerly. "I am not in the least tired. It is all so wonderful, so beautiful. I feel as if you ought to be in a kilt, with a broadsword in your hand and an eagle's feather in your bonnet."

He laughed. "I don't know about the broadsword; we shall have to dispense with that, I'm afraid; but you will see me in a kilt, all right, to-morrow. Come and look at the corridor. A good many of the family portraits are there; and it's on your way to your room, where, I expect, Janet, your maid, is anxiously awaiting you. Diana, if you tried with all your might, you couldn't realise the joy, the delight, your presence here gives me. I feel—oh, what is the use of my trying to tell you what I feel!" He drew her to him and crushed her against his breast. "And to think," as he bent and kissed her, "that I shall have you beside me all my life, that you will move about these rooms and bless them with your presence; that I shall only have to call 'Diana!' and you will come to me!"

As they went up the great stone staircase, he told her lightly of the fight that had once taken place on it between some of the Clan Glenaskel and another clan which had succeeded in gaining an entrance to the castle.

"Some of them got in, right enough; but, I believe, none of them ever got out again. Behold the portraits of the family. Rum-looking lot, aren't they?"

"Some of the women are very beautiful," said Diana.

"None so beautiful as my darling's portrait will be," Dalesford returned. "There's a place for her there, by the organ. My father was talking the other day of having you painted. It must be done." He saw Janet standing in the doorway with an anxious look on her face. "These are your rooms, dearest. I hope you will like them."

He stood in the doorway and looked at her fondly as she gazed round amazedly.

"Oh, Vane, how beautiful! And it's my favourite colour, too! Why, how did you know it?"

He laughed. "Ask the governor. He got it out of you. Oh, he's as artful as a magpie when he likes. But I'm glad you're pleased, dearest."

"Pleased!" she echoed. "Oh, Vane! it is all too good, too beautiful."

Janet had discreetly vanished into an adjoining room, and of course Vane took advantage of the fact.

"Nothing in this world could be too good, too beautiful for you, Diana," he said. "And now you will rest, dearest, until it is time to dress."

Diana had left Mrs. Burton very much better; but she had implored her to telegraph, and the telegram was lying on the table. It was very short; just a few words—

"I am quite well; do not be anxious about me. Enjoy yourself and be happy.

MARY BURTON."

Janet insisted upon her young mistress lying down for a while; but Diana found it difficult to rest, and was soon up and dressing. She listened for the gong, but in place of it there arose the weird, impressive strains of the bagpipes.

She went downstairs, and found Vane waiting in the hall; and he looked up at her with love and admiration in his eyes; and with just cause, for surely no more graceful or more beautiful woman, not excepting even those of the Glenaskel family, had ever descended those historic stairs. She still wore black; but the great Parisian master had composed an evening gown for her which, in form and texture, accentuated her lissome figure and the healthy pallor of her face. Vane smiled at her proudly, and, drawing her arm within his, led her to the drawing-room.

The piper was still filling the castle with the strains of the half-martial, half-joyous music, and, marching round the hall, he now appeared at the door of the drawing-room. He was a giant of a man, six feet two or three, and broad in proportion; he held his head high, his eye flashed fire, he moved with a proud and masterful step, as if he were leading a host to battle; and he led the way to the dining-room, and walked round it twice as the company took their seats.

The meal was a stately one. How could it be otherwise, seeing that the table was laden with silver plate, upon which royal eyes had rested and from which royalty had eaten; that a servant in rich livery stood behind every chair, and that the distant sound of the bagpipes, playing on the terrace, kept up a weird and impressive accompaniment to the conversation?

It might have been too stately a meal but for Mabel and Bertie, who, seated at the end of the table, were full of chatter and laughter. To both of these young people, state and ceremony were just an elaborate joke; and, strange to say, the earl, instead of resenting their levity, regarded them with an indulgent eye. In fact, the old man was far too happy to be critical or censorious; for was not his only son and heir seated near him, and was not the young girl he loved, his future daughter, close beside him; so close that he could talk to her and touch her hand, fill her glass and press upon her some one of the many dainties of the elaborate meal?

Little wonder if Diana, as she sat in the great drawing-room, listening to Mabel's light chatter, asked herself if she were moving in a land of dreams, and if it were actually the fact that she, the schoolmistress of Wedbury, was sitting there in this vast castle, its future mistress. Perhaps she realised it, or nearly realised it, when she and Dalesford walked up and down the terrace which overlooked the ravine, with its torrential river tearing in a silver gleam between the ridges of pine.

She was so tired that night that she slept until the bagpipes proclaimed the hour of rising. It was an early hour, for life moved at no sluggard pace at Glenaskel. The invited guests were expected, and the serious business of shooting and fishing was commencing. In the evening, several of the guests arrived, a murmur of excitement ran through the vast place, and guns and fishing-rods were very much in evidence.

Vane, in his kilt, with the eagle's feather in his bonnet, moved among his guests. Diana found herself plunged into an atmosphere of Sport, with a capital S. No one talked of anything but grouse and salmon. The men went out soon after breakfast with gun or rod, and the women joined them at luncheon-time, and ate the meal on hillside or in valley; and the talk was of nothing but the bag or the creel. Mabel and Bertie were the most enthusiastic of the enthusiasts; and Mabel was carried beyond herself with delight when she succeeded in landing, with Bertie's aid, a twenty-pound salmon.

Diana neither fished nor shot; but she bore her part in ministering to the needs of the sportsmen, and won not only Vane's, but the earl's approval.

"There is no need for you to shoot or fish, my child," said the old man, with fond pride; "that you are here is quite sufficient. It's all very well for that tomboy, Mabel, to go with the men and land her salmon or fill her bag; but it is quite enough for you to appear at lunch and to give them their tea when they come in. And you do it beautifully, my dear. No one could do it better."

Isolated as the castle of Glenaskel seemed, there were several other residences, mostly those of noblemen, within a reasonable distance; and the earl decided that a formal dinner-party should be given.

Invitations were issued which embraced all the families of the neighbourhood. It was, as Vane laughingly declared, a gathering of the clans.

"You ought to know all the people, my dear," said the earl to Diana. "Vane is very fond of this place; and I think you also are already?"

"Yes; yes, indeed," assented Diana. "I have never seen any place so beautiful; have never known, imagined, people so nice, so lovable as the people here. If I go down to the village they treat me as if they had known me all their lives, as if I belonged to them and were one of them."

The old man nodded. "So you will be, my dear," he said. "In fact, they regard you as if you already belonged to them. This feeling of clanship seems strange to you, no doubt. I don't know that I myself fully comprehend it. There isn't a man, woman, or child who wouldn't lay down his or her life for any one of the family; and, of course, they already regard you as one of the clan. But, touching this dinner—now, my dear child, you will not think me intrusive or presumptuous if I venture to make you a little present for the occasion."

Diana looked at him and shook her head apprehensively. "You are surely not going to make me another present!" she said. "Scarcely a week, a day, has passed without you're giving me something. Seriously, Lord Wrayborough, there must be a limit to your generosity and my gratitude."

He laughed, and drew her arm within his. "My dear, I have only given you a few trifles not worth mentioning; and you must not refuse to accept my gift, this thing that I want you to take and wear on this occasion. Come with me and you shall see what it is."

He offered her his arm in his courtly fashion, and led her across the hall and into the room which he called his own. It was one of the smallest rooms in the castle, lined with books and furnished in a solid and simple way. Diana had never been in it before, and she looked round her with interest; an interest which increased as the earl, taking a bunch of keys from his pocket, unlocked a door by the fireplace, and, signing to her to follow, entered a still smaller room, in which there was very little besides a large safe. Selecting a key from the bunch, he opened this, and, taking out a casket, carried it to the adjoining room, and, unlocking it, threw back the lid, and, with a nod and a smile, invited her to look at the contents.

With her hand on his shoulder, Diana bent over the box, and was startled and surprised to see that it contained a quantity of diamond ornaments. She had no idea of their value; indeed, no one but a connoisseur could have estimated their worth; but she knew, at a glance, that they were very splendid; and, with an exclamation, she looked from them to him questioningly. The earl smiled and nodded.

"These are not the family diamonds, my dear," he said. "I suppose that you ought not to wear those until you are married—"

"Oh no, no!" said Diana earnestly.

But Lord Wrayborough laughed. "I don't know that I care very much about strict etiquette," he said; "but I do know that I want you to wear these, at any rate, at this dinner-party. As a matter of fact, I don't think the family diamonds—they are at the bank in London—are as fine as these. Take them out, my child."

Diana lifted the gems reverentially, and looked at them with girlish delight and admiration. There were a tiara of splendid proportions, a necklace and pendant, bracelets and old-fashioned earrings, several rings, and a spray which could be used as a brooch or an ornament for the hair.

She took them up one by one and held them to the light, exclaiming, in a subdued voice, at their magnificence. While she was doing so they heard Vane's voice in the hall. Diana ran to the door.

"I am here, Vane. Oh, come and see!"

He came into the room and put his arm round her and looked smilingly at the priceless gems.

"I thought that was what it would be," he said. "If the whole world belonged to my father, he'd melt it down for you.—I suppose you are going to give them to her now, sir?"

"Yes, I am," said the earl. "She shall wear them at this dinner-party."

Dalesford took up the tiara and placed it on Diana's head, and drew back and gazed at her with worshipping eyes.

"You look like a queen, an empress; doesn't she, sir?"

The earl gazed from one to the other with delighted satisfaction.

"She shall wear them, Vane. There is no woman in the world who could wear diamonds better than Diana does. Put on the bracelets, my dear; and the necklace. I suppose you can't put on the earrings, because your ears are not pierced? Quite right—a barbaric fashion. I'll have them made up into something else, eh, Vane?"

Gradually they got the whole of the suite on her, and, drawing back, looked at her with smiling wonderment and admiration; for, though blushing and with her eyes modestly downcast under their gaze, she "carried" them well, as the earl had said she would.

"My dear Diana," said Vane, "you will create a sensation.—I don't think," to the earl, "that there are many finer diamonds than these, are there?"

The earl shook his head as he commenced to collect the various pieces of the magnificent suite. "As a matter of fact, I don't think there are," he assented. "One of the English ducal families possessed a finer suite; but it was broken up. We have kept ours intact, for a wonder. They were your mother's," he added, in a low voice, "and Diana shall wear them on the twenty-second."

He gathered them together, replaced them in the box and locked it, and took it to the safe. Vane looked round the small room absently.

"I suppose they're all right here, sir?" he said. "I'd no idea they were here. I thought they were at the bank."

"No," responded the earl carelessly. "They have always been here. I had quite forgotten them until our dear girl came upon the scene."

"They are quite safe, I suppose?" said Dalesford.

The earl shrugged his shoulders. "Oh, quite. Why shouldn't they be? It's a very good safe; they've always been here. What should happen to them? I don't think any one but ourselves knows where they are. The windows are heavily barred; and there has never been a burglary at Glenaskel."

CHAPTER XVII

NINE SOVEREIGNS

DESMOND MARCH first saw the announcement of his cousin Dalesford's engagement as he was returning from a race-meeting at Hurst Park.

He had had an extremely bad day; had not only failed to spot a single winner, but, as is often the case with men of his temperament when luck seems dead set against them, he had heavily backed each succeeding loser.

He had had a run of bad luck lately at cards as well as at racing; and as he crowded into the railway-carriage with half a dozen similar men, he was filled with the rage and despondency which, like vultures, tear at the vitals of the unsuccessful gambler; but his face was little paler than usual, and he carried his head erect and smiled with his usual nonchalance.

One of the men produced the inevitable pack of cards, and it was while Desmond March was spreading a sporting paper over his and his companion's knee, to serve as a table, that he read the short paragraph which contained such significant and lamentable news for him.

For a moment or two he stared at it, holding his breath, his long hands closing over the cards spasmodically. The shock was a sudden and severe one, though he ought to have been prepared for it; for it was almost certain that Dalesford, the heir, would marry. Of course there had always been the chance that Dalesford might break his neck out hunting, be drowned in his yacht, have a fit, or meet with some other fatal accident; and remote as the chance might have been considered by a disinterested person, Desmond March had cherished the hope of it.

The marriage of Dalesford, the advent of a son and heir, would not only ruin Desmond March's future prospects, but would work him immediate ruin. He was always in debt, always living from hand to mouth on his winnings at cards or at races, on loans from the Jews raised at exorbitant interest; and his ill luck of the last few weeks had plunged him deeper into the mire; so that, as he talked and laughed with his companions and played with an apparent carelessness and sangfroid, he had all the sensations of an animal driven into a corner and at its last extremity; but even when the man beside him saw the paragraph, read it out to the others, and joined in the chorus of commiseration, Desmond March still kept a smiling and unmoved countenance.

"Oh, Dalesford was bound to marry some time or other," he said. "He was not likely to keep single for my sake, confound him! But the game isn't up yet; all sorts of things may happen; and I may yet romp in at the finish."

It was not until he reached Hans Crescent that he allowed the mask to slip from his face, and, pallid to the lips, lay back in his chair and stared vacantly before him. To tide over his difficulties, to enable him to go on for even a few months, he would need a large sum of money; he knew that the Jews would not only refuse to lend him another penny, but would be soon swooping down upon him for that which he already owed them.

He had only recently wrung from Mr. Starkey five hundred pounds, his allowance from the earl was not due until the end of the quarter; and even if he could succeed in extorting another hundred or two from the same source it would be as a drop in the ocean of his liabilities.

He arose presently and began to pace up and down, stopping now and again to help himself from the decanter of brandy which stood on the sideboard. He was desperate, and quite ready to do any desperate deed. In the drawer of the sideboard was a loaded revolver, and once or twice he glanced towards it. But as he turned in his pacing he caught sight of his pallid face in the mirror on the wall: he was too young to die; there must be something he could do, some loophole of escape from the meshes which surrounded him.

Of course there was flight; but Desmond March, during his pleasant runs on the Continent, had met men who had sought that refuge from their trouble; he had seen them wandering about the streets of some foreign, fifth-rate watering-place, had come across them in a "silver-hell," or caught sight of them, seedy, unshaven, out-at-elbows wretches, slinking furtively among the crowd at a disreputable race-meeting. Could it be possible that he, Desmond March, the nephew of the Earl of Wrayborough, the man who was not far removed from the earldom itself; should sink to such depths of degradation?

And yet what hope was there of anything better for him? He could not dig, and, though he was not ashamed to beg, there was no one from whom he could beg, no one to help him. Not a single one of the so-called friends, the men who had drunk and gambled with him, who had shared in his plunder of some innocent lad or monied fool, proud of the distinction of playing with Mr. Desmond March, would stretch out a hand to save him from perdition itself. There was no woman—

At this point of his bitter reflections there rose before him the sad, sweet face of the girl who loved him, and of whose love he had taken advantage. Yes; there was one woman, and one woman only in the world, who would be sorry for him, who would give her life if the gift could help him to a moment's happiness. The thought of her, though it awakened no remorse, for he was steeped in selfishness to the very finger-tips, intensified his craving for sympathy, the sympathy of some human being.

He had promised to go round to Garner Street, but without any intention of keeping his promise; but now he thought wistfully of the loving welcome that would await him; and, putting on his hat and coat, he left his rooms and took a cab to the shabby little street that was like a backwater in the great London tide.

She heard and knew his step on the stairs, and came to the door to meet him. She had been at work, and the shaded lamp fell upon her half-finished drawing;

one corner of the shade was raised, and the light shone upon his face; she saw its pallor, something worse than pallor, the deep lines of care in the handsome face, the hunted, desperate look in the usually brilliant and laughing eyes, and she drew back her head and scanned his countenance with tender anxiety.

"What is the matter, Desmond?" she asked. "Are you ill? Has—has anything happened?"

"Yes," he said; "something has happened. I have just had bad news."

She drew him to the shabby arm-chair and actually put a cushion at his back; then she knelt on the ground beside him and, resting her arms on his knee, took his cold hand and pressed it between her own, lovingly, consolingly.

"My cousin, Lord Dalesford, is going to be married," he said; his voice was husky, and the forced smile simply twisted his lips into a more haggard expression. "That will cut me out of the succession. Of course I might have expected this; but it has knocked me rather hard; for it comes on top of a run of bad luck, devilish bad luck; and I am out of sorts and can't play a losing game as I used to do. I've had a rotten bad time at Hurst Park to-day; and, upon my soul, taking one thing with another, I'm as near stone-broke as a man could well be; and shall soon be completely stone-broke, ruined, thrown into the gutter—I, Desmond March!" He laughed, a laugh that made the girl catch her breath. " 'Pon my soul, I've half a mind to think it a pity I didn't put a bullet through the brains that have been so little use to me, instead of coming whining here."

With a swift movement she put her hand upon his pale lips. "Ah, no, no; don't say that, Desmond!" she said in a low voice. "When did you have anything to eat last? All those hours! Ah, yes, I thought so! Wait!"

She ran to the sideboard—ran is scarcely the word—she glided swiftly, noiselessly, as if she knew that every movement, every sound, would jar upon his strained nerves. There were only the remains of her last poor meal; she brought it out, and, swiftly and noiselessly as she had moved before, she laid a tray and brought the food to him. He had sent in some whisky many months ago; the bottle had been untouched; she found it and mixed him some spirit and water.

He tried to eat, but could not; but he drank a little of the whisky-and-water, and a faint tinge of colour stole into his pallid cheeks.

"That's better," he said; "but it is a shame to worry you with my troubles, Lucy."

"No, no," she responded, quickly and softly, with a woman's joy in the fact that the man she loved had sought her in the moment of his trouble. "Whom should you come to, but me? And, ah, how I wish I could help you!"

" 'Fraid you can't, my child; very much fear there is no one who can. Looks to me as if I shall have to make a bolt for it or provide the coroner with a job—"

"No, no," she interposed, with a shudder. "Why shouldn't you go away, Desmond? Why shouldn't you give up this London life; this—this trouble to live, to keep up appearances? Why shouldn't you go away and—and—" her voice broke, the colour flooded her face, then left it pale; her eyes were fixed on his with a terrible anxiety, a keen longing—"and take me with you? I'd try to make you happy, Desmond. And I could help, too. We could go to some place on the

Continent, where few of our English people go, where living is cheap. Let me give you some more whisky. Smoke, Desmond! Where are your cigarettes?" She got the case from his pocket, opened it, and extended it to him lovingly, lit a match, and held it to the cigarette; and he leant back and smoked and looked at her with a curious kind of hesitation; as if he were actually considering the possibility of yielding to her prayer.

"We could be very happy there in a quiet way. I am earning more money now, getting better prices for my work; and I am sure I could manage. You can't think how clever a little housekeeper I should prove. And you would have your allowance; and, of course, that would be your own to spend as you liked; I could keep the house going on my earnings quite well. Oh, Desmond, think of it, only think of it! You and I *together*, always, away from this horrible London, where I am always so unhappy—excepting when I am with you; and where you, too, Desmond, are unhappy, are you not? And"—her voice grew lower, would have been inaudible if she had not crept still closer to him and almost laid her cheek against his—"and you would marry me, Desmond, wouldn't you? I'd make you a good wife, I'd make you happy; oh, I couldn't fail to do so, for I love you so much, so much!"

The man's heart was stirred, not so much by pity for the girl, who was almost a child, kneeling beside him and trying, like a child, to woo him to the right path, the path of restitution, atonement, honour, as by the picture of peace, of rest, which her words had painted.

His lids drooped, his mobile lips worked and twisted the cigarette to and fro and in a circle, and he let his arm drop round her waist.

"'Pon my soul, Lucy, I might do worse." It was of himself only he thought, of course. "Yes; it's rather a pretty picture you've drawn, a deuced pretty little picture; you are an artist in words as well as with paint and pencil. And you think we should be happy, eh?"

He smiled down at her with the condescending smile which the man of his character bestows upon the woman who has placed herself entirely in his grasp, the woman who is at his mercy.

"Yes, yes," she said eagerly, her colour coming and going, her eyes glowing with the anticipation of a happiness which seemed too great to be possible. "You're afraid that you would miss your clubs, the race-meetings, and the society of London; but see, Desmond dear, what happiness have they ever brought you; how many times have you come to me tired and weary of all the gaiety and the men and women of your set, people of rank? You told me that they always bored you, and that you were glad to get away from them! Give this new life—and—and me a trial, Desmond; just a trial! If you grow tired of it and me,—ah, well, you can come back. I only ask you just to try it. Desmond, how soon could we go?"

She looked eagerly into his eyes, for she saw that he was brooding over her suggestion, that it was not unwelcome to him; and her soft hands stole round his neck caressingly, her parted lips touched his cheek.

He roused himself from his reverie, and, with a little shake, smiled at her.

"Yes; I'll give it a trial, Lucy," he said. "Hold on!" as with a cry she drew closer to him and whispered anxiously—

"Now, Desmond! At once!"

"Not at once," he said. "There are things I want to clear up; things I must see to. In a day or so. Now, don't look so disappointed. You've got my promise."

She might have reminded him that she had bitter reasons for mistrusting his promises, but she did not; indeed, she kissed him lovingly, and with a patient sigh rose from her knees, and, going to her working-table, opened a drawer and took out a tiny leather-covered box.

"What's this?" he asked, as she pressed it into his hand and drew his fingers over it. Blushing and downcast, she raised her eyes to his imploringly.

"Take it, Desmond. I—I don't want it. I have some more—a little, but enough to go on with; and there is some owing to me I shall be able to get. Pray take it—to please me, dear!" she begged him. "And, indeed, it's as much yours as mine! Think of the money you used to spend on me"—"before you got tired of me," she was going to say, but checked the words—"before you got into difficulties! Don't refuse, Desmond. It will make me so happy to think that I—I may have been of some use to you; the lion and the mouse, you know!" She laughed tremulously. "Be a good lion, and take it, dear!"

The man reddened, and he opened his hand, shaking off her fingers roughly; then he hesitated, his lids fell to cover the shame in his eyes, and with a forced laugh he said—

"What! Your little savings! Well, well, if it will please you, Lucy;—and, upon my soul, I believe it will!—I'll accept the loan for—for a day or two. And I don't mind admitting, my child, that I am completely stumped! But you're sure you don't want it?"

"No, no!" she assured him eagerly. "I was only saving it for—in case—for a rainy day."

She had been saving on the happy chance of his making one day a sunny one for her.

He dropped the little box into his overcoat pocket and stayed with her for some little time; but the whisky, her sympathy, the presence of the box in his pocket, had "bucked him up," and very soon he was anxious to be gone. And she knew him too well to attempt to keep him; indeed, as soon as she saw he was desirous of going, she told him that she wanted to get back to her work, mixed him some more whisky-and-water, and kissed him with a smile in her eyes and on her lips.

"Soon, Desmond!" she whispered lovingly. "You will not break your pro—you will not change your mind?"

"Trust me!" he responded confidently, he whom man or woman had never trusted without rueing it.

He walked to his club and dined, and when the footman's back was turned, took out the box, and, glancing round to see that no one was looking, opened it. It contained nine sovereigns.

He laughed with a contemptuous pity, put the gold in his pocket, and, crushing the cheap little box in his white hands, flung it into the fireplace, as he went to the smoking-room.

Some men were standing talking, and they looked round as he entered in his slow, graceful way. One of them was the Captain Mortimer whom Diana had seen in the dog-cart on the night she had rescued Dalesford, and he nodded and looked at Desmond March with a kind of reserved scrutiny.

"Hallo, March," he said. "We're just going into the cardroom for some baccarat. Will you join?"

Desmond March was about to decline, then he remembered the nine sovereigns in his waistcoat pocket, and nodded. The men seated themselves at the table and play commenced. March looked quite cheerful and perfectly self-possessed, so much so that Mortimer felt it safe to venture on a word of condolence.

"Bit of a blow for you, March—Dalesford's engagement," he said, in a low voice—they were seated next each other. "Glad to see you're taking it like a man."

March shrugged his shoulders. "Is there any other way of taking it?" he said.

"Awful bit of bad luck!" Mortimer remarked. "I'd have rather bet on Dalesford's funeral than his marriage. Such a reckless fellow. Did you ever hunt with him?"

"Never had that honour," replied Desmond languidly.

"Ah, well! Rides like the devil himself. I always feel as if he were going to break his neck."

"But he doesn't. I'm unlucky, as you say."

"And it isn't only when he's hunting. Did I ever tell you of his accident coming home from a mess-dinner at Lowminster last year?"

March shook his head, and seemed intent on the game.

"Yes; a narrow squeak that must have been. He was riding that night, and he fell off his horse, so they say. But I don't know. It looked to me as if he'd been in some kind of a fight, and Grayson, who was passing along the road next day, saw that it was cut up with a horse's hoofs and a man's footsteps—"

He stopped suddenly, for March's face had gone suddenly pale, and he looked straight before him, as if he were fighting against some weakness.

"Anything the matter, March?" Mortimer asked quickly.

Desmond March recovered from the attack, whatever it was, and turned to him laughingly.

"Nothing, thanks," he said coldly. "The room's confoundedly hot, I fancy. But I interrupted your interesting story"—with a faint sneer.

"Oh, it's nothing. I'd finished," said Mortimer. "I was only going to say that there was a kind of mystery about that night's work.—Open the window, there, please."

Desmond March won from the commencement of the game, and, with only a few exceptions, won all through. It seemed as if poor Lucy's little savings had broken the run of bad luck which had of late pursued him. The stakes increased as the play went on, and, as the dawn struggled between the curtains, Desmond March rose, the winner of a large sum.

Now, your gambler lives for the moment, and seldom for more than the moment; with his pockets stuffed with notes and gold, his face flushed with the excitement and the champagne he had drunk freely, Desmond March felt very differently from the Desmond March who had gone whining to a woman for comfort—and had borrowed her savings.

After all, was the game up? Luck had swung his way again; it might continue in his favour, something might turn up. Anyway, flight was postponed for the present; and in the glow of his good fortune the vision of Lucy's pale face, the memory of her sweet, pleading voice, irritated and irked him.

Of course he would pay her back the nine pounds. But to do so he must go to her; and she would expect him to keep the promise she had cajoled him into making. He'd send it to her. But, heartless as he was, even he shrank from so brutal an act. Ah, well, she must wait.

CHAPTER XVIII

DESMOND'S TOOL

IT was the afternoon of the day of the dinner at Glenaskel; the dinner and the dance, for Dalesford, prompted by Mabel, who had discussed this addition with Bertie, had suggested that they "might as well do the thing properly," and kill two birds with one stone; and Diana, who had, of course, been consulted by Lady Selina and the earl, had, equally of course, welcomed her lover's proposal, as she would have welcomed any suggestion of his.

Mabel and Bertie were returning from the river with some sea-trout in their creels and a wealth of happiness in their hearts; and the boy, as he strode beside her with his pipe in his mouth, glanced now and again at the girlish face with its piquant, half-parted lips and radiant eyes.

"I suppose you'll give me a dance to-night?" he said, after a long pause in the conversation.

Mabel broke off in her soft whistling of "Ye banks and braes," and looked at him with a mischievously innocent air.

"I don't know. Can you dance?"

"Can I—" He took the pipe from his mouth so that he might give vent to his indignation. "Can a duck swim? Of course I can dance. What did you take me for?"

"If I took you for anything, it would be for a course of lessons in manners," she retorted smoothly. "But about the dance. I will see. You are doubtless aware that my card will be pretty well filled up—you see, I'm one of the ladies of the house, and everybody will have to ask me, for duty's sake—"

"I'm asking for pleasure, Mabel," he put in, not unadroitly. "The thing will be spoiled for me if you don't dance with me. And you know that. But never mind. I daresay I shall get some partners; don't worry on my account."

"I'm not worrying in the least, I assure you," she retorted, smiling at him in an exasperating fashion. "I've ever so many other things to think of. There's my dress, for instance. I can't make up my mind between a white silk and a pale blue crêpe de chine."

"Wear 'em both," he suggested.

"The white becomes me best, but then I look ever so much older in the blue; it's almost long."

"Let down the white one."

She ignored this valuable suggestion, also.

"And Captain Fairbourne says that blue is really my colour."

Captain Fairbourne was one of the "guns," a young linesman who had fallen a victim to Mabel's girlish spells and impish humour; and if Bertie were capable of hating anyone, the aforesaid captain would have been that ill-fated person.

"What's Captain Fairbourne know about colour?" he remarked, with a toss of the head. "He'd much better confine his expression of opinion to the goosestep and musketry drill."

"Strange how civilians always dislike a soldier," observed Mabel reflectively. "Can it be envy, I wonder? Is this a walking-match? If you are going to tear on like this, I must ask you to go on alone."

"I beg your pardon," he said. "Sorry I was walking too fast for you; but you do make me mad sometimes."

"Only sometimes?" she queried, smiling up at him. "Perhaps you will be so good as to tell me when you are sane, so that I may know when to begin; for I think I rather like you when you're a little—just a little—mad."

"Do you—Mabel?" he responded eagerly, the gloom of his boyish face relaxing. "That's good news! But I like you all the time."

"Even when I tease you?" with a sideways glance.

"Even when you tease me—by flirting with that conceited redcoat, Fairbourne."

"I never flirt," she declared, reddening.

"Never?"

"Well, not to speak of." She faltered a little. "If you consider that I am flirting if I speak pleasantly to any other person than a conceited cock-sparrow of a schoolboy—"

"Now, that's unjust, and—and not, like you, Mabel! I'm not conceited, and you know it."

"I call a person conceited who contradicts everyone who holds a different opinion from his own. And I saw you looking in the glass as we went through the hall this morning."

"I did; but it was because I wanted to look at your new fishing-hat without your seeing me do it."

"Isn't it a pretty hat?" she said, beaming up at him, so that the boy longed to take her in his arms and kiss the face beneath the hat. But he checked himself, and, boy-like, took refuge in banter.

"Oh, it's all right," he said. "But you might wear it straight."

"Isn't it straight!" she asked. "Please put it right, will you!" she requested, as boy to boy, and with a childlike look in the blue eyes raised to his.

Poor Bertie slipped his pipe in his pocket and set the coquettish hat straight, his hands trembling a little, his lips tightly set, and his eyes fixed carefully on an imaginary spot in the centre of her forehead; for he felt that he needed all his strength to resist the temptation to kiss the half-parted lips so close to his.

"There you are," he said roughly and a little huskily. "You ought to have a nurse with you."

"Oh, I find a young bear quite as good," she retorted sweetly.

"Well, don't forget that some bears can dance," he said, "and to-night remember this one. I shan't mind pinning up your dress or tying your pinafore. I suppose it will be a splendacious affair?"

"Rather!" she assented enthusiastically. "All the nobility and gentry of the Borough Road. And, oh, Bertie, you wait until you see Diana's dress! And she's going to wear the old diamonds Uncle Edward has given her!" She cast her eyes up to heaven, as if she were in the ecstasy of some glorious vision. "I tell you, my dear boy, that there has never been seen anyone so entirely unsurpassable as Diana will look to-night."

"The Queen of Sheba?"

"Her Majesty was not in it with our Di!" declared Mabel, with absolute finality. "It's— But what's the use of trying to describe a ball-dress to a stupid boy!" she broke off in despair.

"Perhaps I shall like your simple little frock as well," he said.

"My simple— And pray, who told you it was simple? At any rate, however simple it may be, it will not be half as simple as you.—Oh, here come Diana and Vane," she exclaimed, as a dog-cart came up the road behind them. "I'll ask Vane to give me a lift: you watch his face!"

The two lovers were looking at each other as they talked in low accents, in slow, lingering speech, and did not see the boy and girl until they were close upon them; then, in answer to Mabel's call, Vane pulled up.

"Give you a lift?" His face fell as he repeated Mabel's bland request; then he laughed and shook his head.

"Not much! A walk will do you two good. The fact is, Mabel,"—severely,
—"you're getting fat for want of exercise."

"Oh, Vane!" pleaded Diana laughingly. But Mabel called out—

"Sold again! Who wants to ride with a couple of spoons? Yah! Drive on, Romeo and Juliet!"

Diana looked back, waving her hand until the dog-cart turned the bend, then she nestled close to Vane again.

"How happy they looked!" she said, with a happy little sigh.

Vane nodded and laughed. "Yes; a pair of children playing at love," he said. "I hope there's nothing serious in it. Sometimes I blame myself for asking the boy down here; he was quite gone enough at Shortledge. There'd be trouble if he meant business, for Aunt Selina would look higher for Mabel, and Master Bertie will be as poor as a church mouse."

Diana was silent for a moment, then she said, in a low voice—

"He may not always be poor. Someone—someone might help him—and her."

Vane pressed her still closer to him, and looked at the downcast face with swift comprehension and gratitude.

"Is there anyone you know whom you don't make the happier for knowing you, dearest?" he said. "Bertie's a lucky beggar! But I'm the luckiest of 'em all! But it's just like you, dear sweetheart, to think of those two kiddies."

"Why, what is money good for but to make those we love happy?" she asked quietly. "And I love Mabel as if she were a sister. I never had a sister," she added, almost to herself. "I have never had anyone but Aunt Mary."

Dalesford was silent for a moment, then he said—

"I don't think I ever met with anyone so entirely free from relatives; relatives are a nuisance; at least, most of mine are. Desmond March, for instance. You don't know anything of your father, Diana? I mean who and what he was? Why he left England while you were so young?"

The question was prompted only by his interest in everything connected with her, and she answered simply—

"No. You know as much about him as I do. Mr. Fielding has told you."

"Yes. He must have been particularly clever to have made that pile of money, that money which I'm always half inclined to be jealous of, Diana."

"Oh, why?" she asked.

"Oh, I don't know. Fancy I'd rather you hadn't turned out a great heiress. Never spoken of it before—rather a—a sore subject—and we won't speak of it again."

"I'm sorry," she said meekly; and he laughed and kissed her.

"Well, so long as you don't do it again," he responded, as if she were apologising for some naughty act. "And you think this idea of the governor's about my going into Parliament a good one?" he asked, changing the subject.

"Whatever Lord Wrayborough says must be right," said Diana.

He laughed aloud at her prompt response.

"His idea is that I shall have some object in life—as if I wanted any other than you!—and that it may amuse you. I ought to have put the second reason first, seeing that he considers you and your inclination before anything and everybody else in the world. If you'd like to see me an M.P., I'll have a shot for it. There'll be a vacancy at Lowminster before long; what's-his-name, the present member, has talked for a long time of retiring. I expect I should make an awful mess of it—got no brains, you know—but you'll have to find them; and you'll have no difficulty. The governor says— But you must be tired of hearing the governor's song of praise in your honour. Here's the lodge, already! We must have come along pretty fast."

The mare had taken her own leisurely pace, but Diana, edging away from him to a discreet distance, did not say so.

"Now, you go and lie down"—he was always wanting her to go and lie down, as if she were an invalid who needed the most tender care—"and have a good rest before dinner. And you dance the first and the third and the fifth and the sixth with me—"

"Yes. They wouldn't"—wistfully—"let me dance them all with you, Vane, I suppose?"

Not since the last visit of royalty had the great castle presented so gala an appearance as it did on this eventful night. The avenue and courtyard were illuminated by the torches of the Highlandmen; and the guests were received by the majordomo and a double file of the house servants in their state liveries, and conducted through the great hall, for this occasion all ablaze with electric lights, to the magnificent drawing-room, where the house-party awaited them.

Many of them had already made Diana's acquaintance, and now renewed their homage; for the girl looked, in her exquisite dress with the diamonds scintillating on her white neck and arms, and nestling amid the priceless lace—also a gift of the earl's—like a queen. And yet, with her queenliness, there was a sweet, maiden modesty, an expression of girlish happiness that struck each one who came up to her; and made strangers, who had been inclined to consider the rumours of her grace and beauty sheer exaggeration, inwardly confess that her devout admirers had reason for their enthusiasm.

The dinner was a function almost regal in its splendour, and even Mabel and Bertie were almost awed into quietude; but when it had run its stately course and the Hungarian band was heard softly tuning up in the music-gallery in the old ballroom, Mabel broke the spell.

"Captain Fairbourne has asked me for the first dance," she remarked to the epergne laden with fruit opposite her.

"Oh!" said Bertie grumpily. "And, of course, you gave it to him?"

"Well, no," she replied casually. "I thought I should like to sit it out and watch the others."

"Not you!" he retorted incredulously. "You watch the others! Well, you can watch them quite well enough while you're dancing; and I'll stop now and then for you to do so, if you like."

So he got the first dance.

Diana also felt inclined to stand still and watch the brilliant crowd, as, a mass of soft and flaming colour, of flashing and glowing gems, it moved about the vast ballroom; but she had to reckon with Dalesford, who, trying not to look too proud and Heaven-blessed, came to claim her.

"The most beautiful woman in the room, my dear Lord Wrayborough," said an old friend and neighbour, as she stood beside the earl and watched Diana.

He turned his eyes slowly from the girl he had learned to love as a daughter, and bowed as if the praise were personal to himself.

"Isn't she! And as good as she is beautiful! My boy is the luckiest Wrayborough that ever danced in Glenaskel. Look at him! He is ten years younger, he radiates happiness—and no wonder, with such a girl for his own!"

"Yes; Vane has changed," she said, as she watched him bending over Diana with love-worship in his fine eyes. "She carries those diamonds well, for so young a girl."

"Diana would carry an imperial diadem," he retorted; and as the pair glided near them in the progress of the dance, he smiled at her fondly, receiving as fond a smile from her in response. "There is no one like her—no one!"

"That sounds like Tennyson—'Maud,' you know," laughed the countess. "But you have every excuse for your enthusiasm, dear Lord Wrayborough. Who did you say she was?" she added with friendly interest.

"Her father was a wealthy merchant named Bourne," he replied. "He is dead: I am her father now, dear lady."

"You are not tiring yourself, Diana?" he asked her some time later. "You are dancing a great deal, my dear, and you have been out with the rods and the guns so much."

But Diana laughed and shook her head as she softly slid her arm in his—it was one of the "mousy" little ways in which she showed her affection for him, ways that filled the old man with delight. "Oh no! I feel as if I could dance for ever; as if—ah, well, try and imagine yourself the happiest girl in the world at her first big dance!"

And to Vane, still later on, she said in a low voice—

"Happy? Oh, Vane, how poor and meaningless the word is to express what I feel! If you knew how good everyone is to me, how full my heart is of joy and bliss. Once or twice to-night I have asked myself whether it is fair for one girl to have so much, such wealth of love, such hosts of friends, such petting and spoiling, while others—"

She broke off, and he saw her eyes glisten with sudden tears; and he drew her out of the glitter and shimmer of the ballroom into one of the anterooms, closed the door, and took her to his breast.

"God give me the luck to keep you always as happy, my angel and my love!" he whispered passionately.

The daylight streamed through the windows before the ball was over; but at last the house-party stood in the hall listening to the last carriage as it rolled away.

"And now to bed, my child!" said the earl to Diana. "Vane, go with her to the corridor and see that Mabel does not lure her to her room for a gossip. She must rest, rest! Good-night, my dear."

As he kissed her the diamonds in her hair flashed in his eyes, and he said—

"The diamonds, my dear; better give them to me to lock up for you. You'll want them for Lady Brandon's dance on Wednesday; after that, I'll send them to the bank."

Laughing and blushing, Diana, aided by Vane's caressing fingers, took off the jewels, and the earl collected them in a heap and bore them off to the safe in the small room adjoining his own.

On the Monday after the day of the ball, Desmond March was sitting over the pretence of a breakfast. The covers from the dishes had not been removed, and the toast he broke absently fell untasted from his fingers. They were trembling, his lips were ashen and drawn, and there were black shadows under his sunken eyes. His run of luck had broken down, and once more he was in the depths of despair. Beside his plate lay a scattered heap of letters, all of them demands, some of them threatening demands, for money. As he looked round the room with aching eyes—he had drunk heavily at the "supper" club on the preceding night—he remembered that the rent was overdue, and reflected that in a short time he would be homeless as well as penniless.

For the first time for weeks he thought of the patient, loving woman whose faith he had betrayed, whose pitiful savings he had taken and squandered. To go to her now—no, not even he was equal to that. There was nothing but flight. But where to fly? Where? Absently, he picked up one of the papers which lay on the table; it happened to be a society journal, and as he turned the leaves wearily his eye caught an account of the great ball at Glenaskel. His face flushed and grew bitter as he read the successful efforts of a reporter still dazed by the splendour he had witnessed from a corner of the music-gallery.

Desmond March set his teeth upon the oath that broke from him. And all this —Glenaskel, Wrayborough, and how much more?—might have been his. Diamonds—this girl of his cousin's, Dalesford's, must have been smothered with them. Great heavens, and he, the next heir, was stone-broke, a defaulter, an outcast. Diamonds! Why, a quarter of the sum they would fetch would tide him over his difficulties. And this girl was flaunting them, would lose them, very likely— he flung the paper from him and groaned.

His valet, to whom, of course, wages were due, knocked at the door and entered.

"The—er—person to see you, sir."

Desmond March stared at him.

"Eh? Oh, tell him to go to—" Suddenly his face flushed, and he caught his breath. "Wait!" he called, as the valet was leaving the room. "I think I'll see him."

A moment or two later the valet ushered in Garling. The short, square figure, the rugged, heavily lined face, looked strangely out of place in the luxurious room, and the man stood awkwardly leaning on his thick stick and regarding in silence the aristocratic, pallid face of Desmond March with a mixture of deference and defiance, of apprehension and dislike.

"So you've turned up as usual," said Desmond March, leaning back and looking at Garling, under half-closed lids. "It's as well you did; for I happen to want you."

"To want me?" said Garling, in his peculiar, husky voice. "What can you want with me? See here, Mr. March, I've come to tell you that this—this game can't go on. I'm tired of it. You took me by surprise that night, and I caved in before I'd had time to turn round. Every Monday I've been here to—to report myself"—his rugged face grew red and his mouth hard and set—"but I don't mean to do so again. I'm—I'm different to what you take me for."

Desmond March nodded towards the door.

"You can go. My man will follow you and give you in charge to the first policeman he meets. Or you can stay and undertake a job. I've got one for you. Which is it to be? Right," as the man, white to the lips, ground his teeth and remained standing. "Now lock the door. Come here, sit there, and listen."

Garling took the chair and kept his eyes on March, as the slave eyes his master, whip in hand; and in slow, measured accents Desmond March set him his task.

In the middle of the recital Garling sprang to his feet, his eyes glowing, his teeth set.

"No, no!" he exclaimed hoarsely. "I won't do it! I can't!—I've left that kind of work! For God's sake, say no more! I'll be no man's slave; I—" he shuddered. "I've had enough of convict life."

Desmond March leant back and toyed with a paper-cutter; but kept his eyes on his man.

"Oh yes, you'll do it," he said. "Where's the risk to you—the Ironmonger, you know! But, risk or no risk, you'll do it. You'll take a—a commission, of course, and you can clear off when the job's done; for I shall have done with you for good and all. Hesitate, you—you convict, and, by God! I'll send you back to Portland!"

With a groan Garling sank into his chair. Then he sprang up and paced up and down with heavy, dragging steps, his head bent, his brows knit; and Desmond March leant back and watched him with a feigned calm that concealed a deep anxiety.—

At last Garling stopped before his tyrant, and, glowering down at him, said hoarsely—

"If I do this—job, it's the last, you say? You'll have done with me—will let me go? You swear it? Swear it!" He laughed a laugh that sounded like the snarl of a dog. "You'd swear anything, you—you fine gentlemen, I know. But, mind! you're driving me harder than you think! I'll do it; but—it's the last; unless it's the kind of job"—he looked at Desmond March with a sudden ferocity—"that I'd swing for!"

CHAPTER XIX

BERTIE COMES A CROPPER

It was noon on the morning following Lady Brandon's dance when Diana awoke to find Mabel sitting beside her bed, regarding her with a smile that was wistful as well as affectionate.

"Oh, I'm late; you're dressed, Mabel!" Diana exclaimed guiltily. "What is the time? So late? How long have you been sitting here? Is it anything you want, dear?"

"I've been here for the last half-hour," replied Mabel. "I did want something, but I've forgotten what it is now. How beautiful you look when you're asleep, Diana! You've been smiling for the last five minutes. What were you dreaming of?"

Diana thought a moment, then blushed and shook her head.

"Dreams are silly things," she answered evasively.

"Yes; they're silly enough even when they're happy," admitted Mabel; "because they're only dreams, you see, and they mayn't come true. But yours are all safe enough," she added, with a mischievous smile and nod. "I'll ring for your tea. Oh, you mustn't think of getting up yet, for Vane has given me strict orders to see that you breakfast in bed."

"I've never done such a thing in my life that I can remember," urged Diana; but Mabel shook her head decisively.

"Them's my orders, miss; and I'm just old enough to know that it's better to obey 'em when Vane gives them. And here's the tray. Are you hungry?"

"Starving," said Diana, sitting up and flinging her long tail of hair over her shoulder. "Is Vane down?"

"Down! Hours ago. Oh, he's quite the Industrious Apprentice now, since a certain young lady took him in hand and reformed him. He was up before the breakfast-bell rang, seeing to the programme for the day. He slaves at it as if he were a Cook's excursionist guide. Vane, who, last year, was the laziest man that ever drew breath! And that reminds me of what I wanted. It's about that troublesome boy, Bertie."

"What has he been doing now?" asked Diana with a smile, and a loving, whimsical glance at the pretty girlish face, as its owner, having seated herself on the bed, was snuggling against Diana and somewhat hampering her fork hand.

"Oh, nothing; it's what he wants to do. He wants me to ride over with him to the Holy Well."

"And you're going to do so, of course?"

"Well—I was; but Aunt Selina has suddenly discovered that I ought not to. She says I spend all my time with him.—So absurd! I'm sure I don't! And she says she won't have me scampering about in country lanes with a young man; as if Bertie were a young man!"

"He's scarcely an old one," said Diana. "And you want me to come with you, I suppose, to play chaperon?"

Mabel nodded and grinned. "Yes; that's it, dear. You and Vane, of course. I thought—that is, Bertie thought—that we might get some lunch at the inn by the Well and make a day of it. It would be awfully jolly—just us four. And we wouldn't interfere with you and Vane, you know. You could ride ever so far behind—" She wound up by giving Diana a hug, and, having got her way, ran off to inform her fellow-conspirator of the success of their little plan for getting so many hours together.

Diana came down in her habit and found Vane patiently waiting for her in the hall. He looked up as she ran down the stairs, and his eyes greeted her with mute admiration, and he scarcely waited until the butler had discreetly withdrawn before he took her in his arms and lifted her off the last few steps.

"I spend most of my time trying to decide in which dress you look most lovely, Diana. This morning I'm inclined to put my money on a habit; but I know that to-night I should plunge on an evening frock. How well, how bright you look, my star! Yes! that's it—you are my star, dearest. Without you my life would be black as—"

"Now, when you two have quite done—don't let me hurry you," said Mabel, from the door, with exaggerated politeness, "but the horses have been waiting for ▯▯▯▯▯, and Bertie says he thinks you must have mistaken this for a moonlight ride."

"This girl will be the death of me," declared Dalesford, with mock despair. "Come on, then. But look here, Mabel, no larks; no giving us the slip with that fellow boy of yours. I have just been listening to a lecture from Aunt Selina— The Delinquencies of Lady Mabel Dashwood. And I've promised to keep an eye on you, young lady."

"Pooh!" retorted Mabel contemptuously. "You've only one pair of eyes, and you can't keep them off your young woman. Besides, as if I couldn't take care of myself!"

The four young people started, talking and laughing with the joyousness of youth with a lifetime of love before them; and presently, as Mabel had shrewdly foreseen, she and Bertie had left the other couple far behind, and were quarrelling and flirting with a charming absence of restraint.

Dalesford seemed even happier than usual that morning, and before they had ridden a mile Diana learned the cause.

"The governor heard from Mr. Starkey this morning," he said, lowering his voice and pulling his horse near to Diana's mare so that he could take her mistress' hand. "He says that these blessed business arrangements are nearly concluded, and that— Diana, do you think you could marry me, say, next week, if these lawyers will let us?"

Her eyes were downcast for a moment, then she raised them and looked at him with infinite love, with so sweet a surrender in them and on her half-parted lips, that his hand closed over hers in a swift grip.

There was silence for a while, then they fell to talking, in a low voice, of their marriage, of the place where they should pass the honeymoon.

"I leave it all to you, dearest," he said. "I should be happy enough if we spent it in a London attic, or a slum in Manchester; anywhere with you would be paradise."

And, of course, she assured him in faltering accents that for her any place, with him, meant an earthly heaven.

"What I should like would be to stroll off by ourselves to some quiet little church away beyond the hills there, and get married quietly and without fuss. But, of course"—quickly, as Diana, blushing, looked doubtful—"of course that wouldn't be allowed. The dear old father has set his heart on a regular grand wedding, with a bishop to do the service, and a perfect crowd at the house. We'll be married here, eh, dearest? He'd like it, and the people—what have you done to win their hearts, you witch? Do you know that they fight in the stables for the honour and glory of saddling your horse; that any man who gets a word from you goes about the place with an air of pride and conceit that renders him insufferable? Why, I saw one of your photographs, those last ones of yours, on Donald's"—Donald was the head-keeper—"mantelshelf. I can't think how he came by it."

"It must have been one of the proofs. I threw them in the waste-paper basket," said Diana, laughing very softly.

"Ah, I see. He declined—you know Donald's stately way?—to tell me where he got it; and when I began to read him a lecture, looked so fierce that I dropped it and cleared out."

"Dear old Donald!" murmured Diana.

"Exactly. So you see that the people would feel bad if we had it at Wedbury. Besides, here we are. Next week, dearest."

"Not next week, dearest. Why, I haven't half my things. Perhaps—the week after—or the week after that—if Aunt Mary is well enough to travel. She is better and getting stronger every day, she says— Oh, Vane, what are they doing?" she broke off, looking anxiously at Mabel and Bertie, who were going across the moor at racing pace, and apparently making for the stone wall of one of the marches.

"I believe they're going to try to jump it," said Vane. "Young idiots!—Hi, Mabel! Hi, you there, Bertie! Hold hard, there's a fall on the other side of that! Hi!"

But the wind was against him, and the two young scapegraces failed to catch his warning and rode on, their laughter blown backward to Vane and Diana.

"Is—is there any danger, Vane?" she inquired anxiously.

"N—o, no, dearest. Don't be alarmed. They can both ride; but that's a young untried 'un Bertie's on, and— You come on quietly; I'll try and catch them."

"I'll bet you what you like you won't clear it," Mabel was panting, as they rode towards the wall. "It's all very well when you London people have to deal with a haw-haw fence; but these stone walls—"

"I'll double you," yelled Bertie, his eyes dancing, the laughter bubbling through his words. "I'll give you ten to one in gloves; my size is seven and a half; yours is fours, I know."

"Fours! Threes, you impudent boy!" retorted Mabel, throwing her mane back with an indignant toss of her head. "Now, look out! Lift him well, Bertie—"

"Hi!" yelled Vane angrily; but his warning shout reached them too late to be of any use; on the contrary, it caused Bertie to unconsciously tighten his rein as they were close to the wall. Mabel's horse, an experienced hunter, cleared the formidable stone wall as cleanly as a bird flies; but Bertie's young one hesitated, jumped a little too low, and, catching an inch of his off heel, stumbled over the wall and threw Bertie.

A cry rose from Mabel, and she tried to pull up; but it was quite a minute before she could get back and fling herself beside the prostrate boy, who looked absurdly long and fearsomely still as he lay with outstretched arms and white face.

With a gesture of utter abandon and terror, the girl put her strong young arms round him and lifted his head to her palpitating bosom.

"I've killed him, I've killed him! It's my fault, it's all my fault!" she moaned. "Bertie dear; dear Bertie, look at me, speak to me! Oh, what shall I do! Is—is he dead?" she sobbed to Vane, who had by this time cleared the wall and got beside them.

When riding with Diana he always carried his flask; he took it out and got some brandy through Bertie's clenched teeth and poured some on his forehead, and presently the boy drew a long and painful breath and slowly opened his eyes.

"Get back," said Vane warningly. "He is coming to."

Mabel reluctantly, and with a pitifully anxious gaze still on Bertie, drew away to Diana, and, gripping her hand so tightly as to cause Diana pain, stood there shivering with apprehension and suspense.

But as Bertie pulled himself together and struggled to his feet, the colour stole back to her face, and, setting her teeth hard, she fought with the shame that crushed her eyelids down.

"Hallo!" said Bertie. "What's up? Is—?" He looked round with an anxiety that matched that which had sat upon Mabel's countenance. "Is Mabel safe? Is she—she's not hurt? It—it was my fault, Vane. I chaffed her into jumping it."

"She's all right; you're both all right, you young idiots!" said Vane, half angrily, as he felt the boy over. " 'Pon my soul you aren't fit to be trusted with anything bigger than Shetland ponies, either of you! Here! take a pull at this while I get your nag. You darned young fool, to force a horse, a young horse, as ignorant as yourself, to take a wall like that!"

"It was my fau—" began Bertie again; but Vane shut him up and went after the horse. Bertie found his cap, felt his head covertly, and went up to Mabel, now quite a different person from the wild, terror-stricken girl who, a minute or two ago, had held him in her arms and wailed over him. She received him with every species of exaggerated scorn and contumely.

"Didn't I tell you so?" she exclaimed. "I told you you couldn't ride. I knew you'd come a cropper; and you have, you see. Perhaps you'll take my advice another time. And I'll have Fownes' gloves, please; and don't you forget the size—threes, not fours. A pretty sight you look with—with the blood running down your face. Where's your handkerchief? Oh," with withering scorn, "take mine; pity Nurse isn't here."

He took the dainty little square of cambric and hastily and shamefacedly wiped his face, and meekly offered to return it. But Mabel shrank away with a shudder.

"Don't offer it to me back, you—you dirty boy!" she adjured him angrily.

"All right," he said. "I won't. You can have one of mine in exchange—"

"For a table-cover, I suppose. Thanks! Oh, how hungry I am! For goodness' sake let's ride on!" she exclaimed impatiently. But the moment his back was turned, her number three hand stole toward Diana's and clutched at it, and her eyes, now dim with tears, sought Diana's imploringly.

"Oh, what should I have done if—if he had been killed?" she murmured. "Keep in front of me for a moment—only a moment, Diana dear. And—and—do you think he heard me? Oh, how could I give myself away so! Do you think—really and truly think—he isn't hurt? Keep near me for the rest of the way, Diana; I'm—I'm so afraid that he might see—"

Diana comforted and quieted her. "Happy Bertie!" she whispered softly. "Do you love him so much, Mabel dear?"

"Love! That mere boy! I hate—!" Her voice, which had begun valiantly enough, faltered, and a little sob caught at it and checked it; and she hung her head and turned away.

Judging by the way Bertie ate at the inn, it was evident that he had not received any mortal injuries; and they rode homeward happily enough, though Mabel was unusually quiet and demure.

As they approached the head-keeper's lodge, Donald, hearing the horses, came to the door and doffed his bonnet. He was a giant in girth and stature, and his ruddy face glowed redly at the sight of the "young mistress," whom he regarded with the frank and fearless devotion of the born Highlander who is not afraid or ashamed to display his respectful affection for the person to whom he owes loving allegiance.

Diana, with a glance at Vane that asked his approval, pulled up.

"I hear you have my portrait, Donald," she said, blushing a little.

Donald shot a swift look from his keen eyes at Vane.

"The master haf told you?" he said, with an upward jerk of his head. "Hech, an' you'll no be minding, Miss Diana. I gave one o' the maids—'tis no matter what I gave. An' ef it's no offence, me leddy, I have a favour to spier."

"What is it, Donald?" she asked.

"It's just that ye'll write your bonnie name at the bottom of it," he said. " 'Tis meself that will be the proud man ef your leddyship will put the writing to it."

"Why, yes, of course I will," said Diana, smiling at him. "Do you know that you are paying me a great compliment, Donald? Go and get it, and I'll sign it and send it back to you; and you must let me put it in a frame, if you really care to keep it."

With a couple of strides or so Donald entered the tiny cottage, and instantly reappeared with the precious photograph.

"Here! give it to me, Donald," said Dalesford. Donald watched him intently as he put the photograph in his breast pocket, then he took off his bonnet to Diana.

"Thank you, me leddy!" he said simply, almost as if he were just acknowledging a favour to which he was entitled; and he stood bareheaded until they had turned the corner.

"The governor ought to have seen that," said Vane, laughing, but with his eyes glowing proudly. "As for me, I'll own to being jealous. I can plainly see who is going to be the chief of the Glenaskel clan! It is getting dusk. Bertie,"—he turned in his saddle,—"you'd better go straight to Mrs. Harvey, the housekeeper, and get her to see to that scratch on your head— What is the matter, dearest?" he broke off, as Diana uttered a faint cry, and her mare swerved. "What is it?"

"I—I don't know," she replied. "Someone, some man, passed between the trees just there; and the mare shied."

"Where?" he asked angrily. "Was it one of the servants? Confound—"

He turned his horse and rode back a little way, peering into the shadows of the trees.

"I can see no one," he said. "Was it one of the keepers, woodmen, dearest? I'll have the fellow hauled over the coals. No one has any right to skulk about the drive—"

Diana laid her hand on his arm.

"Don't be angry, dearest," she said. "Yes; I daresay it was one of the keepers. I am not frightened; there is no harm done. See, there is Lord Wrayborough. What care you take of me!"

At the foot of the stairs she remembered Donald's photograph, got it from Vane, and held it in her hand as she talked to Lord Wrayborough; who, as usual, wanted to know all the details of the ride, how she had enjoyed herself, and whether she was sure she was not tired. She told him of Donald's purchase of the photograph and his request, and the old man, proud and pleased, drew her into his room.

"Bravo, Donald! Fine fellow that, eh, Diana? Compliment! I should think so. And he behaved like a gentleman, eh?"

"Like a prince!" said Diana.

"Here's the pen and ink. Write it large and plain. That's it. Hem! Pity he hadn't waited a little; you could have written 'Diana Dalesford.' What?"

He put his hand on her shoulder and pressed it lovingly, and did not move it when the butler, at the open door, said—

"Mr. Fielding has arrived, my lord. He would be glad if Miss Bourne could see him."

"Fielding? Eh, Diana? What?"

"Oh, I'll come directly," said Diana, and, dropping the photograph on the table, she left the room and followed the butler to the library.

CHAPTER XX

BEFORE THE JEWEL SAFE

MR. FIELDING rose as Diana entered, and, smiling at her with a fine mixture of the paternal and legal, held her hand and patted it.

"Don't be alarmed, Miss Bourne," he said. "My sudden and unexpected visit has no evil import. May I say that you are looking both well and happy?"

"Alarmed! I am delighted, Fairy Godmother!" responded Diana, laughing. "I suppose you flew here on your broomstick? Yes; I am quite well, and quite happy," she added frankly, but with a blush and a sudden glow in the eyes that always met his straightly.

"No evil import; but on business, of course. I would wait until this evening or to-morrow before bothering you, but it is just possible I may receive a wire that will take me back by the night mail."

"Oh, poor Mr. Fielding!"

He nodded and sighed. "Yes! Taking all things into consideration, a lawyer's life is not an easeful one, my dear Miss Diana. But to business! It is connected with your father's estate. Do sit down"—he put a chair for her, and sat opposite, leaning forward a little, his eyes, guarded now, fixed on hers. "Our investigations into the amount and character of your father's property have taken a great deal of time, as you may easily understand. Neither his will nor the few papers he left behind him gave any list or clue to his investments or holdings, and we had to hunt them up. Now the man we sent out—a very capable and reliable person, of course—made a strange discovery."

Diana listened gravely and with intense interest. Her father, his career, his very fate, were for her invested with a deep and tragic mystery. He seemed intangible, almost mythical, to the daughter who had not until lately heard his name mentioned, who had almost forgotten that she had ever possessed a father.

"It was this," continued Mr. Fielding. "It appears that your father had a partner, a man named Brown; this partner was with your father when he died. They were up in the mountains, almost if not completely alone; and those who were near them in that wild locality knew nothing of them. I believe that the two partners were prospecting for gold, or, perhaps, examining some new investment or speculation. However, your father died there, and soon afterwards the partner disappeared—well, that is scarcely the fair word to describe his departure; for there was nothing secret about it. He was very much affected by his partner's death, and he spoke openly of leaving the country, of coming to Europe."

"Poor man! Ah, yes, I understand. He was with my father when he died. Could I not find him, Mr. Fielding? I should—should like to see him," Diana said in a low voice.

Mr. Fielding nodded. "As usual, with woman's wit and directness, you have put your finger on the spot, my dear young lady," he said approvingly. "We, too, want to see this partner of your father's; for, on going over his accounts—your father's, I mean—we find that just before he died he had sold his partner, Mr. Brown, several properties, shares in mines and companies, and so on; and it is rather difficult to trace the money your father ought to have received. It amounts to a very large sum, very large; and, of course, we want to know whether Mr. Brown paid, and where the money has gone. Do I make myself clear?"

"Quite," said Diana. "But—but you don't suggest that Mr. Brown didn't pay my father?"

"N-o," replied Mr. Fielding. "That would be going rather far—very much farther than I should care to venture; for, you see, your father was too keen a business man to part with such valuable properties without receiving payment; and, as his accounts were very loosely kept—indeed, we have had to construct them for ourselves in the kind of way the famous naturalist constructed the megatherium from a single bone—it is quite possible he invested the money as soon as he got it, or buried it, or—or gave it away. As Mr. Brown realised these properties before he left South America, and we can't trace him, it's difficult to come to a decision. And now, this is my business to-night: Will you accept the estate as it stands, with this question of Mr. Brown's indebtedness left open, or will you wait until we can track him down—if that is not an inappropriate expression?"

"Wait?" said Diana.

Mr. Fielding nodded and smiled at her.

"Yes; postpone the wedding, I mean. Because you will have to do so if you do not care to leave this question open. But," for Diana's face had gone crimson and her lids drooped, "even without this money, which Mr. Brown may or may not owe, you are an extremely wealthy young lady. If you will glance at these figures—this is the total at the bottom—"

He handed her a paper, and Diana, looking at it, uttered an exclamation.

"You think it is enough?" he said with a smile. "You won't trouble about Mr. Brown, and will not keep Lord Dalesford waiting?"

"No," she whispered. "I—I promised him—in a fortnight—"

Mr. Fielding rose and took both her hands.

"A very sensible decision!" he said heartily. "Let me wish you every happiness, both of you! And there's every prospect of my wishes coming true. The marriage settlements shall be completed at once, and—"

A footman knocked, and, entering, carried a telegram on a salver to Mr. Fielding, who groaned aloud.

"As I feared. Just time to get a snack before I start on my return journey. I must have a few words with Lord Dalesford. Is there anything I can do for you? No? Have you everything in the world you want? Ah, well, you deserve it."

"Why, Fairy Godmother?" Diana asked, as she held his hand.

"Because— Oh, never mind! Good-bye!"

It was a quiet house-party that night, for they were all feeling the effects of the ball of the preceding night; but the Wrayborough family, and the earl and Mabel especially, were happy and complacent. Vane had told them that the wedding-day was fixed; and the earl was in the seventh heaven of delighted satisfaction. After dinner he sat for some time beside Diana, holding her hand now and again and patting it, as if she were a beloved child who had been more than ordinarily good.

Early in the evening she went up to her own room and poured out her heart to her Aunt Mary. The letter was just a song of happiness, of wondering bliss; and when she heard Vane's voice calling her in the corridor, she went out to him with a light in her face which struck him silent, as if with awe.

The night was fine, though dark, for there was no moon, and he coaxed her on to the terrace, where they paced up and down or stood in a cosy, sheltered corner rapt in the lovers' silence that is so much more eloquent than words.

He had drawn one of Lady Selina's thick shawls round her as they had gone out, and as they re-entered the hall by one of the back doors she slipped into the earl's room so that Vane might take the shawl off her. While he was doing so— and how long the simple action took!—she fancied she heard something drop; but a passing footstep in the hall startled her out of his embrace, and she forgot to look for it, whatever it was.

The earl drove her to bed early, and just as she was falling asleep she remembered the little tinkling sound that had struck her as Vane had taken the shawl from her shoulders, and wondered what had caused it. She fell asleep while she was still wondering; but awoke presently, and with a start; for her brain, that mystic piece of machinery, had been at work while she slept, and had whispered, "Aunt Mary's portrait!"

It was a miniature which an artist in Paris had painted for Diana; an exquisite piece of work, and so small that Diana wore it as a pendant.

She sat up, asking herself whether it was the portrait that had dropped, and, after a minute or two she got out of bed and went to see if it was on the table. It was not there, nor was it on any of the other tables or in the places where the maid would have been likely to put it. Diana was now convinced that it was the miniature that had fallen, and she tried to tell herself that it would be quite safe where it had dropped in the earl's room until the morning. But she was uneasy about it and could not sleep; when she closed her eyes she pictured the servant sweeping it away: the thing was so small that a sleepy housemaid might easily overlook it.

She grew so restless in her anxiety about it that she sat up and thought of ringing for Janet, her maid; but Diana was one of those women—they are not too plentiful, by the way—who consider the comfort and well-being of their servants; and she was reluctant to awaken the girl and send her down. Why, it was much better for her to go herself, for she was already awake.

She got out, and, slipping into her dressing-gown, opened the door and listened. The great place was wrapt in silence, a silence broken only by the ticking of the big clock and the crackling of the logs in the fireplace in the hall. She stood hesitating, feeling a little nervous, and half dreading the journey from her room, along the corridor, down the staircase, across the hall into the earl's room. It seemed fearsome and weird in the dead of night—the turret-clock chimed two as she listened—in that intense silence.

But presently, ashamed of herself, she, womanlike, passed out quickly, and as quickly went down the stairs and across the hall. Her movements were absolutely noiseless, for she wore her felt bath-slippers, and trod like a thing of air, a flitting vision of girlhood trembling on womanhood. As noiselessly she pushed open the door of the earl's den, and found that it opened only a little way, and some obstacle stopped it. She looked round and saw a small wedge of wood lying against the door. It was within reach of her foot, and with her foot she pushed it away, and, without asking herself why it was there and how it had come there, she entered the room, turned up the electric light, and began to look for the miniature.

She had not to search long, for she saw it lying under a small table where it had rolled when the shawl had broken the slender, threadlike chain. With a sigh of relief she picked it up, pressed it to her with a girlish gesture of relief, and was passing out again swiftly when she heard a peculiar noise in the adjoining room.

She stopped dead short and listened. It was a strange sound, a scraping noise, with at regular intervals a "tick, tick," as of clockwork. Oddly enough the noise did not suggest burglars to her, the idea of a burglar in Glenaskel Castle, filled with servants, surrounded by stalwart retainers, savoured too much of the far-fetched and ridiculous. It occurred to her that a cat had got shut up in the room and was scratching to get out; and, without a single tremor of nervousness or a thought of dread, she glided to the door and opened it.

Then she stood transfixed, struck motionless, almost pulseless, by horror and terror. By the light of a small dark lantern which stood on a chair she saw a masked man kneeling before the safe, upon the lock of which he was at work with a curious-looking tool which revolved as if moved by clockwork. He was so intent on his operations, her movements had been so noiseless, that he had not heard her, and was unconscious of her presence. And in that moment, while she was struggling against the deathlike faintness that threatened to overwhelm her, she saw his figure plainly, saw that his face was half concealed by a mask, and that he was a squarely built, strong-looking man of past middle age.

Her heart seemed to cease beating, she felt choking, and, with her hand at her throat, as if to release her voice, she uttered an inarticulate cry.

At the sound the man looked round quickly, and, springing to his feet, was upon her, one hand clapped on her mouth, the other seizing her arm. His face was thrust close to hers, his teeth, from which the lips were drawn like those of a dog, threatened her horribly. Diana knew that she was face to face with death, but the spirit that had done Vane such good service in the lane at Wedbury rose within her, and she struggled with the man. He wrenched her round, and, in doing so, brought her face into the stream of intense light from the electric lamp.

With a cry, a low, hoarse cry, his hands fell from her, and he staggered back and leant against the safe, his arms thrust out as if to keep him off her, the pallor of his face below the mask a stony white, his eyes gleaming through the mask with a mixture of terror and amazement.

Diana, half-dead with terror, and yet conscious of a kind of rage, opened her lips to cry out; but before she could do so he held out his hand imploringly.

"Don't—don't call! Don't! Be silent, for—for God's sake! You don't know what you're doing, you don't know who I am! Look—" he caught up the lantern and flashed it on a photograph lying on the floor. It was the cabinet she had signed for Donald and left on the table of the next room. "Look! Is—is that your likeness? Answer me 'Yes' or 'No'! But I know. It is! You are—you are—" he moistened his lips and his voice broke hoarsely on the words,—"you are Diana Bourne!"

Diana made no reply, but, taking advantage of the man's strange emotion and still stranger exclamation, though they evoked a vague wonder and surprise in her, she turned and sprang for the door.

To her amazement the man made no movement to stay her.

"Yes, go!" he said, with a gesture of resignation. "Give the alarm. Have me arrested. I'm after the diamonds here right enough. I shan't try to escape. Give the alarm—if you like. But—but you won't, if you've a heart in your bosom, my girl!"

There were such misery, such anguish, so acute a despair, in the rough, hoarse voice that Diana stopped short and looked at him over her shoulder. She was white to the lips; but her eyes met his steadily; for, strangely enough, she felt no fear now.

"Why should I not?" she asked, and her own voice sounded unnatural in her ears, as if it were the voice of someone else, someone else she had never known. "Why should I not? You are a thief—a burglar. You have come to steal the diamonds. You are appealing to me for pity. You appeal in vain." Then, womanlike, she glanced off. "What are you doing with my portrait? Why do you ask me my name? It is some trick to stop me. It will not avail you. Before you can escape—" At that instant the question struck across her consciousness: Why did the man not escape through the window by which he had entered, and which was partly open? "Why should I not have you arrested—you thief?"

His head had sunk on his breast, and he was looking at her strangely through the holes of the mask. Suddenly he tore the mask from his face, flung it aside, and, with a gesture of resignation that was not devoid of dignity, said, almost inaudibly—

"Because you are Diana Bourne,—my daughter.—I am your father!"

CHAPTER XXI

GARLING'S CONFESSION

"I AM your father!"

For a moment or two the words carried no significance with them, and Diana stood staring at the face the man had revealed, with a benumbed sense with which one passes through a nightmare.

Then, as she tried to move, to laugh, to utter words of anger and scorn, something in the man's face struck her; something familiar, haunting, oppressive. In its rough-hewn features, heavy brows, dark eyes, there was a resemblance to—to whom? Not—oh, surely not to Aunt Mary! She tried to thrust the hideous suggestion from her, told herself that it was born of the excitement, the hysteria of the moment; but it would not be so thrust away, and clung to her with horrible tenacity; and she could not speak, could do nothing but stand staring dumbly at him in a silence that seemed to be suffocating her.

"Have you nothing to say? Won't you speak to me?" Garling asked at last, in an almost inaudible voice, thick and hoarse and laboured. "You—you think I am lying?"

She found her voice, and, with flashing, scornful eyes, with a gesture of indignant repudiation, replied—

"Yes. Why have you said it? What was your object? It is a cunning trick, I suppose. You wanted to gain time. You cannot escape; the moment you move I shall ring that bell, alarm the house—"

His lips writhed. "It's no lie. It's the truth," he said, his eyes falling before hers, his hand dragging across his forehead to wipe away the big drops of sweat that had gathered on it. "I don't wonder at your thinking it a lie. It's—it's hard to believe. I—I wish now I hadn't told you, that I'd kept my mouth shut and taken my chance. But it's too late now. You know the truth; miss. Though you stand there a fine lady in this grand place, you're my daughter, right enough."

Wildly, ghastly impossible as the thing still seemed, there was a tone of sincerity in the man's rough voice which struck a chill to Diana's heart. She watched him with a shuddering intentness, with a sense of evil which increased each moment.

"My father is dead," she repeated mechanically, unconsciously.

"You thought I was, they all thought I was," he said. "It was a mistake. I—I planned it. It wasn't me that died; but my partner, poor Stevie Brown. We'd trekked from Chaquetta—"

142

Diana started. The queer name of the place which she had first heard of from Mr. Fielding went home.

"Chaquetta?" she echoed.

He nodded. "Yes. That's the place where I made my money. We'd trekked from there to the mountains, where we expected to find gold. My partner fell ill —fever got in the plains, and through drinking bad water; and he and me were a'most alone in the wildest spot on God's earth—"

"Why do you tell me this?" she broke in impatiently, scornfully.

He hung his head, then raised it and looked at her with dumb appeal and deprecation.

"I'm—I'm trying to explain, to show you," he said meekly. "It was while Stevie was dying that the notion struck me that I could let it go that I died myself. You see, I—I wanted to come back to England, to—to see the little gel as I'd left there—"

Diana sprang to the bell.

"You are lying to me, concocting a story to gain time! Ah, yes, you are expecting help from some confederates. Ah! Help!"

He had leapt toward her and seized her arm before she could press the bell, and he drew her, with as little force as possible, away from it.

"Don't, don't for your own sake! I—I don't care! I'd as soon be lagged as not. But it's different for you. You're a grand lady—at home here—though how I can't understand! Don't ring, don't call, till I've proved to you who I am and who you are."

Diana dragged her arm from his grasp and shrank back, shuddering from the pollution of his touch.

"Go!" she said. "I will not give the alarm.—The diamonds are safe? You have not got them?—I will not give the alarm until you have had time to escape. But go while my patience lasts!"

He shook his head. "I'll go presently. There's no danger while you keep quiet, missie. You still think I'm lying, that I'm playing a trick on you? God help me, I wish I was! Prove it? How am I to prove it?"

He looked about him with the grotesque helplessness of the illiterate man unaccustomed to logical expression; definition; then suddenly he saw the pendant lying on the ground where it had fallen from Diana's hand when she had seen him. He picked it up absently and mechanically glanced at it, and as he did so he uttered a faint cry.

"Why, it's Mary!" he said thickly. "It's Mary's portrait!"

"You—you know it!" escaped Diana's trembling lips.

"It's my sister Mary—Mary Burton," he responded simply. "It's the portrait of your aunt, the aunt that brought you up, missie."

Diana staggered and pressed her hand to her forehead.

Was she dreaming? Was this a hideous nightmare? Would the whole horrible scene fade away presently and leave her, panting and trembling from the effects of it, in her dainty bed in the luxurious room upstairs?

"That's who it is," he said, still gazing at the miniature. "She's altered, o' course; yes, she's older and seen a deal o' trouble, trouble of my making"—he drew a long breath; "but I'd have known her anywhere. Is—is she here, missie—Diana?"

Diana felt as if she were choking.

"She is not here!" she gasped.

"I beg your pardon, missie—but—but it's my own sister, my sister Mary as I left you with—"

A low, despairing cry; a moan of horror, broke from Diana's white lips.

"Oh, it isn't true! It cannot be! Oh, God help me! God help me!"

He gazed at her, as she stood with wild, dilated eyes and clasped hands, and his thick lips writhed and worked pityingly, remorsefully.

"Don't take on, dearie," he murmured in his guttural voice. "Don't fret about it. I'll—I'll take myself out of your sight. I'll go at once, and I'll never touch you again."

"Yes—go!" she gasped; then she wrung her hands. "But—but if you go, I—I must go. You—you are my father—"

"That's so, dearie," he said quietly, remorsefully. "It's the truth; you know that, feel that? How should I know Mary's—your aunt's portrait? How should I know *you*?"

"And—and where you go I must go!" she gasped with a shudder, scarcely knowing what she said. "O God, it is cruel! Help me to think—to think of—"

Garling started and held up his hand. "Shsh!" he whispered. "That's—that's a dog outside! My ears are quick. If—if he scents me—"

"Go—oh, go!" she panted. "Go while there's time. And I—I, oh, what shall I do, what shall I do?"

Still listening, with his eyes turned sideways in a horrible fashion, he crept to her and laid his hand on her arm.

"Speak low!" he whispered in her ear, his hot breath on her cheek. "I'm going. You'll stay here. Don't be afraid! I'm not going to worry you. I've—I've seen you, and that's enough. Lord, how beautiful you are, and how—how grand! Like a young queen—"

She shivered. How often had Vane used the same words!

"And, mind you, whatever happens, I hold my tongue. Not to a living soul while I'm living myself will I let on that I've found my daughter. No, no! I know what's due to you, I know the difference between us. And you can trust me, missie—Diana. Let me call you that once, I shall think of you by that name; I shall—" His voice broke, and he turned away with a gesture of grief and despair that was not lacking in a kind of grotesque dignity. It was the father speaking in him.

Diana fought for calm, prayed for it.

"I—I must see you again," she said with an unnatural stillness, which belied the heaving bosom, the distraught eyes. "Can you—dare you—wait about the place, somewhere in the neighbourhood, where I can meet you?"

He looked doubtful, and shook his head; then he drew himself up.

"That's—that's kind of you, missie. You want to see me again? I'll risk it. Yes, I'll risk it!" He thought a moment. "There's a little wood by the river, below the woodcutter's hut. If—if you're of the same mind to-morrow, I'll be there, miss, at seven o'clock in the morning." He saw her glance at the safe, and he nodded reassuringly. "That's all right. I'll fix things nice and neat, just as they were, and nobody'll know if they don't go to the safe. Will they be likely to?"

"No, I think not," she answered almost inaudibly.

"Right," he said with a nod. "Don't you be frightened an' upset, dearie. You won't see me again after to-morrow. You'll forget as such a man—"

He waved his thick arm with an action as of sweeping the gruesome fact of his existence away, and, turning to the safe, rubbed the spot on which he had been working with an oiled rag; then he carefully but swiftly removed the filings from the floor, and, going to the window, as carefully pushed aside the bar, the bottom of which he had neatly cut through with a file. Here he paused and looked over his shoulder at the motionless figure, the white face, the eyes that followed his every movement as if she were fascinated by horror and loathing, and, drawing a long breath, he crept slowly, hesitatingly, towards her.

"Won't—won't you say 'good-night,' just 'good-night—father'!" he pleaded in a hoarse whisper. "I'd like to hear the word from you once, dearie! My little gel that I've thought of, dreamed of—!"

She tried to speak, to say "good-night," but her voice seemed frozen, and she flung up her hands and shrank from him.

With a gesture of apology, of hideous meekness, the meekness of a beaten hound, a jail-bird, he turned from her, stepped on to the window-sill, and dropped from her sight. She heard the faint, very faint sound of the bar slipping back into its place, then all was silence.

How long she stood, staring vacantly before her, she did not know; but at last she started, awoke from the awful spell that held her, and, with a shuddering glance round the room, turned off the light and went upstairs. Her last steps were uncertain, faltering ones, she staggered as she shut and locked the door, then fell fainting across the bed.

When she came-to the dawn was breaking, and the terrible reality of her position came crushing down upon her. She felt that but for the swoon her mind must have given way, and that she would have passed into raving hysterics; even now, as, weak and trembling, she sat up and hid her burning, aching eyes in her hands, she was assailed by the dread of brain-fever, of some seizure in which she should reveal the horrible truth.

For in her heart, at the back of her throbbing brain, lay the conviction that the man had not lied, and that she was indeed his daughter.

At such moments the mind, like a slave too hardly pressed, revolts and refuses to perform its wonted task. She could not think, could not think even of Vane. She tried to do so, tried to picture the misery, the shame, that would overwhelm him and crush him as they were crushing her; but she could not see him clearly; she was moving, living, in a land of shadows, in a phantasmagoria too grotesque, too monstrous, for belief. She, Diana Bourne, Vane's affianced wife, the daughter of—

With unsteady steps she dragged herself to the washstand and bathed her face until the burning forehead felt as if it were bound in ice; then she slowly dressed herself, choosing one of her plainest dresses, and putting on a hat with a thick veil she had worn for motoring. Now and again she looked at herself absently in the glass: was that white-faced woman with the dark shadows under her eyes, the strained lips, still quivering with horror, herself?

And she was going to meet the man whom she had last night detected in his vile work; she was going to meet—her father!

The clock chimed the quarter to seven, and with a start she looked round the room, holding her head with her hands in the vain effort for self-possession, for concentration of mind. She moved to the dressing-table on which lay the jewels, the trinkets she had worn last night. They represented a large sum, they were the tangible evidence of the vast wealth she had considered here; some of them spoke eloquently of Vane, of the earl, who had given them to her with loving words, loving caresses; but she shuddered as she looked at them, remembering those other gems which her father—her father!—had come to steal.

Half blindly she selected those which she herself had bought, and others which Aunt Mary had given her, found her purse, and put it and the jewellery into her pocket. She stood and looked round her again at the bed in which she had slept and dreamt of the man she loved. Oh, why did not her heart break at the thought of him? Was it because she could not think clearly? Then, lingeringly, she opened the door and passed out.

As chance willed it, Janet, her maid, came out of her room at the same moment.

"Oh, miss, are you dressed—are you going out?" she asked.

Diana fought for self-possession, even succeeded in forcing a smile.

"Yes. I did not sleep very well last night, Janet," she said, and her voice sounded strangely in her own ears, as if it were the voice of some other person. "I—I was restless. I am going for a little walk." She paused, and Janet, with a lady's-maid's eyes for details, set straight a lapel of Diana's jacket. As she did so, she felt Diana tremble.

"Why, you're trembling, miss," she said with concern. "Oh, do let me get you a cup of tea before you start."

"No, no!" said Diana quickly, and with a smile that she herself felt must appear forced and unnatural. "I won't have any tea. I shall try and sleep when I come back. Don't disturb me."

CHAPTER XXII

DIANA'S FLIGHT

She went down the stairs, feeling Janet's anxious eyes following her, and, crossing the hall, went out by the back door. It was a lovely morning, and the sun shone on the lawns and fell athwart the hills violet with heather and golden with gorse. The beauty of the scene was an added pang to her tortured heart; all her life she would remember that view which she and Vane—where was Vane?—why was he not by her side to help her, to sustain her?—had looked at together.

Slowly she passed through the shrubbery, glancing at the barred window of the strong room and shuddering as she averted her eyes, and, skirting into the path that led to the wood, quickened her pace. She must not keep him waiting. He was in danger, terrible danger; and, he was her father!

She gained the little wood, paused to see if she had been seen, followed; then, threading her way among the thick trees, suddenly came upon him.

He was seated on a fallen tree, his square chin sunk in his hand, his eyes looking gloomily, yet expectantly, before him. In that moment no detail of his appearance escaped her. She saw that he had changed his clothes, and was now dressed like a workman in his Sunday best; noticed the massive head, the thick limbs, the great hands, the short, stubbly hair. And—she asked God to forgive her —every fibre of her being shrank from him.

He heard her when she was some way off, and, springing to his feet, held out his arms, his lined and rugged face lit up with a smile of welcome. Of welcome!

Then, as he saw her wince and draw back, he let his arms fall to his side, and, with a gesture of resignation, motioned to her to sit down.

Perhaps only half consciously, Diana had been schooling, nerving herself for the ordeal; she was, in appearance at any rate, calm and unmoved; and she signed to him to seat himself beside her; he sank on the trunk of the tree, but at a little distance from her. It was Diana who broke the silence.

"Tell me—tell me everything," she said in a low voice, glancing at him for an instant, then fixing her eyes on the tree in front of her. "Keep—keep nothing back. I—I can bear it. You ▢▢▢my father?"

He inclined his head. "Yes; I'm your father," he said in his deep, guttural tones. "You've been wondering why I left you. I'd—I'd rather not tell you; but I've got to, I suppose."

He glanced at her, and she made a gesture of assent; almost of command.

"I was a locksmith by trade when I met your mother," he said. "She was an Italian. Her father was one of these socialists, anarchists, and had fled over here

147

to England—there's a lot of 'em hiding away in London and the other big cities. I met her when I was doing some repairs to a lock at a house where she and her father were lodging; and we fell in love. I was"—he raised his head for a moment, then dropped it again—"I was a decent-looking chap then, and—and honest; and I loved her true. But she was afeared to be seen with me; for her father, with all his queer notions, was a swell in his own country, and we had to meet on the sly. We had to be married on the sly. But we were happy."

He paused and stared before him with half-closed eyes.

"We were happy, though we had hard times. She was rather delicate; and, what with the want of firing and proper food, she fell ill. There was a general slackness in my trade, all the trades, that winter, and I couldn't get any work, though I tramped miles for it, and wasn't particular what I did. There was no work to be had; and I'd come home of a night and see her half starving. There was no one to help us, for her father had died of the same complaint, consumption. The doctor said that she'd get all right if I could take her to the proper places abroad and could give her nourishing food. And it was hard work to earn a crust! I watched her dying by inches until I was near mad at the thought of all the money that was being wasted in London every day, every hour, all round us. And one evening a man I met in a public-house and who knew something of me offered me—work. It wasn't honest work, but it was of the kind I could do. I learned afterwards that he'd had his eye on me for weeks past, and just chose his time to speak. And I—I closed with him. It was well paid, that work of his, and I did several—jobs for him. But the money came too late. A week after you was born, dearie, my wife, your mother—died."

His voice broke, but he recovered it and went on moodily—

"The day of the funeral, while I was sitting with you on my lap, wondering what I should do with you, the—police came."

Diana shuddered, and pressed her lips tightly together to check the cry of horror that rose to them.

"I was wanted for—for a job I'd done on a safe at a bank." He cleared his throat. "They offered to send the child—that's you, Diana—to the workhouse; but I got my sister Mary to take you—and I swore that if ever I came out I'd turn honest and be a credit to you—"

"And you—you broke your oath!" she said almost inaudibly.

"Wait till you hear it all," he said meekly. "I had a hard time in—where they sent me. It was a long sentence, for they proved the other jobs against me, and no wonder. Ah, well, it was more than flesh an' blood could stand, and I tried to escape. I did nearly get off, but they caught me and brought me back; and I served my time and came out with a ticket o' leave. You know what that is, dearie?"

She made a gesture in the affirmative and set her teeth hard.

"It gives you the right to live like a free human being while you report yourself—an' do you know what that □□□□? That you're spied upon and suspected, with by the police as the cat plays with a mouse. Honest life! I tell you"—he raised his huge, heavy hand and let it fall with tremendous weight and force on the log—"that not one 'ticket' in a thousand—ah! not one in ten thousand—can stand it. I made a bolt for it and left England. I'm strong—they used to call me The Ironmonger"—the touch of pride in his voice made Diana wince—"and I'd no difficulty in working my passage out in a sailing ship. I wanted to see you, to see you bad; but I wouldn't. I kept away from you because I'd sworn not to go near you until I was fit to claim you, to kiss you.—Don't move! I'm not going to touch you, missie—Diana, I mean. I know what's due to you. I struck luck in the new country after a time, and at Chaquetta there I was the richest man in the place. Everything fell into my mouth like a ripe plum, jest like a ripe plum. I'd sent money home to your Aunt Mary for you, and I wanted to send more; but she wrote and told me not to, that you was earning good money yourself; and the notion came to me that I'd come home when my ticket had run out, and bring the money and lay it at your feet—and make a great lady of you."

His voice grew thick, and he glanced at her wistfully for a moment, then averted his eyes.

"The longing got a hold on me, such a grip-hold that the days seemed weeks, and the weeks like years. The waiting got on my nerves; I'd a terror on me that I should die before my ticket was out, die without seeing you. Then my partner and me went up to the mountains, as I told you last night; and he fell ill and died. We were alone; no one knew our names; it was easy to pass him off for me, to give out that I was dead and so leave me free to go where I liked, to come back as Stevie Brown instead of Benjamin Bourne, or Garling, as the police called me. So I made a will and stuck it among his traps, and took his name. It worked all right, didn't it? You got the money?"

Diana's lips moved.

"That is, all I left for you; I kept some of it, pretending that I'd sold some property to Brown. I'd have passed on every penny to you; but I didn't want to be driven by poverty to—to the old life. You understand, dearie?"

Yes; she understood plainly enough. And every word he said went to prove his identity, to strengthen the evidence contained in his resemblance to her aunt; in the unmistakable sincerity of every accent and expression.

"Then I made my way slowly, bit by bit, to England, and began to search for you. I'd got your London address, for Mary wrote to me now and again; she'd told me that her husband and her little child was dead—"

"Yes; she died after Aunt Mary took me. I never saw her—to remember her," said Diana, more to herself than to him. "Poor Aunt Mary!"

"Yes; she's had a cruel, hard time, too," he said with a nod and a twitch of his lips. "It's the poor as suffers every way. Well, I went to the address in London; but you'd gone and no one knew where you were. I had to ask on the quiet, because, you see," he cleared his throat, "my ticket wasn't expired; and—and they could lag me if—"

She made a gesture to check him, and, with an apologetic jerk of the head, he went on—

"At last I heard by accident that a gel with your name had got a berth as a schoolmistress at a place called Wedbury; and I went there. But you'd gone again; and no one seemed to know where.—And now you're here—and—and we've met; and—and it's all of no use; for you know what I am; that I ain't fit to speak to you, breathe the same air, leave alone claim you as my daughter. It's all of no use, and I might as well have stopped out there in that God-forsaken place, or—or shot myself!"

His head drooped and his hands gripped each other. There was the bitterness of despair in every line of his face, in every huge, clumsy limb.

"All of no use. You, my own little gel, are ashamed of me—and rightly; you a fine lady—and you'd rather I'd died as you thought I'd done."

Diana tried to speak one word, only one word of denial, of comfort, of sympathy with his agony of disappointment; but she could not. There was silence for a moment, as her aching brain struggled to realise the situation; then she said—

"But if you kept some of the money, as you say—oh, how I wish you had kept every penny, all!—why were you robbing—doing what I saw you doing last night?"

He raised his head and looked straight before him, and an awful change came over his face, which was darkened by an expression of unutterable hatred and fury.

"I was waiting for that," he said slowly and in a low, hoarse voice. "Seeing that I'd kept back money enough, and that I'd made you rich, what was I working that safe for—what was I running my neck into a noose for?"

He unlocked his hands and flung out his arms with a curious action.

"Must have been mad, it seems to you, missie? Looking back on it, I'm 'most inclined myself to think I was. And yet, what could I do? Don't be hard on me till I've told you. But"—with a long breath—"you won't understand; you haven't seen him, heard his voice—the devil! He's the worst devil I've ever met; and I've been to Portland, where there's worse devils than there is in hell."

Diana uttered a low cry and held up her hand to stop him.

"I beg your pardon, missie," he said meekly. "But you just listen. One night, the night I'd heard you'd gone to that place in the country, school-teaching, I dropped into a place I knew in London. I was lonely and down on my luck, and it was one of the few places I could venture to be seen in; a low drinking and gaming place. No, no, I didn't want to drink or play. It's years since I've done either. But I wanted company, lights, the sound of voices and laughter; and I knew I should find 'em there. I went in, knowing the password, and just looked round, meaning to take a drink and go out again. Some of the people there were playing, playing cards; and a couple—a gentleman, a swell, a real swell, was plucking a lad, a mere boy, as he'd fuddled with liquor. I knew the gentleman, though I'd seen him only once before in my life; but it was at a time I wasn't likely to forget —the day they caught me and brought me back to prison. He was standing beside the governor when they dragged me in half-famished and torn and bleeding —and that fine young gentleman stood there and laughed and sneered at me."

He loosened his neckcloth as if he were choking, and waved his hand with a rough apology for his emotion.

"I knew him again; and I was turning away when he spotted me and signed to me to stop. I'd a mind to take no notice and get out of the place; but—I couldn't." He looked from side to side with a helpless expression. "I don't know why, but he seemed to hold me, to—to ☐☐☐me stop. You see"—deprecatingly, and as if he were trying to explain his powerlessness to himself—"when a man's been used to obey orders, a word or a look, just like a dog, it comes hard to refuse, to stand up for himself. And this gentleman—" he stopped again, as if in despair of making Diana understand the peculiar influence that had mastered him. "He's a devil," he said, between his teeth. "He went on playing and kept me there against my will. Then he made me promise to report myself to him every Monday—and I did."

"Why?" Diana asked with weary surprise. "Why did you not leave England, go back, go abroad out of his reach?"

Garling looked at her. "I wanted to see you, to see my gel," he replied simply. "He said he might want me. I thought it was only a threat, that he was playing with me, a cruel kind o' game; but one Monday he told me—he gave me my job. He was hard up—his sort of gentlemen get a run of bad luck sometimes and get driven into a corner. He said he was stone-broke, and he knew where these diamonds were, and I was to get them—"

He paused under Diana's start and gaze of amazement and horror.

"But—but you could have refused, could have taken flight—"

Garling shook his head and smiled grimly.

"No, dearie. If I'd refused—and I did try to, God knows!—he'd have set the police on me. And there's no getting away nowadays without a fair start and wonderful luck. He'd only to drop a line to Scotland Yard, and the hue-and-cry would have been out; every port would have been watched, and I should have been lag—caught and sent back to finish my time. No; there was no help for it. But I made him swear that it was the only job he'd expect of me, that he'd let me go after it was done. I was afraid of him; but that wasn't all. As I said, I wanted to see my daughter. Why"—his hands clenched and his face worked—"I'd have gone through fire and water to see you. I did go through worse than that; I risked Portland and a life of hell in coming back."

He was silent for a moment or two, and sat gazing at the ground moodily, almost listlessly; then he lifted his great head.

"An' now I'll go again. I'll get out of the country. And I promise you, missie, you shan't see me any more. You're a great lady now. Was you visiting here, at this grand place, dearie?" he asked meekly, with a kind of wondering awe.

Diana was silent for a moment. She could not bring herself to tell him that she was—ah, no, she was not now!—had been engaged to marry Lord Dalesford.

"Yes," she said, her head bent.

"That's all right; that's as it should be," he said with grotesque satisfaction. "You're a lady, every inch of you; you take after your mother—though, strange to say, you ain't like her in looks. You stay on here, just keep on as you've been going. There's plenty of money, and if there wasn't I could make some more. I've got the knack of it." He raised his head with a humble kind of pride. "I'll send you more, ever so much more—"

Diana turned to him with a gesture of despair.

"This money, ah, this money!" Suddenly: "Why did you not offer some to the man, the wretch who—who drove you back to crime?"

Garling shook his head.

"It wouldn't have been of any use. He'd have bled me to death, and spent every penny. He'd have wanted to know how I got it, have learned where I'd been, have dug up the past, and found out about ⬜⬜ I'd rather work as his slave for the rest of my life than he should do that."

The simple statement went to Diana's heart; and she flung up her hands before her face, crying—

"Oh, what shall I do, what shall I do?"

"Just what I say, missie," he answered for her. "Go on as you've been going. No one will know. I'd rather have my tongue cut out—beg pardon, dearie; my rough way of speaking ain't fit for a lady to hear. No, no; don't you be afraid. I shall never ask to see you again—"

"But don't you see that—that," she said with suppressed anguish—"that my place is by your side? I am your daughter; and wherever her father is his child should be. I must go with you. Yes, I must go with you!"

He sprang to his feet, his arms outstretched, his rugged face working; then as, despite herself, she shrank back from him with a faint cry of terror, he stopped and let his arms fall, as he had let them fall once before.

"Don't you think that, Diana," he said quietly; "I'm an ignorant man, but I know better what's due to you than that. ⬜⬜ come along and live with ⬜⬜! Why,"—his voice grew hoarse—"you couldn't do it. It wouldn't be right. Why, I might be took at any moment. When I go to this man that's got the pull of me and tell him I've chucked the job—" He stopped and shrugged his shoulders significantly. "No, no! I'll go my way, and you'll go yours, missie. And if you give me a thought once and again, why, think of me as if I'd really died out there in the wilds. Think of me—not as—as you saw me last night, not as you see me now, but as the honest man as worked hard to scrape some money together for his little gel, to make a lady of her."

"Ah, don't you understand?" Diana cried with a choking sob. "It is because you worked for me, because you were driven to—to do this for my sake, that I cannot leave you."

He waved his hand and smiled grimly.

"It 'u'd break your heart," he said with the simplicity of insight and conviction. "You couldn't stand it. Every time you looked at me and heard me speak— No, no! From this moment we're standing here, I want to be as good as dead to you. That's just it—dead. As I ought to be. Why, I ain't fit to touch you. Me drag you down to what I've sunk to! No, dearie; I'm bad, cruel bad, but I'm not as bad as that."

They stood in silence. During the whole tragic interview he had been listening warily, and his eyes had scanned the wood with keen watchfulness. Now, as he heard a labourer whistling as he skirted the wood on his way to work, Garling drew himself up and looked at his watch.

"People beginning to get about," he said in a low voice. "I must be off. I'm going to walk through the lane to the junction. I can catch a train there. If no one goes to the safe or the window, nothing will be discovered till I'm clean out of the country. It's—it's good-bye, dearie. Good-bye for ever."

Duty called to Diana; but, as if he saw in her eyes the struggle that was going on within her, he shook his head.

"No, no; I go alone. I'm—I'm your father, and I tell you that—that I won't ☐☐☐you with me. Good-bye!"

His hoarse voice broke as he turned away, and Diana went to him slowly, as if her limbs were leaden.

"Good-bye," she faltered. "If you wish—if you—"

"No," he said, understanding her. "No; I'm not fit to touch you, dearie, much less kiss you. Think—think—no, don't think of me. Try and forget!"

He was gone, and Diana sank down on the tree, over-whelmed with despair. What should she do? Whither should she turn to escape from—herself, from the self which had become loathsome, degraded?

To go back to the castle—to Vane—was impossible. Vane! She could think of him now. And the remembrance of his love, of his perfect, passionate love for her, his pride in her, was a torture almost too great to be borne.

He must never know the truth. The shame that made every vein in her body burn must not touch him. He must never see her again. Let him think what he would of her, let him curse her as the most false, the most faithless of women; but he must not know how vile a creature he had nearly made his wife.

The daughter of a criminal, a convict! To think of it, to dwell upon it, meant madness. She must find relief in action or break down utterly, and so reveal the awful truth.

She looked at her watch. An hour, an hour of dreadful torture, had been spent; and time—time was so priceless. She tried to form some plan; but her only idea was one of instant flight; and, impelled by the terror of discovery, by the passionate desire to spare the man who loved her, she staggered to her feet and went giddily, uncertainly, through the wood towards the railway station.

As she went she tried to piece together the jumbled, hideous puzzle of her fate. She knew now the cause of her aunt's nervous apprehension, of her agitation when Mr. Fielding's first letter had come. She knew now why that astute lawyer had, with pitying consideration, slurred over the story of her father's career. Those remittances, the money that had come in the days of their poverty, had come from her father. And the vast fortune, some of which she had spent so lavishly, the immense sum which she knew the lawyers were settling upon Vane, all, all had come from that crime-stained hand, the hand of the common thief and burglar.

Her father! Half blinded she made her way, fighting, praying, for sufficient strength to carry her into hiding, to some place where she could be alone to cower under her shame and ease her broken heart.

There were no other passengers at the little station and the porter eyed her curiously as he touched his cap.

She turned away and bit her lip to bring back some colour to it, and forced a smile, as she said—

"I am going to London on—on sudden business. Will you get me a ticket, please?"

The man got a ticket, told her that the train was overdue, and, looking round, asked for the luggage.

She told him that it would follow; and when the train drew up he put her in a first-class compartment, shut the door quietly and respectfully, and stood by the window, in case she should have any further use for him.

It seemed to her as if the train would never move; but at last it left the station, and, leaning back, she shut her eyes that she might not see the turrets of the castle, the house which held the man she loved better than life itself; the man she was leaving for ever.

CHAPTER XXIII

DALESFORD'S LETTER

DALESFORD happened to breakfast alone that morning. Lady Selina always partook of an apology for that meal in bed, and Mabel and Bertie had scrambled through a hasty repast of fish, ham and eggs, and the Scotchest of Scotch marmalade at eight o'clock, and had gone off fishing; fishing, because Lady Selina, while laying an embargo on the two young people walking or riding alone together, had forgotten to include angling!

Dalesford, as he took up his letters, looked wistfully at the empty chair beside him, then sighed with a thrill of satisfaction as he reflected that in a little while, a few short days, he would be entitled to take up his darling's breakfast, if she desired to have it in her room. A few short days! He looked before him musingly, his heart glowing within him at the thought. To have the right to be with her always; never to part again; to be able to call her whensoever it pleased him, to gratify her every wish, to be able to say "my wife"!

And he had laughed at matrimony, had pitied the amorous husband! But then he had so much greater an excuse than most men; she was so beautiful, so sweet, so altogether to be desired. Why, there was not a man who did not envy him, not a man who knew him who did not consider him the luckiest man on earth. His pearl among women! He was glad she was resting; but he wondered whether she would be late in coming down; and he felt particularly lonely.

He had arranged to drive her to a distant part of the estate, to meet the factor and discuss with him a proposal to cut down some trees; and he was looking forward to a long morning with his beloved. Not many months ago Dalesford would not have dreamed of meeting the factor on business; but, as Mabel had said, love had wrought a marvellous change in him; he had caught from Diana a novel and surprising regard for small details, and the people on the estate were delighted at the interest which the young laird was showing in his future property.

When he had finished his breakfast, he lit a cigar and went down to the stables and ordered a dog-cart with Diana's favourite horse; a dog-cart, because it did not necessitate a groom, and he and Diana would be alone. He remained at the stables, looking at the horses and talking to the head man, for half an hour; and as he returned to the house he met Janet coming down the stairs into the smaller hall. She had some lace, which she was going to clean, in her hands, and she dropped his lordship a little morning curtsey.

"Good-morning, Janet," said Dalesford. "Is your mistress in her room still?"

Janet hesitated a moment, then she replied directly to the question. It was not her place to explain that Diana had been out, but had, as Janet thought, returned.

"Yes, my lord. She is asleep. That is, I knocked at the door and got no answer. My mistress did not have a very good night—"

Dalesford looked anxious instantly.

"But she's sleeping now, my lord; and I thought it better not to disturb her."

"Quite right," he said approvingly. "Don't wake her, Janet. She has been doing a great deal lately; far too much, I'm afraid. No, no, don't disturb her."

He wandered about the hall and the smoking-room with patient impatience; they came to tell him that the dog-cart was ready, and he nodded and went out, and stared at it in the way men have when they are waiting. Then he consulted his watch. It was a fairly long drive, the factor was a busy man, and it would be scarcely the thing to keep him waiting—novel consideration for Dalesford to display!—and perhaps the drive would be too long for Diana if she were tired and overdone. He would go up and suggest that he should go without her, and that she should keep her bed until he returned. Going up two stairs at a time, he stopped outside her door and listened. There was no sound within the room, and, concluding that she was still asleep, he sighed and went down again.

"Tell Miss Bourne that I thought it best not to disturb her, and that I will be back as quickly as possible," he said to the butler, as he got slowly into the dog-cart, and, with a wistful glance at her window, drove off.

It was past two o'clock before he got back, and the butler met him in the hall, and, with a grave face, said—

"The earl would be glad if your lordship would see him in his writing-room."

Dalesford nodded, and strode quickly across the hall. At the drawing-room door he paused and looked in. He had failed to see Diana on the terrace; perhaps she was in there trying some music or reading; but the room was empty, and he went on to the earl's. The old man was seated in his chair with the paper, behind which he almost hid his face, as he said, with a cheerfulness which instantly struck Dalesford as forced—

"Oh, you've got back, Vane. Have you—er—seen Diana?"

"No," replied Dalesford. "Where is she? She is not—ill?"

"No, no," said the earl quickly. "She—she is out somewhere; with Mabel and young Selby, very probably. Really"—testily—"these young people must not be allowed to—to ramble about the place in this irresponsible way, without leaving word where they are going. Of course Diana is with them, but— Here is a telegram for you, Vane."

He handed it across the table, and Vane murmured "Thank you," but did not open the ugly envelope; he was too absorbed in Diana.

"She was asleep when I left this morning," he said. "She was to have gone with me; but I thought she was better resting." As he spoke he took out the telegram, and the words died on his lips, to be followed by a sharp exclamation.

"What is it, Vane? What is it?" demanded the earl quickly and nervously. "What a hideous invention the telegraph is! I've not yet got used to it. It seems to me that people should find time—"

"It is from Diana," said Vane almost to himself. "She is in London."

"Diana—in London!" echoed the earl with amazement. "In London? Surely, Vane, there is some mistake."

"Listen, sir," said Vane; and he read the telegram aloud—

"I am going to London unexpectedly, and will write from there.
DIANA."

The earl frowned, but drew a breath of relief; Vane stood staring at the telegram with a surprise too keen to permit of reflection or conjecture.

"Tut, tut!" said the earl. "Gone to London unexpectedly. What—?"

"Mrs. Burton must be ill," said Vane in a low voice. "And yet, no; Diana would have said so, would have been sure to say so."

"She must have heard some news, received some message," said the earl. "She has not been seen for hours; I can find no one who has seen her the whole of the morning—indeed, since last night."

Vane went to the bell and rang it.

"Ask Miss Bourne's maid to come here, please," he said to the servant.

"Ah, the maid!" exclaimed the earl. "Of course. How quick you are, Vane!"

"Where Diana it concerned—yes," responded Vane with a smile. "Janet will tell us all about it. Don't be alarmed, sir; there is no cause for anxiety."

"I'm not alarmed," retorted the old man irritably. "Good heavens, why should I be? There is nothing ominous in a lady going to town suddenly. Depend upon it, she has received an important communication from her modiste or the man who is making her boots." He laughed, and Vane nodded and smiled; but neither of them looked reassured; and Vane went to the window and drummed on the pane until his father got him away by asking him to look at a business letter he had received.

Presently Janet entered. She looked pale and frightened; for both the earl and Vane, though kind and courteous to their servants, as became their rank and breeding, were held in awe by them.

"Oh, Janet," said Vane, as casually as he could, "did your mistress leave any message for me?"

"No, my lord," replied Janet in a low voice. "I—I have not seen my mistress since she went out early this morning—"

"Early? What do you mean by early?" asked Vane involuntarily; and he would have recalled the hasty question, but it was made; and it seemed to be the last straw to Janet's endurance, for she began to cry in a subdued fashion.

"A little before seven, my lord. I met my mistress ready dressed, coming from her room; she said—"

"Why do you cry?" asked Vane rather sternly, as she paused to check a sob. "There is no cause for alarm. Your mistress has wired to say that she had to go to London suddenly."

Janet fought with her agitation, and hastily wiped her eyes.

157

"Oh, I'm so glad, my lord! I—I mean that my mistress looked so ill this morning that I was afraid—that I thought something might have happened, some bad news—"

"You appear to indulge in singularly baseless apprehensions, my girl," broke in the earl reprimandingly. "Lord Dalesford and I sent for you in case you could add anything to the information which the telegram gives us; a telegram is necessarily short. Your mistress had a restless night, and, waking with a headache, went out for a walk. She was better, I hope, when she returned?"

"I—I—don't know, my lord," replied poor Janet, ready to sink into the earth under the sternness of his voice and glance; for the earl, aware of her affection for Diana, had generally a smile and a kindly word for her when he met her. "My mistress did not come back."

"You told me that Miss Bourne was asleep when I asked for her after breakfast," Vane reminded her.

"Yes, my lord. I—I thought she had come back and gone to bed again. I listened at the door and did not hear her moving; and she had not rung. She had told me not to disturb her—and she sleeps so lightly that I was afraid to go in, to open the door even."

"Has your mistress taken any luggage?" asked Vane as casually as before.

"No, my lord," replied Janet, beginning to threaten tears again. "That's—that's what's upsetting me so. She must have gone to London without anything; and without me to take care of her—"

Vane nodded by way of dismissal, and Janet, fighting with another attack of tears, was leaving the room when the earl called her back.

"It is a very terrible thing that your mistress should make a journey to London, to visit some friends, without her luggage; but it is not so terrible as to serve as an excuse for your weeping, my girl. Be good enough to dry your eyes—and hold your tongue."

Then—the worm, especially the loving worm, will turn—Janet flashed an indignant glance at the grand earl.

"My lord, I—I don't deserve it!" she said. "I—I never talk of my betters, especially of my dear mistress."

There was silence when she had gone, then the earl said—

"Seven o'clock; no telegram could reach here until half-past eight or nine."

"Eh? What, sir?" Vane said. "No telegram? She may have met the man bringing one that came last night; she must have done so."

"Of course, of course!" exclaimed the old man, welcoming the suggestion. "Or—or one of the other maids, Janet being out of the way, may have taken it to her room."

"But she did not come back to the house," said Vane absently. Then suddenly he drew himself up and, with a hauteur he seldom displayed, said—

"'Pon my soul, sir, we're discussing this little journey of Diana's as if there were some mystery in it. We are both rather absurd, don't you think?"

"Yes, yes; we are, Vane!" responded the earl gratefully. "Deuced absurd! And it's all so explicable. The child met the man with a telegram saying that a relation was seriously ill—Mrs. Burton, very likely. Diana may, in her flurry, have forgotten to put that in—"

"Yes. I think I'll run up to town, and down to Rivermead—"

"No, no," said the earl, with a return to nervousness. "I would not. She may have gone somewhere else, in quite a different direction. The letter saying where she is will reach us to-morrow, and you can go to her and bring her back. You can take Mabel.—Well, what is it? Come in!" he broke off testily, as someone knocked at the door.

Lady Selina entered.

"Oh! sorry to disturb you, Edward; but have you heard anything of Diana?"

Vane looked at her calmly, and even smiled, as he said easily—

"Oh yes. She has run up to town on some sudden business—she is going to be married, you know, Aunt Selina. And I am going up to-morrow to travel back with her. I'll take Mabel, please. Perhaps you will tell her that she's going?"

Lady Selina opened her lips, but changed her mind, and with a nod went out.

"Now, sir, we'll leave it at that," said Vane with quiet decision. "I think I'll take a gun or two and try that West Spinney. Something will have to be done with it, by the way, this winter; the cover wants thinning."

The two men talked about the West Spinney with unnecessary earnestness for some minutes, then Vane went out.

He shot until the light faded, then he tramped home and dressed and came down to dinner outwardly serene and smiling, but fighting with the vague dread, the shadowy fears that gathered about him. It was hard to be compelled to listen to, and answer, Mabel's questions; and as she followed him into the smoking-room with them, his restraint almost gave way, and, with a roughness unusual in his treatment of her, he bade her go and see about her packing—or flirt with Bertie.

"I shall have time for both, thank you, Vane," she retorted haughtily. "Good heavens, I hope no one will be so desperately in love with me as to become transformed by my temporary absence into a perfect bear.—Bertie, shall we play just one game of billiards?" she asked that quite willing young gentleman, and marched off with him, her head aloft, her "red-ripe" lips pouting.

Vane sat up late that night, smoking alone and hard, and thinking of Diana and her sudden journey. A cloud of darkness and gloom seemed to have fallen on the whole place; the hours dragged along with weary, tardy feet. Great heavens! what should he do if—if anything happened to her, if for some unimaginable cause she disappeared from his life!

Calling himself a nervous idiot, he at last went to bed—to lie awake and count the hours as he had counted them in the smoking-room. But he would not get up earlier than usual, and when he got down and went for his accustomed walk before breakfast, he would not stroll to meet the postman.

Indeed, when the letter-bag was placed beside him, he did not hasten to unlock it, but helped himself to some bacon before doing so, though there was already some on his plate. Mabel and Bertie were at the table, and he opened the bag and tossed them their letters. Among his was an envelope, a plain, cheap envelope, addressed to him in Diana's handwriting. He took it up, feeling Mabel's eyes upon him, but he could not open it.

"Diana—she has written?" asked Mabel eagerly.

He nodded, took up his letters and left the room. When he had reached his own den he opened the letter and read it with feverish haste. For a moment, as he read, the room seemed to spin round with him, and he looked up in a dazed, bewildered way, as if he were not certain of the meaning of the words he had been reading. Then he looked down again, re-read the uneven, broken lines, blurred here and there, as if with tears, and at last sank on to the table and, still holding the letter, stared before him, as a man stares when he has received from judge or doctor his death-sentence.

The minutes passed, struck out with a thin, shrill note by the finger of Time with its scythe in the antique French clock—the only sound that broke the intense silence, save that of his laboured breath; then he straightened himself, and, walking slowly, as if his feet were shod with lead, went down the hall and up to his father's room. The earl's valet met him at the door.

"Yes, my lord; the earl is awake."

Vane went in and approached the bed. The earl was sitting up, with a cup of chocolate before him. He put it aside and looked hard at Vane with keen apprehension, then averted his eyes, and, in a low voice, said—

"You have heard— Wait! Is—is it bad news? Your face—"

"It is bad news," said Vane huskily. "I—I do not understand it. She—she has gone."

"Gone! What—what do you mean? No, no!" as Vane held out the letter. "I cannot see. The—the light is bad. Read it—you."

Vane's voice refused to come at his command for a moment or two; then, almost inaudibly, he read—

> "LORD DALESFORD,—I have left the castle. I have made a discovery which renders it impossible for me to be your wife, impossible for me to see you again. I know how hard it will be for you to believe this, to accept it; almost as hard as for me to write it. But it is the bitter truth. Between us there has opened a gulf which nothing can ever bridge. Oh, if I could only tell you! But I cannot. And for my sake you will not, if you can still love me, if you can bear to think kindly of me, ever seek to learn the cruel thing that has separated us for ever. We are separated, and while life lasts, from this moment. If you still retain one gentle feeling for me, one spark of the old tenderness you have lavished on me, you will grant the request that I make: that you will not follow me, seek to find me; but think of me as one who is dead, as indeed, indeed, I must be to you. I am suffering—oh, when I remember all the love you have lavished on me, when I think of your father, who has been a father to me— But I cannot write any more. Grant my prayer, and let me hide myself from your sight and from the sight of all who have

**loved and cared for me. You will do this? It is I, Diana, who loved
you so dearly, who pray to you.**

DIANA."

An intense silence followed the last words of the piteous letter; and father and son stared before them, each avoiding the other's eyes; but Vane heard the old man breathing thickly, and knew that the blow had fallen on his heart very heavily.

The earl was the first to speak.

"What—what does it mean?" he asked in a quavering voice. "Where has she gone, where does she write from?"

"There is no date, no address to the letter. The date-stamp is London, sir. She —she must have bought some paper directly she arrived in London, at some shop, and written it there."

"But—but what has happened?" asked the old man with a gesture of impatience, of resentment. "She is in some trouble, of course. But what can it be? She must have heard some news yesterday morning—a telegram."

"There was no telegram," said Vane. "I asked at the post-office."

The earl uttered a cry that was almost one of rage.

"I—I hate mysteries! And a mystery in connection with Diana! It—it is an outrage; she is so—so pure, so simple-minded in her goodness—the very type of an honest Englishwoman, the perfection of breeding, of all that we mean by 'lady.' Mystery—it is too vulgar to be connected with Diana. Of course she has gone to her aunt, Mrs. Burton."

"I am not so sure of that," said Vane. "I think not."

"Of course you will go and see; you will find her," broke in the earl feverishly.

"Of course. But—I don't think that I shall find her; and if I do—"

The earl raised himself—he had fallen back—and stared at him angrily.

"You will bring her back, Vane. Do you understand?" he said almost fiercely. "You will bring her back, wherever she is, whatever has happened. I will hear from her own lips the meaning of this letter. If she is in trouble, here"—he struck his breast—"is the old man who loves her like a father. Let her come to me.— Why the devil, sir, do you stand gaping there?—I beg your pardon, Vane; I humbly beg your pardon! Forgive me! I forgot myself. I know you are suffering." He looked at Vane's white, haggard face pityingly.

Vane nodded. "I will find her if she is to be found; but I doubt my ability to bring her back," he said. "Diana would not have written this, would not have killed the heart in my body, without sufficient cause. This is not the outburst, the raving, of an hysterical woman. Diana is the last woman to give way to hysteria. There is some cause, some terrible reason, for her flight, for her—I was going to say—desertion. She has said that I am not to follow her, that nothing would induce her to be my wife, to return to me; and—I know Diana as well as love her, sir."

"What do you think it is?" asked the old man in a whisper.

Vane shook his head. "I can't even guess; I can scarcely think. My brain is in a whirl. I feel— Bah! Think!" He laughed slowly, a laugh which made his father wince; for there was a touch of the madness of despair in it. "Think! I am like a man walking in the dark—with the devil at my elbow! I will order a special, and get to London. You will say nothing, sir?"

"No, no! And—and tell her, Vane, that *I want her*. That she has taught me to love her as my own daughter, and that her place is here, here by the side of a very feeble old man! Bring her back by force, if necessary!" He fell back and covered his face with his trembling hands.

Vane smiled grimly. Force and Diana! He sent down to the station to order the train; then went to his room and told his man to pack a small portmanteau. On his way down, dressed for the journey, he met Mabel.

"I shan't want you, after all, Mab," he said with ghastly cheerfulness. "Diana is with her aunt; I'm going to join her there."

"I knew it was that!" exclaimed Mabel. "She is worse, I'm afraid. Oh, Vane, I'm so sorry for her and poor Diana! It will put off the wedding, I see by your face."

"Yes, I fear so," he assented. "Be a good girl."

He paced up and down the smoking-room with feverish impatience until the man came back; it would take an hour and a half to get a special.

Wondering how he should endure those ninety minutes, ninety ages of inaction, Vane went into the hall and met the earl. His face looked white and drawn. Beckoning Vane into his own room, he said, in a shaky voice—

"Take those diamonds up with you, Vane. I can't bear to look at the safe—to think of her as she looked with them on. Take them to the bank. Here is the key —my hand shakes—"

Vane inserted the key and endeavoured to turn it.

"Wrong key," he said; but the earl shook his head.

"No, no, it's the right one. Never mind, never mind!"

Vane tried to take out the key, but it stuck fast.

"Something wrong," he said, and mechanically he knelt on one knee and examined the keyhole. "Someone has been tampering with the lock. It has been cut by a sharp tool, a drill."

"What!" cried the earl. "Do you mean that a thief has been at work; that the diamonds, *her* diamonds, have been stolen!" He rang the bell. "Send for Donald!" he said sharply to the servant. "Tell him to bring an axe, an iron bar. Her diamonds gone!"

"What does it matter, sir?" said Vane with weary indifference. "If she has gone—" he made a gesture of despair.

The servant found Donald about the house, and brought him. The giant drew himself up and saluted.

"Open that safe, Donald!" said the earl.

Donald looked at it with an impassive countenance, and shook his head doubtfully.

162

"I'm thinkin' that's easier spiered than dune, laird," he said. "But it's auld, and may yield. Stand ye back; laird, and gie me my swing."

They stood back, and Donald swung his axe and struck the safe upon its lock. The key had partly turned it, and the tremendous blow shot back the bolts.

The earl went to the safe, and, with a cry of surprise and relief, took out the jewel-case, unlocked it, and showed the jewels to Vane.

"They are here!" he said. "You are mistaken in thinking—"

"No, the safe has been tampered with; these are steel filings"—Vane pointed to a little heap that had fallen to the floor of the safe. "Someone has been here."

Donald strode to the window, and, examining the bars, displaced the one that had been sawn through.

"The Master's reet, laird," he said. "It haf been a thief." He sprang on to the window-ledge and looked down. "The footmarks have been left, ye ken."

The father and son exchanged glances, and the earl with a "Thank you, Donald, that will do. You will say nothing of this, please," dismissed Donald.

With a grim nod Donald saluted again and went out; and Vane and the earl stood looking at the jewel-case in Vane's hand.

"Do you understand; can you make anything of it?" asked Lord Wrayborough in an agitated whisper.

Vane shook his head. The matter seemed so small, so trivial a one compared with that which was breaking his heart, that he was surprised at his father attaching any importance to it.

"Some burglar has been at work and was disturbed," he said. "You will instruct the police— No! Better say nothing about it, sir. It will attract attention to —to Diana's sudden departure."

The earl looked at him with flashing eyes, with indignant amazement.

"Are you connecting this—this burglary with Diana? You must have gone mad, Vane!"

Vane made a gesture of denial. "Connect it with Diana? How, sir? How can it concern her? No, I meant that it would be better not to call attention to anything that has happened here lately."

The earl drew a long breath. "Forgive me, Vane. I—I—my head is spinning round. You are right. We'll say nothing about it. Donald can be trusted. He is as secret as the grave. I'll lock the door. But all the more reason now for taking the diamonds to the bank. We must keep them safe for her, Vane! Isn't it time you started?" he broke off impatiently.

Nothing shall be said of Dalesford's journey to town. They cleared the line, in as far as they were able, for the special, and he reached Rivermead late that same night. As he went up the avenue, through which he had walked—how often!—with Diana's hand or arm linked in his, he looked round as if he were moving in a dream. There was a dim light in the hall, and in answer to his ring a servant, with widely opened eyes of surprise, dropped him a frightened curtsey and said that Mrs. Burton was in; and she led him to the drawing-room. Mrs. Burton was lying back among some cushions in a chair by the fire, her eyes closed, her hands folded in her lap.

She started at the sound of his name and leant forward, gazing at his face, white and haggard with sorrow, and that which is harder to bear than sorrow—suspense.

"Diana!" broke from her thin lips.

He took her hand and bent over her. She looked so ill, so frail, that he almost feared to tell her; for he knew by the tone of her cry that Diana was not there.

"Diana is not here?" he said, as quietly as he could.

"No," she responded. "Is she—has she—"

"She has left Glenaskel," he said, drawing a chair near her, and looking at her with a forced smile. "She left suddenly, so suddenly that we feared you were worse."

She was silent for a moment; then she said—

"She did not tell you where she was going?"

"No; she sent me a telegram and then a letter. In neither did she explain why she had left me so suddenly. She is in trouble. I will read you the letter, though it is sacred to me; but you must know what she says, so that you can help me to find her."

He read the letter and looked at her waitingly. She had grown paler, whiter, than before, if that were possible, but her eyes were fixed on the opposite wall, and her thin lips were drawn together with, as it seemed to Vane, an expression of determination.

"I cannot help you," she said hoarsely. "I cannot help you. Diana—Diana is her own mistress. Oh, my God, gone! Gone! She is free to come and go as she pleases! I am not answerable; I"—her voice rose suddenly to a thin cry of resentment, of complaint—"I warned her; I opposed this marriage, Lord Dalesford. From the bottom of my heart I warned her. But she would not listen. She turned a deaf ear. She went her way, and it has led her— Oh, my child, my child!" The shrill note died into a wail; but suddenly she stretched out her hand as if to ward him off. "I will say no more, I will answer no questions. I do not know. I know nothing, nothing! She has gone of her own free will and accord. She did not come to me. She will never come back to me! Never, never!"

Vane, sick at heart with dread imaginings, tried to calm her.

"Tell me this, only this," he pleaded huskily. "Is she in any peril? Is she—? Heaven and earth, what can I ask you? It is all a dark mystery, an accursed juggle! Surely, surely you want to see her, to have her back, to restore her to me! I love her. Do you hear? I love her, though you do not seem to do so.—Oh! I beg your pardon! Forgive me, but—"

She had risen and was looking down at him, fear, resentment, a strange mixture of emotions, depicted on her white face and in her dilating eyes.

"I do not love her!" A laugh of ghastly mockery distorted her face. "I do not love her! You do not know what you are saying."

"I don't," he said with a groan. "I am half mad with my anxiety, Mrs. Burton. But, for God's sake, bear with me—and help me! Only tell me where I can look for her."

She had sunk down again, calm now, or what seemed like calm, after her passionate outburst, and she turned her face from him and stared at the fire as she replied, with dogged sullenness—

"No; I can't help you. I do not know where you should look for her. If Diana has gone into hiding from you, you will not find her, Lord Dalesford. She—she is clever. She knows what she is doing. You will go to the police, I suppose?" she asked suddenly.

Vane shook his head. "You know I cannot do that." It seemed to him that she drew a breath of relief. "I cannot drag my dear one's name in the mire of a police hue-and-cry. I must find her myself, unaided—if you still refuse to help me."

"I do not refuse," she said, with the same dogged manner. "I am powerless. You do not know Diana."

"I do not know her?"

She shook her head. "No. If she has resolved to hide from you, to have done with you, nothing will move her. I know the blood, the temper that is in her."

He was silent a moment, then he rose.

"I will go. I have already wasted much time. If you hear from her—"

"I will write to you, if she does not forbid me," she said.

He shook her hand, and she let it lie in his limply, lifelessly; then he left her, telling the maid, as he went out, to go to her mistress; for he feared that Mrs. Burton would collapse when he had gone. He stood looking at the lawn, the river, with an anguish beyond words; then went back to London to begin his search.

CHAPTER XXIV

ONLY A BEGGAR

FORTUNATELY for Diana, she had to change at Perth; fortunately, because as she walked along the platform she saw a woman on one of the seats nursing a little girl, who was crying fretfully, as if in pain; and Diana, who never could listen unmoved to the cry of a child, went up to the woman and asked her what was the matter with the little one.

"She's ill, miss," said the mother. "I'm going to the hospital for a trouble of my own, and I'm taking her to her aunt to take care of while I'm in."

Diana winced, but smiled bravely.

"You look ill and tired."

"I am that, miss."

"Let me hold her for you while you go to the refreshment-room and get some milk. We'll all go."

Too touched for words by the young lady's kindness, by the angelic pity and sympathy in the beautiful eyes, the sweet, sad voice, the woman, with a threat of tears, handed her the child; and Diana got them some milk and a bun for the little girl. It seemed to her that a watchful and merciful Providence had sent her the mother and child to divert her from her own great, overwhelming sorrow; so, very wisely, she went into a third-class carriage with them, and insisted—"I'm well and strong; and I'd love to have her"—upon holding the child, who, as fascinated as her mother by the "booful lady," lay with her curly head against Diana's bosom and listened to the story of Cinderella, until she fell asleep.

The mother herself also dozed, but sleep held aloof from poor Diana; she lay back with wide-open eyes, and drew pictures of her past happiness with the pencil of grief and despair.

When they reached the terminus, the woman took the child from Diana.

"God bless you, miss," she said. "You've got a kind heart. You're fond of children; may He send you many of them to love and to love you in return."

For the first time since the blow that had shattered her life, Diana's eyes filled with tears; a lump rose in her throat, and she could only shake her head and smile the smile that covers a broken heart.

Diana was no daintily reared exotic, to be blown hither and thither helplessly in the sudden blast of misfortune. The experience of her early days came back to help her; and she made her plans. Just before she and her aunt had gone to Wedbury, they had put up at a small boarding-house in Bloomsbury, and she now took a cab and had herself driven there; stopping at a stationer's to write to Vane the letter, every word of which she had gone over in her mind during the journey.

The landlady had a vacant room, a small room at the top of the house; and, remembering Diana, accepted her as a boarder. It was not until Mrs. Parsons looked round for the luggage that Diana recollected that she had nothing but the clothes she was wearing; but Mrs. Parsons, on being told that Diana had come up so suddenly that she had no time to bring anything, offered to lend her some of her daughter's things; and at once brought them. Diana would have liked to rest, but after she had had a cup of tea in her own room, she went out and purchased a few articles—the cheap things which are to be found in the shops of the great thoroughfares in that locality; and as she did so, the sense of unreality, of moving in a dreamland, almost confused her.

It was not until she lay in bed, exhausted mentally and physically, that the full weight of her sorrow came crushing down upon her and racked her weary, aching head. Vane! It was Vane who was uppermost in her thoughts. What must he be suffering now, and how much keener still would be his agony—for she measured it by her own—on the morrow, when her letter reached him?

Vane! She should never see him again. He would learn to forget her—ah, no, no, surely not! Not forget her! He would remember her, if in the remembering he were forced to curse her for wrecking his life, breaking his heart. And the earl and Mabel—they, too, would think hardly of her for the wrong she had all unwittingly done the man they loved. It was after these that she thought of her aunt. She, too, would suffer, would wonder what had happened to cause Diana to disappear. For she could not go to her aunt, who must never know, who was not strong enough to bear, the secret burden which Diana must carry to her grave. She would write to her—yes, she would write; a line of farewell, a prayer for pity.

And her own life? She closed her eyes and stifled a moan that rose from her tortured heart. Well, life, too, was a burden one must carry until one laid it in the grave and found rest.

She thought of her father. She had looked for him—with fear and trembling —at the junction; but she did not see him. The remembrance of him, the square figure with its huge head and doglike eyes, haunted her, and made the silence of the room almost unendurable. God forgive her! That she might never see him again was the prayer that cried from every fibre of her aching heart.

She was ill and weak in the morning, and the servant, a young Cockney girl, with a wide, kindly mouth and cheerful smile, brought her a cup of tea and some toast.

"I see as you looked a bit tired and knocked out, miss, last night; and I thinks to myself, 'she'd be all the better for a lie in bed in the morning.' You just drink this, miss, and turn over and get another snooze. Lor', how pale you look! An' you up from the country, too, ain't you?"

"Yes," said Diana with a sigh.

"Ah, I've never been in the country; but they talks a lot about it, them as have been there. A cousin o' mine was sent away to one o' them 'Omes, 'Omes for conval—conval—something or other; and she came back lookin' as if she'd bin a-washing 'erself in coffee. 'Well,' I sez to 'er, playful like, 'you may 'ave got yer 'ealth, Jermima, but I'm blest if you ain't lost your compleckshon!' But there! There ain't anythink the matter with ⬚⬚⬚⬚, miss. It's like ivory. What name, miss, if any letters come?"

Diana had given the name she had resolved on in the train—Mary Kendale—and the girl, remarking, with a nod, that she was christened Geraldine Araminta, but was called Polly for short, drew the clothes round Diana, patted her in a motherly fashion, and left her.

Diana lay still for an hour or two, trying to force her thoughts away from Vane to her own future. To live she must work, and she must find work quickly; for she, who had spent her childhood in poverty, knew that her small stock of money, and the sum which she would get for her jewellery, would soon be exhausted. She could teach—she knew that; but who would employ her without references? She had her certificate, and that would help her, if she could account for her life since she had gained it. When she went downstairs to the shabby room, that smelt of countless dinners and the cigars that the gentlemen boarders smoked after their evening meal, she found the room empty.

There was a morning paper on one of the chairs, and she took it up and eagerly—if the word is not ill-chosen, seeing that Vane, Vane, came between her and the paper—scanned the advertisements.

There was one by a schoolmistress who needed a teacher of drawing; and Diana read it through twice wistfully; and presently put on her outdoor things and went, by 'bus, to the address given. As she reached the door, she found a dozen or more women—how alike they all seemed, stamped by the hallmark of genteel poverty, poverty eloquent in their shabby but well-cared-for clothes, by their air of eager anxiety!—standing about the steps; and Diana took her place on the fringe of the group and waited, with head bent. At intervals a maid-servant opened the door, an applicant emerged, and the maid beckoned the next. At last, after half a dozen had entered and come out again, the servant called out—

"The situation's filled."

The disappointed ones turned away without a word, and Diana turned with them. As she did so she knocked against a girl who had been standing beside her, and Diana, seeing that she had caused the girl to drop a portfolio she had been carrying, earnestly begged her pardon, and, stooping, picked up the portfolio and held it out to her.

The girl took it, and looked up at Diana with shy, wistful eyes; they were as blue as a child's, and shone sadly in a pale, pretty face; so sadly that Diana said impulsively—

"I'm afraid a great many of us are disappointed."

"Yes," said the girl, with a sigh which she checked as if ashamed of it. "Yes. But I think we are most of us used to it. Did you notice how we turned away, as if we expected it?"

Diana nodded. "Poor things!" she said involuntarily.

The other girl looked at her curiously, shyly.

"Are you not disappointed?" she said. "But perhaps it does not matter to you as much as it does to some of us?"

"Oh yes, indeed it does," Diana replied. "I want work very badly. Are those your drawings?"

The girl nodded. "Yes. You have not brought yours?"

Diana started, and looked, and felt, foolish.

"I—I have none. Oh yes! I can draw, but I thought that they would let me try. It was stupid!"

They had walked on, and the girl now stopped.

"I am going to take a 'bus here," she said. "Good-bye."

"Good-bye," said Diana, and she held out her hand.

The girl started slightly, a faint colour came to her pale face, and, as if confused by the friendliness of a stranger, she merely touched Diana's hand, and, with an inarticulate murmur, hurried on.

Diana thought of the girl a great deal that day, and for many days after, when she, herself, was growing despairful of getting employment. For she found that in the Great City one could get anything and everything but one's daily bread. Day by day she trod the weary, flint-strewn path which he and she must tread who seek work in a town where for every place there are a thousand applicants.

She soon had to leave the comparative comfort of the boarding-house, and, descending the scale of lodging-houses by quick degrees, took refuge in an attic —it was a descent, though she had to climb three flights of stairs—in a dingy house in one of the river-side streets. With some of the money that remained she had bought a second-hand typewriter, and by a piece of good fortune had succeeded in getting some employment from one of the institutions which give out copying-work.

It was badly paid, for the supply of typewriting does not correspond with the demand, and the market is cruelly overstocked; but, by writing early and late, she earned just enough to keep body and soul together.

The winter was almost upon her, she was insufficiently clad and fed; and, as she had no money to spend on newspapers, and no time to read them, she did not see the agonised appeals which Vane inserted almost daily. Indeed, if she had seen them she would not have responded. The memory of the past was so great an agony that she tried to kill and bury it, to forget it in the daily, hourly struggle for mere existence.

But for the children—the grimy house was a rabbit warren for them—she would have lost heart altogether and let herself slip into the grave which despair digs; but at her worst and cruellest hours she could find some consolation in nursing a sick child, or feeding, with a share of her own scanty meal, a hungry one.

Desmond March had arranged to meet Garling at the night house near Leicester Square on the second night after the robbery, to share the spoils; and he went down there in a state of excitement and desperation, which he concealed behind his debonair manner and easeful smile.

The appointed time arrived, but his slave and tool did not put in an appearance, and, after waiting until the vile place was upon the point of closing, he went back to his rooms and ate his heart out until the morning paper came. With trembling hands he turned over the pages, but his bloodshot eyes could see no account of a burglary at Glenaskel Castle. What had happened? Had Garling failed? Had he sold his "master" and given him the slip?

As the days passed, and Garling did not appear, Desmond came to the conclusion that the man had betrayed him and escaped, and he began to make stealthy preparations for his own flight. Indeed, he had completed his arrangements and was on the point of leaving England when he saw a paragraph in one of the society papers. It was a discreetly and cautiously worded hint that the engagement between Lord Dalesford and Miss Bourne had been broken off; and that Miss Bourne had left England for the benefit of her health, and was likely to remain abroad for a lengthy period.

Desmond March drew a long breath and clutched the paper spasmodically. Was it true? Was he going to have another chance?

It seemed as if he were to have more than one; for as he was walking down Pall Mall that afternoon, his head more erect than it had been for weeks, a brougham stopped abreast of him, and a woman's voice said—

"Mr. March?"

Desmond started slightly and went up to the brougham. A young woman with a plain, commonplace face and a nervous smile and blush held out her hand.

"You haven't forgotten me, I hope?" she said with a simper.

She was a Miss Bangs, the daughter and heiress of a late eminent soap-boiler, one of the women who had gone down before Desmond March's fascinating face and manner. A little while ago, before Dalesford's engagement, she had almost proposed to Desmond March; but he had failed to respond; the earldom was then apparently near, and he was not down on his luck. But circumstances alter cases; and now as he pressed her hand he assured her that he had not only not forgotten her, but had thought of her every day since she had left London.

"Is that true?" she said, blushing still more redly, and with a smile of gratification widening her mouth. "Then come inside and let me drive you home for tea. I've still got my sister-in-law as watch-dog. So you've been thinkin' of me? Really, now!"

"Of course I'll come; delighted!" he said; and he opened the door, and was stepping in when a thin, girlish figure paused on the pavement behind him, and a voice he knew so well cried despairingly—

"Desmond!"

He heard it, and, with his hand on the door, looked towards her. Lucy waited, her eyes seeking his imploringly. She had not seen him for weeks, since the night he had promised to marry her and go away with her, the night he had taken her poor little savings. Surely he would leave this woman and come to her for a moment, would speak to her, at least!

"Who is that? What does she want?" asked Miss Bangs, with contemptuous surprise.

Desmond March shrugged his shoulders.

"Begging, I suppose," he drawled; and he took a shilling from his pocket and tossed it toward the white-faced girl with the piteous eyes. Then, as she recoiled with a low, heart-broken cry, he turned and entered the brougham and was driven away.

CHAPTER XXV

MABEL'S TERMS

"CAN nothing be done, my lord?"

It was Mr. Starkey who put the question, as he sat on the edge of his chair in the earl's room at Wedbury. It was in the afternoon, and the shaded lamp threw its greenish light upon the old man's face, and revealed its pallor and the hollows grief and disappointment had dug in it.

He shook his head and drew his thin white hand across his brow with a weary gesture.

"Nothing, I should say," he replied. "I have not seen Vane for weeks, for months. Have you?"

Mr. Starkey gave a low negative.

"I—I have heard of Lord Dalesford," he said hesitatingly.

"So have I. Who has not?" said the earl bitterly. "He must be mad; and if he is not already so, will be. No man could lead the life he is leading for long. They tell me—Captain Mortimer told me—that he is terribly changed—the shadow of his former self—and that he looks as if he were going to—" His voice broke, and he shaded his eyes with his hand. "I was afraid that it would end in this way. We Wrayboroughs take things seriously where our hearts are concerned: you know that, Starkey."

"And it is the awful suspense, uncertainty," murmured Mr. Starkey. "It is that which has told upon Lord Dalesford. I should have thought it impossible for anyone to disappear so completely." He went on, after a pause, "Especially so beautiful, so distinguished a young lady as Miss Bourne."

The earl nodded.

"Yes. And God knows every effort to discover her has been made; no stone has been left unturned."

"Mr. Fielding?"

"No; he cannot help us. He has done everything short of employing the police—though I think he has gone even as far as that—but has been as unsuccessful as the rest of us. She may have left the country—no, I agree with you," as Mr. Starkey shook his head. "We should have been able to trace her at one of the ports."

"And Mrs. Burton knows nothing?"

"Nothing. Or, if she does know anything, will not disclose it. She persists in remaining dumb to all our entreaties. She has left Rivermead and gone, no one knows whither. Heaven help us, we seem to be in an *impasse*; and my poor boy — But I beg your pardon, Starkey; you wanted to see me on business?"

Mr. Starkey nodded. "Yes, my lord. It is about the Sunninglea property. I have some good news—"

"Good news! Is it possible?" murmured the earl in bitter irony.

"The railway company has come to our terms for the land they want—terms which I myself thought exorbitant—and the syndicate for the promotion of the developing company has made us an offer which exceeds even the sum I intended asking. In fact, the place has proved a small Eldorado for us. It will enable us to clear off the heaviest mortgages at once, and may turn out a perfect gold-mine, one of the kind of properties which have enriched the Devonshires and the Grosvenors. It is a singular and a curious thing—I mean the fluke, the mysterious way in which we bought back the property."

The earl pondered a moment. "I don't even remember the name of the man who bought and resold it to us," he said pensively. "By the way, ought he not to have some share in the profit?"

"He is not legally entitled to any, he has no claim on us," replied Mr. Starkey. "And—here is a mystery again—I made some inquiries about him of the solicitor who acted for him. Strange to say, he informed me that it was the only business he had done for his client; and that he knows nothing about him or what has become of him."

The earl made a weary little gesture. "You will do what is right, of course," he said. Then after a pause he sighed heavily. "The good fortune comes too late, Starkey. If—if—all had gone well, and—and Vane and Diana had married, it would have been a handsome dower for her. As it is— Have you written to Vane?"

"Yes; but I am sorry to say I have received no answer. I called at his rooms, but his man told me that Lord Dalesford would not see me; that he was asleep, and the man dared not wake him. He said that"—he stopped, but the earl signed to him to go on—"that Lord Dalesford saw no one, was not fit—not well enough —"

Mr. Starkey coughed and lowered his eyes.

The earl bit his lip. "He will not answer my letters, or Lady Mabel's," he said in a low voice. "There is nothing to be done, but—but wait."

"And hope for better days, my lord," said Mr. Starkey.

There came a knock at the door, and Mabel entered, followed by Tubby, the pug. The shadow of the Wrayborough trouble had fallen athwart her, also; and she looked pale and anxious.

"I've brought you your tea, Uncle Edward," she said. "I met Parker outside with it. How do you do, Mr. Starkey?" she added, seeking his eyes eagerly, anxiously; but he shook his head; and, smothering a sigh, she turned to the earl and poured out his tea, drew a low chair close beside him, and sat with her arm resting on his knee. He stretched out his hand and laid it on her head caressingly.

"No; Mr. Starkey has no good news of Diana or of Vane for us, Mabel," he said, for his still quick eyes had caught her inquiring glance.

173

She looked from one to the other sorrowfully.

"There will be no good news of Vane until we find Diana," she said in a low voice. "And it is not only because he cannot find her that he—he is so heart-broken, but because he knows that even if he did find her the trouble would remain. She would not come back to us."

Both the men looked at her thoughtfully. Great sorrows are not discussed freely, and little had been said, though much had been suffered by the Wrayboroughs through the mysterious disappearance of Diana, and Vane's outbreak of wild despair.

" 'Out of the mouths of babes and sucklings,' " said the earl. "Why do you say that, Mabel?"

"It wasn't I," she said with a sudden blush. "It was Bertie. He says that Diana would not have gone away if something terrible had not happened; he says that the cause of her flight was a discovery so awful that she could not tell it, and that while the cause remains she will not appear; he says that if she were to come to Wedbury to-morrow, it would not make things better. Bertie says—"

"Bertie appears to have said a great deal," remarked the earl drily, "and I imagine, from the freshness of your quotations, that he has only recently given utterance to his *obiter dicta*. When did you see him last, Mabel?"

"He is in the drawing-room with Aunt Selina," replied Mabel with a fine air of propriety. "He called to ask how you were."

"And the rest of the family, no doubt," said the earl. "He is home for the Christmas vacation, of course, and, equally of course, he spends a great deal of it with—Aunt Selina. Tell him, with my compliments, that if he cares to shoot over the preserves he is more than welcome."

"Oh, thank you, Uncle Edward—I mean, he will be very glad, I'm sure," she faltered.

But she did not offer to go, and presently the earl said—

"Are you not going to tell young Selby, Mabel?"

"Oh, he'll wait," she responded with serene confidence. "Let me give you another cup of tea, dear. Mr. Starkey will have his with Aunt Selina, won't you?"

She re-seated herself, and remained apparently quite content for some minutes, then she rose and left the room demurely; but went down the stairs two steps at a time. Bertie was in the hall, and she beckoned him on to the terrace.

"Uncle Edward's compliments, and you can have the shooting," she said.

Bertie's face lit up. "Hurrah! He's a good sort, the earl, Mabel. Given me the shooting! I—I wish he'd given me something else."

"Men are never satisfied," Mabel remarked to the evening sky. "What is it you want now?"

"The one thing to make me happy for life," said Bertie, drawing nearer to her. "If he'd only give me you, Mabel!"

She tried to meet his ardent gaze with one of astonished indignation, but her eyes fell and her voice faltered as she retorted—

"I'm not given away—with the shooting, thank you."

"And I'm not rich enough to buy you," he said sorrowfully. "I'm very little better than a pauper; and you're disgustingly rich, I know. Oh, I know! But I'm going to the Bar, and I mean to work hard, to succeed—"

"I should think you would," she put in thoughtfully. "I've heard Vane say that the thing you want most at the Bar is—er—confidence. I should imagine you had plenty of that."

"I wish I had—where you're concerned," he said with a sigh. "That's just it. If I could feel sure that you—you cared for me just a little—just enough to promise to be my wife if—when—a year or two ahead, when I've felt my feet."

"I've felt them often enough," she murmured. "They're large enough."

"Ah, be serious, Mabel!" he pleaded. "It's fun to you; but it's—it's life or death to me. I—I love you so very much, you see."

"Do you, Bertie?" she said in a low voice, with a sudden tenderness in her downcast eyes.

He caught her hand and held it in his warm one.

"You know I do!" he asseverated. "I love you with all my heart, and I shall never love anyone else. I know it's like my cheek, but—but—I can't help it. Mabel, give me a word, only a word; just say: 'I'll marry you when you've made your way—' "

She seemed to be melting; then suddenly, as if she had remembered their common sorrow, she drew her hand from his.

"No, no," she said resolutely, but with a little catch in her voice. "I won't let you make love to me, I won't promise—anything, while we're in such trouble. I can't think how you can be so heartless."

"Heartless! Oh, Mabel, and you know—"

"Wait till Diana comes back to us, till all is running smoothly again between Vane and her; then—then—ah, well, I'll see. But, oh, Bertie, I'm afraid it may be a long while before that good time comes; perhaps never! No, I won't let you kiss me! I can't think of love while we're so unhappy. Oh, Bertie, you're a clever boy—at least, I've heard somebody say so. Why don't you find her?"

She looked at him with a momentary revelation of her love for him; then, pushing him away, turned and fled.

CHAPTER XXVI

LONDON NIGHTS

VANE was taking things badly. He was not, alas! anything like the high-minded hero whom we meet in fiction—but very seldom anywhere else; there was little or nothing of the stoic in him, and, half mad with despair, knowing, as Bertie had shrewdly opined, that even if he found Diana she would not return to him, he sought forgetfulness after the fashion of men of his class.

He had lost her; and with her his life had lost its savour, and had become worthless. Diana could find some salve for her breaking heart in her work, in her love of the children whom she tended and comforted; but there was no such consolation for this man of the world; and he fell back into the old, foolish, profitless ways from which he had been roused and rescued by his love for Diana.

The old haunts knew him again. He rejoined the band of men who seek the pleasure of the hour, and live for that only. But, unlike most of them, he took the pursuits with a grim seriousness, with an object—forgetfulness—which even while he was amongst them separated him from them. So relentless was his pursuit of the waters of Lethe—that stream which evades us as surely, as tormentingly, as the flood that ebbed from the lips of Tantalus—that he gave himself no rest; and even the wildest and most foolish of his set were outdone and out-paced by the man who seemed able to do without sleep or food; and to whom no dissipation brought physical weariness.

He played, and played with the stolid indifference of the gamester for whom the game is the thing, and the winning or losing of no account. He drank, but drank as a man drinks who strives to drown thought; and so great was the strain on his nerves that the wine failed to bring intoxication. His days were spent in a whirl, the few hours that were left of the night in an attempt to gain forgetfulness in sleep—an attempt that proved futile; for when the broken, unrestful sleep came it was haunted by dreams of his past happiness, by visions of Diana—Diana with sorrow-laden eyes which dwelt on him in reproach and hopeless love.

There were some decent men in his set who watched his downward career with regret; and one or two of them had ventured on a remonstrance, but had been met with so stern and fierce a rebuff that they had been effectually silenced.

"If Dalesford has made up his mind to go to the devil—and it looks as if he had—no man alive can stop him!" said Mortimer gravely. "Of course a woman's at the bottom of it. That engagement of his was broken off, you know; and he's taking it badly. Seems funny, seeing how many other fish there are in the sea; but"—with a shrug of the shoulders—"Dalesford's just the man to want one particular fish, and run amuck if he doesn't get it. He seems to hate the sight of women, by the way— Hush, here he comes!" he broke off, as Vane entered the cardroom of the Apollo.

He was very white, there were black shadows under his eyes, and he looked thin and emaciated; but he was as erect as of old, and his eyes shone with an unnatural brightness—the baleful gleam of insomnia. He nodded to the men, and, going to a corner, lit a cigar and took up a newspaper. They let him alone for a time, then Mortimer crossed the room to him and asked him to play; and Vane, looking up at him as if awaking from a dream, rose and went to the table. Strangely enough, he usually won, and his luck was still with him this evening; but he seemed scarcely conscious of his good fortune, and played with phlegmatic, stolid indifference and an impassive countenance.

Now, while they were playing, a man entered the room from a door behind them, and, ordering a drink of the footman, glanced at the players. Two or three of Vane's party looked up at the man and then at Vane; for the new-comer was Desmond March. He appeared to be in excellent spirits; was carefully dressed, as usual, and sauntered across the room with his peculiar debonair and graceful gait. As he reached the table at which Vane was playing, he paused, nodded to the other men, and regarding Vane with a cordial smile, behind which, however, lurked the suggestion of a sneer, said—

"How d'ye do, Dalesford?"

The men held their breath, and stared before them expectantly, but Vane raised his eyes for a moment only; then, as if he had neither heard the greeting nor seen the man, he returned to his cards and went on playing.

Desmond March drew a long breath, smiled so that his white, even teeth showed between his lips; then, with a contemptuous shrug of the shoulders, went on to another table.

Vane's face had not moved by a hair's breadth; but a dull kind of rage was burning in his heart. It was the first time for years that Desmond March had dared address him publicly: how low he, Vane, must have sunk for March to have ventured to intrude upon him!

After an hour or so, during which time he could hear March's voice and low laughter quite plainly—and both voice and laughter held a note of triumph in them—Vane rose.

"I'm going," he said rather curtly.

"Oh, stay for another hand, Dalesford!" urged one of the men; but Vane shook his head.

"The room is too hot and—crowded. There are too many men here to-night."

There was something in his voice and in his manner which checked any further insistence, and they watched him as he went, looking neither to the right nor the left, out of the room.

Desmond March also openly watched him.

"My amiable cousin been losing?" he said over his shoulder. "No? Doesn't like my company, is that it? Well, I'm not particularly keen about his; and, by — I don't think any of you will be afflicted by it long. Looks to me as if he were going either to the family vault or a private lunatic asylum. There's insanity on the maternal side of the family, you know."

The bitter remark was received in silence; for Vane was liked and trusted, and Desmond March was both disliked and distrusted; but presently Mortimer, as the party went into the smoking-room, said—

"March seems to have got on his feet again. I thought he was utterly stone-broke."

"Not a bit of it," retorted another man with a laugh. "He has got hold of that Bangs girl—a million of money, they say. Oh no, no; Desmond Marches take a lot of killing."

"Most curs can swim and are hard to drown," remarked Mortimer laconically.

Vane left the club and went along Pall Mall slowly, purposelessly. The night was early yet, and he dared not go home, for the solitude of his rooms was intolerable. How much longer would it be before Desmond March, the gentlemanly blackleg, stepped into his place! What did it matter? Life was over, ceased the day his eyes fell on Diana's letter of farewell. What did it matter who bore the old title and the historic name? Men were divided into two classes, the knaves and the fools, and there was little to choose between them.

There was a moon, but the sky was flecked by scurrying clouds, and he watched them, half conscious of the symbolism they conveyed: his life was hurrying on like these clouds to a last and greater darkness. Unwittingly his steps took the direction of the river, and, looking up, he found himself on the Embankment. The night was a bitterly cold one, and even the outcasts and homeless ones, who generally find refuge on the hard seats, had been driven to more sheltered spots; but Vane did not feel the cold; the fever born of fast-lived days and sleepless nights was in his blood; and presently he dropped on to one of the seats and gazed moodily at the lights on the river. He was looking at one of the most beautiful and marvellous sights in the world, but he was blind to its marvel and its beauty, for he was seeing dimly, vaguely, the face of the woman he had loved and lost. A policeman passed and glanced at him doubtfully; then, thinking it might be one of the members of the House of Commons, which was still sitting, he paced slowly on.

After a time Vane felt drowsy. The cold air, the swish-swish of the river as it lapped against the great stone wall, lulled the overstrained senses, and, folding his arms across his breast, he fell into the first sound sleep he had had for weeks, for months.

Only a little while before Diana had risen from her typewriter, with a sigh, and had gone to her attic window and looked at the clouds driven across the moon. She had been working for many hours, her head was hot and throbbing, her hands stiff and aching. She opened the window, and the cold air seemed to woo her while it revived her.

It would be well if she got a little exercise before trying to sleep. Mechanically she put on her outdoor things—all too worn and thin for such a night—and went softly down the narrow stairs. Drawing her shawl closely round her, she passed out, walking quickly out of the dreary street on to the Embankment; but she was arrested by the sight of a small boy crouching in a corner of one of the recesses. He was awake and shivering with the cold, his head sunk on his breast, his hands clasped together, as if for warmth. Diana, with an inarticulate cry of pity, bent over him, and at her touch he started and shrank, thinking it was his natural foe with the perpetual "Move on!"

"No home, nowhere to go?" said Diana. "Oh, poor boy, poor boy! It is too bitter a night for you to sleep here; and it's too cold to sleep, isn't it?" She took some coppers from her purse—there was little else there!—and put them into his grimy hand. "Run to the nearest lodgings, dear," she said.

The boy clutched the money and, staggering to his feet, drew his rags together, stared at her, as if he thought he was dreaming, and without a word of thanks, shuffled—he was too stiff to run—across the road.

Diana looked after him; then, with a sigh, walked on. The clouds had obscured the moon, and the darkness was relieved only by the mockery of a light which disgraces the greatest and richest city in the world; so that she was passing with but an inattentive glance the man who was asleep on the seat—indeed, she was quickening her pace—when suddenly the moon emerged, and its light fell full upon the face of the sleeper.

She knew him instantly. With a low cry she stopped, and, her hand pressed to her heaving bosom, gazed at him with unutterable love and pity.

This Vane, her Vane; this white, haggard-faced man! This emaciated figure the form she had loved!

The tears welled to her eyes, every fibre of her being called to him; and, by an ungovernable impulse, she sprang to him. But before she had touched him with her pitying, longing hands, she remembered. She stifled his name upon her lips and drew back. For his own sake she must not wake him, must not let him see her; for she knew that if his eyes met hers, if he touched her, though only with a finger-tip, she could not leave him again, let whatever of shame and remorse follow.

She stood and looked down at him as a mother looks at her fever-wasted child, as a wife looks at her husband doomed to death, as a lover looks at the wraith of her dearest and best beloved.

O God, how hard life was! How cruel Fate! That she should be within touch of Vane, and yet not dare, for honour's sake, to wake him!

Stifling the cry of her heart, she crept nearer—even while she strove to fly—and, bending over him, touched his cheek with her lips; then, affrighted, she flew like a guilty creature dreading detection.

Vane stirred slightly and his lips moved.

"Diana!" he cried hoarsely. "Di—!" Then he awoke with a start and looked before him with dazed eyes and a strange sense of reality in his dream.

For fully five minutes he stared vacantly at the lights and shadows of the river. At last he rose, and, thrusting his cold hands into his pockets, went to the edge of the Embankment wall and gazed below. The cold, the intensity of the dream, the seeming reality of the touch of her lips was making his heart throb painfully. Suddenly the full consciousness of the unmanly part he was playing smote him. God forgive him! All these months he had been sullying the memory of her love, had been seeking to drown in drink and dissipation the remembrance of the woman whose purity and goodness should have been sacred enough to keep his life—wrecked as it was—sane and clean. Sane? Yes, that was it; he had been mad. But he was mad no longer. Something—what was it?—a prayer of hers uttered as he slept there?—had touched him, stirred his conscience to the depths, recalled the manliness to his heart; and he was alive to the shame, the horror of his life since he had lost her.

With trembling hands he got out his case and lit a cigar; but he could not smoke. As he flung the cigar into the river the policeman returning on his beat spoke to him.

"Going home, sir? Bad night!"

Vane looked at him strangely.

"Yes," he said; "I am going home."

Diana went swiftly, shaking and trembling with emotion, towards her lodgings; but suddenly she stopped. If her touch, her kiss had awakened him, and he should follow her! With a cry of fear and yet longing, she turned aside and went in the direction of the Strand. It was crowded by the people—the happy, laughing people!—coming out of the theatres, some of them gaily on their way to supper; and, shrinking from the noise and the excitement, she passed from the big thoroughfare into one of the quiet streets. A drunken man, lurching towards her, addressed some hiccoughed words to her, but Diana scarcely saw or heard him. All her heart and mind had room for was the white, weary face she had seen in the moonlight.

Still walking on, absorbed and lost to place and time, she found herself on Waterloo Bridge. The crowd had melted, the Bridge was empty, and she stood alone at the Strand end of it, breathing painfully.

As she stood a woman passed her: a thin, wraith-like figure with its head bent, its hands clutching its cape across its bosom. Diana glanced at her; there seemed something familiar in the thin face, the fragile form. In an instant, absorbed as she was, she remembered the girl she had spoken to in the crowd of applicants for the situation of drawing-mistress, the girl with the portfolio. With a shock of surprise and pity, Diana stood and looked at her, for the face that had passed by had been eloquent of want and despair.

The impulse born of pity—and a vague fear—prompted her to follow the girl, who, hearing Diana's footsteps, paused a moment, then crossed the road, and, with a faint cry of anguish, sprang on to the stone seat in one of the recesses, and from thence to the parapet itself.

Diana called to her in terror-stricken accents, but the girl, taking no heed of the cry, flung up her arms with an awful gesture of despair and dropped into the river.

Diana stood for a moment frozen to the spot with horror, then she cried aloud, as she thought, for help; but her voice was as frozen as her form; and it was not in answer to her frenzied appeal that a man who had been coming along on the other side of the bridge, dashed across to her, demanding hoarsely—

"What is it?"

Diana, without turning her head, and gasping for breath, pointed downward. He craned over, must have seen the figure on the water, upon which the moon at that instant was beaming, and without a moment's hesitation, he turned and ran down the bridge steps. Diana, feeling sick and giddy, fled after him, and was in time to see him seize a boat and push out into the stream. The boatman and he pulled like madmen toward the spot where the girl had gone down, and presently Diana saw the man who had come up to her on the bridge almost fling himself over the boat, clutch at something with both hands, and lift it in.

The whole terrible occurrence had taken only a minute or so in the action, and Diana had scarcely recovered from her first shock before she was bending over the still form from which the water was running.

"Is she dead?" asked the boatman callously. "Sometimes they are and some-times they ain't."

"No, she's alive," said the man who had rescued her. "I can feel her heart."

"You got her pretty sharp, mister," said the boatman. "It's a case for the per-lice," he looked up and down the river. "There ought to be some of 'em near—"

"No, no!" said the man quickly. "No need for the police—poor soul! I've got some brandy"—he pulled out a flask. "Here's a sovereign for you—will you get a cab? This lady will help us."

He turned to Diana, stared at her, then shrank back, murmuring—

"Diana!"

She looked up—she was on her knees supporting the girl's head—and saw that the man was her father.

In his recognition of her he seemed to have lost consciousness of the girl ly-ing at his feet, and stood gazing; but Diana's gentle heart was lavishing its pity on the frail form resting on her bosom.

"The cab!" she said.

"Right!" he responded hoarsely, shaking himself and pulling himself to-gether. "Help me lift her. Quick! There's a police-boat coming!"

Between them, and quite easily, for their burden, alas! was scarcely heavier than a child, they carried her up the steps, at the top of which the boatman had al-ready got a cab waiting. The cabman showed a certain amount of reluctance, but Garling slipped a coin into his hand, and, supporting the girl, Diana and her fa-ther got in.

"Where to?" said the cabman.

"It will have to be a hospital, I'm afraid," said Garling moodily and anx-iously.

"No, no! My room—I live near here!" said Diana, and she gave the cabman her address.

Not a word passed between Garling and Diana until they had carried the girl to the attic and placed her on the bed; then Diana, gently signing to Garling to go outside, said, with ashen lips—

"Wait!"

The fire was still burning, there was some hot water, and Diana undressed the girl and bathed her cold limbs; and when she began to breathe painfully and heavily, wrapped her in the blankets and held her hand tightly; for she knew how terrible would be the first moments of returning consciousness. They came at last, and in a voice scarcely audible the girl wailed—

"Where am I? Oh—God forgive me!"

Diana's arm went round her.

"You are here with a friend, quite, quite safe! Lie still—oh, one moment, I will leave you for only a moment."

With trembling haste she warmed some milk, and, raising the frail form, made the girl drink it. At first she refused, but, melted by Diana's tender eyes and gentle voice, she yielded at last; and fell back on the pillow with a sobbing sigh.

Diana sat beside her, giving her more of the milk at intervals, and presently the girl's eyes closed and she fell into the deep sleep of exhaustion. Then Diana opened the door. Garling was leaning against the wall, his head sunk on his breast, his hands thrust in his pockets; the whole attitude of the square, short figure was one of utter dejection. He started at the sight of Diana, and; following her into the room, glanced towards the bed questioningly. '

"She has come-to and is asleep; but she is very weak. Oh, poor girl! poor girl! If I had been there a moment sooner—"

Her eyes filled with tears, and she bent over the bed to hide them.

Garling looked round the room with its meagre furniture and poverty-stricken aspect.

"Diana!" he said in a hoarse, reproachful whisper. "Why—why are you living here, alone, and in such a place?"

Diana's face flushed and her eyes were downcast; then she lifted them and looked at him sadly, steadily.

"I see; I know!" he said with a groan. "You wouldn't be beholden to me for —for anything, not even for food. That's a typewriter; you get your living—?"

"Yes," said Diana in a low voice. "I earn enough—" she faltered as he looked round again significantly. "I am content. Ah! you did not think that I could take —"

"My money?" His rugged face worked. "My girl, you were wrong. The money I gave you was honestly earned, every penny of it; yes, every penny of it. But you couldn't know that, seeing me at—at work that night. And you've left your grand friends and live here, in an attic in the slums! My God, I am punished! My own daughter livin' from hand to mouth; half starving, maybe, while there's thousands an' thousands, ay, a million lying ready for her! Why"—his voice dropped and he sank back to the rough form of speech of his early days —"them clothes are thin and old and not fit for this weather. And you—you as are used to every comfort and luxury— Diana, it's—it's hard on me!"

Diana turned her head away. It was not for her to remind him that the children must suffer for the sins of their fathers. But, indeed, he did not need the reminder.

"It's a hard world and a cruel," he said brokenly. "And it's full o' misery. That poor girl there—" he drew near the bed as he spoke and looked down at the white, pinched face. "Why!" he exclaimed in a whisper, "I know her! I mean I've met her before. It's the girl I saved from being run over."

Hurriedly, disjointedly, he told Diana of his former meeting with the girl they had rescued.

"I took to her the first moment I saw her," he said, gazing at the face with its still wet hair clinging to the marble-hued forehead. "She was so pretty, so—so like a little, innocent child. I wanted to help her, to keep sight of her; but she was proud and wouldn't take more than the half-sovereign, and wouldn't tell me her name. Seems as if everybody was too proud to be helped by me, Diana. Yes; that's my punishment, I s'pose. But"—almost fiercely—"you've got to let me help her now. She'll want good, nourishing food an' firing, and a doctor."

"Yes," said Diana very quietly.

His face cleared a little. "I'll see to it," he said. "I'll get"—then his brow darkened—"no; I can't be seen in it," he said moodily. "I'm in hiding. I only go out o' nights—living in a quiet place in the slums over there"—he jerked his thick thumb over his shoulder in the direction of Lambeth. "In hiding from that —that man I told you of, the man who forced me to try for the diamonds. Well, well!" as he saw Diana shudder. "We'll forget that. Ah, no, you can't, I know. And no more can I! That's the worst of it between you and me, my gel; there's no forgettin'! And you're living here like a pauper; left all your friends—half fed, badly clothed—"

He broke off with a groan, and, sinking on to a chair, hid his face in his hands. Diana wanted to comfort him, but she could find no words, could not force herself to lay her hand on his shoulder as she wanted to do. He was her father, but she still shrank from him, still inwardly shuddered at the sight of his face, the sound of his voice. She could only look at him and try to accustom herself to his presence.

Presently the sick girl moved uneasily, turned and opened her eyes.

"I am still here," she said faintly. "How good you are to me! I've seen you before. Yes; I remember. But for you I should have been lying dead in the river there. Oh! why did you save me? I wanted to die. I had nothing to live for, nothing, nothing!"

Diana quivered. How often had that cry been hers?

"Hush!" she whispered. "There is always something to live for, dear!"

"Not for me," moaned Lucy, turning her head away. "I am not fit to live. I will go home." She raised herself on her elbow; but Diana gently forced her back again.

"Not yet," she said softly. "You will stay here with me until you are better, stronger. I shall be glad, very glad to have you, for I am all alone."

"Who is that?" asked Lucy fearfully, as she caught sight of Garling.

"My—my father," said Diana with a choking sensation. "He—he helped me bring you here. There is no need to be frightened, dear."

"I will go home," said Lucy faintly; then she sobbed out, "Home! I haven't any! They—they turned me out—I had no money, not a penny—I've slept in the streets for—for ever so many nights—" her voice broke and she clung to Diana with the terror of the homeless.

Diana soothed her as one soothes a child; indeed, she seemed more child than woman.

"Hush, hush! You are here, safe and in good keeping."

"Good—good!" The white lips caught up the word. "Ah, you don't know! I'm not good! I'm not fit for you to touch. Let me go!"

She began to struggle, and Diana, half frightened, turned to Garling; but as he came to the bed the fragile figure ceased to struggle and fell back.

"I'm hot—and I was cold a little while ago," Lucy panted. "Hot! So hot! I'm burning!"

"Fever," said Garling.

Diana nodded. "A doctor!"

He bit his lip and hesitated. "Better not; not yet. Wait a little while. Hush, listen! She's raving, poor girl. Yes; I'll get a doctor."

As he turned, Lucy's voice, at first incoherent, grew clearer, and, extending her hands imploringly, she cried, in a piteous, heartrending tone—

"Don't leave me, don't desert me. Oh, keep your promise, dear! You loved me once. I'm not altered. I'm the same, and I love you, dear; oh! I love you; take me away with you, and—and make me your wife! You promised, promised faithfully; and I've waited, waited so long! Ah, don't be cruel to me, don't desert me!"

There was a pause; then suddenly her arms fell to her side, her head sank, and with a deep sob she wailed—

"He's gone. He will never come back; he's tired of me. Oh! I knew it from the first. God help me! He has gone!"

Garling looked at Diana, and Diana turned her head away and sighed.

"Some scoundrel," said Garling hoarsely. "I'd—I'd like to have him here! She's very bad. I'll fetch a doctor."

CHAPTER XXVII

LUCY'S DEATH

GARLING came back quickly with the doctor, who stood and looked at the delirious Lucy with pursed lips and the keen eyes of a man who has to diagnose more cases in a day than the ordinary practitioner sees in a week.

"Brain-fever, following on shock to a system completely run down by—yes, I should say want of food and exposure to the cold and wet." He gave the necessary directions; then, as he edged toward the door and his next patient, he said, in answer to Diana's anxious inquiry, "Will she pull through? Ahem! shouldn't like to say. All depends upon how thin the metal has worn; and it has worn pretty thin, I'm afraid. Good-bye. Look in to-morrow."

Lucy raved for some hours, then sank into the coma of insensibility; and Diana sat beside her and held her hot, wasted hand. The fact that the girl had been betrayed had in nowise dried up Diana's pity and charity; indeed, it had increased her pity and made her desire still more keenly to help the victim of a man's selfishness and cruelty. Diana had seen too much of the world of late to turn from a fellow-woman who had erred for love's sake; and she was now too skilled a student of the human face divine not to know that, wronged though she might have been, the girl was still pure at heart.

In the morning Garling came round from his hiding-place in the neighbourhood. He had brought ice, and wine, and delicacies suitable for an invalid, and hung over the bed examining the flushed face eagerly.

"If there's anything that can be done—if there's anything money can get, tell the doctor to mention it, only mention it," he said with sudden eagerness. "I've set my heart on saving her. Poor little thing! And you, Diana; you aren't going to turn from me, and refuse the things my money can buy?" he pleaded. "I tell you, I swear to you, it was come honestly by. When she's better you'll leave this place," he looked round almost savagely, "and let me make life comfortable for you?"

Diana was spared a response; for, fortunately for her, the invalid moved uneasily; and Diana went to her. The doctor came again, but still declined to give any opinion; though Garling pressed him hard and offered him a fee which made the doctor suspicious. But he had too many of the criminal class among his patients to attach much importance to the character of this rough, brusque man, and pocketed the money without question or comment.

Garling came in and out during the day, and, after looking at the sick girl, sat beside the fire, brooding.

"When she gets better she shall go away to the sea-side. Wrong time of the year? Not for the South. We can take her. I forgot; you wouldn't come, not with me."

"Yes; you forget," said Diana in a low voice. "I offered to go with you."

"I know, I know," he assented hoarsely. "You did, but—I saw your face. And you know what I am; she doesn't," he jerked his head towards the bed. "And she needn't know. I'll take care of her as if—as if she was you." He was silent a moment or two, then he said, more to himself than to Diana, "The man—I want to meet him. Yes, and I may some time."

After one of his long silences, he said suddenly—

"Where's your Aunt Mary?"

Diana shook her head. "I do not know. I have not heard."

"I understand. You've hid away from everybody because you're ashamed of me. And you're too proud to take a penny, a mouthful of food from me. But you're right, my gel! Pity I didn't die instead o' Brown. Pity!"

He said "Good-night" soon afterwards, and went out. At the end of the street he stopped and looked round him restlessly and wistfully. The silence and solitude of the den in which he was hiding were to be shunned as long as possible; instead of going home he went up the road and past the House of Parliament. The policeman, little guessing the true character of the man he was aiding, stopped the traffic so that he might cross the road. Among the vehicles was a hansom cab with a gentleman inside, who was leaning forward and regarding the passers-by absently, but as his glance rested on Garling, his eyes opened with a quick light in them, and, putting up the trap-door in the roof, he said swiftly—

"Follow that man there—the short one. See?"

"Right!" said the cabman, and he turned up toward the Park after Garling.

Presently the gentleman alighted, told the cabman to wait, and stepping quietly up to Garling, laid a hand on his shoulder, saying quite calmly and pleasantly—

"How do you do, Bourne?"

Garling started, and, turning with a swift movement, raised his hand as if about to strike; but the gentleman seized the hand and shook it, as if it had been offered for the purpose.

"Mr. Fielding!" gasped Garling hoarsely.

"Splendid memory yours; almost as good as mine," responded Mr. Fielding with a nod. "Strange, meeting you here! Are you busy, engaged? If not, perhaps you will come to my office and have a chat?"

Garling, with a look of resignation in his working face, made no refusal, and Mr. Fielding, linking his arm in his, led him to the cab. The clerks were gone, the office in darkness, and Mr. Fielding let himself in, lit the gas, and waved Garling to the chair on which Diana had sat.

"And how are you, Bourne?" he asked.

Garling eyed him stoically, and with a touch of resentment mixed with awe.

"You knew I was alive?" he said sullenly.

186

"Not exactly 'knew,'" confessed Mr. Fielding, with a touch of regret and self-reproach. "I only guessed, surmised. Why should your daughter run away and hide herself unless she had heard you were alive or seen you? And that partnership business was—thin. It was merely conjecture by deduction. Understand? And how is Miss Diana?"

"She is— How do you know I've see her—know where she is?" Garling demanded.

"Well, I know now, if I didn't a moment before," said Mr. Fielding with a grave smile. "Poor girl! Is she well—safe and well? I ask for personal reasons, Bourne, for I am fond of her; and I've suffered not a little remorse on her account. You see, I'm the cause of all the trouble."

"You? You mean me."

Fielding shook his head. "No; you couldn't help not dying; and though I think you might have refrained from turning up again—"

"You're not a father," said Garling huskily. "You've never pined for a sight of your gel, the child you left."

"No. Oh yes, I can make allowance for your paternal feelings, my good fellow. Troublesome things these same feelings. In your case they have ruined your daughter and wrecked her life."

"I know it," said Garling with a dry sob. "And you don't know all—how completely I've done it." He was thinking of Diana's discovery of him "at work" at Glenaskel. "What's to be done, Mr. Fielding? You'll help me? You always have."

Mr. Fielding shrugged his shoulders. "Afraid I can't help you here," he said with genuine regret. "I tried to play amateur Providence once, and I've made a mess of it. Of course I ought to have told Lord Dalesford of Diana's—er—parentage before they became engaged."

Garling started. "Do you mean to say that she was going to marry a—a nobleman, a swell?"

Mr. Fielding nodded. "Yes. The only son of the Earl of Wrayborough. She would have been a countess if you had not—er—inconveniently come to life again."

Garling wiped the sweat from his face.

"And—and—you kept it from them?"

"Yes," said Mr. Fielding, shrugging his shoulders again. "I thought that it would be safe to do so; I thought—no, I didn't think of anything but Miss Diana's happiness," he broke off with fierce self-reproach. "I laid the flattering unction to my soul that the secret of your—past was buried with you, and that if it leaked out after her marriage it would not matter. I was wrong, of course; both Mrs. Burton and I were wrong."

"Ah, yes; Mary!" said Garling. "She kept the secret, too. Where is she?"

"She is living in a little village near London," said Mr. Fielding. "I don't think I'll give you her address; it would only distress her to see you, to know you are alive. Though"—he mused, his eyes flashing keenly—"I shouldn't be surprised if she'd guessed it. All along she had been nervous, apprehensive. At any rate, she must guess the cause of Diana's flight. Let me see, you said Diana's address was—"

Garling shook his head. "I daren't give it you," he said uneasy. "She wouldn't like it; she—she wants to be alone."

Mr. Fielding nodded and sighed impatiently. It irked and distressed him not to be able to disentangle this ravelled skein; he, the clever Mr. Fielding, found himself helpless and impotent in this tragic case.

"I'm afraid she's right," he said reluctantly. "The sins of the fathers—I beg your pardon, Bourne; I did not mean to rub it in. Strange, the conviction that money can do everything is nowadays as strong as, nay, stronger than, any religious belief; and yet here's a case where money—and a million or more, eh, Bourne?—can't help us."

"I wish I was dead!" groaned Bourne.

"So do I," said Mr. Fielding. "Pardon, pardon! But—you're alive, you see. By the way, aren't you in—er—some little danger? Wouldn't it be rather awkward if you were seen?"

Bourne nodded gloomily. "Yes. I've a 'ticket' only."

Mr. Fielding pondered for a minute or two.

"Better leave the country," he said gravely. "No, that will scarcely do; for if you were to die in sober earnest we shouldn't believe it. Oh, I don't know what to do with you! Or for her. And I tell you frankly her future is my first consideration. The sweetest, dearest girl— O lord! Bourne, it's hard on her. And the man who loves her. He is taking it badly, and is going to the dogs. Really, if you were quite heartless—which I see you're not—you might be moved at the wreck and ruin you have all unwittingly caused. You will have actually affected the line of a peerage; for Lord Dalesford will never marry, and the title will go to his cousin, Mr. Desmond March.—Why did you start and swear, Bourne?"

Bourne had done both; and now sat staring at the lawyer's troubled countenance.

"Desmond March! Is that his name?" he asked hoarsely.

Mr. Fielding nodded. "You've heard of him? If you have, you have heard of the choicest specimen of the scoundrel and the blackleg to be found even in this scoundrel-ridden city. Yes; he will get the title, and his marriage will bring the money to clear the estates. The wicked flourish as the bay-tree—pardon, Bourne, I meant nothing personal—and Mr. Desmond March, who ought to be standing in the dock at the Old Bailey—tut, tut!—is going to marry an heiress. But this does not interest you. I only mentioned it to you to show you how far-reaching was the trouble you have caused. And you are living at—?"

Bourne shook his head doggedly.

"No; if you can't help me and her—and I don't see how you can, Mr. Fielding—I'd rather keep in hiding, even from you. God knows what we can do, where we can go!" He sighed heavily and rose.

"All this money, now, Bourne?" asked Mr. Fielding, as he went with him to the door.

Bourne turned on him fiercely. "Curse the money!" he said.

Mr. Fielding shrugged his shoulders. "Well, we'll wait a bit. Don't do anything, or leave England, until you have seen me again. Good-night."

He held out his hand, but Bourne, after a moment's hesitation, shook his head and passed out.

Mr. Fielding returned to his room, and, sinking into a chair, sighed heavily.

"Yes; amateur Providence is a risky part to play," he muttered; "especially when the dead come to life again; and one is dealing with human hearts—and a woman's among them!"

Garling, when he went round to Diana's the next morning, said nothing of his meeting with Mr. Fielding; he knew that it would cause Diana useless suffering; but he regarded her with an acuter and respectful pity, a still more intense remorse. But his resolution to leave England and take the sick girl with him had grown stronger.

"Do you think she's getting better?" he asked as he stood and looked down at her.

Diana shook her head. "I'm afraid not. The doctor came in the night—he is anxious. She is so weak." She sighed as she gently forced some milk through the scarlet lips.

"And—and her mind's fixed on her trouble," he muttered. "Go and lie down. I'll watch her."

Diana reluctantly went to the chair bedstead he had sent in, and, stretching her weary limbs on it, closed her eyes for the first time since Lucy had been brought to the attic. She must have fallen into a half sleep, for suddenly she was awakened by the sound of a knock. Garling started and looked from her to the door.

"It's not the doctor's knock," he said with the certainty of a man whose sense of hearing has been trained by years of dread of detection.

"May I come in?" said Mr. Fielding, and he entered.

Diana hushed the cry that rose to her lips and shrank back, white and trembling. Mr. Fielding took her hand and patted it, smiling and nodding at her as if he were soothing a frightened child.

"Yes, I've found you, my dear," he said, with his odd mixture of the legal and paternal manner. "By chance"—he had been watching in the neighbourhood since the early morning—"I happened to see your—Mr. Bourne, and followed him. No need to speak, my dear. I know all. Who is this?"

Diana told him of the rescue of the girl. "We do not even know her name," she said.

Mr. Fielding looked down at her, Diana's arm still held within his, and shook his head.

"Poor girl! Still the same tender heart, Diana!" he added, nodding at her. He drew her a little aside. "And don't you want to ask me about—about some old friends?" he said.

Diana drew a long breath and shook her head.

"I saw—him the other night. Oh, Fairy Godmother!" her voice broke. "I am past even your help; but if you could help *hm* !"

189

Mr. Fielding cleared his throat and frowned; it was not pleasant for the clever man to acknowledge his helplessness.

"I want you—Mr. Bourne," he said. "I am glad I have found you. I'm afraid I can't—well, put things straight; but don't you forget, please, that I am still your legal adviser. Will you come, Bourne? What a devil of a job I have had to track you!" he said after they had reached the street. "If my proper practice should ever go I shall take up the detective business. I want you to come to my office."

Garling hesitated, but Mr. Fielding hailed a cab, and gently but firmly pushed him into it.

As they entered the outer office, Mr. Fielding said—

"Wait here for a minute or two, will you?" and passing into his private room, he took off his hat to a bent, veiled figure that was seated in the clients' chair.

"Glad you've come, Mrs. Burton," he said. "I've some news for you that will surprise you!"

Mrs. Burton raised her veil. Her face was deathlike in its pallor.

"You have found Diana?" she said, moistening her dry lips. "Take—take me to her!"

"Yes; I have found Diana," assented Mr. Fielding, with a cheerfulness that was meant to have a restraining effect. "You will be glad to hear that she is—er—well, as well as we could hope. Thinner and paler, yes. But"—with a shrug of the shoulders—"what could you expect? For, you have guessed, of course, she knows who and what her father is."

Mrs. Burton looked at him strangely.

"Yes, I thought so," she said in an expressionless voice. "It was the discovery that sent her into hiding?"

"And she has discovered that her father is alive," said Mr. Fielding softly.

"Benjamin—alive! Oh, my God!" cried Mrs. Burton.

"Alive and well. It seems that the report of his death, the certificates, were applicable to his partner, who—"

Mrs. Burton rose and faced him with an awful mixture of despair and defiance.

"He is here," she said. "Take me to him!"

Mr. Fielding opened the door and beckoned Garling in.

For a moment or two brother and sister looked at each other; then Mrs. Burton gasped—

"Benjamin!"

"Mary!" he said. "Yes; I'm alive—worse luck! I want to thank you for the care of my gel, Diana. She's told me how good you've been to her, how you've kept the secret. It was my fault that it was ever found out; but I'm grateful to you, Mary."

She seemed to be struggling for breath and speech. At last the gasped—

"Take—take me to her."

Mr. Fielding had slipped out of the room and ordered a cab, and they drove to the house in which Diana was lodging; and during the journey Mr. Fielding told

Mrs. Burton as much as was necessary of the plan by which Bourne had deceived him.

They went up the rickety stairs as quietly as possible, and Diana opened the door to them. She flew into her aunt's arms, and Mrs. Burton pressed her to her bosom and bent to kiss her; but suddenly drew back and eyed her almost with fear.

"You have found me, Aunt Mary!" sobbed Diana, struggling with her sobs because of the sick girl lying there. "And I am glad, though I ought to be sorry."

"Yes, I have found you," said Mrs. Burton chokingly, as if she were fighting down her emotion. She turned suddenly and glanced at the bed. "This is the girl Mr. Fielding has told me about? She looks ill—very ill. You must come away, Diana, come with me. I—I have every right to you."

Garling turned. He had been bending over Lucy with anxious, careworn eyes.

"You've every right? Not now, Mary. She—God help her—she's my daughter."

Mrs. Burton looked at him fixedly and drew her lips together, as if to stay their tremor.

"No, she's mine," she said in a low, expressionless voice.

"Yours!" said Garling, staring at her. "Yours? Ah! yes, you mean that you've been a mother to her."

"I *am* her mother," said Mrs. Burton in a hollow voice, the voice of a person whom despair has made callous and insentient. "When you left your child I meant to do my duty by her, but—but I was always respectable; and my gorge rose at her—a convict's child! I sent her out to nurse. The people grew fond of her and adopted her—they gave her their name, treated her as their own—I saw to that, I've no need for reproach—and—and—oh, she was well cared for. And when the money came—here is my sin and here is my punishment," she looked at Diana, who stood gazing at her in breathless amazement and terror—"I spent it on my own child."

Mr. Fielding stepped forward. He did not look astonished, for if the stars had fallen he would not have expressed surprise: but he took Diana's hand and held it firmly.

"We were poor, Diana and I, well-nigh starving, while your child I knew was well cared for. I spent the—money on Diana. As she grew up I learned that you were making a great deal of money, that you were rich and—and—I pretended that Diana was your child."

Garling leaned against the mantelpiece, his hands clenched at his side, his eyes fixed on Mrs. Burton's glassy ones.

"And *my* child, my own child, where—where is she?" he demanded hoarsely, fiercely.

Mrs. Burton shook her head. "I do not know," she said. "You can kill me if you like, Benjamin. I have sinned; I have sinned, and I am ready to bear my punishment. I do not know. I lost sight of her. The people who adopted her came to London—"

Diana was conscious of, rather than saw, a movement on the part of the girl lying on the bed.

"Hush!" she whispered breathlessly, warningly.

Lucy's head tossed from side to side with the restlessness of fever, her parched lips opened; and almost before Diana finished giving her some iced milk, she was talking.

"We'll go!" she said with a glad note in her feeble voice. "We'll go away together. And we'll be married. No, no, I forgive you for the past, I forgive you because you are good to me now. I shall be your wife at last, Desmond, I shall be Mrs. Desmond March—"

Garling, who had been standing by the bed looking pityingly down at the fevered face, started and bent lower.

"Desmond March!" he said in a hoarse whisper. "Why—My God!—"

"Hush! hush!" warned Diana. "She is coming-to. Stand—stand back."

"We'd better go outside," said Mr. Fielding in a hushed voice; but Mrs. Burton lingered, staring at the girl as if fascinated; and Garling remained standing by the head of the bed as if incapable of moving.

Diana raised Lucy to her bosom and smoothed the hair from the thin face. Presently the blue eyes opened, a painful, puzzled expression came into them as she gazed up at Diana's tender, pitiful face.

"Where am I? Ah! yes, I remember. You are the girl who brought me here. Have I been very ill? I'm—I'm sorry!" she sighed. "Will you tell me your name?"

Diana drove back her tears and forced a smile.

"My name is Diana. Diana—" she paused and looked at Mrs. Burton.

"It is—a—pretty name," said the sick girl faintly.

"And yours? Will you—do you care to—tell me yours?" asked Diana, and she bent her lips nearer to kiss her.

Lucy put up her hand, a hand too feeble to push Diana's face away.

"Don't," she faltered so faintly that the others could scarcely hear it. "I'm—I'm not fit. You don't know. I'm—I'm not married as—as I ought to be."

"Oh, my dear, my dear!" breathed Diana, the tears rushing to her eyes.

"Yes; I'll tell you my name. It is Lucy, Lucy Edgworth— Oh, who—what is that?" she broke off, for Mrs. Burton had uttered an exclamation, a cry of surprise, terror.

" 'Lucy—Lucy! Edgworth!' It's the name of the people who took the child. It's—it's— Oh, my God!"

Garling thrust her aside, and leant over Lucy, who had sunk back as if exhausted.

"Keep—keep back!" he said hoarsely. "She's—she's my child! I—I knew it. My child! My little gel! My own little gel!"

He bent lower over her, his hands waving, as if itching to touch her, to grasp her, catch her to his heart; then suddenly he drew back with a cry of grief, of despair. For he had seen death too often to fail to recognise it.

Lucy's eyes had closed, and a faint tremor ran through her frail form. Diana raised her in her arms and held her, while Garling's laboured breath alone broke the silence. Presently the weary eyes opened again and looked at Diana with a pathetic gratitude; but gradually the intelligence faded from them, she sighed, not sorrowfully now, but with a serene joy and peacefulness which was even more pathetic; a smile, like a flicker of winter sunshine, lit up her face; and, opening her lips, she murmured something.

Garling fell on his knees beside the bed that he might catch the words, and heard her whisper sweetly—

"I am ready, Desmond dear; quite ready. We will go away together; your wife, your own loving wife. Oh, Desmond, how happy we shall be!"

The voice ceased, and her eyes closed on the vision of happiness which had brightened the last moments of her sad and sorrowful life. She was dead.

Bourne rose, tugging at his collar as if he were choking, his eyes staring before him with a savage longing for vengeance, with a nameless horror on his face, as if the shadow of hell itself were passing over him.

"Desmond! Desmond March!" came hoarsely from his parched throat. "My child—Desmond March!"

With his hands stretched out, as if he were blind, he thrust aside those who were in his way and staggered from the room.

CHAPTER XXVIII

MISS BANGS' CONVERSION

"I AM going home," Vane had said to the policeman on the Embankment. He caught the night mail, and, there being no carriage to meet him, for he had not telegraphed, he walked from the station in the grey light of the early morning.

The butler, who met him in the hall, started and allowed an exclamation to escape him, an exclamation of surprise and dismay; for even so strong a man as Dalesford cannot pass through the fiery furnace of dissipation in which Vane had lived for the last few months scatheless; and he looked wan and haggard, the shadow of his former self.

"Don't disturb my father," he said. "I will go and have a bath."

He went up the stairs quietly; but the earl was awake; he knew his son's footsteps as he passed along the corridor; and he called to him.

Vane stopped, hesitated for a moment, then opened the door and went into the room. The earl was sitting up, his eyes fixed hungrily on the door, but he said not a word as his hand closed on Vane's.

"You've—you've come back at last," he said, after they had looked into each other's eyes for a moment or two. "Caught the night train? You—you look tired. Yes, yes! I'm—I'm glad you are back, Vane; very, very."

He fought for composure, fought with the shock Vane's appearance caused him, and forced a smile.

"I'm afraid I woke you, sir," said Vane, in the voice which had been habitual with him of late; the voice from which all the old joy and gladness in life had gone, leaving it weary and toneless.

"No, no; I was awake. I don't sleep very well now—not in the morning. Oh yes; I'm quite well—quite; a trifling cold now and then—gout, I daresay. You're looking"—he hesitated a moment over the flimsy falsehood—"well."

"A little off-colour," said Vane, with a shrug of his shoulders. "I shall pick up here soon enough."

"Yes, yes; Mabel is here—she'll be glad. Your Aunt Selina, too. I—I think I'll get up."

"No, no," said Vane, laying a restraining hand on the arm of the old man, for in his excitement he made as if to get out of bed. "Wait until after breakfast. I'm going to have a bath. I'll look in as I go down."

Both of the men hated "scenes," and though they both knew that Vane's return was something like that of the Prodigal, they mutually shrank from any signs of emotion, even while their hearts were drawn to each other as, perhaps, they had never before been drawn.

The earl nodded. "You must be tired—the long night journey—you must rest. Get some breakfast—" He stopped and dropped back with his face turned from Vane.

Vane had his bath, and when he went down found Mabel waiting for him at the bottom of the stairs.

"Oh, Vane!" she cried, as she noted the change in him; then she bit her lip and flung her arms round his neck and pressed him to her with girlish and yet maternal abandon. "I'm so glad you've come back! We've missed you so! It's such a long time, you see. Have I creased your collar?" with a laugh that belied the tears in her bright eyes. "Never mind; I don't do it often, do I? We're not a demonstrative family. But I'm so glad! And Bertie will be glad; he's coming here to lunch after shooting. Come in to breakfast. Aunt Selina's hurrying up; but we won't wait. We'll have it alone as we used to do in the old times."

There was rejoicing in the servants' hall as well as "above stairs" at the return of the son and heir; there was a flush on the butler's face as he hovered about Vane, and the footmen cast respectfully welcoming glances at him as they served him with discreet assiduity.

Mabel chatted away to him on home and local topics as if Vane had only been absent a few weeks, but her eyes when they sought his face covertly grew troubled and anxious; for she saw that though he had returned he had brought no good news with him, and that he only made a pretence of eating—he who had been used to make of breakfast a solid and substantial foundation for the day.

Presently, after the servants had left the room, he caught one of those covert glances, and, looking at her steadily, said—

"No, Mabel, there is no news."

"Oh, Vane!" she cried in a low voice. "I had hoped that you had found her!"

He shook his head and went to the fireplace, holding his hands over the logs, so that his face was turned from her. She went to him and put her arm over his shoulder with tender sympathy.

"And you can discover nothing?" she whispered.

"Nothing," he said.

As he spoke the earl entered; he had not been able to remain in bed. Vane turned to him as if suddenly nerved for a painful task.

"I have just been telling Mabel that there is no news of—Diana," he said in a low, dry voice. "And I have searched—" He paused. "Even if I had found her, I should have gained nothing but the relief from suspense. Diana will come back to us of her own accord or not at all. I know her. There is no more to be said, and"—his voice broke for a moment, then he steadied it and went on bravely —"no more shall be said. Ask Aunt Selina, all our friends, to respect our silence, sir."

The earl bowed his head.

"My poor boy!" he murmured inaudibly. "But you are right. I, too, know Diana, and feel that, while the cause of her flight remains, she will not come back to us. And—and—your plans, Vane? Have you made any; you're going abroad, perhaps?" he added with an attempt to hide his anxiety and dread; for the companionship of his son meant much to him.

"No," said Vane quietly. "I intend remaining with you, if you'll have me, sir."

The earl checked the cry of joy and relief that sprang to his lips.

"Are you sure that it is—wise, Vane? Change of scene and—"

Vane smiled grimly. "I've tried it, sir," he said. "No; I will stay here and play my part—like a man, if I can. I've been behaving more like an hysterical woman up to now—Beg pardon, Mabel; a woman would have known better than to seek forgetfulness as I have been seeking it. But that's done with." He made a gesture of renunciation. "That's a fool's game, and unworthy of—the woman I love and shall love till I die. No, no, I won't say any more!" he broke off, as the earl's lips twitched and his eyes filled with tears. "How are the birds this year? Bertie getting good sport? I wonder whether he has found any snipe in the lower marshes? There used to be a good many; but they fell off last season. That's the worst of draining. Shall we take a drive, sir, or aren't you up to it?"

"Yes, yes; by all means!" responded the earl eagerly. "We'll meet Bertie Selby and pick him up. Where has he gone, Mabel?"

"To the western woods," she replied, as promptly as if she were his keeper. "He'll be so delighted to see you. Don't be late for lunch. I'll tell them to have some of your favourite curry, Vane."

Happier than he had been for many a sad and weary month, the earl sat beside Vane and talked about the estate as they drove along the well-kept roads to the western lodge; but he talked and listened with an occasional sinking of the heart; for he saw that Vane's cheerfulness was only forced and assumed, and that the iron had eaten deeply into his heart. It was difficult for the father to realise that this thin, haggard-faced man, with the grave, preoccupied air, was the Vane who had taken life so easily, as if the world had been made for him, and the sun bidden to shine that he might bask in the warmth and gladness of its rays.

Presently they heard the sound of a gun, and came upon Bertie. He exclaimed at sight of Vane, but he, too, saw that there was no good news, and abated the eagerness of his greeting. But Vane's manner plainly indicated that he wished to avoid any expression of sympathy, and Bertie quickly caught the proper tone.

They talked game all the way home, and through the lunch, at which Lady Selina, who had received a hint from Mabel, bore herself as if nothing were the matter, and Vane had merely returned from an ordinary visit to town.

It was not until Mabel and he were alone that Bertie gave vent to his feelings.

"How shockingly ill and changed he is!" he said in an awed voice. "He looks years older, and—have you noticed his eyes?"

"Of course I have," said Mabel impatiently; "but I don't let him see that I have; and don't you. What we've got to do is to treat him as if nothing had happened. Not to fuss over him, mind! If there's anything Vane hates it is fuss; and at the first sign of it he would be off."

"I suppose it's all a question of time," remarked Bertie sadly.

"Oh, is it?" she retorted ironically. "How long do you think it would take a man to get over the loss of Diana?"

"I know how long it would take me to get over the loss of—you, Mabel," he said.

"Oh, do you? A few months, I imagine. But fortunately for you the question doesn't arise. You can't lose what you haven't got, you know."

"Oh, Mabel, if you'd only give me the right—" he pleaded.

"Now, don't talk nonsense," she caught him up. "I'm too busy—busy thinking of Vane, and wondering what I can do to help him, to think of anything else."

Vane took up his new life with a quiet resignation which was indicative of the change that had come over him on the night Diana, unknown to him, had found him asleep on the Embankment and kissed him. He interested himself in the affairs of the estate, or, if he did not interest himself, he discussed them with the earl and Mr. Starkey, and visited the tenants and work-people. Mr. Starkey had no difficulty now in getting a hearing from Lord Dalesford, and was both surprised and delighted to find that his lordship possessed a capacity for mastering details and figures however intricate. His new mode of living did not cost a third of his old reckless and extravagant one, and he joined Mr. Starkey in planning economies and cutting down those expenses which might be spared without decreasing the comfort of the people on the estate.

Vane had always been popular, for the English tenant and labourer will regard his landlord and master with respect and affection even when that landlord and master is rather hard; and the Wrayboroughs had always been, if anything, too generous and lenient. Little wonder that the tenants' and people's liking for "the young master," as they called him, grew to genuine affection when they found that he cared for their well-being and spent most of his time making their lives more prosperous and comfortable; so that Vane, as he rode or walked over the estate, met with a warm and hearty greeting from all; and especially from the children, who quickly came to look upon him as a friend—a friend, however, who was to be regarded with an affection mixed with awe.

Often, as he passed the little school, in which a new mistress reigned in Diana's place, he would turn back and look in at the children with a smile on his grave, sad face; and not seldom he would pick up some mite of a boy and give him a lift on Jess; or walk through the woods with two or three children as close to him as they could get, while he asked them about their lessons, their games, the birds' nesting, in the manner of a true though older chum.

They missed him when he went to visit the other estates; and when he returned, the news went round the village and was received with anticipatory joy.

Sometimes Mabel or Bertie accompanied him on his walks and rides; and Vane talked and laughed, if not with the debonair carelessness of old, with an assumption of cheerfulness; but he preferred solitude, and spent many hours of the day on Jess, or tramping through the covers with his gun. And it was then, when there was no eye to see him, that he yielded to the spirit of sadness, the black shadow of memory that held him in thrall; it was at such times that he communed with the past, and his heart was filled with an aching longing for the girl whom he could not forget.

For the rest, he played his part with a manly fortitude, and, though he would fain have lived to himself and his memory of the days that had fled, he did not shirk his social duties. At the earnest request of the hunt he took over the hounds, and did his duty by them; and it was, perhaps, when he was riding after a good fox, with a keen scent and an open country, that he found most relief from the black care that darkened all his days. He did not discourage the earl's natural desire to display hospitality, and dinners were both given and accepted—the old-fashioned dinners at which the earl shone so conspicuously; and Vane in genial courtesy would run a good second to his father. But when the guests had gone, Vane would stand in the hall and look out at the night with thoughts that wandered toward the dinners at which Diana had been the acknowledged queen; and long after the rest of the household had retired he sat up in the smoking-room with his pipe—the old briar he had so often smoked when Diana was by his side —and gave himself up to the past.

Where was she? Should he never see her, hear of her again?

Sometimes he would go up to London; but his old haunts of folly and sin knew him no more. He would look in at his club for his letters, scarcely staying for half an hour, then wander about the streets, the quiet streets of the poor, his head bent, but his eyes searching every woman's face; and now and again he would see a face and a figure that were like Diana's; but as he got nearer the resemblance would fail, and his heart would sink. On one of his visits he heard that the marriage of Desmond March with Miss Bangs had been fixed for an early date; but the news did not interest him. Indeed, nothing was really of interest to him; and his old London friends, when he met them, were chilled by the aloofness of his manner, and presently began to avoid him.

And all the time the loving hearts of Mabel and his father were aching for him. They saw that he was only playing a part, the part of the Spartan boy who strove to conceal the stolen fox that was gnawing at his breast. The earl had grave cause for anxiety; for he was too often assailed by the dread that Vane would never marry, and that the title would pass to Desmond March, the blackleg, the man whose evil reputation stank aloud in the old man's nostrils.

To women Vane was always courteous, far more courteous and well-mannered than he had been in the old days; but it was too evident that no one of them, be she as charming and beautiful as she might, could warm his bereaved heart with the glow of love.

"One doesn't love a Diana for nothing," said Mabel with womanly shrewdness. "There is no one like her; no one. Vane will never marry anyone else."

"It isn't likely," Bertie responded with warm concurrence. "Do you think that I could ever marry anyone else but—but one person in the world?"

"That's another question; and one that doesn't interest me," retorted Mabel. "Besides, you don't know what you may do—when you're a man."

Of course the sudden and complete disappearance of Diana was discussed in the servants' hall, and, though it was with bated breath and genuine sympathy that the servants talked over the matter, for Diana had won the hearts of every man and maid of the Wrayborough household, the subject was carried to the outside world; and by a natural coincidence it reached the ears of Miss Bangs—through her maid, who had a cousin at Wedbury.

Miss Bangs, whose breeding, unfortunately, was not equal to her wealth, encouraged her servants to gossip; and she listened with open ears—and mouth—to the story of Diana's flight; and an hour or two later, when Desmond March paid her one of his frequent visits, she said—

"Have you seen your cousin, Lord Dalesford, lately, dear?"

"Oh yes," he replied with a smile and a shrug of his shoulders. "Saw him in town not long ago. He looked awfully seedy, and was walking with his eyes fixed on nothing, like a man in a dream. Oh, I'm afraid his appearance is not very hopeful for me—for us," he added quickly, to hide the thought that, in the event of Vane's death, Miss Bangs would perhaps have no cause to interest herself in his succession. "He's the sort of man to live to ninety—unless he breaks his neck by an accident. But he looks only the shadow of his former self, confound him."

"Perhaps he's fretting after his lady-love," suggested Bangs, with a giggle.

Desmond March hated her when she giggled, but he pricked up his ears and asked her what she meant; and Miss Bangs retailed her maid's tittle-tattle.

"Quite a romance!" he said; and he went to the window and looked out with a gleam in his eyes. "So that's what he is looking for?" he said thoughtfully. "She's never been heard of, you say? Rather strange, isn't it?"

"Very," assented Miss Bangs, delighted at this display of interest by her fiancé, whom she usually found not easy to interest. "I wonder he doesn't set the police to work."

Desmond March smiled. It was not worth while explaining to Miss Bangs that the Wrayboroughs were not in the habit of placing their private affairs in the hands of the police.

"Oh, he'll find her presently," he said. "Find her, and make it up and marry her—it would be just my luck."

He left the house soon afterwards, and as he walked along his lids drooped and the eyes behind them were sharp and hard, like those of a bird of prey. He was tired of Miss Bangs, whose infatuation for him filled him with disgust—and made him, much to his annoyance, think of Lucy. If that love-sick cousin of his were only out of the way, he, Desmond March, would be saved from Miss Bangs. If he were only out of the way! The words kept repeating themselves at the back of his brain for the rest of the day; haunted him even while he was playing cards at the Apollo; and kept him awake as he lay at night staring into the darkness. Then suddenly he turned on the light and sprang out of bed and stood with white face and quivering lips as if he had seen or heard something that had filled him with terror.

The paroxysm passed quickly, and with a laugh he went to the spirit decanter and poured out some brandy.

"It's—it's madness!" he muttered as he set down the glass. "Sheer madness. And yet—and yet—if it could only be done!"

CHAPTER XXIX

IN THE DARK

ONE morning Vane took up the post-bag, and unlocking it, began to sort out the letters.

"They look uncommonly like bills, Mabel," he said as he handed her batch across. "Except this one. Bertie's handwriting. He's a good correspondent—he went to London only the day before yesterday."

Mabel coloured up and affected to disregard the letter.

"Oh, I asked him to get me something, and, of course, he's forgotten all about it and is writing to say so. He's a nice boy, and I rather like him, but I wish he had some brains— Oh, what is the matter, Vane?" she broke off, for, looking up, she saw that his face had gone white.

"Nothing," he said, but his voice was husky and shook. He looked at his watch. "I must go up to town on business," he said. "Will you order the dog-cart for me? I must catch this train."

There was only just time to drive to the station, and he got into the train as it was moving. Not once, but twenty times he looked at the letter which had moved him so greatly, and at every perusal his heart beat more quickly. From the terminus he took a cab to Mr. Fielding's office, and found him alone and on the point of leaving.

He looked hard at Vane as he took his hand.

"You have heard news?" he said.

Vane nodded and returned the lawyer's gaze inquiringly.

"You, too, have heard, know—" he said swiftly.

Mr. Fielding narrowed his eyes and shut his lips tightly.

"Whatever I may have heard or know, Lord Dalesford, I am pledged to silence."

Vane made a movement of repressed excitement and laid the letter on the table. Mr. Fielding took it up and read it, his eyebrows rising.

"So she has written!" he said. "I did not think she would; for only yesterday she bound me to secrecy. But a woman always does the unexpected."

"You can tell me no more than this? Can throw no light on the letter?" asked Vane with eagerness.

Mr. Fielding shook his head, then read the letter aloud. It was scarcely a letter, for there were only a few lines—

"I am leaving England, but I cannot do so without seeing you once again. I will be at the end of Spencer Street, by the river, at Chelsea, to-morrow night at ten o'clock; and will explain everything. Destroy this. D."

"It is strange," said Mr. Fielding musingly.

"It is typed; the envelope also is typed," said Vane.

"Yes; so I see. There is a reason for that. Miss Diana has a typewriter.—No, no; I cannot tell you any more! My lips are sealed. I can only ask you to wait until ten o'clock this evening. Please God the dark cloud that has hung over her young life and yours may be dispelled."

"God grant it!" said Vane. "For her sake I must respect her confidence in you. It is joy enough for me to know that she is alive—and well?"

Mr. Fielding shook his head. "Not another question, I beg, my lord!" he said.

Vane inclined his head. "Give me the letter," he said; "she bids me destroy it."

As he tore the paper across, Mr. Fielding made a motion as if to stop him, but checked himself; and Vane reduced the letter to fragments and dropped them on the fire.

"You will not have long to wait," said Mr. Fielding. "I hope you will go and eat something; you look—"

Vane smiled gravely. "I trust at ten o'clock my troubles—and hers—will be over," he said significantly. "Yes; I will get something to eat. It is probable that you will see me to-morrow morning—both of us."

Mr. Fielding drew some papers towards him and bent over them; but he could not work; and at last he got up and, calling a cab, had himself driven to Alpha Street, the street in which Diana still lived.

He heard the click of the typewriter as Mrs. Burton opened the attic door to him. Both women were in mourning—poor Lucy had been buried three days now—and both were looking worn and weary. Diana had rented a second room, and Mrs. Burton presently went into it, leaving Diana and Mr. Fielding alone.

"How late you are working, my dear!" he said. "Is it necessary, is it generous?"

She shook her head as if she had answered the question before. "You want to see me? Is it about—Mr. Bourne? Have you seen him?" she asked in a low voice.

"No," he replied. "No; I have seen someone else—Lord Dalesford."

Diana looked up quickly, then her head went down.

"Is—is he well?" she asked in a faint voice.

"Well? Oh yes. Better than he has been for some time—of course!" he answered.

She glanced up at the "of course." With a little nod at her, he said, rather sharply—

"Why did you change your mind and write to him?"

He had considerately turned away to the fire, and he did not see the start and the flash of surprise in her eyes.

"And why, if you had decided to see him, did you not meet him at my office instead of making an appointment at the end of Spencer Street, and at night?"

A few months ago Diana would have exclaimed with amazement and repudiated any such appointment; but she had waded through the waters of a bitter experience; and she was on the alert, the defensive. She remained silent; and Mr. Fielding shrugged his shoulders.

"I see you do not mean to tell me. Ah, well, I am glad you have acted as you have. If you had seen Lord Dalesford, the joy, the hope, in his eyes, notwithstanding his suspense! But his suspense will be at an end at ten o'clock to-night!"

"To-night!" Diana's lips formed the words, and she glanced at the cheap clock on the mantelshelf.

"Shall I go with you?" asked Mr. Fielding. "I think I ought to do so; to be near if—if you should want me."

"No," she said in a low voice. "I will go alone. I wonder whether I shall ever be able to thank you for all you have done for me?"

"If you really feel any gratitude for my poor and quite inefficient services, my dear," he said promptly, "you will act on the advice I gave you when—when we discovered whose child you were, and at once make Lord Dalesford happy. He has suffered agonies through no fault of his own.—There, there! Don't cry! I can't stand that, as you know. Go and meet him and let him bring you to me in the morning. Oh, my child, don't wreck a good man's life—to say nothing of your own—for a mistaken sense of honour. Honour! 'Pride' is the word. There, there! Sure you wouldn't like me to accompany you? It's a lonely spot you've chosen."

"No," she said again; "I will go alone."

When he had gone she sat and gazed at the fire, her heart beating painfully fast. By whom had the letter been written? She could think of no one but Bourne. Had he sent the letter with the intention of bringing her and Vane together again? Had he? It was impossible for her to conjecture the reason, solve the problem; but there was one thing plain to her. She must be at the place mentioned, even if she did not disclose her presence.

Vane walked to his club, and while the chop was being served, went into the library and got a London Directory; for in his excitement he had omitted to ask Mr. Fielding where Spencer Street was.

He forced himself to eat the chop, and drank a little wine; smoked a cigar afterwards, and tried not to look at the clock or listen to its striking of the slow pacing hours.

At last it was time he started! He sprang up with a flush on his face, his eyes shining, his heart beating fast. A footman helped him on with his coat, and as he gave him his hat said—

"A cab, my lord?"

"No—yes!" said Vane.

He told the man to drive him to the large thoroughfare from which Spencer Street struck, and leant forward with painful eagerness. Discharging the cab, he walked quickly down the street, and found himself in a small, open space close to the river.

The night was dark, and the faint gleams of a feeble gaslight in a dingy street-lamp just revealed the squalor of the place. In front of him some barges were moored to the shore; at the end of the street was a hoarding round the tottering remains of a ruined house. There was no one in sight, no sign of life save that supplied by a cat crawling toward some scrubby shrubs that grew in the garden of an empty house.

Vane shuddered as he thought of Diana, whom he would have screened from every ill wind, every evil sight, coming to such a spot. But it did not matter; he would take her away. Lady Selina was stopping in town; he would take her there. Yes; she should not leave him again!

A wheezy clock in the tower of a neighbouring church chimed the quarter to ten. He sighed impatiently. Would she be late? No, he felt that she would not. He proceeded to pace up and down, and had come to the end of the street when he heard footsteps behind him. Quite convinced that he was not deceived, he turned —to meet a tall figure that flung itself upon him with one hand upraised.

In the murky light Vane caught the gleam of steel in the menacing hand, and instinctively gripped the arm of his assailant and tried to shout; but a strong arm was across his throat, pressing it to the point of suffocation, and he could only struggle in silence.

He was weakened by illness—and, alas! past dissipation—and the man who had attacked him had the advantage of him. Setting his teeth, Vane tried to free his neck and wrench round the arm with the knife; the two men swayed from side to side, giving and taking inch by inch, foot by foot, as the unknown foe tried to free his arm and force Vane to his knees or on his back. And moving thus, they came directly under the light of the lamp, and Vane saw that he was struggling with Desmond March.

The signs of recognition flashed in his eyes, and his lips framed the name. With a tremendous effort, inspired by fierce indignation, he pressed on Desmond March's breast with such force that March felt his breastbone giving, and with a snarl like that of a dog he, too, made a fearful effort and swung Vane round and almost to his knees.

At that moment, the critical moment, they both heard the scream of a woman; and a girlish figure, after pausing for an instant, as if transfixed with horror, rushed towards them.

Vane looked round and saw that it was Diana. His terror for her unnerved him and caused him to release his grasp. Desmond March shook it off, and with another snarl struck downwards twice. Then, as Diana flung herself upon him, he hurled her away and darted up the wharf. But suddenly stopped, for a man—a short, thick-set man—was coming towards him; not running, but slowly, and bent, as an animal is bent when it is about to spring.

He was almost upon March, had almost got his hands at his throat, when March swerved aside, dashed across the road, and sprang upon one of the barges.

The man followed, but, in his blind rush, his foot slipped; and he fell into the hold; and Desmond March, leaping almost over him, gained the quay, and in an instant had disappeared.

So desolate, so unfrequented, Was the spot—the bargemen were drinking at a neighbouring tavern—that Diana's cries for help met with no response for some minutes, and in a frenzy of terror and anguish she knelt beside Vane, essaying to stanch the blood that flowed from his wounds, and every now and then calling upon him in distracted tones.

At last a policeman heard, and came running to the spot, flashed his lantern on the white, drawn face against her bosom, and blew his whistle.

"Let me see him, miss," he said. "Why, he's a gentleman! And he's badly hurt, I'm afraid; stabbed in two places."

He looked at her suspiciously, and when, in a hoarse whisper, she said, "Yes, I saw him do it; he has escaped," he shrugged his shoulders.

"It's a nasty place, this, miss," he muttered. "Scarcely a night but what there's something happens; and it isn't the first time highway robbery with violence has been done here. His watch is there, all right; and his money, too—I suppose you came up in time and frightened the man off? I wish my mate would come! Ah, here he is!—Gentleman been stabbed, George, badly stabbed, I'm afraid. You get a cab at the top of the street and we'll take him to the hospital. You'd better come, too, miss. I'll try and stop the bleeding with my handkerchief."

The cab came rattling up, and Vane was lifted in, and with his head still on her bosom was driven slowly to the hospital.

She was, of course, shut out of the examination-room, but she threw herself down on the bench in the hall, and one of the policemen stood near her, as if on guard.

But presently the door opened and one of the house surgeons came out to her.

"Yes; he is alive," he said, answering the anguished inquiry of her eyes. "He has been badly stabbed; and but for your coming up as you did, I've no doubt that—Ah, you're not going to faint? Porter, a glass of water!"

Diana put it to her lips, then rose, fighting against the deathly stupor that threatened to overcome her.

"Can—can I see him?" she asked almost inaudibly.

The surgeon hesitated. "It's not usual; he is in a very critical condition. Well, I'll see."

He went away, but returned very quickly.

"Well, just for a moment," he said. "You will not speak?"

Her lips formed an assent, and she followed him into the room, and, closing her eyes for a moment, went up to the bed on which Vane lay. Then, with clenched hands and throbbing heart, she bent over him and looked at his white face, as if her soul were in her eyes.

The surgeon touched her arm, and she followed him into the hall again, where the policeman was waiting for her.

"We have found the gentleman's card-case," said the surgeon. "You will like to know his name; he is Lord Dalesford. Let me see, that's Lord Wrayborough's son. We shall, of course, communicate with the family at once."

The policeman drew nearer.

"I shall have to trouble you to come to the police station, I'm afraid, miss," he said. "I've kept the cab."

At the police station an inspector asked a few questions, and Diana was dismissed.

A guarded telegram was sent to Lord Wrayborough; and he and Mabel reached the hospital in the afternoon. Vane was conscious, but so weak that he could scarcely speak, and they sat beside him in speechless fear as long as they were permitted to remain, and than went sadly away.

CHAPTER XXX

VANE'S CONVALESCENCE

As the clock struck the following morning, Diana, closely veiled, was among the small group of persons waiting in the hall; and presently the surgeon came out to her.

"I'll give you ten minutes," he said gravely; "and I'm afraid I shall have to cut those short if he is at all excited. He is better, but—oh, very weak, of course."

Fighting for calm, striving to bring the colour to her white lips, to drive the agony from her eyes, Diana followed him into the room in which Vane lay.

The nurse went to the other end of the room, casting a meaning glance at Diana, who sank on her knees beside the bed, and, taking Vane's hand, laid it against her cheek in silence. He trembled at her touch, but controlled himself, for he knew that if he showed any excitement they would take her from him.

"Diana! Come back to me! Come back to me! Oh, my dear, my dear!"

"Hush!" she said, her eyes filling with tears, her lips quivering. "Yes; I—I had to come; if—if only for last time. Oh, Vane, Vane!"

He smiled at her.

"Not the last time, dearest," he said. There was silence for a moment, then he whispered, "The second time you have saved my life, Diana. And you think it does not belong to you—even now! You—you weren't hurt, dearest? The dread has haunted me, tortured me, even when I was able to think of nothing else."

"No, no," she said; then suddenly but firmly, "Vane, *it was the same man*! I saw him distinctly! Though only for a moment."

He nodded almost carelessly. "Yes; it was my cousin, Desmond March."

"Desmond March!" she bit her lip to keep back the cry.

"Yes; Desmond March," he said. "How did you find out that he had written to me? Mr. Fielding—? Ah, yes! Clever fellow, Desmond! Nice cousin! I didn't think he'd go as far as this. And yet"—he sighed—"He's a bad lot, Diana. But you have told no one?" he asked with a touch of anxiety. "No, no, of course not!"

She shook her head. "No—I—I waited until I had seen you. I will do as you wish."

"Yes," he said with a smile. "From this time on, dearest. Diana, why did you leave me?"

"Because— Hush!" she faltered. "There is not time, and—and I must not excite you."

"All right," he said easily. "I can wait. It's enough for me that you have come back to me. How long the time has been!—All right, nurse," he said with a smile, as she came up to them looking significantly at her watch. "Give me another minute. This young lady is going to marry me when you've turned me out warranted sound."

The blood rushed to Diana's face, and she fought with the mingled joy and misery in her heart: the joy of listening to his voice, of seeing his face; the misery that rose from the thought that she would soon hear and see him for the last time.

Something in his voice, as it hesitated and broke, touched the nurse, and, even while shaking her head, she drew back. He tried to rise on his elbow, but Diana stretched out her hand and laid it on his breast. He winced, then smiled up at her.

"I'll get up, right up, if you don't kiss me," he said with a touch of fever in his eyes.

What could she do? She bent and slowly let her lips touch his, her eyes streaming with tears. The nurse returned to the bedside with stern resolution in her face.

"You must go now," she said. "I can't let you stay another minute, not one single moment!"

Diana, dropping her veil to hide her face, touched the nurse's hand gratefully and went out. As she was passing along the corridor she saw an old man approaching, leaning on the arm of a young girl. Diana drew back and slipped into a ward, and waited, trembling, until the earl and Mabel had passed.

Immediately Vane was strong enough the detective was at his bedside; but he was surprised, and not a little disappointed, to find that his lordship could render him very little assistance towards the arrest of the assassin who had attacked him. It seemed that Lord Dalesford had no capacity for description, and no very clear idea of the kind of man his assailant was.

As he got better—but how slowly he progressed!—visitors came more frequently. The earl and Mabel lived only to count the hours they spent away from him. The earl would sit and hold his son's thin, wasted hand, scarcely speaking, but every now and then turning his pathetic eyes on Vane, as if to assure himself of the improvement in his condition. And Mabel, though she was not so silent and told him the news with characteristic comments, looked at him with a vague questioning in her glance. But Vane held his tongue. It was not yet time to speak.

Lady Selina came frequently; but her chief desire was to get Vane to the house in Grosvenor Square, "to be nursed," as she put it emphatically, ignoring the fact that he was being nursed with that absolute devotion and skill which can only be obtained at a hospital, with its staff of famous surgeons, and its band of self-sacrificing women, whose unselfish lives shine out like stars in this murky, selfish world of ours.

Of course Bertie came; and always came when Mabel was unaccompanied by the earl, and as invariably expressed surprise at seeing her. Vane would lie back and listen smilingly to them as they tried to hide their love-making under a mask of quarrelling and arguing, a mask so palpably transparent that it made even the nurse laugh.

Diana's visits were carefully timed, so that she should not meet the others. As Vane got stronger, her manner gradually changed. With her joy in his recovery was mingled the sadness of the coming parting; it was like a dark shadow on the happiness of the last few fleeting weeks.

"I am going to get up to-morrow, dearest."

"If you are good," said the nurse sternly. "I mean if you will sit still and not insist upon walking about."

"Avaunt, tyrant!" retorted Vane. "Do you know, Di, that if she had her wicked will she'd keep me here for the next six months. I'm afraid she's fallen in love with me. Oh, nurse, think of that other poor young man who trusts you so entirely! Oh yes, nurse, I love you very much; but, you see, I'm engaged, like yourself, so that, 'alas! it can't be.' "

The nurse laughed. "Lord Dalesford is the most impudent patient I have ever had," she said to Diana. "I don't envy you."

Diana tried to smile, but the tears came into her eyes as she turned her head away. Should she tell him to-day, tell him that she was not fit to be his wife, that, though she was not the daughter of a convict, she was his niece; had lived on his money; was contaminated by his relationship? Not to-day. Let her have one more day. Her plans were made, her resolution irrevocable.

He felt her trembling more than usual at their parting that afternoon, and he looked with loving scrutiny into her eyes. But she slipped from his arms and left him without a word.

Some time later that same day the nurse came into the room and, after a moment or two of watchful silence, said

"There is another visitor, Lord Dalesford. It is a man—he will not give his name—who says he wishes to see you on a matter of the greatest importance. I have been down to the hall to see him, and I think from his manner it *is* business of importance. Will you see him for a few minutes only, if I let him come up?"

"Let 'em all come!" said Vane cheerfully; for in another day or two he would be out and able to "look after" Diana. Never again would he lose sight of her. It was of this he was thinking.

The nurse went down, and presently returned and ushered in the visitor.

"A quarter of an hour," she said, as she closed the door on them.

That night Diana, bending over Mrs. Burton, kissed her and said, in a low but firm voice—

"Mother, we are leaving England the day after to-morrow. I have not told you before because—I was afraid of Mr. Fielding, of—of everyone. But no one must try to stop me. We must go; we must!"

Mrs. Burton inclined her head.

"I understand, Diana," she faltered meekly. "I shall be ready."

CHAPTER XXXI

MR. BOURNE'S WILL

DIANA worked at her typewriting that night and early the next morning; for her money was running short and she had refused to accept any from Garling.

But every now and then she looked up and gave her misery a breathing space; it was so hard to give up Vane, now that she had seen him again, had spent so many hours beside him—hours in which her love had been intensified by its very hopelessness.

She finished her batch of work and posted it on her way to the hospital. Vane was dressed, and his hat and coat lay on a chair, as if he were going out.

"Yes, dearest, they are going to throw me out!" he said with a laugh, as he drew her to him and seated himself beside her. "The carriage will be here directly, and we will go—"

She drew away from him and looked at him piteously.

"Not—not I, Vane!" she murmured. "I—I have come to say good-bye. But I —I have something to tell you, something I must tell you before we part. You— you will be good to me, Vane, you will not try to keep me—make it harder for me to part from you?"

"Oh, I'll be good to you," he said gravely, but with the smile, the tender smile, of loving confidence still in his eyes. "What is this you are going to tell me?"

"The reason why I went away, why we must say good-bye for ever," she faltered, bravely trying to keep the tears from her eyes and voice.

"No need, Diana; I know," he said very quietly.

She started and looked at him.

"You know!"

"Yes. I had a visitor after you left yesterday. His name is Benjamin Bourne."

Diana shrank back with a little cry; but Vane took her hand and held it tightly.

"He—he has been here—he has told you?" she panted.

"Yes; everything. Diana, if anything could make me love you better than I do —which isn't possible—the knowledge of all you have gone through would do so. And you could think—dream—of leaving me again? Oh, my dear, how could you?"

She looked at him with wonder and surprise.

"But—but I must!" she said in a low voice. "Vane, do you think I—love you?"

"I know it," he responded, "and the knowledge makes me the happiest and proudest of men, dearest."

"I should love you very little if I consented to drag you down to my depths," she said with a catch in her voice.

"What depths?" he asked calmly.

"I—I—am related, I belong to that man. Ah, I must not speak, think, unkindly of him! He was generous to me, Vane. I must not forget that."

"You're not likely to. And why should you?" he asked as coolly as before. "Benjamin Bourne is a very good sort of man. By George! he's a man to admire; a man who went back on his past and trod it underfoot. Not many of us can do that, Diana; few of us could make such a sacrifice as he made for the girl he thought his daughter."

She went white. "You—you don't know, Vane, that—that I found him at Glenaskel—trying to steal—"

"The diamonds? Oh yes. He told me the whole story. I think he kept nothing back. Perhaps *you* don't know that he was driven back to the old path, to play the burglar, by my fine cousin, Desmond March, Yes; Desmond had a hold on him and used him—as Desmond March would use any man in his power—unmercifully, ruthlessly. Poor Bourne! I took to him. I could sympathise. His child—his real child—that poor girl! Desmond March again! There is a bad reckoning to be made up between the two men. I hope"—his face and voice grew grave and apprehensive—"they may not meet. Bourne is leaving England—for ever. Oh, he's a fine fellow. And how he must have suffered!"

Diana regarded him with wide-open eyes.

"A—a convict!" she said in a whisper, her head bent.

Vane nodded coolly. "I know. But what has that to do with you and me, dearest?"

She was silent with amazement.

"He turns out to be not your father; but even if he had been, I shouldn't have given you up.—But we won't discuss it," he broke off as the nurse entered the room. "Carriage waiting, nurse? Right. Don't look so mighty glad to get rid of me. I may come back, you know. You see"—with a glance at Diana—"I've been so happy here; happier than I've been for weeks past."

"I hope you will take care of yourself, Lord Dalesford," said the nurse. "You must not take a chill, or do too much for some time. You have been a very good patient—at least"—checking herself, with a smile—"as good as could be expected for a man. Yes; take care of yourself."

"Thanks very much; but here is a young lady who will save me the trouble. I'm going to be taken care of for the rest of my natural life. Good-bye, nurse. I won't try and thank you."

Nor did Diana try; but she went back quickly and kissed her; and there were tears in the eyes of both women.

Dalesford found that he was not so strong on his pins—as he put it—as he expected; and he had to lean on Diana's arm; or said he was obliged to do so.

211

The carriage was waiting, and the footman and coachman touched their hats respectfully and eagerly, and regarded their young master with anxious and curious eyes.

As the carriage drove off Diana seemed to awake to the fact that she was being carried away.

"Where are we going?" she asked in a low voice, as they sat hand in hand: for how could she refuse to let him have her hand when he had only just come through the valley of the shadow of death, and was still weak?

"Home," he said. "The governor and Mabel were at the hospital just before you came; and I told them that I should bring you home to lunch."

"Oh, Vane, Vane!" she breathed with a long, wistful sigh and a shake of her head.

"You should have seen the governor's face. He is not given to shouting, as you know. Mabel did that for him. She screeched so that the nurse came running in and chucked them both out!"

"And—and the earl? Oh, surely—surely, he will not be glad to see me, *me*!"

"Well, you'll soon find that out for yourself; for we shall be there presently."

"And he knows—?" she whispered, with bent head.

"Everything. And he said— Oh, well, it's his deal now; and you must wait."

They reached the house in Grosvenor Square, and Mabel ran down the steps and fell upon Diana as soon as the footman had the carriage-door open, calling her name and kissing her, holding her at arm's length and regarding her with loving reproach and infinite joy.

The earl was seated in the drawing-room, but he rose quickly and came towards them and held out his arms to Diana; the tears were in his eyes, though he smiled and patted her on the back as one pats the back of a child who has just stopped short of falling off a wall or drowning herself.

"You wicked girl!" he said. "What a fright you've given all of us! And you're paler and thinner—tut, tut!" He drew her to a chair and sat beside her, holding her hand. "And you must tell us your adventures, eh, Mabel?"

"You know?" said Diana in a low voice.

The old man nodded.

"Yes, I know, my child," he said softly.

"Then you will help me—against him?" she murmured, glancing towards Dalesford, who stood regarding her and his father with an air of serene satisfaction. "I want to say good-bye. I and my mother are starting with a colonisation party for South Africa to-morrow, Lord Wrayborough."

The earl smiled and slowly shook his head.

"My dear, I understand. Do you think we do not know and understand and sympathise with you? But, indeed, you mustn't go. You belong to us—belong to Vane; and it would be a great misfortune if we were to lose you. It would mean —ruin to the house of Wrayborough."

"Misfortune—ruin, if I—I went?" said Diana, in troubled perplexity.

The earl touched a bell.

212

"Will you ask Mr. Starkey and Mr. Fielding if they will be so very good as to come to us here?" he said to the footman.

Diana rose and shook hands with both men as they entered, but there was a clinging pressure in the hand she gave Mr. Fielding.

"I am very glad to see you, Miss—Burton," said Mr. Starkey with a respect that was as genuine as it was profound. "Your lawyer, my friend, and I have been discussing some business matters of yours—and Lord Dalesford's."

"They are going to show you how imperative it is that you should not—jilt Vane," put in the earl under his breath.

"You may not be aware," said Mr. Starkey, addressing Diana, "that the Wrayborough estate is in an extremely embarrassed condition. But, yes, no doubt Lord Dalesford—"

"Oh, I've told her, long ago," said Vane with a touch of impatience. "Look here, Diana, but for your uncle, Mr. Bourne, we should be up a tree, on a rock, stony broke. But he came to the rescue. It was Mr. Bourne who sold us, at a nominal price, a merely nominal price, the Sunninglea property—property which will result in an enormous profit and a continuous and increasing revenue."

"If we hold it," said the earl softly.

"Furthermore, Mr. Bourne has made a will—" began Mr. Fielding, but Diana shrank back and murmured—

"No, no! I—I cannot take it. Oh no, no!"

Mr. Fielding smiled rather grimly.

"You are not asked to do so, my dear Miss Diana. The will leaves everything Mr. Bourne possesses to Lord Dalesford."

Diana looked from one to the other.

"But—but you will not—" she faltered, and yet with a secret hope.

"Won't I?" said Vane "Why not? You won't take it. Why shouldn't I? The money was gained"—his tone grew emphatic—"honestly. Oh, I know—know the whole of his life. I shall take it on one condition."

Diana raised her heavy lids.

"That you share it with me—as my wife. If you refuse, I decline the Sunninglea property, and the money left me by the will."

"And we are ruined," said the earl gravely.

Diana looked from one to the other of these amiable conspirators for her happiness.

"It's for you to decide on the future of an ancient house, my dear," said the earl.

She turned to him, her eyes swimming.

"And I—I—so shamed, so shamed of—"

Vane strode to her and stopped her with an imperative gesture.

"No, no. Not even from you will I hear that, dearest," he said. "You speak of shame because there is a dark spot in the life of a relative. What about *us*? And our past! Heavens! Do you know how we got our peerage?" He glanced at the portrait of a lady, a lady of the dissolute Court of the second Charles, and bit his lip. "No, no; it isn't safe for *us* to dig up the past."

The earl inclined his head. "It is true, Diana. You see, my dear?"

"But the world—your people?" stammered Diana.

"Here comes the world, here comes one of them," said Vane, as the door opened and Lady Selina entered. She had been well coached, of course, but even if she had not she was too much a woman of the world not to desire a marriage which would literally save her family from destruction. She went to Diana and kissed her.

"My dear, I am so glad to see you!" she said; and she said it with such evident sincerity that Diana broke down.

"Oh, what can I do?" she sobbed.

"Marry me to-morrow morning," responded Vane promptly, as he put his arm round her. Then in a lower voice he said to the others, over his shoulder, "Run away, all of you!"

CHAPTER XXXII

THE QUAYS OF AMSTERDAM

ONE night, a week later, Desmond March stole back to his rooms. He looked white and haggard, for he had been in hiding and had had a bad time.

In the dingy purlieus of Brussels, where he had been hiding, Desmond March had fancied that every footstep was that of the detective who was coming to arrest him; for he knew that he had been recognised by Dalesford and Diana and by Garling. But the days passed and no one came with the dreaded warrant, and, according to the English newspapers—with what feverish anxiety he scanned them!—the police had come to the conclusion that the attack on Lord Dalesford had been made by a common cutpurse, whom Lord Dalesford could not identify.

At this intelligence Desmond March began to pluck up courage. So Dalesford was not going to put the law in motion! Afraid of the scandal, the shame that would stain the family name! Well, then, he, Desmond March, could return and brazen it out.

Yes; he would venture back. If Dalesford and the girl would not give evidence, he was safe. He scarcely condescended to bestow a thought on Garling. *He* was powerless and not worth consideration.

It was evening, a murky evening, as he unlocked the door and stole up the stairs, and, with a sigh of satisfaction, looked round the luxurious rooms. A pile of letters stood on the table, and he looked them over. There were two from Miss Bangs, and he opened one at hazard, for the envelope contained some hard substance. It was the engagement ring he had given her; and it was enclosed in a curt note—

"Miss Bangs returns Mr. Desmond March's ring, as she wishes to terminate her engagement with a man of whose real character she has been fully informed."

"Vulgar fool!" he muttered with an oath. "But five minutes with her will put it right. Who has told her? Dalesford? Curse him, I'll be even with him yet!"

He summoned his man, had a bath and changed, and with an affectation of his old debonair manner, left the house. He had dined on board the steamer; he would go to the silly fool of a woman at once.

He took a cab and reached the grand house in which Miss Bangs lived, and rang the bell confidently.

"My mistress is not at home, sir. She is on the Continent. No, I don't know when to expect her. Not for some months, I think. No, sir, I've no address. I think she's in the South."

Desmond March went down the steps with a sudden sinking of the heart, and was calling a cab when a man came from out of the shadows and stood beside him. Desmond March stared and stepped back; then he pulled himself up and laughed harshly, contemptuously.

"Ah, Garling," he said. "Glad to see you. Are you shadowing me?"

"That's it," said Garling. He spoke quite calmly, but his face was livid and his eyes glittered with a subdued ferocity. He had shrunk in girth, and his head was thrust forward as if it were bowed by a heavy grief.

Desmond March laughed again. "Blackmail? My friend, you don't know your man. Clear out; move off, or by— I'll call that policeman there and give you in charge, you—you convict!"

Garling did not move his eyes, with the savage light in them, from the pallid, haggard face.

"No," he said; "there's no escape for you there, Desmond March. That's the road to the gallows."

"He's not dead!" exclaimed March unwittingly.

Garling moistened his lips.

"No; he's not," he said.

A cab came up slowly, and, hailing it, Desmond March got in, not hurriedly, but leisurely. Garling got in beside him. Desmond March looked at him and bit his lip.

"What is your game?" he said between his teeth.

"Yes; I'll tell you," responded Garling in a dull, impassive voice. "I'm going to keep beside you until the hour of reckoning. It may not come to-night, or to-morrow, or the day after; but it will come. I am waiting for it."

"Ah, well, one must humour a madman," said Desmond March. He coolly lit a cigar and lay back comfortably on the cushions.

Presently the cab drew up, and Desmond March got out leisurely. Garling followed him and stood with his hands thrust in the pockets of his pilot-jacket, his head bent, but his eyes under their shaggy brows still fixed on his companion's face.

"Coming in? No? Going to wait outside?" asked Desmond March jeeringly. "All right; suit yourself!"

He walked upstairs and looked down at the street from behind the blind. Garling remained for a minute exactly as he had been left, then went slowly away.

Desmond March laughed, and, going to the sideboard, got some whisky.

"Fellow looks mad," he muttered, "raving mad. What's it matter? He can't open his mouth; he's in no hurry to go back to stone-breaking; and a word from me would send him there. Pooh!"

He threw himself into a chair and took up a paper and turned it over listlessly. This paragraph met his eye—

"Thanks to a splendid constitution, Lord Dalesford's recovery from the dastardly attack made upon him by one of the too numer-

216

ous street ruffians has been rapid. He has left St. Jude's Hospital, and is now staying with his father, the Earl of Wrayborough, at Wrayborough House, Grosvenor Square. It is much to be regretted that the police have not succeeded in finding any clue to the man who committed the murderous outrage. Surely the criminal population ought to be more closely under police surveillance."

Desmond March laughed and gnawed at his lips.

"Means to keep his mouth shut! No scandals! Quite right, my dear cousin.—I wonder if that madman is still there? I can't afford to appear in a row, a struggle in the public streets, with a lunatic convict. Better clear out again for a time. Yes; I'll go back to that infernal Brussels. I'll lie low for a bit."

He went into his dressing-room and changed his evening clothes for a travelling suit, and, with the collar of his ulster turned up as far as it would go and his travelling cap dragged down to meet it, went down the stairs, opened the door, and cautiously looked out.

Garling was not in sight; and, with a sense of relief which enraged him, he called a cab and was driven to Liverpool Street.

He was in time to catch the Harwich boat-train, and he hung back watching the few passengers until they had gone from the station to the quay. Garling was not among them. On board the boat Desmond March went stealthily to a point from which he could scan his fellow-passengers; but he saw nothing of the square, shrunken figure, the livid face and bloodshot, menacing eyes.

There was a fog on the Scheldt, and the boat moved slowly, sounding the fog-horn continually.

The fog was still thick when the steamer reached Antwerp. The day had turned to night; the electric lights made the darkness seem denser at places untouched by the lamps, and Desmond March, as he stood leaning over the deck-rail, peered into these black spots with a vague apprehension creeping on him. He was almost the last of the passengers to land, and he was passing to the train which stood waiting, when he saw a figure move slowly down the gangway and stand on the quay.

It was Garling—Garling with no attempt at concealment in his dress, no up-turned collar or screening cap. Desmond March stood for a moment as if uncertain what to do; then he stepped out of the rays of the electric light into the shadow. Useless to go aboard the train with this madman as a fellow-passenger. He would wait where he was until the train had gone, and then—ah, well, he had meant to go to Brussels and thence to one of the small, out-of-the-way Belgian towns; but he could remain in Antwerp or—or return to London.

He stood—he was ashamed to crouch—behind a high pile of bales, and heard the train start. He remained in hiding for another minute, then he stole out.

Garling was waiting for him on the other side of the bales.

Desmond March opened his lips to cry out, but checked himself, for Garling did not attack him; simply stood with his hands in his pockets, his eyes blazing redly in his impassive face.

"Curse you!" gasped March. "Why do you follow me? What do you want? Come a step nearer and I'll call the police; there are a dozen here. Yes, by God, I'll stop your little game; you're carrying this mad freak of yours too far."

Still not a word, not a movement of the menacing eyes.

As Desmond March moved towards the quay, the officials turned out some of the lights; the passengers had gone, and the place seemed deserted. Confused by the sudden darkness where a moment before there had been at least partial light, Desmond March blundered uncertainly forward.

The next instant an arm was thrown round his neck and across his mouth; he was borne to the ground with an irresistible force, and Garling's knee was on his breast. Desmond March could not see the face above him, but he could feel the hot breath, could almost feel the savage eyes. He could not speak, for the huge hand was upon his lips, forcing them out of shape, driving them against his teeth.

"At last," said the impassive voice. "We're at our reckoning, Mr. March. You want to know what I've got against you? I'm going to tell you. I've been waiting to tell you. Oh, I could wait. I'm used to it. I've learned patience in a hard school. And you don't guess why I'm going to kill you? That's—strange; yes, that's strange! You don't think of *her*—not for a minute, not you! What's just one girl to you! You won't care when I tell you that she's dead. What's it matter to you whether Lucy Edgworth lived or died; you'd done with her, hadn't you? Well, she's dead. She flung herself over a bridge into the river. It's a pity there wasn't an end of her there, a pity for you that I picked her out and brought her home to die. A pity, because, you see,—I'm her father."

Frantic with terror, Desmond March struggled; but as vainly as if the knees that pressed on him were a ton of steel.

"Her father. Strange, isn't it?" said Garling, not jeeringly, but almost solemnly and with the terrible calmness of insanity. "Her father. And me a rich man, too. Worth a million. And she'd have had it, if I'd known she was my child in time to save her. And you'd have had the money you'd sell your soul for, you —murderer. Pity, eh? If you'd only known!"

He paused and looked down at the face—now stained with purple patches—beneath him, looked down almost absently.

"That's what we've got to reckon up, Mr. March. My girl's ruin and—murder. For you killed her, you know. For myself—I'd cry quits; though you drove me hard, Mr. March; very hard. But my girl, my innocent, pure-hearted girl! Ah!"

The roughly-hewn month opened, the fangs shone whitely in the murkiness, the huge hand was raised—and fell. Fell with such deadly force that it spurred the shrinking soul in the quivering body to one great, superhuman effort. Incredible as it seems, Desmond March freed himself from the horrible incubus of the down-pressing, life-crushing knees, and struggled to his feet. He would have screamed for help, but his throat was too parched for any sound save a gasping sob to issue from it; but he writhed and flung up his arm in impotent rage and fury, the blood streaming from his battered face and severed lips.

With a snarl, the guttural cry of the madman, Garling closed on him, lifted him bodily, as if he were a bundle of straw, and, edging nearer and nearer the brink of the quay, poised for one moment, then plunged over with his burden into the dark waters beneath.

When the bodies were found—almost side by side—the face of Desmond March was unrecognisable; that of Garling calm and peaceful, as if he had passed to death from sleep.

CHAPTER XXXIII

"TILL ALL'S BLUE!"

IT was the deep voice of Donald, as he stood in front of the great stone steps at Glenaskel, his fingers on his beloved pipes, his gigantic figure drawn to its full height, his eyes, even as he addressed the throng of Highlandmen under his command, peering through the twilight toward the bend of the road along which the carriage, bringing Lord and Lady Dalesford to their Scottish home, might come in sight any moment.

"Ye'll understand, laddies, ivery mon is to wave his cap and shout when the carriage reaches where I'm standing. An' ye'll not rush forward an' frighten the bonny young master's wife. I'll hev ivery mon mind his manners. But ye can shout an' ye can wave till—till all's blue!"

"Ay, ay, Donald!" came the response.

"And, mind ye, there's the laird and Miss Mabel hev got their een on ye from the hall window. Be gay, but canny, laddies!"

Strung up with excitement, the crowd responded again, and swayed this way and that, their eager eyes fixed on the spot at which Donald was gazing.

In the hall the excitement was as great as that which prevailed outside. The earl, leaning on Mabel's arm, strove to look calm, and not at all impatient, but every now and then he glanced at the clock, even while he chided Mabel for doing the same.

"I've sent Bertie to the lodge gates," said Mabel. "They'll be sure to stop a moment to speak to the children—Diana couldn't pass them, you know—and he'll have time to run here and give us notice. Uncle Edward, if you tremble so I will not let you wait here; you shall go into the drawing-room. Ah! what's that?"

"That" was Bertie sprinting up the drive with the speed of the runner completing his last lap. Nodding excitedly to Donald's eager inquiry, he ran up the steps and burst into the hall, panting—

"They've come; they're at the lodge. Diana is talking to the children—"

"What did I tell you!" exclaimed Mabel, her bright eyes sparkling. "She isn't to be trusted where children are about. Fancy being kept waiting by a parcel of kids!"

"Mabel!" murmured Lady Selina; but on this occasion Mabel was impervious to rebuke; indeed, there was no time for expressions of regret and penitence, for suddenly the wild notes of the pipes broke out, and the carriage with its four white horses, with ribbons by their glossy faces, with heads erect, as if they shared in the general joy and were proud of their share, came round the corner.

Up went the caps, out rang the deafening cheers, and, alas, alas, for discipline! the ranks were broken and the great Highlandmen pressed forward to catch a sight of, if possible to touch, the bride and bridegroom.

The hall door had been flung open and the earl came forward, his hands already held out, his whole attitude eloquent of a loving welcome.

They all held their breath; Donald's notes of wild joy faltered for a moment, then broke out again with tenfold vigour as Vane, bareheaded, helped out the girl for love of whom every heart was beating high.

At sight of her, a little pale, but as radiant as Vane, the caps went up again, and the men crowded so closely that they scarcely left Vane room to lead her to his father. She took the trembling hands held out to her; then, with the tears filling her eyes, drew closer to the old man and kissed him.

It was Mabel's turn now, and she flung her arms round Diana and hugged her in true girlish fashion, scarcely yielding her to Lady Selina, who stood beside her ready with a warm, if a less enthusiastic, greeting.

"And here is Tubby, too!" said Diana, trying to strike a lighter note. She caught up the pug, who was yapping himself into a fit, and held him for a moment, then her hand stole into Vane's.

Once before she had been welcomed to Glenaskel; and she had then been able to thank them. Surely now a few words were due to them?

They seemed to know what was passing in her mind, for they were silent for a moment and pressed round the steps, gazing up at her eagerly. She opened her lips, but no sound would come, not a single word.

But silence is golden; and they understood, and the roar of cheers, the "God bless ye, my leddie!" showed that they appreciated her incapacity to thank them in words.

The house-party consisted of the family only, and the evening dress which Diana wore for the occasion was of black, and there were no diamonds; for, as it must be always in this chequered, transient life of ours, the shadow of death touched, though it did not darken, the sunshine of happiness. The ill-fated man who had taken the vengeance of Heaven into his own hands had died while working that vengeance upon his daughter's destroyer. And Mrs. Burton had passed peacefully away in Diana's arms.

After dinner they all peeped into the servants' hall and heard Donald propose the health of the young master and mistress; they went to the great window on the corridor and looked out upon the fierce flames rising from the bonfires, and heard the shouts and laughter of the people; they sat, almost in each other's pockets, listening to Vane telling of the happy honeymoon; and it was, as of old, the earl who drove Diana to bed.

"You must be tired, my dear," he said, with the little tone of authority which proclaims the love behind it. "It's been a trying day for you. You should be in bed. Vane will agree with me, I'm sure."

Vane laughed as Diana rose obediently.

"You manage her very nicely, sir," he said. "She's not half so obedient to me. I'll get you to give me a few lessons."

He put his arm round her and kissed her.

"Really, Vane, you ought to be ashamed of yourself!" said Mabel. "Before me, too! And you've been married—how long? come along, Diana!"

"I know what that means," said Vane, as they went out. "Those two will sit up in Diana's room chattering until I drag Mabel out by the hair of her head. One cigar, sir? Come on, Bertie. We mere men may as well have our gossip."

An hour later Mabel, coming out of Diana's room, saw a figure sitting on the stairs in an attitude of patience and expectancy; it sprang up at the light sound of her footsteps and came toward her with flushed face and eager eyes.

"Bertie!" she exclaimed, with half-serious indignation. "Why are you sitting there? Why don't you go to bed? What are you waiting for?"

"What I've been waiting for ever so long," he replied, in a low voice. "Come in the alcove, Mabel."

"No, no," she breathed quickly. "I must not. Everybody's in bed.—Well, the other end of the corridor, then; Aunt Selina can't hear there. What is it? I can't stay more than a moment, just one moment."

"Oh, Mabel!" His ardent eyes were all aglow, his face was pale with doubt and hope finely compounded. "You promised! You said when Diana came back, when everything was all right again. We've got her back, and everything and everybody's all right—excepting me. Mabel, won't you say that little word I want to hear so badly?"

"I'll say three words, and you ought to hear them, even if you don't want to: 'Go to bed.'"

"Only a moment more. Mabel, dearest, dearest, the sweetest girl in all the world! Oh, Mabel, I love you! Say you'll be my wife!"

She tried to stare him down with a fine assumption of maidenly indignation.

"Is this the time of night— Besides, what's the use? They'd never consent. You foolish boy, have you come into a fortune?"

"Yes!" he responded, so swiftly, so loudly, that she started and looked round apprehensively. "Yes! I'm a rich man—or I shall be; or you will be—it's the same thing. Vane's just been telling me—oh, what a stunning friend he is, Mabel! —he is going to settle ever so much on you, enough to let you marry me—if you want to. And—and you do, Mabel dear; don't you?"

Perhaps she was so amazed that she did not know that his arm had gone round her and that his lips were perilously near hers. Indeed, her answer was so muffled that it must have been spoken under difficulties. But he caught it, and, pressing her to him, rendered any further speech from her impossible.

"Isn't he a brick?" he said presently, in an enthusiastic whisper.

"Vane? You silly boy," she retorted, raising her head and looking at him with a proud and tender light in her pretty eyes. "It's Diana, of course! But she didn't say a word to me, while I was in there with her. What are you grinning at, sir?"

"Yes, it's all Diana," he said. "She told me to wait for you on the stairs. Diana! Oh, she's—she's—"

"An angel—and a brick, too!"

THE END

www.ingramcontent.com/pod-product-compliance
Lightning Source LLC
Chambersburg PA
CBHW012150260626
47155CB00020B/3555

* 9 7 8 1 4 7 9 4 9 9 8 5 4 *